I0736710

ENTANGLED

A HAVEN REALM NOVEL

MILA YOUNG

DEDICATION

To all the wonderful readers who've supported me from my first Haven Realm book. This one is for you...

CONTENTS

HAVEN REALM SERIES

Hunted (Little Red Riding Hood Retelling)

Cursed (Beauty and the Beast Retelling)

Entangled (Rapunzel)

More on the way...

ENTANGLED
A Haven Realm Book

Tangles of death, danger, and monsters. Rapunzel and her sexy shifters must escape a witch's vengeance.

At the tender age of eight, Elliana's life was shattered, her freedom stolen, and her destiny forever altered—all while locked away in a tower guarded by a formidable gargoyle.

Determined to break free, Elliana embarks on a daring quest to unearth a hidden weapon powerful enough to vanquish her stone captor once and for all. To succeed, she must summon the aid of three enigmatic shifters: a cunning dragon, a fierce lion burdened by secrets, and a devious tiger.

But time is running out, for the malevolent witch who cursed her is returning to seal Elliana's fate.

As Elliana's journey unfolds, the lines between loyalty, love, and survival blur. Amidst the magic of dragons, lions, and enchanting hair, she must find the strength to forge her own path and seize a unique 'Happily Ever After.'

HAVEN REALM
and the Seven Territories
WHITE PEAK
UTAARA
TERRA
THE EDEN
DARKWOODS
TRITONIA
WILDFIRE

HAVEN REALM

The realms of Haven warred for ages upon ages, laying devastation upon its lands and its residents alike. To put an end to the death and destruction, the realm was divided into seven kingdoms, one for each race, ruled by nobility, entrusted to maintain the truce. Over centuries, kingdoms rose and fell as the power of the ruling noble houses waxed and waned. And the peace between the lands persevered. But a corruption is growing, bringing darkness to the realms, and threatening the return of war and suffering to Haven.

PART I

CHAPTER 1

$\mathcal{A}$s I climbed out of the tower window, I rubbed my swollen lip and winced from the sting. My back pinched from the whippings I'd received last night, but I didn't stop. Today, I was breaking free. I would risk everything to escape my captor. To gain freedom. To stop the insanity that developed over the past eight years from eating away at my mind.

The sun dipped behind the horizon of trees, smearing the sky in bloody streaks. In the distance, the bastard who beat me each time I left the tower sailed through the sky. He also attacked anything that came near the tower. His stone wings flapped, and his hideous gargoyle mouth gaped open. He dove toward birds, picking at the food I'd placed near the woods yesterday for a distraction so I could escape. I'd left enough food scattered in the field for dozens of disturbances as more animals would be drawn to the scents.

My stomach churned, and my hands shook, but I couldn't sit back and do nothing. I scaled down the makeshift rope comprised of bed sheets tied together.

The witch with purple eyes who had shoved me into the tower eight years ago had never returned to check on me or even bothered to barricade the only window in the tower. Why would she when she'd compelled a freaking gargoyle to watch over me? I was clearly a nobody, and she probably forgot about me. Then again, she'd made sure I had food magically appear in the tower, as if she intended for me to sit there for eternity. I'd attempted to escape so many times, each ending in a beating and me getting tossed back into the tower. I hated her, and one day, I'd get my revenge.

Hurry! This is your chance, my subconscious repeated in my head, as she always did. Reminding me of my mistakes, what I should do, and other nagging things. But this time, she was right about getting a move on. The voice in my head had been there ever since I was thrown into the tower. I called her my make-believe friend, but I wasn't stupid and knew it was my twisted mind dealing with my loneliness. Yes, I spoke to myself, and my mind responded, but she offered me a sliver of company. Anything to stop the insanity of being on my own.

I scrambled out of the window, the bag on my back bouncing about as I jerked downward.

Behind me, the gargoyle glided toward the tower's roof, and I froze. Sweat drenched my skin, and my shirt clung to my skin as I trembled. My arms ached from holding on, but if I moved at all, he'd see me. I squeezed my eyes shut, praying he'd leave and go kill some defenseless animal in the forest.

Stone fragments cascaded down from the roof. I opened my eyes.

He vanished, and I slid down in haste. But all at once, the fabric slackened in my hands, and I fell, my arms flying outward. A yelp pushed against my throat. The rope fell out of the window, along with the table I'd tied it to. I hit the enormous shrubs with a thud, the air in my lungs gushing out. I groaned. The material landed on me in a heap, and I covered my head with my arms. The table fell inches from me. A loud crack of wood sounded as it broke into dozens of pieces.

My heart raced, and breathing seemed impossible. A shadow fell over me, and I rolled beneath the bushes. My skin prickled as I pictured the monster coming for me, striking me until I writhed in my own blood.

But nothing came.

I peered out from my hiding spot to find the gargoyle rushing after more birds. So, I scrambled to my feet and careened around the tower. Stubs of ruins dotted the field, and I leaped over them, the wind ripping at my clothes. I pushed the bag strap up my shoulder, my ridiculously long hair stuffed inside.

Never stop. This is your chance.

My pulse pounded in my ears. Goosebumps crawled up my legs. I looked back. No sign. The creature would be distracted long enough for me to put distance between us.

On a previous escape, I'd run into someone. A magic caster who'd agreed to create an incantation to finish off the gargoyle, but I'd had to collect it from her home. It had come with a hefty cost of ten thousand gold coins, which could buy a small mansion. Of course, I didn't have the money, which I had made clear to the witch, but I'd guaranteed her I'd repay her in installments. Otherwise, she'd come for my blood. If her spell worked and got rid of the gargoyle, I'd be free from my prison, meaning I'd take any job to earn the money I owed.

I burst into the thick forest. The gargoyle would find me soon enough. He always chased me down after a while, and I figured he somehow sensed wherever I went. Who knew how, but I despised the notion of being connected with him in any way. And now, I needed time to reach the witch's home. Dread squeezed my lungs because the last time I dealt with a witch, I ended up trapped in a tower. Could I really trust another magic caster?

Night fell over the woods. I jumped over a dead log and dodged a low-hanging branch. When I finally reached the track in the forest, I swung left and darted. My lungs burned for air. Around the next bend, I spotted the back of a carriage. My ride.

It stood near Ghost, a tiny town only open at night for anyone who dared to venture into the depths of the Darkwoods. No one lived here, as it was an entertainment center for those looking to gamble, get drunk, or find a woman for the night.

But I'd also discovered that the carriage traveled here from Tritonia with deliveries of rum. The black vehicle rolled forward, the wagon covered with a tight canopy, and the back flapped open. Perfect. I pushed forward, but they moved too fast.

"Wait!" I called out, running after them. "Please, wait!"

The cart vanished into the shadows, and I cried out in frustration. Stopping in the middle of the track, I gasped for air, and my stomach somersaulted.

He'll come for you. Keep moving.

I scanned the empty woods behind me, trembling. Ahead was the tiny town, huddled amid the lush green trees with basically two main businesses—a tavern and a masseuse house. I heard the beat of horses' hooves, then rushed forward when another carriage emerged from behind the tavern. Laughter belched out from inside the building.

Two terrifying black stallions pulled the covered carriage. Each had two red horns on their brows and snorted fire. No rider guided the beasts. I shuddered and recoiled.

Dragon horses. Larger than the average horse, they were fast, and once they learned to follow a path, they traveled it without stopping for anyone. I'd read about them in books because the witch who had locked me up had a sense of humor. She'd filled the tower with furniture, magically generated food, clothes, and walls full of books. Maybe she'd figured if I was away from the world, I might as well read up on it.

Move. Get ready.

"Yes, I know." I rushed along the path where it merged with the path leading out of town and waited behind a tree.

The moment the cart passed by, I leaped into the back, where the covering flapped in the wind. Dimness greeted me inside, and I scrambled forward on hands and knees as the carriage bounced beneath me. Empty wooden boxes were tied to the edges of the carriage, so I pushed myself into a corner and curled up, hugging my knees. I prayed the gargoyle hadn't sensed me leave yet, and we'd travel fast enough to avoid the monster… at least for longer than ever before.

* * *

THE MOON CRAWLED behind the gathering clouds, plunging the open field into a murky darkness. I'd jumped out of the wagon a while back and crossed the woods in haste. Only a few stars freckled the black sky. I pushed one leg in front of the other, despite my ragged breaths and aching muscles. I'd been on the run for the past day.

Never stop.

A quick glance over my shoulder and a shiver clawed up my spine. No silhouette shifted through the forest at my back. The sky remained silent, peaceful. No movement. That didn't mean shit. He always came for me, found me, and beat me. I gasped at the thought and sprinted faster. I had to put distance between me and him.

Gripping the straps of my backpack, I raced toward the lights amid the lofty trees ahead. They sparkled like fireflies. Wakefield, the village in this godforsaken Tritonia realm, was my destination. Sweat beaded across my upper lip. I wiped it away, hating the humidity, as the insects tried to chew off my eyelids. I'd been on the run for most of the day and night. But this was my chance to break free from my prison, to never be locked up or forgotten again. Desperation crept through me.

A growl screeched through the hot, stifling air behind me.

I flinched as I turned around, my breath caught in my chest, and my hand fell to the dagger on my belt. The unforgiving place lay silent, swallowed by the night, and my earlier reassurance ebbed away.

Never stop! This time, if the gargoyle catches you, he'll shatter more than your bones.

"Yes, you're right," I mumbled under my voice, thankful she was speaking to me. I felt less alone.

I trembled and kept running.

Salvation is near. Yes, you can do this.

Flamed torches lined the street in the distance, and I closed in on them. A briny, salty scent found me. The ocean lay close— the place where pirates plundered, witches ruled, and mermaids lured you to your death if you dared enter their watery realm.

But I'd risk that and more to gain liberty. To stop the insanity eating away at my mind and the torture destroying my body.

Desperation pressed on my heaving lungs. My captor was somewhere on my heels.

Tick tock. Tick tock.

"Enough!" I had it all planned out.

Evade the guardian.

Collect the spell to eradicate him.

And put an end to my incarcerated life.

Shifting the heavy bag across my back, my hair too long and cumbersome to not keep contained, I trampled the grass and foliage, hurrying closer to the village. I emerged from the forest. Huts riddled the tiny village, their windows dark, as if unoccupied.

A dozen homes flanked the wide dirt track. No fences, just shrubs and flowers. By daytime, the place might have resembled a quaint town, but now, I might as well have stepped into a nightmare. I couldn't stop shivering from the feeling of being watched.

Just get this done quickly. Move fast.

Bones tied to a rope dangled from the front porch of one house, and with the sudden gust of air, they clattered, announcing my arrival to the homeowner. Enormous oaks with branches fanning out wide stood like a wall behind the houses. They rustled and seemed to whisper on the warm breeze that whirled around me.

Hurrying onward, I ignored the three cats prowling across another lawn, watching me with their lamp-like eyes. Their brown-black fur fluttered in the wind. They weren't skinny, so someone fed them well.

The silence stroked my skin like a cold wind filled with jagged edges. I breathed heavily, scanning the makeshift road. The witch had given me instructions, and I'd followed them to a T. Travel the thick woods of Tritonia. Check. Overhead, the glorious silvery orb hung full. Check. Creepy town where witches lived. Check. Yep, this was the place. Now to find the house with a single burning candle sitting on the windowsill.

Stop overthinking everything. Keep moving.

I rolled my eyes and marched past a double-story building covered in tiny bones… wait, no! I squinted for a better look. Shriveled vines, barren of leaves.

The wind swept against me, bones rattling, the felines yowling. Creepy-ass naked dolls were scattered on a lawn, and I ran past. "Please don't come to life."

I strangled the bag straps over my shoulders and approached the last home on the road. A single candle sat on the front windowsill. This was it.

My flesh rippled into goosebumps, and I glanced behind me. The street lay abandoned. No shadow following me.

Do this fast.

"You don't say." I marched down a rocky path across the yard toward the porch. The stairs creaked beneath my steps, and I knocked, praying I hadn't made a mistake and picked the wrong house. I really didn't need to upset a witch tonight.

I took another glance around, but there was no sign of my pursuer.

When the door groaned open, I spun to face Vanore, the witch I'd met in Darkwoods who'd promised to help and whose smile now offered me hope. I breathed a sigh of relief. Her expression morphed into one of pity, but I didn't care. If that made her want to aid me, then yep, she could feel sorry for me until the cows came home.

The swirled tattoos across her cheeks and brow creased when she smiled again, revealing two gold canine teeth. Her skin was deeply sun-kissed, and her eyes were as dark as tar, matching her dreadlocks. She gripped the waist of her mauve dress, her sleeves long and ruffled.

"Ey, Elliana girl, thought you'd break our arrangement." She spoke with a burr where the letter 'r' trilled each time she pronounced it. She reached out, taking my elbow, her grip iron strong. "Let's get inside." She stared at something behind me. "Nothing good comes of lingering in doorways."

When I turned to look behind, she dragged me into her home and slammed the door shut. I should have panicked, but I was desperate, ready to trust anyone who offered salvation. And in the grander scheme of things, I'd take my chances with the witch with a softness in her eyes.

A strong smell of spices and burned wood permeated the air. To my right lay a battered brown sofa in the sitting room. Jars of various herbs and a large bowl brimming with white and black feathers sat on the coffee table. Curtains with holes covered the windows, and only one remained open with the single candle on the sill. More candles littered the fireplace mantle, though I doubted it ever got cold enough in Tritonia to require a fire.

"Nice place." My gaze settled on the dead crow on the floor near the foot of the table, its legs in the air. It was bigger than my foot. Was it dinner or for a concoction or some good luck charm?

"Me mama left the home to me, and her mama to her. Been in the family for five generations, and now this place is mine." Her voice deepened, and I turned to find her rummaging through a tall wicker basket for dirty laundry, but I somehow suspected she used it for other purposes.

"No man getting their stinking hands on me home neither!" She snarled the word *man,* and I figured she had unresolved issues. But that wasn't my problem because I hadn't met any men in years, beyond what I remembered as a child about my dad and the people he'd visited to make his deals. He was a grand thief renowned for his abilities in the Darkwoods realm. I'd never known my mother, and he'd refused to speak about her. But Dad would take me on every heist, using me as his excuse for trespassing on anyone's property if anyone caught him. I would fake-cry so people would think he was settling an upset young kid who had wandered onto their property. But most of the scum he'd dealt with would rip him off when it came to payment.

That was a lifetime away now because when I'd been eight years of age, he'd made the grave mistake of stealing from a witch, and my life had changed forever. He had paid with his life, and I was thrown into the tower and kept in there by the stone guardian. Not a day went by when I didn't think about the day when I would hunt the witch down and make her pay.

Vanore made a clicking sound with her tongue, and I refocused on her.

"Most men are bastards," I added to fill the silence.

"Ey, you right there. They decide with their dick first, then the consequences of what they did come later." She glanced over. "How old are you? Fourteen or fifteen? Old enough to hear such talk." Diving back into the wicker basket, she sighed.

"I'm sixteen." Most days, I felt like a child who had no clue about life beyond the things I read in books, but now I was enjoying Vanore's company and her interacting with me as if I were normal. "Sounds as if you've met some bad men." I strolled over to the cabinet and studied the array of tattered books stacked on top of each other. Most had missing spines or covers, but the ones still bound had titles like *Magic for Sailors*, *Controlling the Elements*, or *Herbs and Aches*.

"They have a split tongue and make better companions as cats." She sniggered, and I recalled the animals outside. Had they once been men who'd cheated on a witch? Poor men, but they'd deserved what they'd gotten if they'd thought swindling a witch was ever a smart move. My thoughts flew back to my father. Stealing from a witch was the worst mistake of his life. Never lie to magical folk. That encounter had led to me getting locked up in a tower.

Get a move on. Remember what's coming for you.

"Shhh. Don't scare Vanore," I whispered under my breath. "She's about to give us a goddamn remedy to all our problems."

"Found it!" she bellowed, and I flinched. "Come 'ere, girl. Stop talking to yourself, or they'll call you crazy."

The strap of my bag slid down my arm as I ambled toward Vanore. "Who'll call me crazy?"

"People." She frowned, as if I were indeed a child who didn't understand the basics. "They ain't understanding different and will judge."

I stiffened. Was I different? Sure, I hadn't lived among the community for years, but I was just like them.

You are different. Don't kid yourself.

I shook my head. "I'm the same."

"Concentrate, girl." The witch grasped my hand and placed a soft pouch in my palm.

I drove away the thoughts, the ones that sometimes had a mind of their own, and focused on the bundle. Black fabric wrapped around a small parcel.

"Put that in your pocket."

And I did.

"Now, we made a deal." Her words darkened, her brow hooding over the tops of her eyes. "I gave you magic ingredients to smite the gargoyle for ten thousand gold coins." She swung her arm out from behind her back with such speed, I didn't see the knife she grabbed until the edge bit across my thumb.

"Ouch." I wrenched my arm back.

Vanore held on tight and pressed my thumb to her mouth, sticking it into her mouth and sucking on my blood.

My brain seized up at what was happening, and my free hand flew to my knife. Her tongue rolled over my flesh, and I withdrew my arm hard, my finger popping out of her mouth. I stared at the bloody cut.

"What is wrong with you? Who does that?" Panic curled deep in my gut. "Th-This wasn't part of the deal."

I retreated until my legs hit the side of the sofa, and I gripped the knife still on my belt. What could I do? Stab her before she gave me a solution to finish the guardian?

She laughed and licked a drop of crimson from her lips. "Need to track you for me payment. And child, whoever put that spell on you was serious. It's tangled with your soul, girl. Ain't something anyone can remove but the caster."

My breaths froze in my chest, and it took several tries to find them again. "You can sense the type of spell it is? Who did it?" I flirted with the idea of this being my salvation. A way to rid myself of the hex. A smile played at the corners of my lips as a weight lifted off my shoulders.

I turned sideways and wriggled the bag on my back, holding up my long hair with one hand. "Stupid strands won't stop growing, and I can't cut them. Trust me; I tried everything, even fire. So please tell me everything you know to break the curse." The pleading in my voice made me cringe.

A flicker of hope sprung through me, and I reached out, my fingers extended for her arm. I clutched onto her as if my life depended on it.

"Elliana, me child." She clasped my wrist the way my dad used to hold on to my hands when I got scared each time we went out on a heist. But the witch's eyes carried sorrow, and it left me breathless.

"I ain't got such insight… only that there's darkness in your blood, the magic prickling me tongue, and its connection to your soul. Whoever did this to you had no intention of ever releasing you. I'm sorry. All I can do is help you with the stone guard and a temporary solution to your hair problems. Pray to the Goddess that my incantation frees you, and the witch responsible will leave you alone, but magic lays inside you. And since I don't understand its purpose, I can't assist you without endangering your life."

My legs refused to hold me as I sank onto the couch.

You have no time to get soft. Get up.

My insides stung at hearing the absoluteness of my predicament. What if this spell notified the witch who'd cursed me? Would she return and lock me up again if I destroyed the gargoyle?

"Sorry, child, but your best bet is to find who cast this spell on you."

I nodded and climbed to my feet. This wasn't the time to fall apart.

"Now, as part of our bargain," the witch continued, "I'll take payment in ten installments as we agreed, and I will come to you every full moon to collect. If you fail to pay, I will slit the veins on your arms and use the blood to warm me rum. Death won't allow you to escape." She smiled her toothy grin, and gone was the sympathy. Just like everyone my dad had dealt with, Vanore was in this for herself. I was a means to getting what she wanted. Nothing more.

I gasped but summoned my courage and lifted my chin. "Deal. Now tell me how to activate the herbs you gave me."

"Good girl. First,"—she counted on her fingers—"you must find an animal for the spell."

I stiffened. "I'm not killing an animal."

"Hush, girl." She waved a hand between us as if I were a pesky gnat. "No killing required. Just do as I say. Second, best you do the incantation outdoors beneath the moon."

"Okay, well, can I do it now? I saw a few cats outside."

"No." Her voice rose. "This must be done where your guard lives, as the magic on you both will be strongest there. Soak the herbs I gave you in water for you and the animal to use together. But first, let the concoction sit in the moonlight for a short while, then—"

A sudden crashing explosion detonated behind me, shards of wood pinging against my back and legs. I shuddered on the spot, both the witch and I twisting toward the entrance in unison. The smashed door lay scattered around our feet.

The gargoyle stood there. My prison guard.

A strangled cry pressed on my throat, and my feet glued to the rug.

His shoulders pushed past the edges of the doorway. Three long strides and he marched into the room.

He found you. Run. Run. Run.

"Bloody hell!" Vanore stammered.

Dread coiled in my chest and clung to my ribs. I dragged Vanore backward by a hand through the house.

"The spell. What're the words?" I couldn't pull my gaze from the gargoyle made of rock, standing still for those few moments as if he had frozen in place. Stones the size of my palm covered his body, allowing his movement. His head was a boulder with empty eyes, a hooked nose, and a buckled mouth. Oversized ears unnaturally pivoted, listening for anyone sneaking up on him. He stared down at me in the dim light with a sadistic grin, as if any second now, the hatred in his expression would burst forth.

"Plague seize you," Vanore called out as she tossed a handful of powder from her pocket at the guard. The contents sparked and bounced against him, but he didn't budge.

"Run, child!" She nudged me toward the back of the house.

I stumbled into the kitchen, gasping. "Vanore, what's the rest of the spell?"

But she didn't answer me and hissed at the monster, "Devil take you!"

The guardian charged and shoved a hand against Vanore's chest. She flew across the room and slammed into the wall, her breaths gushing out with a grunt. Powerful and final. Being hit by the side of a mountain wasn't something one got up from. Vanore slumped to the ground in a heap and didn't move.

"Vanore!" My body was wracked with shivers. I ought to have dragged her to her feet, made sure she was all right. But the gargoyle now faced me, and it made more sense to lead him away from her so he wouldn't hurt her further.

My heart hit the back of my throat, and I whipped around, sprinting across the kitchen and ripping open the back door. Panic snaked over my skin.

Outside, the hot wind buffeted me. Without a thought, I swung left and dashed past the house and onto the road, dread chewing on my confidence.

Told ya. Told ya. He'll punish you.

Numbness took hold of my thoughts, and I ran, crossing the dirt road.

Pounding footfalls closed in on me, but I didn't dare to look back.

Icy daggers stabbed my heart.

He grabbed my bag with such force, I was hurled backward, hitting the ground with my ass. He ripped the bag off my arms. My hair burst free from the bag and splayed around me, swallowing me in its golden threads.

But when the gargoyle towered over me, I cried out and dragged myself away, picturing my punishment and how I'd failed. Was Vanore dead because of me? I choked on my hitched inhale.

His wings unfurled from his back, the sound of crushing

stones grating in my ears. Magic had this creature flying with stone wings when it shouldn't have been able to. They snapped out wide and lengthened to six feet on each side, blotting out the moonlight. Claw-like daggers tipped the ends of the bat-like wings.

"Please don't do this. Stop!" I backpedaled farther.

He stormed after me, his clawed hands seizing my ankles, his nails piercing into my skin.

I yelled out in agony, grabbing the dagger from my belt and stabbing it into a crevice between two stones in the center of his chest. The knife met resistance. I shoved it in there with two hands, hearing a satisfying squish as the blade sank deep enough to make the gargoyle hiss.

He knocked my arms aside, and the sting lanced across my hands as he plucked the weapon free before hurling it into Vanore's yard. There wasn't any blood. The wound hadn't even slowed him down.

A rush of air beat into me as we lifted off the ground, him dragging me upward, legs first.

My world swayed upside down. Dread swam in my stomach. Below, the town remained silent without a single person coming to my rescue. Would someone check on Vanore?

You've done it now. Yes, you're in fucked-up shit here.

I blocked out the words as we coasted over forests and rivers and towns in Tritonia. The wind colliding with me had me swaying back and forth with each flap of the monster's wings. Every inch of me throbbed with terror. Part of me had hoped I could cast the spell at Vanore's house and then be free. But that was me being idiotic—to think anything could go well for a change.

Tears blurred my vision. They ran up and over my brow and into my hair. I'd spent the last eight years alone, and it was killing me every day just a little more, erasing my inner light with shadows of darkness. The rest of the world went on while I remained frozen in time, my life drifting away. I didn't worry about where I'd end up in the afterlife because I already lived in Hell.

Dizziness captured my head, and everything faded.

Branches slapped my face, and I woke startled. I must have been upside down for a while. Now, we flew over treetops, and up ahead, I spotted my prison. A circular tower stood erect amid the rubble of destroyed ruins.

I writhed, needing to escape. I didn't want to go back there. The structure with a wide-brimmed flat roof soared over most of the trees circling the open land. Moonlight lit the moss clinging to the sides of the stone walls. Woodland surrounded the open area like a great army, watching my demise.

I wriggled in his grip for escape. We sailed toward the over-sized window, the only way in and out of the tower. He tossed me through the window as if I was a rag doll.

I slammed into a wall and crumpled to the ground, groaning from the sharpness zapping over my spine.

A shadow fell over the window. The gargoyle hovered there, not a sound, as if proud of his catch.

But the moment his wings snapped flat against his sides, and he hopped inside, I screamed. "Please, no! I promise not to leave again."

In his hand he carried a branch, and when he whipped it across my legs, I bellowed from the acidic sting. He never used his hands because stone would kill me, but breaking me was allowed. Permitted. Endlessly encouraged.

He snatched my leg and hurled me to the other side of the room. I crashed into my table and fell down, the table's legs snapping under my weight. I sobbed. The pain was a spider web, spreading over me intricately and viciously.

When the branch connected with my back, I yelled and arched. I couldn't think beyond the agonizing strikes ripping me to shreds.

CHAPTER 2

I lay on my back in a pool of my own blood. A silvery hue stretched through the darkness inside the tower. My breaths wheezed with each exhale. My mouth tasted as if I'd been sucking on coins. Tears pooled at the corners of my eyes. I sobbed loudly, loathing how many times I'd been here—useless, defeated, trapped.

This wasn't how the night should have gone. Every inch of me screamed from the sharp ache in my cuts, and I couldn't even wriggle the toes on my left leg. What bones had the bastard broken this time? Desperation clung to me, the kind that pleaded for the end to come. I shut my eyes and lay there, letting my spinning head claim my thoughts.

* * *

I STARTED to wake as a light breeze brushed my cheek, my eyes flipping open to sunlight. Morning already? I pushed myself to a sitting position, and it felt as if my skin was splitting with each movement. Dried blood layered my arms while my foot lay at a weird angle. I hiccupped a breath as I reached over to move it. Excruciating pain sliced through me, stabbing the arch of my foot and racing up my leg. I cried out, curling in on myself, hating that the wound would take months to heal, hating the monster who gave no shit, and I was pissed with the universe for sending no one to help.

My dad had taught me to be quick with my hands, to steal the shirt off a person's back without them noticing. I might have been young, yet he'd said I was the best. But when I'd turned eight, a lunatic man under the witch's instructions had killed him, and my world had ended. I'd never forget him or his wild, white hair and eyebrows. After that, the witch with purple irises shoved me into the tower, and she'd set the devil perched on the roof to watch me, wait for me to escape so he could beat the shit out of me. I was paying for my dad's sins, but the price was too high. I dreamed of having friends, settling down in a real home, and once and for all, eradicating the gargoyle. But they were fantasies.

Told you to be careful.

"Shut up!" I didn't need snarky remarks from myself right now.

Broken chairs and a shattered bookshelf surrounded me. Books lay scattered across the enormous room. They had found their way to the foot of my double bed, near the unlit fireplace, and into the small exercise section to keep my body moving and my head sane. The whole place was an oversized room with all the necessary amenities and food that replicated the moment I removed it from the pantry. The wood fire did the same, and even hot water magically ran from the bathroom and kitchen taps. Everything I could want while I rotted my life away. The witch didn't intend for me to starve or die... She needed to keep me alive for a reason I didn't understand.

Who the fuck knows why?

Was it to punish my father for stealing her wig made of real gold strands? Clear as day, I remembered the witch ordering her henchman to take my dad into the woods. I screamed for him to stop, to leave him alone. Moments later, the white-haired monster had returned, holding my poor father's head. I'd fallen to my knees, and my world had shredded. Grief surged through every expelled breath, tears never stopped, and all I could picture for weeks afterward was his decapitated head. His lifeless, open eyes, and how I hadn't been able to do a thing to save him. The hole in my heart would never heal, but instead of grief, I now craved revenge.

So why had the witch offered me a comfortable life? Was it guilt for making an eight-year-old child see her dad's decapitated head? All because he stole her gold wig. That couldn't be worth a person's life.

Was that why she had cursed my hair? As a lesson? It kept growing and was impossible to cut. I suspected it was meant to slow me down from running away.

But unlike my previous escape attempts, this time, I'd brought something back. I slid my hand into my pocket and pulled out the magic bag from Vanore. Thankfully, my injuries hadn't been in vain. I prayed Vanore still lived.

Now, I needed an animal for the spell and knew where to find one. So I dragged myself backward on my ass to the open arched window. Groaning, I rolled onto my knees, grasping the windowsill with a death grip, and propped myself up on one foot, letting the wall hold my weight. I gasped for air, waiting for the waves of throbbing in my foot to subside.

Outside, woods surrounded the clearing. The place I called home. Below were old remnants of a castle—a wall, an arched doorway, the floor plan still visible from up here despite the weeds and flowers that now swallowed the landscape.

These woods had apparently once been home to the first human kingdom established in Darkwoods after Haven Realm had split into seven territories. That had been long ago—ancient times—and this location reeked of history. My books explained the land had once been grand and blossoming with vegetation, the most beautiful flowers. Castle walls dripped with precious crystals and gold. Except the royal lords had been greedy and overworked their staff with no compensation, despite having rooms piled high with jewels. When everyone rebelled, the family was attacked by enemies frantic to take their place. So, this kingdom had housed the first royal family to fall. The remains were evidence of the price paid for corruption.

Some books stated the youngest son of the royal family had

escaped death and ended up marrying a fae princess. So maybe the fae regal families weren't as pure as they insisted. I smirked. Snobs, the lot of them.

The skies were a patchwork of clouds. Birds flew overhead, but down below not a creature stirred. Once night came, my little furry friend would arrive. I'd bring the little furball into the tower and do Vanore's spell.

Now, to clean and bandage myself. Determination plowed through me—tonight, I'd eradicate the gargoyle problem once and for all. Even if I had to drag my leg behind me, that monster would never lay a hand on me again.

* * *

THE PARTIAL MOON hung low in the tapestry of stars overhead, but my gaze lowered to the base of the tower. I had to be close to fifty feet off the ground, and most nights, I dropped food to the ground for the only friend who visited me. And tonight, I was going fishing.

Sitting on a seat to help with my foot, I wore so many bandages, barely an inch of my skin was left exposed. The bowl of water and herbs from Vanore's brew sat on a small stool nearby beneath the moon's light.

How do you know this will work? What if you're using the herbs wrong?

"Zip it. I may not know what I'm doing, but I'm not sitting here feeling sorry for myself anymore. I'll try anything." Plus, Vanore had said the herbs and water were to be used by both the animal and me. *So we either splash ourselves or drink it.*

I hung half out the window with my hair dangling over the edge. It didn't reach the bottom, so I'd knotted a longer strip of linen with a fish tied to the end of my hair. The food was stinky enough to bring out most critters in the woods but also delicious, served with tomatoes and bread.

Bait set, I slouched forward, elbows resting against the windowsill, and waited. I had all the time in the world and could both laugh and cry at how pathetic that sounded. My thoughts flew to Vanore. She hadn't given me all the instructions on casting the spell or what to do with the watery concoction and animal. No killing, that was clear. I'd spent the afternoon reading, but my books didn't reveal a thing about spells cast with herbs. Since I used them for cooking, I was going with the theory of eating them.

You sure about this?

"Yes! No time for your doubts."

Staring out into the darkness, the cypress and oaks swayed in the wind, as they had hundreds of times I'd studied them, and I wished someone… *anyone* would visit the ruins and defeat the gargoyle.

Rustling came from below, and I glanced down at the ginger cat with three legs rubbing herself against a nearby shrub. She must have lost one of her front legs at birth or in a fight, but it didn't stop her from attacking lizards and bugs. The first time she'd appeared, she'd been skin and bones, so I'd fed her every night, and now she was plump and healthy. Luckily, she wasn't noisy and never grabbed the gargoyle's attention.

"Hello, princess. Look what I have for you. Yummy fish." I jiggled my hair. I figured it was easier to capture her this way than go down there and chase her without the gargoyle noticing. Plus, with my injured foot, I wasn't sure I had it in me to climb down the tower.

The cat lifted her head and sniffed the air, then pounced on the snack. I jerked my locks upward, but she missed, as I'd pulled up too fast.

Take your time.

I lowered the bait once more. She prowled closer, crouched low in hunting mode. Perfect.

A quick shake of the morsel.

The cat leapt after her meal, and I lifted my hair. She captured the treat with a claw, getting caught in the fabric, and I held my breath.

Yes.

I wrenched my hair up, one arm after the next, drawing her

up into the tower. But halfway up, she bucked and fell into the bushes.

"No!"

She stood there amid the bushes, chewing on something. The fish. I'd never tried getting the cat in the tower before because I'd had no reason to, so maybe this wasn't going to be as easy as I'd hoped.

"You dirty scoundrel." With a sigh, I drew my hair up and tied another piece of fish to the end, then dropped the tresses out the window again. She'd eat all night if I continued to feed her.

Once again, I shook the offering. She attacked the swinging meal, and right when she jumped for it, I towed her up fast. This time, she panicked, but her claws were caught, entangled in my hair. She kicked and thrashed, twisting herself around my tresses like a fishnet capturing a mermaid.

"Don't struggle. I won't hurt you." In haste, I pulled her toward me. She fought and hissed. I beamed with excitement. Part one of my plan was falling into place. Now, I just prayed to the heavens the rest worked out as easily.

"Come on, princess. I have something delicious for you to drink if you come inside."

You sound creepy when you say it like that.

"Oh, keep quiet."

The feline hissed, and I drew her through the window without hesitation. Her claw swiped the air, catching me on the arm. I flinched, dropping her. She crouched there, stomach flat to the floor, her eyes round disks peering out from the tangle of my golden hair. Blood bubbled on my arm, with the flesh itching already.

In haste, I shut the wooden shutters. The room glowed from the candles I'd lit up across the fireplace mantel.

The furball screeched and tossed about in my hair. I leaned closer to release her from the tangled mess, but she burst free and spun to face me. Her ears peeled back, and her lips curled over her fangs. Her menacing yowl echoed through the tower.

"Look, I'm sorry for taking you, but it's just a temporary

thing. All right, I'm lying, as I'm not sure how this will go, but I need your help. Please. And in exchange, I will feed you and you can live here. I'll build a ladder, so you have a spot to stay when it rains." I clutched at straws, guilt pulsing through me for drawing a poor cat into my problems, but we weren't that different—both alone, imperfect, and desperate for survival.

"I won't harm you. How about I get you some food?" I shifted toward the kitchen, but she recoiled against the chair holding the bowl of herbal water. At that exact moment, the bowl rocked forward, and the contents splashed toward the cat, who glanced up with her mouth open mid-meow.

The concoction hit her face and fell into her gaping mouth. I lunged toward it, arms stretched outward, catching the bowl with half the spell remaining. "Shit!"

The cat darted under the bed, and my heart beat rapidly.

Drink it now, too, or you'll waste the opportunity.

I gulped the water. Grittiness assaulted my tongue, and tiny bits got stuck in my teeth, but I swallowed the briny, soil-tasting drink and held back the gagging reflex.

Smacking my chest, I spat out a chunk that clung to my throat. A tiny piece of… *What is that? Please don't let it be a bone.* I inspected the thin stem near the candle and heaved a sigh of relief. Only a twig. I stumbled onto the chair, my foot pinching with pain and my stomach gurgling.

From beneath the bed came popping and noisy sniffing… not sounds a tiny feline should have made.

"Are you okay under there?"

A piercing ache stabbed me in the gut, and I clasped my arms around my middle. Panic swirled in my chest. I'd drank the spell without a second thought. What if I'd done the incantation wrong? My scalp itched as I tore at my head, unable to stop. The insatiability had me gritting my teeth.

"Hell!"

The orange furball scrambled out from under the bed, screeching as she crazily scratched herself. She clawed behind an ear with such vigor, she fell onto her side. It was then that I realized "princess" wasn't a girl at all. Geez, he had huge, round… I gawked and looked away. Not that it mattered when we resembled chimpanzees doing the itchy dance.

She... *he* meowed and glared at me with a look of *What have you done to me?*

"Sorry, this is new for me, too." I raked my nails across the back of my head, relief lasting mere seconds. Heat bubbled in my chest, and I sweated like a beast, so I flipped open the window shutters. The cool breeze did little to help, but when a tingle started at my spine and climbed upward, I froze.

I exchanged glances with the ginger cat when golden sparks danced across his back. And at once, a lightning bolt zapped in from the heavens and struck us both in the chest.

Thrown to the ground, I writhed and screamed as my vision darkened. What the fuck was the spell doing?

PART II

CHAPTER 3

5 YEARS LATER

Five years of returning home before sunset, and you'd think I would have learned my lesson. Nope. I still ran, thumping the forest floor with each rushed step, lungs pumping furiously. I cursed myself for arriving home late again.

Told you not to steal the book, but no... Now you'll get beaten.

"Shut up. That's not helping." My heart pounded as I sprinted down the dirt track I used every night. Five years ago, I had messed up Vanore's spell. Instead of eradicating the gargoyle, the incantation had turned him into an impenetrable statue during the night—he couldn't see or move. But when the sun rose, he snapped back alive, and if he didn't sense me inside the tower, he hunted me down.

The sky grew bluer. Once the first rays climbed over the horizon, the stone gargoyle would awaken and savagely attack me when he found me outside.

Of course, I had visited Vanore's home two times and left her notes, but she hadn't been home. Both times, her neighbors had explained she'd gotten injured and had taken an extended vacation by the sea. She'd never come for her payment either, and it worried me to know I'd caused her harm. Still, her home was too great a distance. After each of those escapes, I'd gotten beaten for arriving after dawn, so I'd given up on going to find

31

her. One day, I'd pay Vanore back and get her to give me a spell that fully worked.

So I'd been working my ass off helping other people solve their problems to make the money. I'd gotten to know many people, shifters, and fae. The trick was discovering what each offered. So, when someone asked for help, I knew who to hire to help them. I ran a referral service and connected clients with people able to do their job.

Despite knowing so many people, I still struggled to make close friends. I ticked the reasons off on my fingers. Telling them where I lived wasn't possible. I could only meet them during the night. Oh, and I spoke to myself. But I didn't care what anyone thought when all I craved was freedom. They could call me "insane" for eternity, but if it gained my freedom, I'd change my name to Crazy.

Bursting free from the dense woodland, I entered the open ruins. The breeze swooshed through my short, cropped hair. I loved the freedom, its heaviness gone, and the way it had over-heated me. A benefit of the spell. Now, I felt as light as a bird. If only I had wings.

The first glows appeared on the horizon with the pre-dawn orange gleam. My skin tingled, and dread filled my veins. I trampled over the knee-length weeds that swallowed everything in the clearing except the tower.

The granite structure stood in the middle of the area, vines curling upward around its base like a snake choking it, and the only way in and out was through the arched window three-quarters of the way up the building. An oversized flat roof of slate reminded me of a cage. A weathervane sticking out depicted a man on a horse slaying a dragon. The poor creature was hunted, just like me.

The monster that haunted my nightmares perched on a raised stone platform in the center of the roof, frozen in place, his granite eyes staring right though my soul. My skin crawled.

Hate him. Hate him. Hate him.

"You and me both."

I stared out over the landscape. Most deemed the ruins

haunted. The truth was, the gargoyle killed anyone who accidentally stumbled anywhere near the ruins during the daytime, which was why I refused to ask for anyone's help. I'd placed signs around the surrounding woods to scare people from the ruins and encourage the myths about deadly spirits living here.

I leapt over rubble and sprinted toward the tower. An orange hue glowed to my left through the trees. My pulse raced, and I rushed up the tower, gripping the grooves I'd chiseled into the stone for my hands and feet.

Halfway up, the sun's rays speared upward from the horizon. My heart galloped, and already the spark of energy prickled over my scalp. Goddess, not yet.

You're too late.

As I climbed the wall, I tried to go faster, but my toe slipped, and I gasped as I dug my fingers into the holes in the wall. Heavy footfalls boomed across the roof.

It's coming for you.

My veins turned to ice. My head itched as if I'd fallen into poison ivy. My hair grew back in fast motion, the tresses already hitting my shoulders. *Fuck!*

Keeping my shit together, I scaled up like a spider, my breath wedged in my throat. The window was in sight, and my golden hair cascaded around me, growing at lightning speed like a waterfall. The weight pulled me backward. With every move, it felt like I was carrying a mountain on my back.

The ledge was within reach.

There were thunderous steps overhead.

I seized the window frame.

A shadow loomed over me. I held back the strangled cry in my chest. I scrambled inside and threw myself in a forward roll. I landed on my back, heaps of blonde hair spreading around me.

The bag I lay on dug into my spine. I gasped for air, unable to move. My pulse drummed in my ears as I listened for the distinct flap of wings, the grating of stone.

After the longest moments of my life, nothing happened, so I exhaled loudly. "Hell, that was close."

Really? You don't say. Tonight's heist wasn't worth the risk. You were reckless.

"Oh, that's where you're wrong. It was completely worth it." I pulled myself up to a sitting position, wrestling my arms out of the bag's straps tangled in my hair.

Movement shifted in the shadows of my abode. Darkness flooded the place, but Gingernuts emerged from the kitchen. His golden fur dragged behind him like a cape, but it grew shorter, magically drawn into his body before my eyes, while my mane grew and slithered outward across the rug like dozens of snakes, wriggling for escape.

At dusk every day, my long hair withered away and regrew at dawn. Yep, the damn spell from five years ago hadn't worked entirely, but it had given me freedom during the night. I embraced it because it offered me time to find a solution to get rid of the gargoyle for good.

Still don't like the cat's name. "Princess" suited him fine.

I laughed. "I disagree. He's a boy with oversized nuts. I'm sure the female cats would love him for it."

He meowed and spun on the spot, pawing at his long fur to keep it from vanishing. But within moments, he'd morphed back into the tabby cat I'd lured into my high prison five years ago. That same incantation not only put the gargoyle into sleep mode through the night but also transferred my long hair to the cat. It wasn't as long as mine, but still ridiculously lengthy. I was left with a short-cropped hairstyle, which I loved. That must be why the witch had told me to get an animal for the spell. But if I knew the enchantment would have made the cat the gargoyle's prisoner, I might have reconsidered, but then again, Gingernuts pranced about at night with his locks as if he were the lion of this castle.

Now, he was my pet, and I adored him.

More like hostage.

"Oh, you're not a captive, are you, Gingernuts?" I used my baby voice as I always did around him.

He lifted his chin, staring away from me as he hobbled past me on his three legs. He pounced onto my hair, rolled himself under the mess, and covered himself with the strands. He was used to concealing himself every time the gargoyle neared the window.

"Come here, you." I snatched him into my arms and pressed him to my chest. "Oh, I missed you so much." I kissed the top of his head, despite his paw pushing against my chin. "Feel like going outside to chase insects? Get some exercise?"

He stopped squirming and looked at me as if I'd declared bath time.

Stop teasing him; he hates the outdoors.

Gingernuts bounded out of my arms and kept meowing. This was quite unlike him. His usual response was to give me a nasty look most mornings when I returned—probably for taking back my hair. The little guy adored the hair too much.

Except right now, he lingered near my feet, looking from me to the left, where I had my bed set up. The morning light crept into the tower, lighting the kitchen to my right and a floor of cushions against the back wall. I'd painted a field of flowers there with dragons in the air and a castle in the distance. I used to imagine I was a princess who'd been locked up, and my Prince Charming would come to my rescue. That never happened, of course.

Gingernuts prowled toward the free-standing wardrobe and kept glancing at me, then the cupboard.

"Did you catch another bird or lizard and put it in there for me?" It wouldn't be the first time I'd come home to find my room drowning in feathers, and all I could imagine was he'd attacked any bird that had perched on the window or some poor reptile that had scrambled up here looking for food. It must have happened a lot because it had become a common occurrence. Last week, I'd found five dead skunks. Yet I didn't have it in me to close the wooden shutters and keep Gingernuts cooped up, as there were no other windows for fresh air.

Not ready for another cleanup, I got to my feet and shoved a hand into my bag. I grabbed a leather-bound book and took it out. Flipping through it, most pages were torn out, but that hadn't mattered when I'd found a section on gargoyles.

You risked our lives by breaking into a lord's house for a freakin' book.

"Not just any book. This could save me." The title read *All Things Undead.* I had no clue what the deal was with the gargoyle, but technically, he was an inanimate object walking around. I would have spent more time searching through the bookshelves because there were so many more texts, but the owner had returned home early. And I had no intention of getting tossed into prison only to have the gargoyle come and break me out before he beat me.

Though I might return later to see what else he had in his library.

Yeah, you help others but still can't find a solution to your problem.

I sighed. "Give me a break. I'm trying." I waved the book in the air. "Hello, Exhibit A. We gain magical intelligence on the gargoyle and how to take it down for good."

Gingernuts was standing on my hair and clawing at my pants. He kept glancing up at me, then at the wardrobe.

"Geez, what's with the wardrobe?" I marched across the room when the door to the tall wardrobe swung open. I flinched and lurched backward, my hand falling to my waist for my knife. Legs planted apart, I was ready for something to pounce out.

Instead, a man with light brown hair falling to his waist stood in my wardrobe, shoving aside my hanging clothes.

"Whoa!" Who in the world was the strange man in my bedroom?

CHAPTER 4

"**W**h-Who are you?" My voice stammered. Shit like someone hiding in my wardrobe had never happened in the past thirteen years I'd lived in the tower. A hundred questions swirled in the forefront of my mind. I touched my waist and drew a blade from my belt because every woman needed protection. Metal never did anything to the gargoyle, but I'd seen other monsters that weren't made of stone, and my dad hadn't raised a fool.

Maybe he can help you escape the tower.

"What are you talking about?" I lowered my chin, speaking to myself, needing to clear my muddled thoughts. Was he going to hurt me… or could he potentially help me with my problem?

Gingernuts was at my side, hissing at the newcomer. I attempted to wrap my brain around a solution.

The stranger emerged from the shadows. He towered over my five-foot-two height. He had to be at least six feet. *Handsome* didn't come close to describing the man-god in front of me. Full lips, a slender nose, a sharp jawline—everything perfectly symmetrical. His strength showed in his corded neck, wide shoulders, muscular arms, and firm chest.

Warmth flooded deep in my stomach. Okay, so the universe might have just delivered one of my wishes—a sexy man all for myself. But I'd grown up on the streets with my dad. I'd seen all kinds of nice-looking people be downright rotten inside.

Even in his black pants and leather tunic reserved for aristocrats, he reminded me of the guards at Brawl. They had one intention—complete their mission regardless of who they stepped over.

So, why the hell was a man who looked ready to wrestle a wolf hiding in my wardrobe? Or was he from one of the royal families in Haven Realm?

Intensity filled his green eyes. His attention swung from me to the window, and he limped toward the exit, breathless. I froze, convinced he'd dive right out of the tower. Instead, he flattened his back to the wall before peering outside. Was he hiding from the gargoyle?

"What are you doing in my home?"

His gaze slid down my body and to the ocean of hair sprawled around my feet.

I wiggled my weapon at him. "Talk unless you want a crash course in flying."

That's right—jab him in the eye.

I lowered my gaze. "What? That's a bit serial killer."

He's in your home, hiding. What if he was waiting for you to sleep so he could rape you?

"Gods, you're so dramatic. Then why would he have come out of the cupboard?"

"You talking to me?" he asked. "Or the fuzzball, or...? I had no idea a crazy woman lived here."

I lifted my head to find Mr. Handsome studying me with a raised brow.

"Hey, don't judge me." I waved the blade in the air between us. "You know nothing about me. And you don't see me making remarks about you, like how you probably work out most nights to build those muscles. Maybe you have something else to compensate for." I wiggled my eyebrows. "Or you perhaps don't have many friends with such an arrogant attitude. Or even how your clothes are torn, as if you've been attacked. You look strong enough to take down a dragon. Yet you're hiding in my wardrobe. So, that tells me you're most likely a criminal."

He took a deep inhale, his chest expanding, drawing my attention to the muscles, and I shoved away the images of him topless appearing in my head. Instead, I studied the cuts across his knuckles and along his strong forearms. Who had he been fighting?

"Listen, Fluffy, you and Fuzzball can relax," he whispered. "I'm not going to hurt you. I just need a quick place to hide, then I'm out of here." His attention returned to the woodland surrounding the field below. Then he stared back my way. "And what is with the hair? Are you going for the title of 'the longest golden locks in the world?' And how come the cat's fur is short now?"

I patted down my hair and found strands sticking outward. Having someone in my tower and knowing I lived here would lead to problems. He'd tell his friends to go and gawk at the freak, then the gargoyle would try to kill them, and I'd feel guilty. Nope, I didn't need that on my conscience.

"Tell me what you're doing here!"

"Keep quiet, Princess," he mumbled to himself, waving me off with a hand as he scanned the forest. He didn't see me as a threat at all, merely treating me as an inconvenience. Who the hell was this man to come into my home and walk all over me?

Fire hit my chest. "How dare you talk to me like that?" I marched up to him and kicked the back of his knee.

That's it. Take him down.

He groaned and fell forward, his arms flying outward for balance to avoid falling out the window. When he dropped to his knees, I lunged after him and swung my blade, pressing it to his throat.

"Speak," I hissed in his ear. "Because I'm crazy, you know, so my knife might slip."

"You're a wannabe princess in a tower, and you have no idea who you're dealing with." His gravelly voice littered my skin with goosebumps—not from fear, but from just how rousingly sexy he sounded. Fine. I had a problem with husky male voices. They were my weakness big time.

"Why are you here, and who are you?" I demanded.

Another loud sigh from him.

"Hurry up and answer," I said.

Stop wasting time. Just jab once and toss him outside. Easy.

"What's wrong with you? You tell me to stab everyone lately."

In a flash, Mr. Handsome grasped my knife-wielding hand and wrenched me forward in the time it took him to leap to his feet.

I cried out as I lurched forward, except his grip never loosened. He yanked me back around, and I crashed into his rock-hard chest.

My breath expelled, but he had already walked me backward at a brisk pace and pinned me to the wall on the other side of the window. Electricity ignited in the pit of my stomach.

I gasped and writhed under him, but he held on to me, and I might as well have been trapped between two boulders. Yet something roused within me—something thrilling and provoking. The way his eyes pierced into me left me curious to understand who exactly this man was. Why I found myself strangely attracted to him when any normal person would have thrown him out the window for trespassing in their home. But I couldn't toss him to the gargoyle. Not when his fingers pressed into my arms, his body plastered against mine, and his breaths sped up.

"My name's Reed." He kept his voice low, as if afraid someone outside would hear him, while he wrested the blade from my hand and tossed it to the floor.

I sizzled with heat at being so close to him, though it wasn't as if I hadn't been with a man. In the past few years, I'd explored the opposite sex, their manliness, and how they stirred something raw within me, and I even dated one for a while. His name was Gage, and I still pined for him. He had been deliciously exciting, but it didn't work out because I couldn't tell him where I lived or why I could only meet him at night.

He'd once followed me home, and I freaked out. I'd screamed at him to never visit my place. I'd broken it off, terrified of what could have happened. Telling him about the gargoyle wasn't an option because he'd confront the creature and end up dying.

Now, with Reed towering over me and his body wedged up against mine, a spark within rallied forward, and I pushed aside my worries for a few moments. I couldn't stop myself from wondering what it would be like to touch *all* his muscles. My body trembled beneath him while my head screamed to get the hell out of there.

Can't believe you're thinking about this now.

"Someone is hunting my pride." His words sliced through my desires, yet he wasn't moving away. "And I took refuge in this tower, thinking the place was abandoned. I mean you no harm. Just a few moments longer to stay undetected is all I ask."

My heartbeat raced as his words sunk in and made sense. I glanced up, noting the recent gash across his chin and another on his collarbone. My thoughts flew to the times I'd run away from the gargoyle and the few people who'd helped by giving me a ride on their carriage or feeding me. They were my heroes because they hadn't pushed me away when I needed help. So, how could I refuse to assist Reed?

He's lying.

"Pride? As in lion shifter?"

He shook himself, and right before me, his pupils morphed into vertical slit-shaped pupils, and a deep growl rumbled in his throat. I stopped fighting and froze as fear chewed on my insides.

"You get it now, Princess."

"Don't call me that. Who's chasing you? Poachers? A king or queen? Or maybe the priestess ruling over the human Terra realm. I hear she's nasty and hates shifters. What have you done to upset them?"

With a quick glance outside, he replied, "My pride members are vanishing, as are other shifters in Darkwoods. Someone is kidnapping them. No bodies are found; they just disappear. This morning, I followed my sister's screams in the forest, only to find a hooded figure dragging her away by a chain tied to her neck. Others attacked me, each wearing a black collar as if they were someone's pet, and I only survived by running like a coward." His voice fell, and he looked away, enough for his hold to slacken.

I shoved him aside and moved to stand across the room, keeping my eyes on him. I felt for his plight.

"So, you hid in my tower to get away?"

He nodded, and only now that he stood in the sun's full glow did I see the real extent of his wounds. The bleeding scratches on his ear and neck, the blood blotting his shirt and pants from cuts, as if someone had slashed him with dozens of knives. My heart went out to him because I understood getting hunted, feeling defeated, and beaten without pity.

"I spotted a ginger cat scaling the tower using the vines that circle the building. It had freaky hair, but not as long as yours now. I didn't care. I only cared about surviving. So, I followed the animal."

What? "Gingernuts, you've been going out at night?" I stared down at him, wrapped in my blonde locks. He stopped rolling through my hair and meowed short and sharp. "You're so busted." This explained all the critters I'd found in the tower.

Reed kept glancing outside, then back at me.

I hated to see someone in fear for their life. "I have a friend who's a beaver shifter and—"

He cocked an eyebrow. "A beaver shifter? Is that even a thing, or are you making it up?"

I scoffed. "Are you being shifterist? Yes, it's real. Anyway, she had someone hunting her down over a year ago for her fur." She didn't know where I lived either or about the gargoyle, as I was too afraid to tell anyone. What if they wouldn't believe me to stay away during the day? They might visit me and get killed.

Reed studied me, his eyes glazing over as the corners of his mouth twitched. Was he about to break into a smile while I told a serious story? "Keep going," he offered.

"Well, the two men were relentless and followed her everywhere until one day they cornered her in the woods. They insisted her fur would bring a princely sum in the Terra realm. If it wasn't for a passing wolf shifter who came to her rescue, she'd be dead. Even today, she's terrified to go outside alone." I swallowed the hurt at remembering her tears, the way she shook each time she spoke of the incident, and studied Reed. He must have felt lost and trapped.

"It pisses me off that people did that to her," I added. "Ruined her life for their own selfish greed. So, I'm sorry it's happening to you as well. I'll help you if I can. I'll get bandages for your cuts." I turned toward the bathroom, glancing over my shoulder. "You can hide in my tower for as long as you need. I won't hurt you."

He cocked a brow, as if he were about to burst out laughing at my suggestion.

"No, thanks. I've intruded enough. I'll leave shortly and not bring danger to your doorstep. I have to find my sister."

"I insist." Not taking no for an answer, I rushed into the bathroom and collected bandages, a towel, and a small container with water.

With everything set on the table, he took a seat on the chair, and I plonked down in front of him. Drenching the corner of the towel, I wrung out the water and took his arm with a gash running from elbow to wrist. I patted down the injury, cleaning the blood. "What did they cut you with? Your skin looks ripped apart."

"A jagged blade. Bastards were not going to let me get my sister back." His eyes hooded, and I kept cleaning him up before wrapping his arm. When shit happened, sometimes silence was the best companion.

"You're very kind," he said in a soft voice and pushed a strand of hair behind my ear. His light touch left me buzzing. "How come I haven't seen you around?"

I shrugged. "I'm more of a night owl."

"Me, too." He offered me a cute smile. "Maybe we can meet up somewhere in a couple of weeks. I'm praying I track down my sister by then."

"Like a date?" Heat rushed up my neck.

"If you want to call it that. I'll come back and see you."

Panic strangled me, and I straightened in my seat. "Maybe

better if we meet in a week's time outside Brawl just after dusk. What do you think?"

"Sounds good."

A dozen questions whirred in my head. Once I finished cleaning and bandaging him, he got up and checked outside.

"I better go."

As I got up, he marched to my side, and without warning, he leaned in, and his lips brushed mine. Soft and quick, but enough to rock me at the core. My heart fluttered, and butterflies swarmed through my stomach. His hand rested below my ear, his thumb stroking my cheek. Our breaths merged before he broke away.

"A little something," he said, his voice strong and deep, "to tide me over until we meet again."

Not ready to let him go, I reached out for him when a huge shadow fell over the window, blotting out the light in the tower. The gargoyle. I gasped.

"Shit. Move!" Panic gripped me. I hauled him away from the window, but within that same moment, he was ripped from my grasp.

He got sucked out the window, his cry echoing through the tower like a ghost's moan.

My heart slammed into my chest, and I darted after him, my hand reaching out for his leg, but it was too late.

The gargoyle had him by the arm and flew across the open land. Guilt sawed on my insides. What had I done? Would the gargoyle beat him senseless? Kill him like the other people? I held my churning stomach.

"Put him down," I screamed, but my words fell on deaf ears. The creature had never paid me attention before, so he wouldn't now. I should have hidden Reed, told him to keep quiet until nightfall. I never expected the gargoyle to hear our conversation.

My eyes were glued on the monstrosity carrying the kicking and thrashing lion shifter. Just above the canopy of trees, he dropped him. My stomach iced over.

The gargoyle swooped in after him and plucked him out before dropping him again. A strangled cry bubbled in my throat. Fear imprisoned me in its straitjacket, and I couldn't do anything but cry.

I contemplated going after him, but then what?

Get beaten again, and how long will it take for your ribs to heal this time?

Swallowing the mountain in my throat, I fell to my knees in front of my window and sobbed in my hands. Hating my life. Hating the gargoyle. Hating that I felt useless and so hopeless.

"I want the gargoyle dead, blown to a million pieces, torn apart, along with this goddamn tower." Every inch of me trembled, but when the distinct flap of the wings sounded nearby, I jerked my head up.

The gargoyle returned, his wide wings sailing through the sky.

I jostled backward and rushed into my bedroom to the farthest corner. His shadow flew over the window and landed on the roof with a thud. I flinched. Heavy footfalls pounded overhead, then silenced.

I slid to a crouched position and hugged my knees, my vision blurred with tears. Was Reed dead?

Forget about him. You're lucky not to get beaten.

But forgetting was an impossibility. Like my entire fucked-up life. My tears rolled free. Breaths came in shallow gasps. Death surrounded my life, and I barely battled to keep my head above water.

Something nudged my leg, and I looked down at Gingernuts, rubbing himself against me and purring. I collected him into my lap and crossed my legs. "What would I do without you? You're all I have."

Hey, and me!

"You don't count because you're just my mind gone haywire."

Heaviness pulled at my puffy eyes, so I climbed into bed with Gingernuts and curled in on myself, unable to stop picturing Reed swinging in the gargoyle's arms. Was he out there somewhere dying? As soon as nightfall came, I'd find him. Until then, I'd pray he held on until I arrived.

CHAPTER 5

"*R*eed!" I woke with a startle, his name screeching past my throat. Sweat drenched me, my hair plastered to my head and neck. Had the gargoyle killed the lion shifter? There was nothing I could have done to stop it.

A balmy breeze swished past my cheeks, and outside, the orange skies darkened. Nightfall approached. On the windowsill, Gingernuts perched like a god, overlooking the land, waiting for the sun to descend so he could claim my hair. He could have it all. Untangling myself from the sheets, I hurried to the bathroom, my hair dragging behind me, coating the floor and cushioning my steps.

Surely, Reed had survived. He seemed agile and would have run, using the forest to dodge the gargoyle. Right? My stomach hurt thinking about him dead.

I passed the wooden panel that portioned my bathroom from the rest of the room. I'd painted it bright yellow to lighten the place, though right now, I felt anything but cheery.

After a quick wash of my face and body, a squawk came from outside. I jolted around, knocking over the bucket. Water gushed all over the wooden floor. "Oh, shit!"

I grabbed two towels from the rack and laid them over the mess, soaking up the water. Everything made me jumpy and unfocused while my chest ached with worry over Reed.

I patted down the hair and glanced in the mirror. Darkness danced under my eyes, so I pinched my cheeks to bring out their color and tried to smile but couldn't. I still looked like I hadn't slept for a week. Lately, I'd woken up exhausted, even though I'd slept through the day. I ought to have slept more, but I refused to spend another second of free time inside the tower.

Something tugged on my hair behind me. Gingernuts was there, kneading his claws into the bundle on the ground.

"Don't worry. This will be yours soon enough."

I climbed into leather pants and a shirt, but the buttons refused to close up. What the hell? I glanced down to see I'd put it on inside-out.

What's wrong with you today?

"Stop talking." I redressed and pulled on a black vest over the shirt, which I laced tightly across the front as I stepped into my boots. With my blade tucked in my belt, I stared outside at the blackening skies. Not long now. I rushed through my routine of feeding Gingernuts dried fish pieces along with a bowl of milk. I prepared myself a plate, too. Bread, cheese, and lard. I couldn't stomach much more. Sitting at the table with my food and Gingernuts eating his nearby, I flipped through the book I'd stolen yesterday from a lord. Opening it flat on the gargoyle page, I read the text and stuffed a piece of bread and cheese into my mouth.

Ah, okay, so apparently, the first-ever gargoyle had been a witch's lover. He had once been a normal human who'd betrayed her, so the witch had turned his heart to stone, making him incapable of ever loving again or feeling emotions. Another witch had found him wandering aimlessly through the sandy realm of Utaara and decided he'd make the perfect soldier, so she'd taken his blood, replicated it, and injected the stuff into dead bodies. Add dark magic, and they'd come to life as stone creatures. The witch had used her undead army to battle enemies on behalf of a royal family in Haven Realm in Darkwoods.

I glanced outside momentarily and took another bite of my meal. This history had taken place right here in the ruins. That was where the gargoyles had come from, though they'd lost the fight because the family had been killed. So, did the witch who'd hexed me have more gargoyles waiting somewhere? Or had she just found one and worked out a way to activate it?

I gripped the book and hurried through the next line... A dragon-tooth dagger could pierce their exterior.

Hell! I choked on my meal and smacked a palm into my chest, then drank down the stuck crumbs with my glass of milk.

"What the hell?" I reread the lines. There was a weapon that destroyed gargoyles? "Son of a bitch. Why didn't I steal this book earlier?"

How will you find such a dragon dagger?

My ex, Gage, was a dragon shifter, but I'd never seen him fully transform. Once, he'd unleashed his wings, which were spectacular, but that was it, and he'd refused to talk about why he wouldn't change all the way. I somehow suspected he had a fraction of dragon blood in him, giving him minimal abilities, but he told everyone he was a full-blown dragon. Regardless of his reasons for potentially lying, he might know where I could find a dragon's tooth.

I'd heard stories that there might be a few dragons living deep in the forest and mountains of the Wildfire realm. No one I'd spoken to had ever seen a dragon, either, and for good reason. They'd burn you to a crisp.

Outside, the sun had almost vanished behind the horizon. Once it had, I'd go and look for Reed.

I kept reading. There was a weakness to the undead army. The spell had softened their hearts. If anyone pierced the organ, the gargoyle would turn to dust and perish.

I gasped and slapped my hand on the table, startling Ginger-nuts, who leaped around and hissed in my direction.

"Sorry, sorry. But, shit! This is it. The freaking demon upstairs is going down." My knees bounced under the table as I returned to the book.

Without the dragon-tooth dagger to smash through the stone body, one had to get close enough to stab a blade in between the moving stones protecting its heart. All before the gargoyle attacked you.

You sure about this? Sounds a bit too easy for my liking.

"Didn't you just read the book? I could use a normal knife." This was the first time I'd found a way to possibly take down the creature. Even if I didn't have a dragon-tooth dagger, I could pierce the heart through the gaps with a normal blade. It didn't come without dangers, but I knew where the best bladesman in Darkwoods worked. For enough money, Dustin would do anything. Yeah, getting close enough to the gargoyle to stab his heart was a dangerous job, and hence, Dustin would ask for a huge payment. He was fast with knives, hopefully meaning he didn't need to get too close to the gargoyle. His throwing ability wasn't something I could replicate, so I would need to count on his help.

Don't get your hopes up. This could fail big time.

On my feet, I paced from the bed to the table, ignoring my negative side. I was desperate and needed a way to eradicate the gargoyle. I'd detail the risks to Dustin, but if things went haywire, he'd have to run to avoid getting hurt. The gargoyle was solid stone during the night from Vanore's spell, but when the sun rose, his body form morphed into smaller rocks that allowed for his movement and revealed gaps for stabbing him. Meaning as soon as dawn arrived, we had to skewer the gargoyle just as he woke up and before he got the upper hand on us.

So tonight, I had to visit the local club, Brawl, where Gage worked as a bouncer, and ask him about a dragon-tooth dagger while I was there to speak with Dustin. I chewed on my lower lip. It had been months since I'd seen him, and each time I did, my emotions ran amuck. Guess that came from breaking up with a man who I adored, but I'd rather risk a broken heart than the gargoyle breaking him.

A few months ago, a drunk had stumbled into the ruins, and the gargoyle had killed him. Reality crippled me. If I hadn't been careful, that could have been Gage. He'd kept insisting on taking me home, and I'd used every excuse under the sun to keep him away. This was why I had to break up with him—for his own safety.

My breath hitched all the way to my lungs. Reed was somewhere out there. Was he still alive? I had to check to make sure he wasn't lying there dead or wounded.

I returned to the book, and at the bottom of the page, a section about only powerful witches controlling a gargoyle ended mid-sentence because the next page had been torn out. *Damn.* But I'd read enough to know what I wanted.

Most ancient spell books had vanished at the time of the old war between the realms, and none were available for sale. So, it was a surprise I'd heard about this text from a client, even if it was tattered and torn.

"Today will be a good day." I smiled and bounced on my toes. "I feel it in my bones."

* * *

THE STIFLING NIGHT air closed in around me as I dashed through the woods, puffing as I ran from the tower.

"Reed, can you hear me?" I gripped a lantern while I scanned the dark undergrowth for him. I could have sworn this was exactly where the gargoyle had dumped him. Around me was debris, ferns growing to my knees, and a few boulders, but no sign of a body. I kept searching, not ready to leave just in case he remained hurt or, worse yet, dead. What if another predator had made a meal of him? Even if it were a wild cougar or panther, such an attack would leave behind a clue, right? Blood or bones.

Sweat drenched my skin, and my heart throbbed as I pictured Reed torn up and dead somewhere in the woods. My fingers curled into fists. I scanned the scrubland, the shadows between trees.

"Reed!" I yelled. "If you're here, say something. Please." I jumped over an oversized dead branch just as an owl hooted overhead. I flinched and plastered my back against a tree. Tonight, the forest seemed darker than usual, as if a black mass collected above on the branches. Or it could have been me, feeling alone and vulnerable.

Cougars attack from behind. We won't see it coming. Leave now.

"You're not helping." Staying on the main track offered a better chance of seeing anything sneaking up on me. Except I couldn't leave yet. I had to keep searching for Reed, so I kept moving through the forest. "Reed!"

After what felt like half the night and coming up short in finding Reed or any evidence of him butchered, I marched out the way I'd come. I sped up, leaving behind the dense woods, thinking I might pay the local lion shifter pride a visit to make sure he'd arrived home all right.

Before long, I reached the dirt track and hurried along, swinging my lantern left and right at every shadow, imagining a cougar leaping out at me. The hairs on my arms stood on end the whole trip, and I looked over my shoulder at every noise. Yeah, this would be the last time I listened to my paranoid subconscious.

Voices reached me before the lights of the tiny town, Ghost, revealed themselves. Ghost had a scattering of tiny huts that reminded me of crouching wolves. Most of the cabins were rentable for a night of pleasure with one of the women working at the masseuse parlor.

If someone weren't looking for the location, they'd miss it in a heartbeat. No one talked about Ghost, but most local men knew it existed and visited frequently. The only reason I'd discovered the place was because I'd gone exploring in the woods and found the area during the night.

I followed the narrow track toward the town. Light poured out of the tavern windows, and a sign, "The Foolish Moon," hung over the entrance. A man slouched by the door, either sleeping or passed out from too much booze. Voices and music boomed from inside while across the makeshift road stood a two-story wooden home with a verandah. Out front were two men studying me with leering glares, guards for the girls working at the parlor.

Neither of those places was my destination. I searched for

the house where anyone with a silver coin or ten could double or triple it in a night. I marched past and headed to the first hut near the tavern. The windows were covered in lace curtains, revealing nothing inside. A garden of yellow flowers filled the front yard. It wasn't much to look at, and I suspected that had been the intention. I set my lantern just outside the house, alongside several others.

Reaching the door, knocked—three quick thumps and a sharp yelp, followed by two slow slaps of my palm to the wooden frame. Yep, one had to know the right way of getting in or you were booted out. Lucky me, I'd dated a bouncer, and he'd revealed the secrets.

The door creaked open to a dimly lit room, and an elderly woman with short, white hair greeted me. Age lines scored her face, and one might have mistaken her as weak. Worst mistake ever. I'd watched her stand up to men twice her size. She owned Brawl, the most popular fight club in the realm. It wasn't illegal, but it was exclusive.

"Girl, it's 'bout time," she said. "Gage's been driving me crazy with his paranoia that you weren't coming back to visit him."

I rolled my eyes and stepped inside, bathed in the strong smell of spices. "He needs to get a life." I hugged Bertha, her petite size all part of her illusion, a feint to make the unsuspecting think they could get past her. The woman was a master in wielding a sword, and she always targeted her victim's ankles.

"Good to see you again. Is Dustin fighting tonight?" I broke our hug.

"He's up first, and they're about to begin, so get in there." She waved me in and added, "All bets are placed at the door now. Too many people weren't paying."

"Makes sense." I strolled through the room with a couch facing an unlit fireplace and down a corridor with a single candle sitting on a side table tucked in the corner. Farther to my right stood a metal door. Instead of reaching for the handle, I tapped the wall to my right. The wall slid open on springs. A set of steps led downstairs, and more candles sat in carved-out pockets in the walls, guiding my passage. As I descended, the door shut behind me. Hoots and cheers found me from lower.

I rushed down the two flights of steps where the air stunk of perspiration and freshly turned soil. I pushed aside fabric draped over the entrance and waltzed into a room four times the size of my place inside the tower. In the center stood an arena surrounded by sandbags and filled with hay. Candles littered the three enormous candelabras dangling from the ceiling, and all around were chairs filled with people cheering. A bald man with way too many muscles flexed his biceps for the audience. A young man dressed in red and green clothing with a hat tipped with bells was blowing raspberries at the strong man, kicking straw at him. Mr. Muscles roared, grabbed the jester by the waist, and tossed him across the room, where he landed behind the chairs. The crowd exploded in applause. I smirked at the theatrics people adored.

"First fight's about to start. What'll you bet?" a woman on my right asked as I turned to find her tapping her fingernails on the chalkboard behind her, on which she had scribbled two names. Dustin Incinerator vs. Cayden the Chaos Bringer. Everyone who attended had to bet with the house as a minimum for the cost of entry.

"One token for Dustin."

I paid and collected my red coin carved with a wolf head on one side. With it in my pocket, I slid into the back row, which was empty and meant I didn't have to make small talk. Don't get me wrong. I loved crowds and mingling and letting myself be carried away with conversations. Anything that made me feel less alone. But tonight, I wasn't here to make friends. I had to stay focused. I'd approach Dustin after his battle to ask for his help.

A loud bell rang, and everyone fell silent. I straightened in my seat as my champion, enormous as a bear with a hairy chest and shoulders, strutted into the pit. I smirked, having seen him fight. Despite his size, the man was fast, which meant he'd be quick when tackling the gargoyle and if he had to escape. I counted on his agility to keep him alive.

Dustin pounded his chest with a fist and roared, giving me shivers. Who didn't enjoy a decent fight? The crowd exploded with cheers… definitely a favorite. He rarely lost a fight, but then, would I expect anything less from a bear shifter? Their kind was rarely seen outside the White Peak realm. I'd met a few in my time, and each had been burly and terrifying.

A few full moons ago, a bear shifter had put out a call to help him with a curse, so I'd caught up with him at a tavern in Darkwoods, and we'd struck a deal. For a huge bag of gold coins, I'd promised him a witch who'd fix his problem. He'd been quick to agree, and one thing I'd give his kind, they took everything seriously—from the six shots of rum he'd drunk without a sign of being intoxicated to his ceaselessly stoic expression to punching out a thug who'd decided on the wrong time to hold up the tavern.

Anyway, Bee had been the perfect person to help the bear shifter with his curse. She was a friend of mine I'd bumped into when I'd sensed her magic the first time we'd met. And damn, that girl was powerful, but she'd said she couldn't help me with my hex because she only did white magic. A load of bull. She was scared of her power—I saw it in the way she trembled and shied away from the topic. I'd had plans to convince her to change her mind over a month ago. I was supposed to meet her at a bar in White Peak to introduce her to the bear shifter. It was risky to travel so far, but this was the highest-paying job I'd ever been offered. So, I'd booked a seat on a super-fast carriage with dragon horses. Except the venture had ended brutally for me. The carriage's tire had snapped and sent the vehicle into a spin, crashing us into a tree. Both horses had panicked and broken free. I'd trekked back home fast but never made it. The gargoyle had found me and beaten me so bad, I hadn't been able to walk for days. I missed our appointment.

Hopefully, she'd helped the bears with their dilemma. I might need to find a way to catch up with her soon and explain why I'd ditched her.

Don't recommend it. She lives in Terra and it's too far. You take too many unnecessary risks.

"Maybe I'll ask her to visit me somewhere in the middle between us." It would give me enough time to return home before sunrise.

"Hey, Sugar Pops, still talking to yourself?" A deep male voice found me, and a ping of excitement filled me as it always did when Gage approached.

He plonked down next to me, his arm brushing against mine, and his warmth was a blanket engulfing me. No matter the weather, his skin sizzled hot. He wore a black shirt with gold buttons, his belt buckle was a golden flame, and even his damn shoes were tipped with gold. Yep, dragon shifters loved their sparkle.

"Heard you've been missing me." I stuck out my tongue at him.

He had the greenest emerald eyes crowned by busy brows. Short, black hair shone like onyx stones beneath the candlelight. His stubble added to his strong appearance—a square jawline, solid chest, and thick arms. But something more always lay behind his gaze, like a hidden treasure just out of reach.

We might have broken up a few months ago, but I still adored him. I should never have dated him. What could I offer? A life of only spending time together at night? How long before I would slip up and the gargoyle killed him because Gage wouldn't back down from a fight? I wouldn't wish that upon anyone. So, I'd made the hardest decision in the world. I'd broken up with the man who treated me like an angel, and it had defeated me, but this was for his safety, not mine. I had a shitty life. And now doubts flooded my mind about asking Dustin to help.

What if things derail fast with the gargoyle?

I planned to put myself in the line of fire to give Dustin a chance to run if the situation got out of hand. The gargoyle always went for me over others. But I prayed it wouldn't get to that stage and that Dustin's swiftness with a blade and his strength would give us the upper hand over the gargoyle. Something I lacked.

"I always miss you," Gage whispered, distracting me from my thoughts.

"Don't, Gage. Please." My chest constricted. We'd forged a bond where we used to finish each other's sentences, where I'd beam with excitement each moment we spent together, where his laughter brought more joy to my life than I'd ever experienced before.

Around us, the audience boomed with cheers. Dustin pumped his fist into the air while his opponent lay sprawled at his feet. I'd missed a great blow, yet sitting next to Gage brought back too many amazing memories—and that wasn't a good thing. Gage always left me tingling, so I'd kept my distance from Brawl to avoid the agony.

"What's been keeping you away for so long?" he asked in his nonchalant way, as if he didn't care that we sat next to each other without me reaching out and taking his hand in mine like we always used to do during fighting matches. I'd squeeze his fingers each time someone threw a punch.

"Been busy with jobs and stuff." I smiled, but the gesture felt fake, knowing I was here to ask Dustin for help with a problem I couldn't tell Gage about. If I succeeded tonight, Gage and I might have a chance together.

The book I'd stolen had said to stab the gargoyle in the heart. That was my focus. Back in the arena, Dustin had his opponent over his head, spinning him as if he were bread dough being tossed into the air. The crowd laughed and screamed for him to slam his challenger down.

Gage's leg nudged mine.

I glanced up at him. "Have you, by any chance, worked out a way to transform into a full dragon yet? I've seen your strong wings that once. Just curious if you managed to change the rest of your body." They were mesmerizing and glorious. Apparently, the only part of him that could shift. I squirmed in my seat, hoping he wouldn't read too much into my curiosity.

He raised an arched brow. "If I had, I'd have flown over your tower to get your attention. I'd collect you and fly you to every realm you've always wanted to visit."

And that right there was why Gage would always be in my heart… He loved hard, and he was loyal. I missed him so damn much, but fear kept me at bay. I couldn't risk his safety until I was free. He deserved better. Heartache swirled unrestrained in my chest, and my head swam with the cruelty of life. Yet Gage looked at me with a smile in his eyes. One day I craved to carry the same positive outlook for my future.

"One of my clients is searching for a dragon-tooth dagger. That's why I ask." I hated lying to him and lowered my gaze.

He rubbed a hand over his jawline, the scratchy sound of his stubble cutting through the silence between the applause. Dustin paraded around the arena, his rival on the ground with a bloody face.

"Wish I could help, but…" His words faded, and I took his hand in mine, squeezing it.

"It's all right. Sorry. I shouldn't have asked." Regret washed over me in slow waves. He'd grown up homeless with no family, discarded as a child, never knowing much about dragon lore.

His brow furrowed, and I stared out as Dustin marched out of the arena. He'd have a few more battles tonight, but before that, I had to speak to him.

I slid to the edge of my seat, my attention on Dustin, who slipped behind a black curtain that surrounded the room in a U-shape.

"Hey, can you get me backstage? I need to speak with Dustin."

"Why?" Gage's face twisted into one of disgust. "The shifter's a murderer-for-hire, and most steer away from him, so what would you want with him? Planning on knocking someone out?" He cocked an eyebrow, staring at me with judgment.

I feigned innocence and placed a hand on my heart. "Such accusations. I might have a job for him for a client." Gage didn't need to know I was the so-called client. "Now, can you help or—"

He got to his feet, towering over me. "He's hired for two things… appearing in a fighting pit or taking someone out. So, what's going on?" His voice darkened, and his eyes narrowed with that inquisitive glare.

"It's not what you think." I licked my lips and kept staring between the curtain and back at Gage, who eyed me with suspicion. "But don't worry. I'll sneak in myself." I got up and slipped past him, but he grasped my wrist.

"Not if I stop you." His grip tightened. "Talk to me, Elliana."

Just freaking tell him already.

I rolled my eyes but couldn't bring myself to reveal the truth because then he'd try to stop me. Or worse, he'd insist on joining us. I couldn't focus if he got hurt, and I was already putting Dustin in danger. Even if I said *no*, Gage would follow. He couldn't sit back and would get involved with taking down the gargoyle, meaning one or all of us would get hurt.

"Look. It's just a client who needs Dustin for a job, and I don't ask too many questions about the tasks, you know that. The less I know sometimes, the better. I collect my money and connect people. It's what I do. Now cut me some slack. Will you help?"

He didn't speak for a long moment. Instead, he studied me, as if trying to see into my thoughts to extract the truth. My palms sweated, and I wiped them down the front of my pants. Lying to Gage never sat right with me. I just hoped that one day I could tell him everything, and he'd forgive me.

"Can't believe I'm considering this," he said. "You know he's a nasty piece of work. I don't want you alone with him."

His words scared me. I'd heard rumors that Dustin murdered without remorse. He was someone who'd take out the gargoyle. And if that meant spending time alone with a man who killed without care, I'd take my chances. Because it meant the possibility of freedom.

CHAPTER 6

Gage knocked on the backstage door in Brawl.

"What?" Dustin barked from inside his dressing room.

"Backstage" consisted of a long corridor drenched in shadows and a few candles from candelabras in the shape of hands on the wall circling the outside of the fighting pit, all concealed by curtains. There were three doors back here. I had no idea what was in the other two, but Gage had led me directly to the one with a punched indent in the wood.

Gage stared down at me, giving me the arched brow look that said, *you sure about this?*

I nodded. Because goddammit, I'd been beaten by the gargoyle so many times that having survived so far, I'd make it through this as well. My priority was gaining freedom, not cowering in fear. Otherwise, I might as well have been dead.

"You decent? Got a visitor," Gage called out.

"Come in already."

Gage opened the door to a small room with stone walls. A long table sat against one end... no, it was too low to be a table. A bed, perhaps, as it had a sheet over it, or maybe space for Dustin to be bandaged if wounded. Speaking of who, the man in question lounged on a chair near a dressing table with no mirror. He had his legs propped up on another seat across from him, and nearby was a small table with a bottle of what stunk like fermented prunes. Homemade vodka. He wore only baggy pants the color of sunrise, reminding me of a genie, but with the way his lips curled into a wry grin, I doubted he'd find my observation funny.

Dustin swung back a shot of the drink that reeked of poison, and I was convinced it could burn away my nose hairs if I sniffed it. He burped, and I scrunched my nose. Damn, he was grotesque.

"You brought me a groupie. A bit skinny for my liking, but she'll do." He rubbed his hands and lowered his feet to the ground.

Fire jostled through my veins. "I am not here for your pleasure. And for your information, I'm considered medium-build."

Dustin boomed with laughter and clapped. "I like her. She's feisty."

"She's here with a proposition for you," Gage said, squaring his shoulders, his voice deep.

"I'm all for being solicited." He remained seated, but his lingering gaze didn't go astray as it sailed down my body and back up, halting on my chest. I resisted the urge to cross my arms and held his stare.

"I'm not here for something like that," I insisted. "Otherwise, I'd be talking to Gage." I turned to Gage, and he winked my way, smirking his devilish grin. Damn, the guy had my insides twirling. "Can you leave us for a bit, please?"

Dustin howled with laughter. "You heard the lady; she doesn't want an audience."

The corded muscles in Gage's neck twitched, yet he didn't move.

"I won't be long... promise. Give us a moment alone." I touched Gage's forearm and gently nudged him toward the door. I'd come to the conclusion that Gage wouldn't go far, so if Dustin pushed his luck, I'd scream for help.

"Little girl, I can promise you that I will need more than a moment. Give us an hour, Gage." Dustin grunted like a boar, and I might have thrown up in my mouth. *Eww.*

Unless, of course, he was the world's most gracious lover, yet somehow I struggled to believe it. Yep, by day, he slaughtered villages without a sliver of emotion, but by night, he seduced females and pleased them to the nth degree. Something wasn't right with this picture.

"I'll be right in the hallway." Gage eyed me for a long moment before marching outside.

I quickly shut the door behind him and turned to the bull of a man with beady eyes, a crooked nose, and way too many scars across his bald scalp. He was someone I'd steer clear of because just the way he stared at me made me sick to my stomach.

He studied me with a confused look on his face, as if waiting for me to strip or dance for him. Not in this lifetime.

I crossed the room and sat on the chair across from him while pulling out a pouch jiggling with money from my pocket. Money I'd saved for years. How much did one pay a mercenary?

His gaze narrowed as he leaned into his chair. He placed his hands behind his head, smiling. "I won't deny a woman the chance to pay me for the pleasure."

"Well, this is your lucky day. Umm, no, that came out wrong." My face burned up, and I fiddled with the cord from the money pouch. "I mean, I have money for you, and you will do a job for me." Did I need to act tough and bargain? At the markets, I always haggled over the best price, but this wasn't me arguing over the cost of a dress.

One of his eyes closed, as if it normally did when he thought. Maybe he'd been hit too many times in the face. "Keep talking."

I swallowed past my dried throat and lowered my voice.

"I need you to take out a gargoyle."

"Come again?" He boomed with laughter, his hand slapping his thigh. "One of the guys put you up to this, didn't they? Who was it? I'm gonna get him back good."

I gritted my teeth. "Can you just pay attention? This isn't a joke."

"There's no such thing as gargoyles."

"Yes, they exist." I raised my voice, then glanced at the door, expecting Gage to barge inside. "You have to stab the creature in the heart." I mimicked the action, yet it worried me that this wasn't going to work. Dustin wasn't taking this seriously, and what if he panicked when he saw the gargoyle? When he realized it wasn't as easy as I'd made it sound? But I didn't want him freaked out, or he'd never take the job.

"Easiest money you'll ever make." I forced a smile.

He scratched an ear and stood, shadowing over me like a giant who could just as easily stomp on me if he so chose. I held back a shiver at his overbearing size.

"I don't work with myths. You're wasting your time." Dustin strode to the bed where a rack of clothing hung, and he reached for a cloak. "Now, unless you're here to suck my cock, fuck off."

I cringed but held back my response and stormed after him.

"All the legends are true. I've seen one myself." I shoved the bag of rattling money against his arm. "One hundred gold coins are on offer. Think of how many girls you could hire with this. Your own harem. Maybe you won't need to fight here anymore."

His attention stayed on the bag of coins despite his frown. "I like fighting."

"Okay, fine, keep the job, but who doesn't need more money, right?"

He nodded, and I stuffed the purse back into the pocket of my pants, bulging like I concealed a ball.

"I'll make an agreement with you," I said. "If I can't show you that the gargoyle is real, I'll suck your dick." That time, bile hit the back of my throat from disgust, and I swallowed past it. "But if I'm right, you kill it and get the coins. Win-win if you ask me." I gripped my hips and lifted my chin, though I'd never let Dustin touch me.

Sometimes, showing confidence was half the trick to winning jobs. I'd learned that by getting people to help my clients with their problems. Like the time I'd convinced a cunning fox shifter to part with some of his tail hairs for a sorcerer. Two unrelated people who I brought together. The magician had gotten the last ingredient for the healing spell for his daughter, and the fox shifter had gained a spell to help him run faster than any wolf chasing him down.

Dustin swiveled his chin from left to right and snatched my arm. He reached out for me with such swiftness, I lost my breath and iced over, and I gritted my teeth.

"Get off me." I pushed against his chest, but it was like trying to move against a mountain.

"Girl, you make a fool of me, and I find there's no creature, you'll do more than suck me off." His large nose scrunched, and lips peeled back over yellow teeth.

My insides curdled like milk, and everything about Dustin repelled me, but I couldn't lose this challenge.

"Agreed." I wriggled out of his grasp. "Now let's go," I hissed.

He swung the cape over his shoulders. "Got a few more fights first. Then we leave."

I huffed, and a sinking sensation rattled through me. I wanted to get this done now. "How long will that take?"

"I finish around dawn."

"No, that won't work." I paced in a circle now. "That's too late. We have to be there to do this before sunrise." I clasped my hands to my stomach.

You're cutting it too short. Forget this plan.

"What about tomorrow? Can you finish earlier?" I asked, hating my pleading voice.

"No can do." He reached over and tenderly cupped my face, as if we had a thing going on, and trust me, nothing would ever happen between us. "Tomorrow, I leave for the Utaara realm, as I've been hired by the sultan as his personal guard for a few weeks."

Scenario after scenario whirred through my mind. I had the perfect man to take down the gargoyle within a tiny window of time. And sure, I could find someone else, but how long would it take to track down a person with precision knife skills and brawn? I didn't want to wait for weeks either because what if Dustin never returned or something happened to him? Nope, I couldn't pass on this opportunity.

"Okay, fine, we do it tonight. I'll wait in the audience. But if you want this job, we need to leave way before dawn. Or no deal."

"Girl, such things can't be rushed. There's a method to my approach." He refilled his shot glass and swung it back.

I rubbed the ache settling across my temples, not interested in getting into the mind of a killer or understanding his so-called methods.

"Let's just focus on you finishing your fights quickly, okay?"

"For you"—he adjusted his package, and I gagged—"I'll try." He headed out of the room, and I followed, finding Gage farther down the corridor arguing with another wrestler, Gage's arms flailing about. Good. Hopefully, he hadn't heard our conversation. But I now had to wait for the meathead to finish his fights.

* * *

"Run." I glanced over my shoulder at Dustin.

"Why rush?" He marched behind me down the narrow track in the woods, not seemingly in a rush, and I suspected this was his normal pace. "I finished my last fight early for you."

Branches and leaves rustled around us through the night, and sunrise wasn't too far away. Prickles hadn't coated my arms yet, but they would soon once the sun rose. Around us, darkness permeated the woods, and only the occasional sliver of moonlight illuminated the track, but I knew exactly where we were. Not far now from my home.

"I appreciate it, but we don't have much time. The gargoyle comes to life at sunrise, and you need to be in place to stab it just as it comes alive if you want to defeat it."

He sighed. "Girl, no one will defeat me. Now you sure you know where you're going? Aren't the haunted ruins this way? Or are you into kinky shit? Because I'm up for it."

"Just zip it and keep moving. This is the right place." I picked up my pace, and his footfalls closed in after me.

You sure you can trust him?

"Not really."

At the edge of the woods surrounding the ruins, he seized my wrist and wrenched me backward. I gasped and pivoted on the balls of my feet as he shoved me up against a tree, his body so close, I inhaled his gross perspiration. Shadows concealed his face… all except his teeth from his open mouth grin. He revolted me.

"Don't think I forgot your promise. No gargoyle and you're mine for the day."

Liar. That was never the arrangement.

"Sorry to disappoint, but you may want to look to your right."

And the moment he did, the shift in his posture switched from proud and stiff to slacking. In the distance stood the stone tower. Moonlight lit up the gargoyle crouched on the roof.

Dustin didn't say a word, but I slid under his arm and rushed into the open area.

"Are you satisfied now?"

He pointed to the tower, teasing me with his glare. "You want me to assassinate a statue?"

"Don't be a dumbass. He comes to life once the sun rises. Now let's get moving."

"Something's wrong with you, right? I heard Gage say you weren't fully there, but this is crazy shit."

I twisted around as he tapped the side of his head.

"He said that?" *Asshole.* Now, I didn't feel so guilty for slipping out of the club without saying *goodbye.* Back in the club, Gage had jumped in to stop a fight between two men. It could have been over anything, like money owed, someone had stepped on someone else's foot, or someone had said the wrong thing. Fights at Brawl happened most nights between spectators.

Next time we see him, jab Gage with your dagger.

"Shut up with the stabbing." I glanced up at Dustin, who smirked, as if I was proving his point.

He laughed loudly and explosively, like a sprung leak in the pipes in my tower. His mocking tone raked claws down my back, but whatever. He wasn't the first person to laugh at me, nor would he likely be the last.

"So, how do we reach this gargoyle?" he asked.

While normally, I let people drown in their own sarcasm,

taking too much satisfaction when I proved them wrong, I didn't have the liberty with Dumballs here.

"Listen, we're climbing up the wall to defeat a monster, so you need to get your head focused. The moment he awakens, he'll try to crush your skull in a heartbeat. So be ready."

"Ahem. So are we going inside the tower? Is that where you live?"

I exhaled loudly. "Are you listening to me? You'll have seconds before the gargoyle comes to life. Its stone exterior will morph into smaller stones, so you must slam the blade into a gap between the rocks just above his heart. That will kill it. Okay?"

Dustin studied the tower with big, goofy eyes, and I grabbed his arm, forcing him into a walk.

"Now, there's really just one rule you must know. If you don't kill the gargoyle in time and it comes after you, run. Don't stop to fight or try to protect me. Just run for your life. Understood?"

"Why would you live out here? It's creepy as shit. What kind of sex games are you into? 'Cause I want some of that."

"Listen to me," I snapped. "Kill this gargoyle, and I'll tell you about my entire life story. Sound good?" Doubt flooded me. If he couldn't concentrate, would he react fast enough when the sun climbed over the horizon? Maybe I was mistaken. I should've spent more time explaining the situation to him back at the fight club. Make him understand this wasn't a game or me leading him to a sexy dungeon for playtime.

"Deal. Plus, you'll show me your tits."

I didn't warrant that with a response and clenched my jaw. By the time we reached the tower, Dustin was still smirking and eyed me as if he were about to be fed ambrosia. I curled my hand into a ball, tempted to smack it into his face.

"Follow my lead," I said. "There are grooves in the wall for your fingers and toes."

I scaled the wall as I did most mornings. Halfway up, the familiar prickling danced down my arms. "The sun's almost here," I called out. "Hurry."

Behind me, Dustin climbed, and despite his size, he moved

with swiftness. At the window, I spotted Gingernuts watching me with intrigue. He hissed at Dustin.

The roof had only a gentle slant going upward to a pointed tip in the center. I lifted myself up, gripping the gutter, and pushed one leg up alongside my hands and then the other. I crawled forward and stood up. Dustin followed suit.

The gargoyle perched on its hind legs in the middle of the roof next to the weathervane, its wings tucked behind its back, its wide eyes and ears upright, as if listening for any sounds. It was as tall as Dustin but wider.

"Fuck, it's high up here." Dustin stood alongside me, sweat beading on his brow. "Didn't look so tall from down below." His shoulders curled forward.

I rushed to the gargoyle's back. "Suck it up and help me push him to the ground."

"What the fuck for? I thought I was just stabbing the thing, and then I was getting a go with you." He smirked my way as he rocked his groin toward me.

"Double eww. Anyway, do you want to face off with this thing up here? We get it down, then you do your stuff."

His nose creased and already the orange glow of sunlight smeared the horizon. "What if we smash it?"

"Just get here already and help me. And you think I haven't already thrown him off before? It never smashes no matter what I do." Together, we wedged the statue from his position, the stone screeching and sliding along the roof.

My pulse raced, and I drove all my weight behind my shoulder. Last time, it had taken me half a night to get him off the roof, but Dustin put his back into it, and the gargoyle slid forward.

The familiar itch raced across my scalp, and I panicked. "Oh, shit. The sun's here. Change of plans. Get ready to stab it."

"Damn, you're one crazy bitch. You better make it worth my while."

But just as his words died, the rock beneath my palms shifted.

"Hurry!" I yelled as my head itched to insanity.

"What the fuck? And what's happening to your hair?" His face paled as he recoiled.

I grabbed the dagger from my boot and pressed it to his hand as my growing hair hit my shoulders. "Stab him as soon the gap appears above his heart!"

But Dustin flinched back, his eyes bulging as he gawked at the gargoyle shifting from solid rock to a creature made up of a myriad of stones, grating against each other as they shifted across the body.

"Do it!" I bellowed, wringing my hands.

Dustin stiffened at first, then launched himself forward, his knife poised for attack. The moment felt like a lifetime—the sun beamed behind us. I held my breath, unable to move.

The gargoyle jerked around. Dustin wavered and slowed. The creature's clawed hand snatched him by the throat and tossed him off the roof. His yells pierced the night. And just like Reed, Dustin was gone.

I screamed, my heart pummeling in my chest as the monster who'd tortured me for years pivoted in my direction, its wings spread wide, and its mouth gaped open, revealing sharpened teeth.

My knees wobbled beneath me, and I lost my footing. I slid and flew off the ledge, praying death collected me before the gargoyle would.

CHAPTER 7

The wind ripped at my clothes and my magical-growing hair as I fell from the roof of the tower. I screamed from the terror slicing at my insides. The world revolved around me as regret punched me in the chest. I should have made Dustin listen, take me seriously, and made him understand how fast he had to act. How his strength and swiftness were what I needed to defeat the monster.

I was approaching the ground fast. Concrete arms swooped under me in midair. I landed with an *oomph*. I battled his tight embrace, flailing widely. "Fuck you!"

In a swift movement, we careened sideways, ascending. I squirmed for release.

Suddenly, the gargoyle arched as if struck in the back, and its wings stopped beating. My heart raced.

We dropped out of the air, and I screamed. My stomach slammed into the back of my throat.

Its grip slackened, and I shoved myself away from the creature. I landed in a line of shrubs, absorbing my impact. The creature smacked the ground.

My blonde hair sprawled over my shoulders and down my back, cascading around me like a waterfall. I scrambled up, despite my head spinning and dread squeezing my chest.

The gargoyle crawled to his feet, the knife's hilt stuck out of a gap between his wings. The creature reached an arm over its shoulder to take out the weapon, but it remained just out of reach.

Dustin swayed on his feet and untangled himself from the bushes catching his pants. He stood at least ten feet away. A gash crossed his brow, and blood dripped down the side of his face. Joy radiated through me that he'd survived the fall.

I grabbed the blade from my belt. "Take the gargoyle down now while he's injured," I yelled as I darted closer, pressing the hilt into Dustin's palm. "Throw it into his heart!"

But Dustin shoved me away and pulled out two thinner blades from his boot, stalking toward the enemy. His shoulders curled forward like a predator's.

I could barely take a breath.

The gargoyle screeched, making strange grinding sounds. I couldn't tell if that was pain or anger because he'd never made such a noise before. But this was the moment to make a change. I'd had enough of being a punching bag and treated like dirt. This ended now.

I gripped the knife in my hand and ran toward the creature.
Stab him. Kill him. Free yourself.

But the gargoyle spun on the spot, its wings flapping, chasing the knife in its back. In front of the gargoyle stood Dustin, his feet firm on the ground, his knees bent, and he hurled a knife, precise and accurate.

I froze.

The blade slammed into the gargoyle's chest, and I cried out with joy, except the monster wasn't falling over. *What the hell?*

It staggered around, and I gawked at the knife dead center in its chest. The creature wrenched the weapon out and tossed it to the ground.

"Stab him in the heart!" I bellowed. If I knew sheer strength would overpower the gargoyle, I'd insist Dustin turn into his bear form, but that wouldn't help with throwing the blade accurately.

The gargoyle jerked toward me, and despite the deadness in

its eyes, I swore a fiery anger stirred behind them. I recoiled, unable to inhale as terror clamped over my lungs.

Leaping forward, the creature snatched my arm with his rock-hard fingers. I fought against the restraint and jammed my knife at its chest with my other hand. The bastard moved too fast. My blade hit its solid chest and skidded sideways.

It whacked a granite hand against my weapon-wielding one, and pain wrapped over my knuckles. The knife dropped from my grasp as I cried out at the fiery agony encasing my arm. I dragged myself away, wriggling to free myself from the gargoyle's hold.

"Let me go!"

Its wings beat, sending a flurry of wind into my face as he lifted us off the ground, dragging me by the arm.

Darkness swarmed my thoughts. I'd rather die than lose again.

I can't live like this. Not again. Not fucking again.

There was movement to the side of me as Dustin hurled himself between us with such strength, I was thrown backward.

Landing on my ass, my strangled cry escaped, and I scrambled out of his reach, my long hair tangling around me.

Near the tower, the gargoyle collapsed onto its side with a thud, a knife sticking out of its chest in the crevice right above its heart.

"Oh, fuck yes!" I bellowed.

Dustin climbed to his feet, dusting off his hands as if this were an everyday occurrence, smirking and giving me a knowing nod.

Warmth exploded through me. I pushed aside locks of hair to see properly before I ran closer, studying the monster who'd kept me prisoner and tortured me for years. Now, it lay there, making a hissing sound as if deflating. Part of me refused to believe it was dead. So many years had passed, and nothing had ever made a difference—until Dustin had destroyed it. I couldn't stop the smile spreading across my face, the leap of joy pumping through my veins that this was really happening.

"Girl, I owe you an apology." Dustin tipped his head toward me. "You spoke the truth this whole time, and I mocked you."

I couldn't find my words at first because I'd dreamt of this moment for so long. Reality refused to settle in, and I tapped the gargoyle with the toe of my boot. No reaction. Was this finally it? I was free?

Happiness flowed through me, radiating me with warmth as I basked under a summer sun.

"Whoop!" I stuffed my knife back on my belt. So many thoughts whirred through my head, all the things I could do now that I was free. "I'll travel to every realm, sleep during the night, visit my friend Bee." But first, I had to go to Gage and tell him the truth about everything. No more lies. And we'd date again as I'd always dreamed, and I'd sleep over at his place.

Dustin wiped his hands down his shirt, his chin high with proudness. "Wasn't as difficult as I thought."

"You did it. Oh shit, I'm free." I jumped into his arms and hugged him, then pulled free.

His hoarse laughter rang in my ear. "You had doubts?"

"Maybe a few." I broke away, bathing beneath the morning's rays, and stared up at the tower, where Gingernuts looked down on us. Was this real? This whole time, I'd remained imprisoned when I should have searched for ancient texts before.

Who gives a fuck? You're free.

Beside me, tiny flakes of rock floated away from the gargoyle's body. He was disintegrating! Dust floated up on the breeze as his body diminished, one inch at a time.

Is it coming back to life?

I stumbled backward and glanced up at Dustin. "What's going—?" But my voice fell flat.

He was staggering around as if drunk, his skin gleaming with sweat.

"Dustin, what are you doing?" Coldness swirled in my chest, and my brain froze.

He looked at me, his eyes wild and fear warping his expression into a painful scowl. His golden skin had sunk in tone to something lifeless, and it terrified me. A panicked ache pressed against my chest.

"Something's wrong with me," he muttered.

I reached out for him, but his eyes rolled back into his head, and his legs buckled. He hit the ground with his knees and fell face-first.

My stomach dropped, and I darted to his side. With both hands, I shoved my weight against his shoulder to push him over onto his back. "Dustin, speak to me. Please." My voice wavered, and an unstoppable snowball of fear slithered to the pit of my gut. "What's going on?" My heart beat harder and faster.

He lay there, unmoving, his eyes closed.

He's dead.

My skin seemed two sizes too small for my body. It strangled me. "Get up. Dustin!" I never wanted him to die, even if he was a disgusting bastard. He was meant to destroy the gargoyle and walk away with my gold coins.

When an electric hum leaped over my skin, I gasped and backed away. *Magic.* My attention swung between Dustin and the gargoyle, whose head was the last thing to evaporate into fine dust.

Dustin screamed as his chest arched upward as he convulsed.

I shuddered and paced back and forth, breaths racing.

Was this part of the spell? A precaution in case the creature was ever killed? The pages I'd read said nothing about such a consequence... *Fuck...* The torn pages. "Oh, hell!"

Right before my eyes, Dustin's body stretched and elongated, his clothes ripping and shredding off him. His skin rippled and transformed from a tanned color to that of granite.

I cried out and recoiled, tears blurring my vision. I wracked with raw sobs, trembling, my insides swelling with dread. The spell was being transferred to him. How the hell did I undo the hex? I paced in a circle, unsure how to save him.

Terror rocked me on the spot. My whole existence meant nothing if the gargoyle only took over whoever killed him. Breaths wheezed when the glint of metal caught my attention from within the grass.

Without a thought, I collected my hair over an arm and picked up the weapon. I charged for Dustin, needing to finish this.

Throwing myself to my knees next to his writhing body covered in rock plates, I raised the dagger and jammed it toward his heart.

His hand flinched and seized my wrist, squeezing.

I yelled at the sharpness shooting up my arm. The weapon fell out of my grip, but I pulled against the restraint, wincing. My brain was on overdrive, my concentration shot.

The monster got up with the ease of a leaf being picked up by the wind.

Dustin's brown eyes were all that remained of him in the face set in stone—the wide jawline, the fangs over the lower lip, the flat nose, the pointy ears. Behind him, wings spread outward like a shadow falling over the world, blocking out the sun and tossing me into darkness.

Fear shackled me, hammering into my head. My throat thickened as I faced a monster bursting with energy, and I was about to become his target practice.

Told you. Told you.

"Please, Dustin. It's me. Don't do this. Please, no."

He snatched my hair and hauled me after him, taking me to the tower.

I tried to drag myself away, wriggling to break the hold the gargoyle had on me. Nothing in my world would ever be right again.

* * *

I FLIPPED OPEN my eyes to the darkness outside and crawled out of bed, groaning. Salty blood filled my mouth from where I'd been thrown against a wall. A sharp pain shot through my back, and I winced. I shuddered from where the bastard had used a belt. He'd tossed me around like a rag doll, but I'd somehow gotten off lightly because my previous beatings had always left me injured for weeks. Maybe it was the gargoyle's recent transformation making him weak. My actions got him trapped inside the gargoyle. Or was he dead? I didn't even know where to begin undoing this… or if it was even possible. He was meant to run the moment he saw danger, but I never anticipated a curse on the gargoyle.

In quick succession, I ran a hand through my short hair, staring at the book on gargoyles on the table. Regret pulsed through me, and I clenched my fists. My stomach hurt, remembering the tragic events. I'd failed Dustin and myself. Tears fell fast, and I sobbed into my hands, hating what I'd done. Hating my condemnation.

Touching my injuries, my fingers came back bloody.

I'd longed for freedom for so long, I'd become blindsided by the first opportunity to destroy the monster. Now, the bear shifter had lost his life. Gage's words filtered through my mind about Dustin being a monster in his own way, killing anyone for money, and the shifter had scared me. But it wasn't my decision who lived or died. By allowing Dustin to die, I was no better than he—a killer. A stabbing ache tightened in my chest, and I hiccupped as another tore through me, hurting across my ribs as tears threaded down my cheeks.

"I'm sorry, Dustin. I didn't mean for any of this to happen."

Agony burrowed deeper within me as reality crashed through me. Not only had I gotten Dustin transformed, but my future had vanished.

I hugged myself because I'd always believed one day I'd destroy the gargoyle and finally be free. I'd been foolish, an idiot. Now, I'd never escape but remain imprisoned, forced to return to the tower every morning.

Pushing myself to my feet, I stumbled to the table and lit a candle. The book I'd stolen sat at the other end of the table, and I dragged it closer to me. I flipped to the pages about gargoyles and reread the whole section, finding no mention of a curse from defeating the monster. The torn pages must have spelled out the consequences of destroying a gargoyle, yet I'd never given the missing information a second thought.

I wiped my eyes, picked up the candle, and hobbled to the bathroom.

I set the candle on a shelf beneath the mirror on the wall and stared at myself. Dried blood marred my cheek and forehead. A darkening bruise appeared under my left eye, and the cut across my temple bled. My skin looked pasty, and my short hair stuck in the air. I pushed it flat across my head.

A tear rolled down my cheek. Anger burned like lava inside me, churning, desperate for destruction, but I was useless. Everything I tried made the situation worse.

You look like you fell off a cliff and got into a fight with a prickly bush.

"Wow, you're full of compliments."

Just saying it as it is. You stuffed up last night.

"Maybe stop talking." The silence engulfed me, closing in around me.

Something rubbed my leg, and I looked down at Gingernuts, staring up at me with huge eyes. Behind him was a long trail of golden hair like a never-ending cape. I reached down and picked him up, despite his wriggling.

"You know I'm going to hug you, so you might as well stop fighting." I tickled his belly as he broke into a purr. With him back down, I got myself cleaned up and dressed, then went to feed Gingernuts.

"Elliana." A male's voice called out to me. I froze midway through feeding Gingernuts. Had I heard right?

Gingernuts headbutted me to finish preparing his meal, so I placed his filled plate on the floor.

"Elliana, you in there?"

I jolted upright and hurried through the kitchen until my back spasmed, and I slowed down. In the main room, I approached the window and glanced down to see Gage with his hands in his pockets, staring up at me as if he was there for a date. And it took everything I had not to let him in without an explanation first.

"What are you doing here? I told you to never come here." Giddiness flooded me at seeing him, at the idea that I might avoid being alone, might distract myself. Of course, I should have known he would come searching for me after I'd left Brawl without saying a word to him, considering I'd told him I'd needed Dustin for a job.

He shrugged. "I had to see you. Want me to come up there?" He wasn't wearing his bouncer black clothes but brown pants, boots, and a short-sleeved shirt. His muscles were on display beneath the open vest he wore, along with a gold chain that sparkled in the moon's light.

"No! I'm coming down." I didn't need him to see how fucked up my life was—the busted furniture, my extremely hairy cat. Gage should have been a spy because he noticed too much and asked a million questions. Like the bruises I hid under my clothes.

In haste, I darted to the bedroom and grabbed several gold coins from the pouch I'd dropped last night near the bed. I stuffed them into my pocket and reached for my dagger on the bedside table. If Gage wanted company, I'd take it. I couldn't bear to be alone, and drowning my sorrows with a drink and a gorgeous man was better than facing the reality of never getting rid of the gargoyle and having basically killed a man.

I swallowed the thickness in my throat, hating the desperation to curl up and vanish from the world.

"Wow, so this is where you live? I expected something grander." Gage's voice filled the tower.

I jostled around as he climbed in through the window, shuddering that he hadn't listened to my request. While at the same time, I was burning up with embarrassment that he'd seen my prison. Would he think less of me?

He studied the paintings I'd created on the walls, the rugs I'd bought at markets to brighten up the place, and the translucent fabrics I'd hung from the cobblestone ceiling in billowing waves. Anything to make the place resemble a home.

I stepped out of the shadows of the bedroom and his eyes fixed on me, widening to round disks.

"What happened to you?" He seized my arms and brought me into the light of the burning candle on the table. "Who did this to you? Was it Dustin? Fucking bastard. I'll murder him. I warned you about him." His voice boomed.

I shivered, and when a tear escaped the corner of my eye, I turned away.

Gage drew me closer, our bodies plastered together.

"Elliana, what the hell happened?" His tone deepened.

This was why I hadn't told him about the gargoyle before. He'd fly off the handle and jump to fix my problems. Damn, I loved that protectiveness in him, but that was why I had to keep him safe from himself. I couldn't bear to see him become a gargoyle like Dustin or get killed trying to save him. Sweat drenched my skin, and the thumping of my heart vibrated in my head. I curled my hands into fists, and my words rushed out loud.

"Gage, just leave it. Dustin didn't hurt me." I pulled myself from his grasp and headed toward my bed, rubbing my eyes, hating that I couldn't control my emotions.

"What is *that*?"

I turned to find him staring down at my cat.

"My pet, Gingernuts."

Gage half-smiled as his gaze followed the cat's trail of hair across the floor and then vanishing somewhere in the kitchen. "Is something wrong with him?"

"No!" I snapped, gaining myself a raised brow. "Haven't you ever heard of long-haired cats?" I huffed, hating that Gage had to see the shithole I lived in, along with the cursed cat I adored so much. The pitiful expression on his face killed me when he looked my way. I'd always worked hard for him to see me as someone strong, brave, and capable of taking on anything. Not this mess who got beaten up and was lost on the inside.

"Okay, whatever. Your cat is freaky." He glanced around my small abode and approached my messy bed. He reached over, taking my hand in his. His touch was soft and warm. "Please, Elliana. Tell me what's going on. It scares me to see you hurt and pushing me away."

I lifted my head to face him, my chin trembling because

facing the truth of my life grazed my skin like a flame. "What does it matter?"

He brought me into his arms with such swiftness, I lost my breath. My bruises ached, but he never squeezed tight.

"I care about you more than you realize," he breathed in my ear. "And if someone is hurting you, I'll fix it. I adore seeing your smiles, hearing your laughter. I hate seeing you cry." He brushed his thumbs under my eyes, and I melted beneath his tender touch.

A spark of passion ignited in me as his body pressed against mine. Somehow, in his arms, the world stopped. No time, no fear, no prison, and most of all, no gargoyle.

Tears kept falling as I remembered Dustin's terrified gaze, that I'd aided in him losing his life. I never wanted to get beaten again. I'd been broken too many times, and now I didn't know if I'd ever feel whole again.

I pulled out of Gage's embrace. His hand took mine, his fingers stroking my inner wrist in that easy way that encouraged me to speak openly. I stared into his green eyes, and a wild expression of terror filled them. Up close, his cheekbones were sharp, and his chin narrow, resembling a dragon's bone structure. Powerful and protective.

He'd always cared for me, perhaps too much, and I'd never understood why. He could have had any woman he wanted, and they'd never been shy around him. Yet he'd never once strayed, and he stared at me as if only I existed. Trepidation strangled me at the idea of placing him in danger. How much longer could I hold on to the anger, the memories, the self-loathing?

So, my words fell before I could rein them in and revealed my sad life—the curse, my father, the gargoyle, years of going mad, and even the time I'd thrown myself off the roof to end my life. For too long, I'd yearned to share them with someone, to somehow end the loneliness that clung to my skin like a jacket made of thorns, always slicing into me and dragging me back to my fucked-up life.

"It's my fault Dustin transformed." A river of emotions

spilled down my cheeks, and I pulled my hand away as I cried into them.

Gage held me and stroked my head.

"Fuck. Why didn't you tell me any of this? This isn't your fault. Some fuckwit punished an innocent child, which boils my blood. And Dustin was a good fighter, but he was a murderer. He's taken so many lives, some deserving, others innocent. You did the world a favor by removing him from our lives."

"That doesn't make me feel any better. It's not my call to take someone's life. But you need to promise me you won't try to take on the gargoyle."

I looked up at Gage to see the fierceness behind his dragon eyes. Dread locked tight in my stomach. I couldn't reverse time or change the past, yet each time I remembered Dustin's demise, my breaths grew shallower.

"Please, Gage," I begged.

He nodded once, as if that was the end of the conversation. He'd stick to his word.

"Don't you dare shed another tear for that loser." He kissed my brow in a way that showed me he cared for me more than just physically. He wrapped his arms around me.

All I could do was try to drive the pent-up emotions into the darkness, and being in Gage's presence gave me the ammunition to never stop trying. I should have trusted him earlier, should have pushed past my insecurities, should have believed he'd never judge me. I inhaled his masculine scent mixed with citrus. I tried to breathe around it but couldn't escape the intoxication. Everything about him was hypnotic.

"So, that's Dustin on your roof, and he comes to life at dawn? Can he be turned back to human?" He rubbed a hand across his mouth.

"No idea. The book I read said nothing about whoever killed a gargoyle taking his place. But when the stone creature vanished, no person appeared in its place. I think Dustin is really dead." I gasped and hugged myself.

"Tell me more about the curse cast on you?"

"I don't know much about that, either, and that's why I've

focused on getting rid of the gargoyle instead. Which failed miserably." My breaths stuttered in my lungs before I released them.

"That's why you asked me about the dragon-tooth dagger last night, right? I may have a lead for you."

Breaking out of his arms, I tried to process his words.

"You know where I can find such a dagger?" I rushed to the table and grabbed my book, bringing it back to Gage. "It says a dragon-tooth blade can slice through stone and finish a gargoyle." And once I got my hands on one, I'd be doing the slaying. No risking someone else's life this time.

Gage collected the book from my hands and turned it the right way. He flipped through the pages, landing on the gargoyle entry. "Where's the rest?"

I shook my head.

He restudied the leather-bound book, his brow furrowed, and his jawline gritted like it did whenever he concentrated.

"First, we need to track down the dagger."

I bounced on my toes, ready to do whatever it took. "Okay, so where do we find one?"

Gage shut the book with a slap and set it down on the table. "I spoke to a friend who knows someone who insists he heard a lion shifter talk about a dragon-tooth dagger."

My mind swam, remembering Reed in my tower and the gargoyle tossing him into the woods before attacking him. I swallowed loudly. I hadn't found his body, so had he made it home safely? And if he'd survived, would he even welcome me?

I wouldn't go visit him.

"I know one, and he owes me a small favor." I let him stay in my tower briefly, so hopefully, he saw that as a kind deed.

"Favor?" Gage's eyes morphed into a honeyed green, slitting into vertical lines for a sliver of a second. His jealousy always revealed snippets of the dragon inside him. "Lions aren't trustworthy, you know that, right? So he probably won't help you."

"Reed seemed decent enough." Maybe I was pushing my luck in visiting him. "There's a pride living across the forest in the open plains, so maybe we can go there and ask if they know him." I spoke fast, and my mouth hurt when I smiled due to my cut lip.

Gage moved close enough for me to feel the heat of his body through my clothes, and his hands fell on my hips. "You should have come to me earlier… should have told me everything about the gargoyle."

I inhaled deeply, not needing to be reprimanded, but I knew his words came from a place of concern.

"I didn't want you to know how I lived or be attacked by the gargoyle." I dropped my gaze. "When I leave the tower at night, I become a different person. Someone strong who can face the world, who has no shackles, who does as she pleases. That's the person you fell for, not the prisoner who's faked her life. I didn't want you to think any less of me."

"I fell for the woman who takes food to the homeless children in town, who reminds me to see the good in others, and who loves me with the passion of a dragon."

My heart rate accelerated. There was no smile on his lips, only the intensity in his eyes that was the start of an explosive blaze of more to come. He kissed me, and my worries faded away. His passion brought a raw fierceness—my breaths coming faster, my skin vibrating with the urgency of what would come next. Our tongues entwined as his hands found the skin of my back under my shirt, and I moaned from the feel of his strong hands touching me.

I winced from the cut on my mouth, and he pulled back. We locked eyes for those moments, his love evident in his gaze. His lips grazed over my cheek, down my neck, not innocently but passionate and demanding.

I shivered beneath him, aroused. He suckled on my earlobe as I moaned, running my hands up his chest, around his neck. I raked my fingers through his hair. In moments like these, holding back seemed impossible. I couldn't move even if I tried.

"Your body and scent drive me crazy. I need you," he breathed into my ear, his electric fingertips gliding across my back. They swept around to my stomach and upward, cupping my breasts. I moaned, weakening at his touch. His fingers pinched my nipples, and I burned all over.

Gingernuts brushed past our legs and meowed, heading toward the window. I caught my breath and came back to reality. Was I ready to do this? Reignite our relationship again? My bruises and cuts ached, reminding me I still remained a prisoner to the gargoyle. I pulled away from Gage, unsure what the right decision was. Making him believe we could be together was wrong. Soon enough, he'd get frustrated with the whole gargoyle situation and try to take it down. I couldn't let that happen.

Gage looked down. "Strange cat, but are you saying that during the day, you have long hair?"

I nodded, though I didn't know if I'd keep the hair if I defeated the gargoyle. "Will that be a problem?"

He turned me around to face the window and wound his arms around me from behind. His chin rested on my shoulder.

"Honey, I can think of some fun ways to use your hair to our advantage." Mirth danced between his words, and right then, I imagined how incredible my life could be if I had a real shot at a future with Gage.

CHAPTER 8

"Is something wrong?" I glanced over at Gage, who'd been quiet ever since we'd left my tower. We'd been speed-walking for a while through the woods and crossed paths with only deer and rabbits. With Gage's senses, he'd pick up on a cougar or other predator stalking up behind us, so I wasn't worried about being ambushed. Still, shadows danced beneath his eyes, and he offered me a weak smile.

My head swam with worry that after everything I'd told him, he now figured I was a basket case, that I posed too much risk, and I was the farthest thing from normal. Was he reconsidering helping me or, worse, being with me?

I finally broke the silence. "Look. You don't have to do this with me. You're under no obligation—"

"It's not that," he said, his voice deep.

"Then what is it?" My voice wavered because, for so long, I'd pushed Gage away, scared he'd get harmed.

He didn't respond at first, and I waited, giving him time. Getting a man to speak openly was as hard as digging a ten-foot hole in the ground with my bare hands. I wrapped my arms around myself to keep from shaking him and demanding answers. Instead, I busied myself with surveying the land.

Around us, the oaks swathed with moss grew sparser, and in the distance, an open field spread out. Lions ruled this territory, and everyone else living here had to follow their law. Many shifters steered clear of the area to avoid dealing with their egos. Lions saw themselves as kings of the animal kingdom. I recalled Reed in my tower, his dread and fury. Learning that someone hunted down his kind had killed me. It was one thing for a group of shifters to live by their own rules, but getting exterminated was monstrous.

Trepidation crept into my chest. What if Reed wasn't with his pride and they confirmed my worst fears that he'd never returned home? Guilt chiseled at my brain. I couldn't undo the past, only try to make amends. I had to believe he was still alive. Or would his pride blame me and make us pay?

Then don't tell them the truth.

I ignored my inner voice, who clearly didn't feel remorse, while I recalled how Reed had pressed up against me and my insatiable reaction to our proximity. Despite my concoction of emotions, I was excited to embrace him and tell him I was sorry for not telling him about the gargoyle right away. Something tightened in my gut. *Please let him be alive.*

"I've let you down." Gage's whispered words floated on the wind.

At first, I wasn't sure what he was talking about until I recalled my question about why he was behaving strangely.

"You're being silly."

We emerged from the forest and stepped into the open plain spanning outward as far as the eye could see. Trees continued on either side of us in a U-shape. Mountain peaks in the distance blotted the starry sky, towering over the land like giants. Enormous oaks with wide branches riddled the landscape, their greenery gleaming beneath the moonlight's silvery glow.

"If I could take my dragon form," he continued, "I'd offer you a tooth to use for a dagger."

Shock rattled through me, and I halted, taking Gage's hand. "You're doing more than I could have asked for by not judging me and for helping me find a solution."

His hooded gaze darkening, he turned away and marched deeper into the field ahead of me.

It never occurred to me how this might have impacted him or his inability to shift. His inability to fully shift had always been a dark mote with him. I rushed after him and took his hand in mine. What I ought to have done was find a book on dragons and determine how to help Gage.

"What about returning to the family who found you in the woods?" I suggested. "We can ask them more questions about what else they found with you. Maybe someone who lived there saw—"

He froze, and I bumped into him.

"Shh. Hear that?"

I glanced around and listened, but all I heard was my pounding heart. "What is it?" I whispered.

"Foliage breaking. Someone's stalking us. We're being watched." He sniffed the air, and I scanned the surrounding woodland covered in the moon's glimmer. Branches swayed in the breeze, grating together, and my skin pinpricked. I suddenly hated being out in the open and vulnerable.

"Surely, they won't hurt us," I insisted, my muscles tense, unsure if I was trying to convince myself more than Gage. "We're not here with the intention to attack." Three animals emerged from the woods to my right. If we ran, how far would we get? When they strode into the moonlight, I gasped at the powerful lions closing in. None had manes... must be females. Powerful paws hit the ground, their breaths steaming in the darkness.

How long have they been following you?

I clenched my fists. Gage stepped in front of me, blocking me from their presence. Two more animals came forward from the forest on our left.

"We're trespassing on their territory," Gage said. "Who are we here to see again?"

"Reed. He's the pride leader, and—"

He snapped around to face me, his frown worrying me.

"You didn't tell me he was the leader. They won't take us to him." His voice climbed.

"Why the hell not? Once Reed sees me, we'll be fine." I bit

down on my lower lip, and my heart throbbed fast. I should have told Gage everything upfront, but I'd assumed we'd walk in and find Reed in no time.

"Lions take no one to their alpha. They protect him with their lives."

His anger surprised me. I didn't know he had a beef with lions.

"Stop worrying. We'll be fine." Then why was I trembling?

The deadly animals were within striking range now, surrounding us. Two had short manes—juvenile males. One roared, his head lifted into the air, making short grunts. Hot air wafted on the wind from his mouth.

I flinched against Gage, who pulled me close and wrapped an arm around me. But this wasn't about being scared. If I intended to find a dragon-tooth dagger, well, I had to get over my fear.

"We're here to speak to your leader," Gage said in a deep voice.

Hadn't he just said that no one gets to see their leader? Or was he trying his luck?

One lioness swiped her clawed paw at the air, snarling in a way that sounded nothing like, *sure, right this way.* The others froze on the spot, hunched low as if waiting for the command to tear us to shreds.

My breaths raced, but I reluctantly stepped forward.

"I met with Reed, and he told me about his kidnapped sister and how your pride is being hunted down."

I prayed my honesty and insight would change their mind. But if Reed hadn't returned to his pride after the encounter with the gargoyle, I might have opened us up to an attack.

Nobody moved, and even the lioness taking charge tilted her head sideways, staring at me as if trying to make sense of my words.

"We don't mean Reed or anyone harm," I added.

The lead female roared and approached Gage, sniffing him. She headbutted him in the leg, sending Gage into a stumble.

The other lions closed in.

My pulsed spiked, and I stiffened. Was this a warning demanding we leave?

Two of the animals turned and wandered across the field, glancing back at us. One yawned, as if she was bored by our presence. The female nudged Gage's leg again, pushing him in the same direction.

"Think they want us to follow them," I said. Together, we marched across the field to the woods on our left. Lions flanked either side of us, and a few fell behind, grumbling. I fought the urge to scream and run, telling myself once I found Reed, we'd be fine.

You keep telling yourself that, but wishes don't make truth.

We entered the woods, trampling foliage and stepping over shrubs. The animals stayed close on our heels.

"Where do you think they're taking us?" Gage asked.

"Their home?"

Before long, we emerged from the woods into an area with scattered foliage, an open meadow, a gurgling river cutting the land in half, and gigantic trees with figures underneath them. More lions. Glowing eyes stared our way. Any chance of escape was now gone. They'd tear us apart before we ran fifty feet.

I swallowed the lump in my throat, counting at least thirty coming our way. Goddess, how big was this pride? Two beasts with shaggy, brown manes approached, and their noses creased as they strutted closer. Nope, they weren't happy.

"Okay, which one is your friend?" Gage asked. "Can you call out to him before they make a meal of us?"

"Reed?" I called out. My voice shook, and I loathed sounding weak, but it wasn't every day I stood amid a pride of animals capable of scratching my heart out of my chest without warning. There was a reason people stayed away from this land—most lions attacked first.

"Why aren't they responding?" I brushed against Gage's arm as we followed the lioness to a seven-foot wooden pole sticking out of the ground. My thoughts swung to being tied up while they took turns taking bites out of us. My muscles froze in place but flooded with the tingling pressure of needing to run. Fleeing was the dumbest course of action, but my brain turned to mush, trying to make sense of how to escape with my head intact.

"Fuck," Gage whispered, and I trembled, my gaze swinging left and right.

I shook my head and refocused on the shithole we'd walked into. Now, I regretted my decision. We should have planned it better.

"What about them?" Gage lifted his chin to more males coming our way. "Any of them the leader?"

"Who knows? They all look the same."

One animal licked his paw, the razor-sharp claws extended. Probably cleaning them for dinner. Dread dug deep into my chest. We were trapped, and no screaming in the world would save us.

My breaths raced.

A male lion grazed right past me, striding elegantly past as if he walked on clouds. His tail flicked me across the ass, and I flinched, twisting around, meeting his large and dark-rimmed eyes. "Reed?"

Another animal glided past, brushing against me, and my skin pinched. When I glanced back, the male had vanished. A female nudged Gage in the thigh, shoving him aside, and I chased after him, but two creatures blocked my path.

"They're separating us!" I cried out, and my teeth chattered. We'd marched in here like fools, offering ourselves as their meal.

They'll hunt you both down. Grab your knife and stab them.

Yeah, smart move. Draw my weapon against a pride of lions. It wasn't as if I could kill them all. Maybe the ones who attacked me if I was lucky.

"Listen, I don't want to hurt anyone. If Reed's not here, we'll leave."

Gage staggered as several females drove him farther away, his reaction blackened by the night. My heartbeat slammed against my ribcage. A chill washed down my spine as I turned around, scanning the area, but there was no way out.

Three animals circled me, each taking turns to whack me with a tail or claw my pants, drawing blood. I cried out as another headbutted me in the leg. Over and over, I stumbled about, treated like a freaking plaything. Were they tenderizing me? Despite the fear clinging to my insides, a fiery rage erupted in my chest. I hadn't come this far to turn into someone's dinner. I curled my hands, and pure adrenaline surged through my veins.

"Enough," I called out. "I'm not your enemy."

None listened, and they broke into a sprint around me. Dust was thrown into the air, blurring my vision and clogging my throat. Bits of dirt and tiny rocks whipped around my legs. Roars erupted from every direction, loud and piercing. All I could picture in my mind was one of them ripping out my jugular with those sharp teeth.

I trembled and reached for my blade.

Everything fell deadly silent. The dust cloud blinded my vision, and I gasped for air. Icy daggers surged right through me because I'd brought Gage into this danger, and now, he'd lose his life because of me.

Through the dust cloud, a lion's head emerged with a long, unkempt golden mane. He sniffed the air, and his green eyes locked on to me. For several moments, he remained quiet and alert.

I recoiled, my hand settling on the hilt of my blade.

Stab it. Kill it.

"Keep quiet. I'm not killing anyone." But I'd defend myself at any cost. Except the animal's eyes were soft and promised safety, and something familiar about them struck me. "Reed, is that you?"

Please let it be him and not someone who'd ask me where their leader was. That would mean the gargoyle had killed Reed.

The lion tilted his head sideways, and at once, a surge of energy crackled over my flesh. The dust settled around us, and the animal's body stretched and cracked, skin splitting. Through it all, he unleashed a deafening roar into the night.

I held still, amazed at how the shifter's body warped, transformed, and regrew new skin that tightened and hugged his human-like figure. I searched for any features to define him as Reed when someone grabbed my arm from behind and hauled me backward. Panic clenched my heart, and I whirled around.

"Hey, stop!" I called out as I stumbled behind a female in a leather vest and skirt, her red hair wild like fire.

"This way," she demanded, dragging me away. I glanced over my shoulder. The male lion had vanished.

"What's going on?" I searched the open plain for Reed, but it was too dark to find his face. Only lions and human figures. Was he even here?

The woman didn't speak as she guided me across the field to an oversized tree. Its branches bowed outward while other limbs reached for the night sky. Each supported perfect white blossoms amid the green leaves.

A sole figure stood beneath its shadows, buttoning up his shirt.

Several torches were lit, revealing his face, his golden hair falling to his waist. Reed stared at me with such hunger in his eyes, I lost my breath. The breeze swished past, doing zilch to cool the inferno burning across my skin. Hair fluttered around his face, giving him a rugged look, coupled with his stubble and parted lips.

My chest radiating as if a flame warmed my soul, I rushed forward to embrace him. "Reed. I thought you were dead. I'm so sorry, I should have warned you about the gargoyle. But you're safe." I held on to his back, his muscles shifting under my touch.

Reed hugged me, arms tight around my waist. He gently rubbed my back, and a light beamed in my heart that had been missing yesterday. He'd never returned to the tower to tell me he was okay, but then again, he'd had more pressing issues, like his missing sister and pride members.

"I like your hair short. It brings out your sweet cheekbones." His breath caressed my neck, sending tingles down my back. I wished I could accept his compliment and parade my neater hairstyle, but it wasn't mine, just a temporary remedy that happened every night.

I remembered our closeness in the tower, the kiss that had me floating on clouds, and those same butterflies now swirled in my gut at his attentiveness, the way his hands had dug into my skin as if he never wanted to release me. In close vicinity to Reed, something turned on inside me. Or maybe it was simply being relieved he wasn't dead.

"Everyone, leave me with the visitors now!" he cried out. He cupped the side of my face, a thumb brushing across the bruise under my eye. His warmth seeped into me, comforting me.

"Who hurt you?" The bridge of his nose wrinkled, as if he might break into a snarl.

The shuffling of feet and grunts faded around us.

"The gargoyle. That's why I'm here." I broke free from Reed's embrace.

My gaze fell on Gage as he approached from the shadows at my side. I breathed a sigh of relief that he hadn't been harmed by the lion shifters who'd split us up. But his expression darkened, and when he reached me, his hand slid into mine, drawing me closer.

"Well, that was a fun welcome." Gage's voice was as sour as sucking lemons.

Reed ran a hand through his hair, pushing the loose strands off his face. "My pride's jumpy, and everyone's a potential enemy before I approve them. These are dark times."

"So, are all these warrior women at your beck and call?" Gage asked, his voice sarcastic. "You lions love your harems."

Reed arched a brow, his gaze falling to our holding hands. "A lion's affairs are not the concerns of a dragon."

"You can tell what he is?" I freed myself from Gage, feeling the uneasy sensation of eyes on us from a distance, and my skin crawled.

"He smells of burned fire. It's clogging my nostrils." Reed's nose crinkled as if he'd just inhaled the worst smell in the world.

I didn't understand the animosity between them.

Gage laughed loudly, likely all for show. "Only thing clogging your breathing is all that hair."

The men glared at each other in a staring contest that could have easily turned into blood and war.

I interrupted them. "*Anyway.* We came to ask for your assistance."

Gage cleared his throat and pressed against my side. "Heard someone say the local lion pride leader knew where to get a dragon-tooth dagger." His words sounded like an accusation—implying that Reed might have killed a dragon.

"You're aware of my gargoyle problem," I added, slicing through the thickening tension. I didn't have time for this macho shit and gave Reed an abridged rendition of my hellish situation—the curse, why I had short hair, and my failed attempt with Dustin and the disastrous outcome. Catching my breath, I said, "With the weapon, I can destroy the gargoyle."

I chewed on my lip, thinking about Dustin's situation, deciding that next time, I would slay the monster myself. No one else would risk their lives.

"This explains your strange cat and you living in a tower in the haunted part of the woods."

"He was in your tower?" Gage rumbled.

Reed smirked, proud of himself. These two would jump into a brawl at any moment. Except Reed had beautiful women around him to select from, and Gage never experienced a problem attracting the opposite sex. So what did they both see in me?

Reed stared from me to Gage. "You have a dragon standing right there, so why are you coming to me?"

I caught the snarl in his voice, and Gage's chest puffed out as his breaths sped. I stepped between them.

"Stop this, please. Reed, I welcomed you to stay in the tower for as long as needed, so I thought you'd extend me a similar generosity. And Gage can't offer his tooth, or he would have."

No one said a word.

"Look. We're both facing problems," I continued. "So I'll do whatever I can for you if you assist me with the weapon. What do you say?"

Reed rubbed his jawline and crossed his arms over his chest, creasing his shirt. "I need to know who's hunting down my pride, but since you didn't shove me out the window of your tower, I'll do my best to aid you." Reed strutted toward the tree and settled down with his back against the trunk.

"Elliana," Reed began, and I sat cross-legged in front of him. Gage knelt on the grass next to me. "There's a collector of artifacts who once mentioned a dragon-tooth knife and a bunch of other items she'd gained from a merchant. He didn't pay her much heed since it was at the local town market, and everyone lied to make a sale. But if she spoke the truth, then one of my friends can help you track down the collector. Kahlo is a tiger shifter, and he once saw the collector as she entered a trap door in a tree deep in the forest. Guess that's where she keeps her collection, so she might have the weapon you're looking for hidden in there."

"Perfect," Gage said. "Tell us where we can find Kahlo, and we'll be out of here."

Reed clapped his hands, and the red-haired warrior hopped down from the branches overhead.

I flinched. Was his pride ready to attack the moment we laid a hand on him? We stood no chance.

"I may have a lead to help your missing pride members," Gage blurted.

Reed's posture stiffened. He released a long exhale, and I faced Gage.

"Do you know something that might assist them?"

Gage shrugged, studying Reed. "I've heard rumors about shifters vanishing. Not just your kind, but others. Panthers, wolves, and bears."

Reed climbed to his feet, his expression growing darker. "What else do you know?"

"I need to be sure you'll help Elliana."

"Go collect, Kahlo." Reed barked and met my gaze. "He's here on pride matters, so you've come at a good time."

I touched Gage's arm. "Tell him what you know."

Instead, he dragged me out of Reed's earshot and whispered, "Don't be so easily led by the cat. They never help others—ever. It's one of their pride rules. So, why would he assist you so easily? I'm telling you that when we have any leads on the other members of their pride, he'll turn on us. So, we get his information on the dagger first."

These past couple of days, I had been through hell, and I longed for things to go smoothly for a change. Instead, Gage was acting like a green-eyed monster, and Reed wasn't any better.

"Let go of me," I replied as if my jaw were wired shut. "He offered to help before you even mentioned the missing shifters."

His mouth opened, then shut again. "But I'm still right. Don't trust a lion. Their priority is their pride at the demise of everyone else. That's why they live out here, away from others. They're a cult."

Reed burst out laughing. "A cult! Really? Is that the best you can do?"

Gage brushed past me, and the humming energy from his body leapt from him to me. Something was happening to his shoulder blades—two bulges pushed outward from under his top, growing in size. He was changing. He pulled off his shirt, but he would only partly shift since that was all he was capable of.

Vast wings fanned outward, fast and aggressive. They were black as night, terrifying, and smudged with gold near the tipped edges of his bat-like wings.

Translucent scales resembling claw-like projections stretched across his shoulders and down his spine, gleaming under the flamed torches. Gage hunched forward, lips curled back, and faced Reed. A wisp of smoke wafted from his nostrils, rising in short puffs.

Within moments, six warriors dropped from the trees overhead, circling us, teeth bared, ready to battle. Reed's arms shifted into large, furry paws, his claws extended. The two men faced each other, shoulders curled forward, growling, ready to battle.

Rage hissed through my body, sweeping against me like waves. I ducked under Gage's wings and placed myself between them.

"What the fuck are you two doing?" Sure, Gage's wings were magnificent and the only ability he had as a dragon, but I didn't for the life of me need to deal with his aggression.

Reed lifted his chin. "Dragon, you have three seconds to tell me about the missing shifters, or my guards will rip you and your delicate wings to shreds. I mean, if those wings are all you shift into, you'll stand no chance against us. And all before you find true love, so you can finally evolve into your true dragon form."

"Wait, what?" I stammered, staring at Gage, who avoided me. I swallowed hard. "Say again. True love? Full form?"

"One," Reed bellowed, starting his countdown.

The warrior women closed in, and their skins shimmered with the telltale signs of their transformation.

"Gage," I yelled. "Stop being a dick. Tell him."

"Two."

I couldn't stop the terror gripping my heart, my brain firing off sparks to run away from the two dumbheads as they got out their aggression. We were in Reed's territory. He'd lost a sister, so hell yeah, he would respond with force. Meaning he had every intention of going through with his threat. And as much as Gage pissed me off, he was outnumbered, and he'd lose this fight.

So, I did the first thing that came to mind. I pressed my back to Gage's chest and faced Reed, hating how quickly things had escalated. The words rolled over my strained vocals. I had no idea if Reed would attack me, but I couldn't let Gage get hurt.

"You'll have to kill me before I let you touch him."

A growl rolled through Reed's chest, his jawline clenching, and the corded muscles in his neck twitched. "Get out of the way, Elliana."

I didn't move from in front of Gage, despite my trembling.

"Fuck, chill your fur balls already," Gage said over my shoulder. "I'll tell you what you need to know. Son of a bitch. Cats! Always whining about something. I just want to ensure you assist Elliana first." He lowered his wings and straightened his posture.

The night air surrounding us thickened, strangling my lungs. I appreciated Gage's protectiveness, but his aggression put us at risk, rather than saving us... by antagonizing an entire pride of lions.

"See." Reed's arrogant triumph showed in his smirk—all pouting lips and the narrowing of his eyes. "Now beg me for help."

"Fuck you." Gage huffed.

I gritted my teeth, snatched his hand, and stepped forward.

"Reed. Gage. Enough. We all want the same thing. To assist each other, so why are you both acting like dicks?"

Reed cocked a brow while Gage breathed deeply and sighed, being the first to respond.

"All I want is the best for Elliana, so I'll tell you everything, but you need to give me your word you'll allow Kahlo to share what he knows."

Reed nodded and flicked a hand at someone to his right.

A man strode out of the darkness and into my line of sight. He wore black pants… that was it. They hung low on his hips, displaying his ripped chest and abs. Tall, sculptured, and damn sexy. Were all shifters built like gods? Damn, his presence stirred up my libido, awakening my lust, tempting me to taste the candy on a stick looking my way. Short, chestnut hair fluttered over his brow, drawing my attention to a healed scar lining the side of his face.

When I met his eyes, I drowned. They captured the greenest meadow, imploring me to dive right in and explore. Something about this handsome stranger had me squeezing my thighs together. I bet he had women fawning over him because I sure was. What was up with the men I'd met lately? Gage, Reed, and now this man… their presence had me burning up. And it was strange how each of them had different shades of sexy green eyes.

"Kahlo, these are my guests." Reed gave a nod in my direction, his mouth curling upward as if he were sending me secret thoughts about what he intended to do to me. Of course, it was completely in my lust-driven mind.

"This is my good friend and a tiger shifter, Kahlo," Reed continued.

The newcomer didn't respond at first, but he scanned me head to toe, his eyes narrowing. In those few moments, time seemed to slow to where his wild stare rested on me as if I were a delectable deer. It felt as if my brain had numbed and struggled to come up with a response. How could someone merely looking at me leave me scorching?

Gage sighed and mumbled under his breath, but only I caught the words, "cat party."

"Kahlo, good timing. The dragon was about to give us an insight into who took the missing shifters." Reed's words darkened in a way that promised war if Gage didn't keep his word.

I gritted my teeth at the whole situation. I ought to have

dragged Gage aside and found out what his problem with the lions was.

Gage stood tall, proud, his chin high. He retracted his wings with such swiftness, it left me in awe. I stepped back as they magically shrank and tucked into the gaping holes in his back. His skin knitted back together without a blemish. My fingers tingled with the urge to touch his shoulder blades. I grabbed his top off the ground and handed it to him.

Reed studied me as if intrigued by the way I stared at Gage. Was he wondering what the deal was between us? Because I had no answer to that or why my pulse kicked up a notch, having Reed's or Kahlo's gazes on me.

"You haven't seen his wings before?" Reed asked, softness behind his words.

"Yes, once before, and they're as majestic as I remembered." There was something sexy about a powerful man with huge wings who looked ready to carry the world.

Gage pulled the top over his head and offered me a devilish wink, making me weak in the knees.

"All right," he began as he clapped once, drawing everyone's attention to him. Always the showman. "Let's do this because Elliana doesn't have all night."

And there he was... my dragon. In control and ready to tackle the problem at hand.

"You go first," Reed said. "We're listening."

I looked over at Kahlo, who remained quiet, but I didn't fail to catch the way he kept watching us as a predatory animal might before attacking. Had I misunderstood his expression as attraction when, for all I knew, he enjoyed hunting down humans and ripping out their throats? I struggled to believe that he was friends with Reed.

Gage rubbed his stubbled jawline and clicked his tongue, telling me it killed him to follow Reed's instructions.

"I never said I knew *who* is running the operation, just that I heard a rumor last night at Brawl. I haven't investigated if it's real. But someone's taken over the old mansion by Sharp Lookout. Someone saw two fox shifters in chains being dragged into the complex."

I swallowed hard at hearing the despair threaded behind his words. It scared him, even if he stood tall and proud. No one spoke, but more figures closed in, materializing from the night. Dozens of faces warped with worry. A mother clasped a child to her hip, and smaller kids lingered among the adults. Families. Elderly. Warriors. They stood together, and their fear coiled around my chest, squeezing. Reed's sister was among the missing, so I could imagine his heartache.

Reed barked an order. "We put together a small team of our finest, and we take the fuckers down tonight. Who's with me?"

Roars boomed, feet stomping the ground, fists in the air. Both the tiger, who seemed alone, and lions alike. That was how they'd take down their enemy—in unison. Something shifted inside me at seeing their bond, despite the fear etched on their faces. My pulse buzzed beneath my skin with an adrenaline that insisted I join them. Maybe it was getting caught up in the hype, but I'd never been part of such a group. I'd only known loneliness and fighting on my own, but what would it be like to be part of such a family? My dad might have gotten me into this trouble in the first place, but he'd do anything for me, and I missed him so much, even after all these years. His jokes and protection and guidance, knowing he'd always catch me when I fell.

Reed's cheer quieted, and everyone followed suit. Then he waved a hand at several of his warriors. "Assemble a team. We go now."

"Wait, wait!" Gage called out, stepping forward, drawing all eyes to him. Even outnumbered, nothing dimmed his unassailable confidence. Backing down was not a trait he embraced. "We made a deal. Now deliver your end of the bargain."

Kahlo nodded, accepting Gage's challenge by approaching him. He slapped a hand on Gage's back. "The collector's bunker is near the border between Darkwoods and Wildfire."

Gage shook his head. "Too vague. That forest is vast and would have us wandering for months to find the right spot."

Kahlo licked his lips and dropped his hand. "It's been a long time since I visited the area, but there was a distinct, acidic smell in the air, and when you sense it, you'll know the place."

Gage huffed, gripping his hips. "Stop pulling my dick and be fucking specific."

I neared Gage's side, not wanting this to go haywire again, and nudged him while meeting Kahlo's eyes. At first, I couldn't find my words, especially with the intense way he looked at me. The twitching at the corners of his mouth readied to break into a smirk. I longed to see that, but Gage nudged my arm.

"Can you show us where it's located?"

"This I will do for you." His smile seemed so genuinely sweet with just the right amount of sexiness, it sent a rush of warmth through me. He reached out and took my hand, his thumb caressing my palm ever so gently. My skin rippled with the electric static, and I drowned in his presence. Did tiger shifters have hypnotic power over people? Because right now, if his tingling touch and stare drove me this insane, I could just imagine what it would be like for him to take me. I gnawed on my lower lip and released a long exhale.

"But not tonight." He bowed his head and released my hand.

Reed closed the distance, and now, all four of us stood in a circle. Three men towered over me. Despite all the fucked-up shit in my life, the guilt of their plight, and the worry that the collector wouldn't help me, a different sensation awakened deep in my gut. An intoxicating electricity had me wriggling on the inside with desire. In such proximity, their scent sent me into a heady trance. There was something about these men I'd never sensed with anyone else. Their presence lit me up from the inside, and their closeness made me nervous, excited, and provoked. Feigning a cool detachment was impossible when three gorgeous men cast glances my way with what I could only describe as fire in their eyes.

Hell, I wasn't a corpse. I had feelings, and I sparked alight at being so close to them. What were they thinking? Wondering what it would be like to kiss me? Rip my clothes off and take me right now?

I can see your thoughts. Heavens, you want them to take turns taking you. I am shocked!

I frowned and whispered under my breath. "Zip it. It's none of your business."

"Sorry?" Kahlo asked.

I stared up at him when Reed responded. "She talks to herself sometimes."

"You get used to it," Gage said. "It's kind of cute."

"Hey, don't talk about me as if I'm not here. Anyway, back to the topic."

Kahlo's gaze remained on me, and I pictured him leaning closer and tossing me over his shoulder before taking me into the shadows. Just the two of us.

Yeah, 'cause you're not sex-crazed around all *these men.*

"I will accompany you, but tonight's priority is finding our missing family members." Kahlo turned to Gage. "Can you give me directions to the mansion?"

For a change, Gage didn't protest and broke into an explanation. Reed collected my elbow and guided me away from everyone.

"Can we talk in private?" he asked, and I strolled with him because curiosity demanded I discover what he wanted. We traipsed along the open field, grass flattening beneath our footfalls.

"What's going on?" I asked. "We're putting a lot of distance between us and everyone else."

"Don't worry. You're safe." He laughed, and the sound danced over my skin like a lover's touch.

"I'm not scared. I'm intrigued."

Reed halted near a tree without leaves, and the faint streak of moonlight lit up the side of his face. Before I caught my breath, he clasped my arms and drew me against him. He pressed his back to the tree and plastered me to his chest.

"Whoa." My breaths came fast. This wasn't a chat, and my insides stirred at being in his arms as they had in the tower. He wasn't shy, and hell, I adored that. Maybe another place and time, we'd... but I couldn't think straight in his arms. I didn't understand what was going on between Gage and me, let alone adding one more man into the mix. Me flirting with images in my head was one thing, but reality never ran smoothly.

He might want a fling.

"I don't see you pulling away." His hands snaked around my back, holding me tight. "I want to know if you're with the dragon."

My words died. I already had so many mixed emotions from the last few days, and my attraction to Reed had me craving his lips again. But I hadn't expected him to be so forward. Was he thinking we were a thing now? Except, I came with massive baggage—the same reason I'd pushed away Gage. I wouldn't force my problems on anyone else. Yet, back in the tower, I was eager to catch up with Reed for a date. Clearly, I was lust-induced and not thinking straight.

"Gage means the world to me, but I can't be with anyone right now." Admitting it out loud was a knife to my heart when my body begged me to goddamn kiss him already. I pushed myself out of his arms.

"I'm not sure what you expect from me. You have a pride to lead, you're probably already promised to several lionesses, and I have a messed-up life I wouldn't wish upon anyone. Well, okay, I lie. I'd force it on the dick who hexed me."

Shadows danced under his gaze, and he moved slightly against the tree. With one knee bent, he put his hands deep into the pockets of his pants.

I lowered my eyes and turned to the fiery glow in the distance with people running about and Gage laughing at something Kahlo had said. Didn't take him long to get chummy.

I shouldn't be attracted to Reed or Kahlo after just meeting them... especially when my heart drummed for Gage. Heavens, what was happening to me?

"Return tomorrow night," he said.

I somehow suspected females didn't say *no* to him often.

"Kahlo will take you to the collector's place."

"Thanks. But what's the deal between you two?"

He stared at me first. Had he seen me gawk at his friend?

"A few years ago, three rogue lions challenged me for my position when I was alone in the forest. By lion law, I either accepted a duel or stepped aside as pride leader."

"Shit odds. Fuck that." My response flew from my mouth. Craven assholes.

He lifted an arm and his shirt to reveal a healed wound from his pit to his waist. I winced and reached out to touch the injury that had healed over. Now, all that remained was a bumpy scar beneath my fingers. But up close, I noticed the cuts on his arms were restored.

"I finished those fuckers, but they left me so injured, I was on death's door. Kahlo found me. He didn't need to save me, but he took me in and cared for me. Ever since, we've been like brothers. We're both coming of age to find a mate to lead alongside us. Without a mate by my twenty-fifth birthday, I must relegate my position as pride leader to the lion shifter from my pride who can win in a battle against me. And that's only a few months away."

Okay, that was a lot to digest, yet funny how my attention homed in on both the shifters being single and needing a partner. So what was wrong with their surrounding females? Did none of them excite them? Or did they consider them too much like family to ever see them as romantic partners? Perhaps they preferred to bring fresh blood into the pride.

It shouldn't have been my focus, especially when I wasn't in the market. It scared me to go there for so many reasons, like why the hell were they interested in me, a woman who talked to herself? It came down to the gargoyle that posed a danger to them if they tried to battle it. Now, if by some miracle, Kahlo's suggestion about the collector having the dragon dagger proved valid, all bets were off.

More than one man at the same time?

"Not at the same time. I don't party that way."

"You talking to me?" Reed asked.

My cheeks flushed, and I looked away. "Shall we return?"

He strolled forward. "Why do you talk to yourself out loud that way? I'm not judging. I want to understand."

"Being a captive since I was young did something inside me. I only had myself to talk to, and one day, the voice inside my skull responded. I didn't question it, well aware it might be me. For the longest time, she kept me company." Admitting the truth should have left me self-conscious, but it didn't. I had gone way past caring what others said about me when I yearned for freedom so bad, I'd do anything.

"Gage's right. It's cute and gives me insight into your thoughts."

I bumped into his arm. "I see. Well, sure hope you share your thoughts, too. Only fair this goes both ways." I flipped my hand in the air between us.

"I've shared a lot with you already, but there's so much more you're missing out on."

"Really?" I nudged his side again, and that time, he stumbled sideways in an exaggerated way. "Let me guess... like kissing you."

You're doing it again. Flirting.

Of course, because I had zero control, I'd gone against my word to keep a distance. But that seemed easier when there had been a physical barrier between us.

"Elliana, you can't handle these lips on you again." His mouth twitched upward, dimpling his cheeks. "Another taste and you'll never let me go."

I chuckled and spotted Gage watching me from up ahead. "You make big promises, Lion-Man."

"And I get what I want."

His response sparked a buzz in the pit of my gut. Something about having a strong shifter like Reed declare he'd claim me turned me into a puddle. It contradicted everything I believed— to let no one control me—but Reed wasn't doing that... nope. This was different. His pledge left me stimulated and awakened with arousal. To have him crave me so much had me swimming in fire.

You know, he might like the whole chasing-his-prey idea. Once he gets you, he'll get bored.

I shoved away those thoughts, preferring to believe he'd

pursue me, capture me, and keep me forever. Yet the lingering worries remained, gnawing at my mind.

With my inability to respond, Reed strolled closer and prodded me in the arm to return to the main tree. Up ahead, Gage strutted toward us, arms still by his side, silent and serious.

"Your dragon comes to protect you."

I was unsure how to take his comment—as jealousy or a veiled insult at Gage. I changed topics and reached out for his arm.

"Hope you find your sister safe and sound."

The sincerity in his soft expression affected me. He was a powerful leader, but he cared for those close to him.

"Please stay safe." I hugged him, my body pressed against his solid form, fitting perfectly together.

His mouth reached my ear as he grabbed my waist. "When this is all over, I'm coming to claim you as mine. I'll show you pleasures and happiness you can't imagine."

My heart pulsed. Would it be wrong of me if I said *yes*? He broke free.

"Have a good night, Dragon." He marched toward the other shifters.

"What the hell was that about?" Gage growled.

"Nothing," I squeaked and cleared my throat. "Let's go. They said they'd take us to the collector tomorrow night."

My brain kept ringing with his words about claiming me as his own. Was he insane? Did he not understand I was stuck in the tower during the day? Plus, I adored Gage. With all the excuses in the world swirling around my head, I couldn't ignore how excited his words had left me. His assertiveness had my libido twisting into a titillating knot.

CHAPTER 11

"That lion has a thing for you," Gage said nonchalantly without a hint of jealousy. We strolled through the forest, having left behind the pride a while ago. "So does the tiger. Saw the way they both stared at you, stripping you with their gazes."

I glared at Gage, who had his hands stiff by his sides, not ready to deal with emotions when, technically, I was pushing everyone aside until I fixed my problems.

"Are you jealous again?"

"Again? Honey, I've been watching men devour you with their eyes since I first met you years ago, and this isn't jealousy but admiration. I'd give anything to watch the lion or tiger take you. But you're still mine."

"What?" I slapped his arm when he reached down and adjusted his package. "Are you getting off on this?" It never occurred to me he'd enjoy watching me with other men. The concept seemed foreign because maybe this whole time, I'd misunderstood his protectiveness for jealousy. Was he into swinging with other couples because, while I'd never contemplated it, now it tickled me inside.

"If we were dating, it wouldn't bother you if I slept with another man?" *Or two?*

"No, but it would have to be someone who adored and

worshipped the ground you walked on like I do." He grinned as his eyes glazed over. "Do you even understand how fucking sexy you are? Those gorgeous curves and that ass. You're on my mind every day. I want to claim you, make you scream out my name until you forget everything else."

There was that word again. *Claim.* I loathed what the witch and gargoyle had done, keeping me in the tower against my will, yet for these powerful men stating they wanted to take me as theirs, I only melted in response. I yearned for them to assert themselves over me in ways that would stimulate me to no end.

You've got one twisted mind.

"Yep, that's me." I shook my head. "Anyway, don't say shit like that, Gage."

"Why? Turning you on too much?" he teased.

I bit down on my cheek and sauntered ahead while Gage laughed. He always pushed his limits, and the scary part was that I loved it. Like the time he'd insisted on making love to me on a thick branch up in the tree where he'd had his house built. Sure, the tree was encased in a thick canopy of leaves, making it close to impossible for anyone would see us, but he had neighbors in other trees. It had terrified me at first, but once we'd started, I hadn't been able to stop, loving the idea that we might be seen.

"Knew it," he said. "You want it so bad." He jogged up behind me as we entered the ruins and headed toward the tower, then he grabbed my arm and spun me around to face him. "Come on, Elliana, admit you're dying to scream with an orgasm, and you're just aching for me to fuck you." He licked his lips, and his sexy eyes were hooded.

I gasped for air, catching my balance as his grin agitated my libido in all the right ways, but I also didn't want to lead him on. "Don't think so." I wrestled free from his grip and moved backward, but my heel caught on a rock, and I stumbled, my arms pinwheeling.

He moved with such swiftness, he might as well have been the wind. His arm swooped under my back, catching me, but instead of bringing me back up, he fell to his knees and laid me onto my back in the lush grass rustling around us. He joined me, his body against my side, his head resting on a bent elbow.

"Damn, that was smooth." I laughed as he blew on his bent fingers before rubbing them across his chest.

The moon's halo reflected in his green eyes. I had no intention of getting up when arousal drove through me unannounced and ready for explosion.

"Elliana." He whispered my name on the wind and brushed away a leaf caught on my sleeve. "Do you want to be with me?"

"Of course!" No hesitation. "But—"

"No." His fingers crossed my mouth. "Tonight, we are free. No restrictions. Nothing. Just us two."

Adoring that so much, I smiled and gave him a slight nod. I longed for the time when every day I could do whatever I pleased.

The overgrown grass swayed, rustling and concealing us. My breaths picked up speed being so close to Gage, having his gaze swallow me. He had always been there for me and never pushed me away, even after I'd walked away from our relationship. With the prospect of Kahlo's help, part of me toyed with letting down my walls, finally falling into Gage's arms, and allowing myself to believe a blissful future was possible.

Reed's words swirled in there, too, about him claiming me, and it excited me to have two incredible men desire me. Unsure how this would work out, I thought back to Gage's comment about watching me have sex with another shifter. Was that just a fetish thing or him willing to share?

Yeah, because the lion will share! And oh, what the hell are you waffling about? Focus on the mission. Eradicate the gargoyle, then you can go all sex-crazy.

With Gage's thumb caressing my collarbone, thinking straight seemed too hard. What could I offer him if I found freedom tomorrow? For so long, I'd craved escape, but now that I might gain liberty, fear squeezed in my mind. What would my future entail? What if I couldn't stop the dread from owning me? Could I be normal? It terrified me that such a simple concept seemed foreign. I'd lost part of myself so long ago. So, who was I?

"Why didn't you tell me about you not turning into a real dragon until you found your true mate?" I asked.

His eyes wandered to the field momentarily, and the corners of his mouth tightened.

"What difference would it have made? I didn't want you to feel pressured or responsible. The love must be real for it to work." He rolled onto his back alongside me and stared up into the speckled night sky.

How could I respond to that? It wasn't too different a reason from why I initially hadn't told him about my own problem. It reminded me of his earlier worries about letting me down by not being able to provide the dragon's tooth.

I lowered my hand between us, our fingers intertwining. We were a lot more similar than I thought.

"Why haven't you found someone who can love you like you were their universe?" I felt stupid asking because deep inside, I wanted to be his goddess, but for so long, I'd driven him away. It wasn't fair to make him wait on the off-chance I escaped my curse.

"Because I'll never want anyone the way I do you." His fingers clutched mine. "I don't get a choice if my heart's already yours."

My stomach twirled, and I stiffened, biting down on my lower lip. "I'm sorry." My throat thickened. "I let you down. Fuck, I'm a selfish bitch. I keep wanting to tell you to stop wasting your time on me. Find someone who can love you better. But I don't because I want you." Guilt iced my gut, and I might as well have been frozen. I yearned to be with Gage as if my life depended on it, but I didn't deserve him. It felt as if a vise gripped my ice-cold heart because my chest ached as though I'd explode.

I drew my hand back and rolled away, hating how my stomach hurt at disappointing Gage when he'd always been there for me.

His arm looped over my waist, and his chest plastered against my back. He held me close, embracing me from behind.

"This was why I didn't tell you. You overthink things, and I don't give a shit about becoming a true dragon. My asshole of a family abandoned me as a child in the woods, so why the fuck would I want to be like them? And you know why I gave that lion shit? Because when I was young and homeless, a pride of lion shifters found me. Instead of helping me, they tied me up like a dog, threw me food, and called me their bitch. They taunted me and pitted me against their teens in battles while everyone watched and cheered each time I fell. I was a fucking child in human form!" His voice trembled behind me.

"Fuck!" I clasped his arms, shocked because he'd never opened up before about his past when I'd pried. "I had no idea. Was it Reed's pride?" I held my breath, praying it wasn't the case.

His response came fast. "No. It was another, but seeing all those lions today brought back anger I'd thought I'd dealt with. I learned long ago that lions look after their own. Anyone else is disposable. Like tonight, you went for help, we gave them assistance, and they left us hanging dry. Their pride is priority."

I couldn't deny what he'd said, but if I were in Reed's position, I'd do the same thing. Priority went to the task with the most urgent need.

"I'm so sorry that happened to you. Shit, it's like we're both broken somehow, you know."

"Must be why I was first attracted to you." He dipped his head and kissed the back of my hand. "You always looked over your shoulder, clearly scared to trust people, and you resonated with me. I'm not sure I'll ever stop caring for you."

I curled into his embrace, adoring his warmth and how he let me see the real him, not just the brave man who'd tackle the world.

"Thanks for letting me in," I said. "It means so much."

"For your ears only, honey." His breath skipped across my nape, warm and ticklish. "I may not trust most people, but for you, I'd lay down my life."

"No!" I pulled his arms around me tighter. "Don't you ever do that."

"I'll never make such a promise." His lips brushed the side of my neck, and a warm spark zipped down my legs. My toes curled as he kissed me in the tender spot beneath my earlobe. "I'd leave my job as a guard, sell my home, and sleep outdoors if it meant saving you. You're all I live for."

My mouth opened to protest, but when his tongue found the length of my neck, I moaned.

"It's unfair of you to tease me."

"I plan to take you right here and show you what you've been missing."

I turned to face him, and his mouth found mine, obliterating every thought. Worries evaporated, and I savored his lips, drowning in my desire to have him move his hands under my shirt and feel me all over. Clenching my hair into his fist, he tilted my head back and licked my chin and down my neck, taking small mock bites of my flesh. Every inch of me sizzled. His other hand pried open the cords of my vest and the buttons on my shirt.

"Touch me," I purred as he dragged my top up and over my head. I sat up and lifted my hands as he drew them off me without hesitation. My breasts spilled out into the cool breeze, puckering my nipples.

Night covered everything, but considering how rare it was for anyone to enter the field, I had no worries about someone walking in on us. Though it might have excited Gage further if someone had.

"Sexy as fuck," he said. "Love your tits."

I collapsed onto my back in the grass, the blades cushioning against me, and surrendered myself completely. Gage followed me, his tongue tasting a breast, sucking and flicking my tight bud. Fire soared south, and I writhed, adoring his attention, his sexiness. I grabbed handfuls of his shirt and drew the fabric over his head, breaking our connection. He never stopped and sailed across to the other breast, tugging on my erect nipple, his teeth gently gnawing on me. My heart skipped, and I moaned in ecstasy as I pictured him pounding into me.

Our breaths raced, and I sensed everything—his quickening pulse, his hungry fingers plucking at my pants, his roaming eyes.

My hips rocked back and forth, grinding against him, drowning in the intensity. Fire enveloped me, and Gage's hands were an inferno.

He knelt beside me, wearing a mischievous smirk. Reaching out, I ran a hand over his strong chest, following the line of thin hair down his stomach and vanishing into his trousers. I moved my fingers to his hardness, pushing the fabric into a tent shape. I shivered in anticipation.

"You're too far away." With a click, I unbuttoned his pants and pulled the front open. His erection popped out, thick and long, greeting me with his musky scent. I adored the way he smelled. It drove me insane with lust. I rubbed a thumb over the tip coated in pre-cum, and he rolled his eyes back, moaning that guttural sound that did things to my insides. He brushed my hand aside.

"No, I'm too close." He stared at me like a starving dragon, eyes alight and vertical slits for a few moments. His fingers hooked into the top of my pants and underwear. In one fast move, he jerked them down my legs and off me with such speed, it left me gasping and rocking backward from the motion.

"Shit, give a girl warning."

He laughed, and I loved the gravelly sound, how the edges of his eyes creased with happy lines.

"Here's my advanced notice. I'm about to fuck you like never before." He moved between my bent legs.

I chewed on my lip and tightened my thighs together, driving home that deep tingle provoking me to an explosion.

His hands hooked under my knees, spreading me, and he hauled me closer. Lifting the bottom half of my body off the ground as if I weighed nothing, he rested my lower back and ass against his chest. My calves rested over his shoulders, his hands interlaced over my stomach, his face right between my legs. I balanced myself by gripping the grass on either side of me.

Breaths coming too fast, the anticipation of what was coming instantly took over.

"Picturesque view from here." He whistled, his eyes locked on to my privates.

"You sure are a tease, and—" I moaned loudly when his mouth clamped around my inner lips. I lost all words, all thought. I arched, groaning. He ate me—the noises he made ought to be illegal, as they screamed raw sex. Nothing compared to having him tongue-fuck me over and over.

I writhed under him, and despite me half-hanging upside down, I didn't care as his lips mashed against my pussy. He gently pulled at my lips and swept his tongue over my clit so fast, I forgot myself.

"Fuck, Gage!" I looked up into his green eyes.

They smiled with arousal. He reached for a breast, kneading it. His tongue was magic, and my skin was a frenzy of static tingles.

At once, I was caught between the intoxication and trying to make the moment last, but it crashed through me like waves, slamming against my libido. I screamed and convulsed faster, harder.

Gage never released his hold as he licked my wetness, moaning his approval.

All tension floated from my body, leaving me spent and floating on a cloud. My smile hurt my cheeks, but I couldn't get enough. When Gage raised his head, his mouth and chin glimmered and winked.

"You taste fucking incredible." He gently lowered me to the ground, then climbed to his feet and removed his pants.

I admired his erect cock, the tightness of his balls, but his shoulders curled forward, and his body shimmied. Something was wrong, and I sat up.

"Gage, are you okay?"

"Honey, I'll be amazing in a few moments." There was a familiar split of skin as his enormous black wings spanned outward, blotting the moonlight and drowning me in complete darkness, all except for the glistening golden tips on his wings.

"Oh, my. I so love where this is going."

His arms found me, and he lifted me with ease, but my attention fell on the iridescent scales spreading across his shoulders. Beneath my touch, they were solid but shifted with Gage's muscles and not slippery at all. For some reason, I expected them to be smooth when, in fact, they were rough. The rest of him remained human. Then there was his cock. That thing had a mind of its own, erect and ready, twitching against my stomach.

"Wrap yourself around me."

I hugged his neck, and my legs hung off his hips as I met his vertical slit eyes, golden and sexy. He kissed my nose, and suddenly, his hardness nudged my opening. I wriggled over the tip, rubbing myself with him.

A gust of wind swirled past as he beat his wings in a powerful down thrust as we moved off the ground. He gripped me tightly, both hands on my ass. I held on as the world grew smaller, and below us stood the tower in the woods. On the roof sat the damn gargoyle. I wished we could fly away and never return, but those were stupid dreams.

"Can anyone see us up here?" I asked.

"Not in the dark, but if they can, we'll give them a show." He kissed me long and deep. Without hesitation, he thrust into me. I groaned into his mouth, my jumping breasts rubbing across his chest.

"Ahh…" The breeze did little to cool me down when his cock filled me. I'd fumbled around with two other men before I met Gage, but I lost my virginity to him and wouldn't change a thing about that.

I rocked up and down on him, meeting each slap, and the higher we climbed, the more my head swirled. His hands fell to my hips, guiding me quick, harder. I clasped his shoulders, lost in a dream of delirious excitement. I moaned at how much he stretched me open with his girth, yet I kept glancing in every direction, fearful I might fall over.

His attention hovered on my bouncing breasts when he pivoted forward. Panic gripped me as I began to fall backward, but he'd already snapped his arms tighter around me.

"I got you, beautiful."

With him still buried deep inside me, I now lay underneath him. We flew as he hammered into me, plunging so hard, I cried out with pleasure. The beat of his wings acted as a harmonic sequence to the thrusting of his dick. The breeze buffered against us, ripping at my hair, doing zilch to cool the inferno between us. A rousing electricity rushed forward with such speed, it spun my head. The explosive spark detonated within me, and I yelled.

"Fuck, yeah!" Gage roared louder and pulsed inside me. His eyes clamped shut as he rode his own wave, both of us bursting with arousal. This was a point of no return. His lips and hands awakened me with every touch.

Except the wind picked up too fast, and my vision twirled. The world came rushing at us. We plunged toward the ground head-first.

Terror dug its claws into my chest. "Gage!" I yelled.

"Trust me," he whispered.

I clung to him, unable to catch my breath, and the whole time he remained inside me. Moments from us splattering into the rocky ruins, he swooped upward and landed on his feet with such grace, I could have sworn he was a bird. He stood upright, and I clung to him like a terrified leaf.

"You all right?" He lifted me off his delicious cock and placed me on my feet. When my knees wobbled beneath me, he kept a hand on my waist to steady me.

The ruins surrounded us, the tower and gargoyle in the distance, and my earlier excitement deflated. I embraced Gage, not ready to return to reality. "

"Please don't leave just yet. Dawn is still a while away."

"I'm not going anywhere. Now or ever."

Just hearing his reassurance and promise, I let myself believe happy endings were a possibility.

CHAPTER 12

When one hooked up with a dragon, the traditional method of sex flew out the window. Who needed that when we freakin' soared through the skies while he'd slammed into me, bringing me to orgasm? Now, *that* was going down in the books as a once-in-a-lifetime experience that had left me exhilarated, scared, and so turned on. Just thinking about it left me desperate for more. We used to have sex marathons when we'd dated, but never once had he taken me into the air.

After Gage left the tower before dawn, I crashed and slept all the way through the day, not waking up sweating in fear.

Now, night cloaked the land, and Gage returned to pick me up. As I climbed down the tower, Gage was waiting at the bottom. We strolled away from the tower, heading toward the lion's territory. Gage said very little.

The cool breeze washed through my short hair. His grip swallowed mine as he looked my way with a sly grin.

I adored how passionate he was, but a niggling worry burrowed through me that I was leading him on. Not because I had any plans to hurt him—far from it. I still wondered how long it might take him to get bored with me. The real problem came down to whether or not I'd finally vanquish the gargoyle. If not, what would we do? Only get together at night? I couldn't ask him to change his life for me. Then, there was the whole attraction to Reed. His words last night had left me stunned and excited to have someone like him pursue me. So how was I supposed to deal with that on top of being with Gage?

Suddenly, that whole pushing everyone away thing seemed easier, far less confusing and painful.

And you were much more focused, too.

Gage broke the silence and distracted me.

"I'm thinking. I'll fly you to the border near Wildfire to search for the collector's hideout, and that way, we'll return before dawn. The tiger can run there, then show us where he lives so we can find the dagger."

"It'll be hard for Kahlo to cover such a distance in such a short amount of time. Maybe we can arrange a time tomorrow where he can meet us somewhere in the woods, giving him time to travel."

"Tigers are fast creatures. He'll be fine." Gage guided me over a gurgling creek, holding my hand to ensure I didn't fall in.

"Let's be civil tonight, okay?" I said. "They're going through hard times."

Gage cut me a curious look. We stalked through the open plain, making our way to the forest line where we'd been taken last night to meet Reed. I kept scanning the land, expecting his warriors to jump out, but they didn't. Did they recognize us and now leave us alone?

"Reed said something to you last night when you went for a walk, and ever since, it's like you care about hurting his or Kahlo's feelings."

"You don't know what you're talking about," I scoffed and focused straight ahead. How could I explain emotions I didn't understand? Reed didn't know me, so how could he presume to claim me? Sure, it flattered me… unless that was how the whole mating thing in his pride worked—find a partner, place your stamp of ownership on them, and take them by force.

"I can see it in your eyes when you speak of him." His narrowing gaze teased me as his mouth curled upward.

"And? Do you see how my stomach flutters each time you touch me, how my world vanishes when you kiss me, how I crave nothing more than to lose myself in you? But I'm terrified. Because if I can't be free, I can't be with you. That isn't fair to you."

I hadn't meant to rant; most of it had come from a place of worry. Most days, my life felt like a magical spell gone haywire. Any moment now, it would rip me to smithereens. For so long, I'd tried to escape and every time I'd tried, I'd failed. So what made this time different?

Told you not to get your hopes up.

I bit my tongue and said nothing more.

Gage drew me to a stop and turned me to face him.

"We'll find a solution."

"That's where we differ. All I can think about is how long it'll be before things somehow get screwed up again."

He threw an arm around me and kissed my brow. "All I was trying to say was that I want to be with you. If that means I see you only at night, then so be it."

Just thinking of the situation hurt my head. I untangled myself from his arms. This wasn't the place to have this conversation.

"We better get a move on." Together, we crossed the strip of forest before emerging into the open meadow that formed the lions' territory. Darkness fell across the barren landscape. No sign of anyone—while last night lions had filled the place. Now, the wind whistled silently.

"Where is everyone?" Gage marched deeper into the field, scanning the area. "Bastards! They ditched us. Got our intelligence and ran."

"No. They wouldn't." Not when I remembered the agony in their eyes, the mothers and kids. That hadn't been fake. "There's no reason for them to. Something happened to them." An ache settled in my gut. "Maybe we should have gone with them last night."

"Elliana's right." Reed's voice came from behind us. I spun as he and Kahlo emerged from the shadows. An excitement bubbled in my chest at seeing both of them. I waited, expecting more shifters to follow, but none came.

"What's going on?" I asked. "How did last night go?"

"It went to shit!" Kahlo hissed, his eyes hooked on Gage. "A spell protected the fucking mansion, and we couldn't enter the boundaries. You didn't hear *that* when you were eavesdropping on customers?"

"Nope." Gage shrugged. "I told you everything I knew."

"So what will you do?" I asked, uncertainty weaving through me. "And where is everyone?" *Please don't be captured.*

"I've sent my pride to the Den." Reed stepped over a patch of overgrown weeds, his face pale and his jaw clenched. "My warriors will keep them protected during the journey. My good friend Oryn, one of the three alphas ruling the wolf realm, will care for them. While they're safe, Kahlo and I plan to destroy the fuckers who are attacking shifters. But I need your help once more."

"What for?" Gage snapped. "We did our part, and you promised to show us where the collector was tonight."

"You've kept your word, and I promise we will too," Reed said as the wind tossed his honey-brown hair against his back like a cape. Funny how I found his long mane attractive. I ran my fingers through my short style, sitting over my shoulders. Back in the tower, Gingernuts adored his tresses. I couldn't wait to find a way to be free of my long hair for good. Then again, I never got a choice in my hairstyle or anything else in life.

"I'll help," I said.

"*Elliana,*" Gage said, but I shook my head.

I'd grown up praying for salvation, and I'd promised myself if I ever escaped, I'd assist anyone in trouble. So, now it was my turn to keep my word. Plus, it might gain me favor with the universe.

A surprised expression hooded Reed's eyes.

"We can wait another night to see the collector," I suggested, smiling at Gage, who crossed his arms. "Those kidnapped shifters are in danger now." I faced Reed. "Tell me what I can do."

Reed's eyes showed the same gentle concern my dad used whenever we'd speak about fixing a problem. "Well, Gage mentioned to Kahlo last night that you are great at sneaking into places undetected. Quick and nimble."

I glared at Gage, who refused to meet my gaze. "Are you pimping out my services?"

"Is it not true?" Kahlo asked, his voice so husky and sexy. Why did he have to sound so delicious?

"We've been watching the mansion most of today," Reed added. "No one entered or left the mansion, but it gave me time to think. Only shifters are being kidnapped. And this section of Darkwoods has very few humans. What if the ward on the house was placed to only keep out shifters? Not humans."

"Sounds like a long shot." Gage exhaled loudly.

"Worth trying before we get a witch involved," Reed added. "Our other option is to ambush anyone in the woods who looks like they're headed to the house on Sharp Lookout and grill them."

You know you'll help them, no matter what Gage or I say.

Of course, I would. Besides, if the ward remained, then I'd lose nothing—maybe get a small shock. And I couldn't walk away from Reed. Sure, it had a little to do with my attraction to him, my admiration of the way Khalo watched me, but mostly it was for those kidnapped. Were they locked up in a prison, terrified? Or being tortured? What else would someone steal another person for?

"I'll do it." The simplest of the options was the most obvious, and it cost me nothing but time to head over to the mansion with the men.

"Okay, we go now," Kahlo said, his hooded eyes fixed on me as they had been the previous night. Had Reed told him I lived in a tower with crazy long hair that vanished at night, guarded by a gargoyle? Yep, my life story sure sounded insane.

"And thank you." Kahlo offered me a slight bow as he had before, reminding me of royalty, full of respect and honor. Was it a tiger trait? Didn't matter when I loved his gesture. I offered him a quick smile.

"This way." Reed ushered Gage and me to join them. We hurried across the barren field.

"What's the plan?" I asked. "Say I can cross the magical barrier, what then?"

"Sneak around and see what you find out. No interacting with anyone. It's just a spying mission to understand who we're dealing with," Kahlo instructed. "At the first sign of trouble, you run, and we'll be there to take on whoever follows. All right?"

"Got it." I nodded, reminded of my missions with Dad. As a team, we'd completed each job. Working with others felt both familiar and comforting.

You sure about this? Sounds risky and could go so wrong.

"I'm sure. What could go wrong?"

"Sorry?" Reed stared my way.

"Just saying it seems like a simple mission. A few days ago, I broke into a lord's home and took a book on gargoyles. Didn't get caught, so this should be a tea party."

"You stole from a royal lord? That was brazen." It was clear from Kahlo's voice that he wasn't judging me, not when he stared at me with smiling eyes.

Damn, he was gorgeous in that dark, brooding way that made me want to sit back and just stare at the way he moved, the way the edges of his mouth twitched when he spoke. And dressing in all black just added to that mysterious side of him.

Then again, the dangerously sexy Reed and protective Gage also had me daydreaming. I wasn't sure I wanted to be anywhere else but with these three. Strong. Handsome. What would it be like to have these three men all to myself?

Crazy thoughts!

I huffed, unsure I could make sense of my emotions, so I focused on the task at hand. The fantasy was mine, and if I wanted to imagine myself with ten men, so be it. I smirked to myself when I caught Gage watching me with a quizzical expression.

With my chin high, I pushed forward and marched between him and Reed while Kahlo took the lead.

Stop staring at his ass.

"Nothing wrong with enjoying the view," I mumbled under my breath.

By the time we scaled the mountain toward the cliff's edge, I was gasping for air, and sweat dripped down my back. Not to mention, my thighs stung. I climbed over two logs and trampled foliage while dodging low-hanging branches attempting to decapitate me.

"I know we're trying not to be spotted, so we're staying away from the main road, but this path sucks balls." A shrub snagged on my pants, and I yanked myself free. Miniature spikes dotted the fabric around my calf while muddy leaves stuck to my boots.

"It's not too much farther, Princess." Reed pushed ahead, with Gage close behind him.

I gritted my teeth. "Princess" implied I was precious and required assistance, but come on, who didn't struggle to climb a steep hill? Clearly not shifters.

"Yeah, easy for you long-legged people," I added.

Kahlo fell back and kept his pace slow alongside me, probably worried I'd slip and slow them down. He reached over and drew me up the steep terrain. That way, I didn't need to grasp branches to avoid falling.

"Thanks."

"I would offer to carry you but figured you wouldn't accept. You seem the independent type who loves to do things for herself."

"Interesting observation. Do you often watch people, then make judgments about them?" I held tight to his wrist as I jumped over a hole in the ground.

His arm sailed across my lower back, speeding our progress. I felt as if I walked on air, and being pressed against his side had me unfocused, except for where we touched. His fingers twitched as if he yearned to draw me closer. I wouldn't complain because something about Kahlo had me fantasizing about him every time we crossed paths.

"Among lions, the strongest warriors are female. They're fierce, fast, and know what they want. Just like you. All you're missing is the ability to move faster."

"With training, I'm sure I can race up this hill," I said. We traveled side by side, sensing every time we bumped into each other, the way the side of my breast brushed his ribs, how his fingers gripped my waist. I wondered what it would be like to be with a tiger who showed compassion but as an opponent would terrify.

You got it bad for these shifters, hey?

"And if I do?" I whispered to myself, but Kahlo gave me a funny look.

We kept trekking. Once we reached the peak where the trees grew sparser, we trudged after the other two, who marched ahead chatting. Were the two now getting along? Was that all it took? Or were they discussing a familiar topic—me? Not that I minded, but I preferred to be in on their discussion.

"I think I know why you talk to yourself," Kahlo said out of the blue. "When I grew up, I lost my parents at a young age. Soon after, I saw ghosts and would talk to them. I know it's not the same, but I figured the reason I spoke to them was because I'd opened myself up to them in my grief." He looked at me and smiled.

His voice carried no judgment, just understanding. While I wasn't ready to take on more relationships right after my night with Gage and Reed's tantalizing kiss and promise, something about Kahlo stayed with me.

He guided me closer to his side with no sign of letting go, even if the path was no longer an obstacle course. I wasn't complaining because being close to these men had me melting in my boots. I was unable to explain it—they twisted my insides into dozens of knots. Crazy, considering no other man had affected me in such a way. So, what was it about these three that had me captivated?

"We're here," Reed whispered, not seeming to mind that Kahlo hadn't released me. But as we approached the other two, I broke out of Kahlo's hold, needing the fog in my head cleared.

Beyond the scattering of greenery lay a large, two-story mansion. It had black stone walls, and from the rear, the place resembled a box with a pointy red roof and a chimney. Fruit trees smothered the backyard, making it impossible to see what was back there. Plus, there were lots of dark corners and places to hide. Perfect. There was no light from the windows, so hopefully, no one would see me enter… if the barricade allowed me to get that far.

Reed approached me. "The magic ward runs along the fence surrounding the property. It electrocuted me and threw me backward, so be careful."

"Wow, that's powerful." Now, I wasn't so sure about this since I wasn't a shifter who had the strength to resist such a strike. I chewed on a hangnail, pondering another way around this.

Told you.

"I'll be right behind you to catch you if the barrier holds. I'll make sure you don't slam into a trunk like I did." The confidence in Reed's eyes helped, especially with the way he rubbed his lower back in gentle strokes.

Except crashing into a tree wasn't what worried me—it was the electricity that could kill me.

Gage was by my side, gripping my shoulder. "You don't have to do this."

Kahlo stood on my other side. Having all three around me gave me the courage to get started.

I stepped out of their circle, then scanned the house and yard in the distance. Only the wind stirred, and the branches rustled around me. They were right that not many humans lived in this area, so the spell might have only kept shifters out. Usually, such hexes could target only a single specific race, as aiming for every kind of race made for a super complicated incantation. But if I discovered the lost shifters and Reed's sister inside the house, I couldn't just walk away. I had to help them. With a deep breath, I ran past shrubs and several boulders up to the metal fence I'd easily climb over.

Gingerly, I reached out.

Stop!

I flinched back. "What is it?" I scanned the area to find no one. Behind me, the men studied me with huge eyes.

Are you sure you want to do this?

"Gah, you scared the shit out of me," I whispered. Okay, do this fast. No more wasting time.

I grasped the railing, cold metal under my palm, and waited… Nothing. I released the breath wedged in my chest and looked over my shoulder.

Gage shrugged while Kahlo nodded and Reed waved for me to climb the fence. Okay, this was happening. I scrambled over and slid behind the apple tree. Up ahead, the darkness drenched the house. No alarms had gone off, so that was fantastic.

I don't like this. It's too easy.

I agreed, and my stomach tightened at the thought. Someone who used a magic ward to keep shifters away would have more security set up. The barrier would not only keep intruders away but also stop any captives from getting out.

Terrible plan. You've done no research into this place. Go back.

I turned to the three men staring at me from within the shadows. I recalled the desperation in Reed's voice when he'd spoken about his missing sister. I had to do this. This wasn't me engaging in battle but gaining information. So I crept toward the house, ignoring the jitters crawling up my spine.

CHAPTER 13

I'd broken into dozens of homes, but no other job left me as swimming in nerves as this one. I wasn't even stealing anything, just doing a recon, yet the whole magic protection spell had me on edge. Not even the lord's home had such security. While this ward wasn't created to keep me out, what exactly were they doing in here to keep shifters at bay? Usually, before breaking into any place, I did my homework and watched the area for a week or two to determine the routine of the occupants, how many lived there, their behavior, and even what day they visited the markets. I constructed a complete pattern of who I was dealing with.

This is why you shouldn't have rushed into this.

"Quiet," I whispered.

I stepped on a twig, and it crunched. Panic struck my chest, and I froze in place, waiting for someone to come rushing outside from the mansion. No one did. I glanced over my shoulder but could no longer see the three men beyond the thick shrubbery and trees backing the property. Perhaps I'd stick to exploring the yard and home from outside, then leave. I could return once I'd worked out what was going on and come up with a clearer action plan.

Reed would protest, and how could I blame him? His sister

and pride members were captured. A single day's delay might lead to their deaths.

Hunched low, I ran to the back of the house just as the lights in a room on the bottom floor illuminated. Luckily, a curtain covered the window. My breaths died as I flattened myself against the wall.

Muffled noises streamed out, so I moved closer and peered inside through a tiny gap in the corner of the curtain. A hooded man sat in a chair on one side, his arms folded, his face concealed by shadows. One leg crossed his other, his ankle resting on the thigh. Why was he concealing his face?

Because he's a psycho, clearly.

Two nude men stumbled into the room as if shoved from behind. Both were riddled with cuts and bruises. One swung around and slammed a fist into someone behind them. The other leaped for the hooded man. But four guards in black attire jumped after him, hammering punches and kicks into both of the men.

I cringed on the inside, stiffening at seeing their suffering.

Yet the hooded figure sat there, unperturbed, watching the fucking show like a monster. He'd done this before.

If you get close enough, jab him with your knife right in the eye.

My pulse pounded through my veins. What the hell was going on in this house?

Both victims heaved for air on their knees, bleeding from new injuries. Hooded Man got up and kicked one in the face with his boot. I gasped and hugged my stomach. He snatched the second man's arm and cracked it over a knee, snapping the bone. The victim's howl reached me, and my chest constricted. I reached for my blade, my arm twitching with the urgency to slam my blade into his throat. His cape slipped open, revealing a solid body wearing all black. He clenched the victim's neck in a vise-like fist. He said something, but I couldn't make out the words. He then tossed the innocent to the ground.

Rage boiled deep in my core, scorching hot as bubbling lava. I clenched my fists, hungry for destruction. I stood no chance against the number of men inside, but the image in front of me sickened me. The same darkness that had swallowed me whole each time the gargoyle had beaten me now fueled my rage.

A bluish energy line surged from across the room and struck both naked men in the backs. They screamed and convulsed on the floor, frothing at their mouths. A surge of blue energy coiled around their necks like a noose. I shuddered, tensing all over. Was someone killing them? I inched sideways to see who'd cast the magic, but my viewing range was limited.

The victims' bodies elongated, their skins tearing and black fur spreading over their bodies like an army of ants on a rampage. They weren't dying, but the ring around their necks must be forcing them into a transformation. I watched, mesmerized, and within moments, two panthers stood in the room.

They staggered as if still dazed, the tiny flickers of energy jumping across their flesh. Must have been how they controlled the shifters, or was it to keep them in their animal form? But why?

The panthers lowered their heads in a submissive manner and slinked toward the hooded figure. They sat at his feet, as if nothing had happened. Was he the dick in charge, using a witch to control shifters? I trembled with anger that this fuckhead dared to take it upon himself to treat others like slaves. At the same time, it scared me to go up against someone with such powers. I stepped closer for a better look, but a branch snapped under my boot.

One of the guards whirled in my direction and marched toward the window.

All the warmth drained from my body, and I jerked away, pressing my back flat against the wall, still as a statue. Bright light streamed out of the window, illuminating the grassy yard from the fabric being drawn back. One movement or sound, and I'd give my position away.

The light faded, and in haste, I sidestepped, keeping my back to the wall, my heart in my mouth. I tensed, desperate to run.

A faint rattle came from behind me. I snapped around to find myself standing beneath a darkened window. Hanging inside was a chime made up of three strings tied with bones. They swayed and clung to each other, as if a breeze moved them. Yet the window remained shut.

My chest turned to stone. A trespass detector—and it had just gone off.

I backed away, my feet growing sluggish. I stared toward my shifters but couldn't see them past the shrubbery as I hurried toward the fence.

When the screech of hinges from a door sounded, I rocked on the spot and jumped behind a tree, holding my breath. The thing about witches was that running from them was useless, and I'd always found negotiation the best course—playing into their egos. Sweat trickled down my back as fear squeezed my lungs.

Stay silent until they leave. Then run.

A breeze sailed past, shaking the leaves and branches overhead.

"Elliana." A female voice sang my name as if it were a lullaby, and goosebumps rose along my flesh at the magic in the air.

My arms trembled at my side, and I bit down on my tongue to stop from screaming.

The soft susurration of her footsteps approached.

"What's my little bird doing out of her cage?" Her words hummed and calmed me like a hot bath on a winter's night. My feet were frozen in place with shock, my heart drumming inside my chest.

Was this the witch who'd imprisoned me in the tower?

Everything swam too fast in my mind. Every inch of me thumped with an urgency to discover why the fuck she'd left me at the mercy of a gargoyle.

Don't. You. Dare.

I reached for the blade on my belt. The only chance I stood against a magic caster was to make the first move. Hit her in the throat or chest. Startle her long enough for me to escape. But then what? If this was the witch who'd destroyed my life, she'd come to the tower. And I had to return by sunrise, or the gargoyle was coming for me. Terror sunk through me because I felt trapped, cornered, and now the predator had found me.

I swallowed past the rock in my throat and raised my knife, listening. Where was she?

Not a sound.

Something crunched to my left.

Do it now!

I jerked around from behind the tree, my sight on a figure closing in, and tossed the dagger, but my blade swished past the woman's head.

Shit!

I sprinted back around to put distance between us. Calling for help was out of the question. I didn't need to put the men out in the woods in danger.

Something snapped around my legs, and I yelped as I fell face-first into a shrub. The prickly branches jabbed my cheeks and neck, catching in my short hair.

Wrenched backward by my feet, I slid over the bumpy ground, grasping for anything to stop me from moving. A boot connected with my ribs, and I cried out, curling in on myself.

"Elliana. You're smarter than I gave you credit for. How did you escape and cut your hair? That explains a few things," she said. "Doesn't matter… but you broke into the wrong property, child."

I glanced up at the witch, who held a glowing white rope. With a whisper from her lips, it moved of its own accord, slithering through the air between us, striking my wrists. I bucked and flung my arms about, trying to shake off the restraints.

"What do you want with me?" My attention fell on her purple irises. "You locked me up for all these years for no reason. You killed my father! And now you're controlling shifters?" I shuffled backward on my ass.

The magical rope wound tighter over my wrists, wrenching them together. Another whipped around my ankles, and I thrashed, screaming louder, but the cord lengthened and slid around me like a constricting python, covering my mouth. Immobile, I lay on the ground, wriggling and glaring at the witch. Fear threaded through me, shaking me at the core.

Perspiration drenched my skin, and the ringing inside my head vibrated in my ears.

This is fucking terrible. What if she kills you or feeds you to the gargoyle?

Those thoughts weren't helping, yet they swarmed through me like a locust plague. I writhed against the cord.

Last time I saw this witch, I'd been eight, and she'd had no front teeth. Now, her golden teeth seemed to glow. She gave a whistle, and a hulk of a man with yellow eyes stomped toward us. Not yellow, but amber eyes with vertical irises, just like Reed's back in the tower. Except this man held his human form.

I moaned behind the ropes, a paralyzing dread spreading through my body like ice.

The witch glanced back to the house, then back at me, worry marring her face. What could possibly concern a witch with such power? The hooded man?

"Pick her up," she said to the guard. "We're going on a quick trip."

I bucked on the ground.

"A trip?" The guard's soft voice didn't match his brawn. "Faye, we were told not to leave the property."

Faye! Too nice of a name for a bitch like her.

"Don't use my name, buffoon. Take her to the basement." She sighed and shook her head.

The man picked me up and slumped me over his shoulder. I jostled about with each heavy step, staring at the fence amidst the fruit trees. Three figures stood in the distance. They must have heard me screaming, but the barrier kept them out, and I was alone. Always alone.

Reality tapped into my brain. I was caught, and I could die. Helpless. That was all I was.

We didn't enter the house but rather hurried to the far end of the property. The world was upside down as the witch opened the basement doors at the side of the home, revealing a faint light and descending steps.

Fuck! They *were* going to kill me and dump my body. I squirmed and kicked my legs as we headed underground. The shifter shoved me higher on his shoulder, his arms like belts around my legs, pinning them to his chest.

The heavy stench of fresh dirt and mustiness assaulted my nostrils. Each moment seemed an eternity as I waited for someone to finish me. But rather, we traveled down a sloped passage through a tunnel, leaving the basement behind. Ahead of us, the witch led the charge, gripping a burning torch.

Tiny fragments of soil rained down from overhead. No one said a word, but we moved fast as I bounced in the man's arms, my gut aching from the angle of his shoulder digging into me. My head swam from the repetitive sway of my body, as if I were sailing on a boat in rough seas.

Fear sat in my chest, eroding every inch of confidence that I'd survive the night.

I closed my eyes and tried to remind myself that I had to live. If I'd made it through all these past years, I would do it again. Whatever the witch had in store, I'd... I hiccupped a breath all the way down to my lungs. Who was I kidding? How long had I been searching for a solution, and just as I'd closed in on finding the dragon-tooth dagger, this had happened?

Tears stung my eyes. I'd been running my whole life, searching for escape. Maybe that had been my mistake. Believing I would ever escape.

I shouldn't have taken this job. Should have told Reed and Kahlo I'd watch the house first for a few days. Now, I was useless to them and me.

We moved for what seemed a lifetime, and my mind swayed in and out of consciousness. But when fresh air stroked my face, I stiffened and glanced around the woods. It was too dark to recognize the area, but we never stopped.

Soon, the dense woodland thinned, and we entered an open field. I lifted my head. A granite wall stuck out of the ground, the base encased by weeds. And up ahead stood my tower. I was back home.

My pulse raced. The witch had no intention of killing me but imprisoning me once again. Best news ever. Imprisonment was better than dying.

He tossed me off his shoulder. I rolled off and hit the ground with a thud. The air expelled from my chest, and I arched from the sharp pain zapping across my shoulder blades.

The witch stepped closer, her disgusting grin widening as she drove the stick end of the torch into the ground near my head.

"Now, let's fix this, shall we?" She raised both arms over me and mumbled something under her breath. She kept chanting, her eyes rolling upward to white pupils.

The ropes melted off my body. I scrambled backward, terror clinging to my chest, making breathing deeply impossible.

"Take her into the tower now!" she bellowed.

"No!" I cried out. "Please, just tell me why you're doing this. What have I ever done to you?"

She tilted her head sideways, studying me with the curiosity one offered a dying animal they'd tortured.

"You, little sparrow, helped your father steal my golden wig. So now you're paying for your mistake."

"You killed him!" I bellowed. I crawled farther away, patting the ground for a weapon, and found a rock. "That was punishment enough."

The man by her side removed his shirt, revealing a barrel of a torso covered in excessive hair. *Gross.* He grunted, his shoulders curling forward. Then, at once, his wings spread out from behind his back, wide and covered in feathers. Brown feathers spread over his shoulders and chest while the rest of him remained human. He'd only partially shifted into his eagle form. I'd never seen one of his kind, as they were rare and lived high in the mountain peaks.

"It's never enough." The witch hissed. "For your father's thievery, I own you."

"Fuck you!"

She flicked a finger at the eagle-man, who marched toward me, and I scrambled to my feet. When he got close, I slammed the rock in my fist against the side of his face. The shifter snarled, smacking my arm aside, the rock falling from my hold. Blood dripped from the cut beneath his eye.

He swooped closer, his body a blur. His arms clasped around my waist as he dragged me into the air, his wings flapping.

I screeched in fear, floundering against him, throwing punches into his head, but he didn't flinch as he dragged me toward my prison. When I grabbed his magic choker, a zap jolted through me. Spams shuddered through me, and blackness crept around the edges of my vision.

Within moments, he'd tossed me through the open tower window, then vanished out of sight. I staggered to the kitchen, flung open my drawer, and plucked out the biggest fucking knife I owned.

I turned, but the witch already stood on my windowsill, the eagle-man hovering behind her.

"You've been dabbling in magic. I taste it on my tongue like dirt." Her nose scrunched. "But no matter. I'll fix that now and return later to ensure you never escape again."

Stab her. Kill her.

Rage scorched me, and I charged at her, my blade raised.

The eagle-man snapped an arm around her waist, snatching her out of my reach, and headed toward the heavens. Two sets of footfalls sounded overhead, and I gasped for each breath. She would bring the gargoyle to life.

I had to circumvent her before it was too late. Kill the witch before she reawakened the gargoyle, end my spell, help the shifters. So I tucked the knife into my belt and scrambled out the window while my skin prickled like it did every time the gargoyle came back to life.

Hatred fueled me to move faster, and I climbed the outside wall. My scalp itched, and I fought the urge to scratch it until I drew blood. But then I scratched, unable to sate the agony.

My hair cascaded around me, dropping fast and dragging me backward from the weight.

My breaths raced too fast, but I scaled up. My arms shook from the strain. I couldn't ignore this opportunity. One hand over the other, I grasped the roof's edge.

A gush of air blew across my back, and I turned just as the shifter sailed past, his arm looping around my waist.

"Release me!" I yelled and flailed my arms and legs as he dragged me away.

He hurled me back into the tower, and I rolled forward, tangled in my ever-growing hair. I hit the back wall and came to an abrupt stop.

Tears blurred my vision, and an inferno chewed me up with fury.

A shadow fell over the window. "Now be a good girl and stay put until I get back." The witch flew away in the shifter's arms. Moments later, the gargoyle swept after them, chasing them away from the grounds.

I collapsed on my rug, devastated. It had taken me years of escaping and getting beaten to find a spell. Now, all my attempts lay wasted and futile. I'd drawn the attention of the witch who'd imprisoned me so long ago, and she was coming back to ensure I never escaped again. The world had shattered around me yet again.

CHAPTER 14

*A*fter a night of no sleep, I slouched on the window with Gingernuts in my lap, staring out into the morning blue skies. The heavens had no right to gleam with such beauty when my life had come to an abrupt stop. All my escape attempts had failed, and this whole time, I'd foolishly held on to false hope. Now, my future lay scattered in a thousand pieces. What was the use of continuing to fight if I always ended up farther behind than I'd been when I'd started?

What about Gage, Reed, and Kahlo? Had they been caught at the mansion? Were they now slaves, wearing those fucking magic rings around their necks? I trembled, picturing them beaten into submission like the panthers had been. And what could I do? Fuck all! Sit here and cry. This was why I'd kept my distance from people and never gotten close—I wore bad luck like skin, and it never failed to fuck me up.

Gingernuts meowed, and I scratched his head. "Sorry, I don't think I'll be able to give you my hair anymore." He stared at me with wide eyes, as if he understood my words, and purred.

"It's just the two of us now." My throat tightened. "Like before."

And me.

"Yep, me, my cat, and my second personality. Talk about messed up."

Last night's events kept leaping through my mind. Faye, the witch with the purple eyes, was a nasty piece of work. Of course, if anyone I knew was involved in the abuse of shifters and kidnaping them, she'd be at its heart. She'd aided the creepy man in the cloak, but why were they stealing shifters? Those panthers had behaved so obediently and loyally after donning the electric choker. Even the eagle shifter who'd carried me home had worn one. Were they creating a group of personal servants or warriors?

A whistle came from the woods, and I scanned the area below. An owl?

Two figures emerged from within the trees and stepped into the clearing beneath the sunlight. My heart shivered. Reed stood alongside Gage. Neither of them appeared injured, but where was Kahlo? My stomach dropped at the thought of him captured.

My thoughts flew to the gargoyle, and dread rocked through me. It would tear them apart. I jumped to my feet, nudging Gingernuts off my lap, and he protested with a meow. "Don't come here!" I called out. "Leave. Now!"

A shadow fell over the window as the stone guardian sailed overhead, its wings tucked against its body as it dove toward the newcomers.

My heart banged against my ribcage.

"Run! Get the hell out of there!" I hugged myself, unable to peel my gaze from Reed hauling Gage back into the forest.

I swallowed hard, watching the gargoyle take a tight turn away from their position. He swept across the field and circled the tower. A long exhale gushed past my lips. I paced back and forth, my mind a buzz.

What about Kahlo? I could never forgive myself if he was harmed. Grief sat on my chest like a boulder, squeezing me from the inside-out. The corners of my eyes stung, and I wiped away the tears.

Would the men now realize coming near me was impossible?

I plonked down on the window's edge and hugged my bent legs.

When a figure burst upward from the canopy of trees in the distance, I dropped my feet to the floor.

"What the hell?"

Huge wings glistened and twinkled like jewels beneath the sunlight in shades of fiery reds and oranges, supported by a normal-sized body.

"Gage!"

The gargoyle thundered after him.

"Gage, get out of here!" I cried out.

But he flew upward, beating his wings, with the monster pursuing him. My stomach locked up at the sight of him risking his life.

Below in the field, I caught more movement. Reed rushed toward me and scaled the tower. Gage was the distraction.

By the time the lion shifter reached the window, my insides grew tighter than my pants when I ate too much. Without a word, Reed rushed over my hair scattered across the floor and hauled me into an embrace. He squished me between his strong arms, and I floated on his musky scents. He kissed the top of my head, my nose, and my lips.

"You're safe. We thought we'd lost you."

"Where's Kahlo? Why are you here?" I glanced outside to find Gage circling the air with the gargoyle on his tail. How long before exhaustion took him?

"Kahlo's safe." Reed's arms wound around me like vines. "We heard your screams, but we couldn't see you behind the barrier. We waited all night, and when no one left the property, we panicked."

"They took me into an underground tunnel, and I passed out until we reached the woods closer to my tower."

"Yes, Kahlo insisted tunnels existed under Darkwoods, and maybe there was an entrance under the house, so Reed and I have been searching for you all night, and we figured we'd try the tower." His words softened, and his mouth fell to mine, kissing me with such intensity, I sensed his trembling. I kissed him back, harder and desperate to merge with him and never resurface.

My legs wobbled from the explosive passion belonging to a man who loved hard and fierce. One touch and I was his.

When he broke away, a chill found me. Outdoors, Gage kept the beast at bay, so I told Reed everything I'd seen and experienced in that place—about the panthers, the magic, and Faye, who'd locked me up in the tower.

His face went blank, and despair filled his hooded eyes. "It's my fault. I should have never asked you to go to the house." His gaze dipped, but his grip embraced me. "I was desperate and angry, but putting you in danger was me being a fucking idiot. I promise you—I will spend the rest of my life freeing you from this tower." His eyes grew wide with terror, and I'd never wish for anyone to carry such a burden, to believe they owed me.

"I made that decision myself." Too many emotions thrummed through me, from worry for Gage and Kahlo to affection for Reed to how they'd risked their safety for me.

"If Faye is coming back for you, we need to do something now," he insisted, his brow pinched. "Tell me where Vanore lives, and I'll visit her. I knew a few people in Tritonia who'll guide me."

"She might not be so eager since I almost got her killed… assuming she survived that night, to begin with. Plus, I still haven't paid her for the first spell. I'd visited her twice, but she wasn't there."

He kissed my nose. "Just tell me where she lives and any other details about her."

A thread of hope pulsed through me that this might work, or was I being foolish in letting myself believe again? However, I didn't waste a moment longer, not when Gage was outside, keeping the gargoyle distracted. I ran to the set of drawers in the bedroom and retrieved a black pouch. "I hope she's still alive, and maybe you can use this to pay for a new spell since the last one didn't work correctly." I handed him the bag of gold coins. "Try to find a carriage with dragon horses. That will be the quickest way to get to Tritonia."

"Don't worry. I've recently made friends with a dragon

shifter." He winked, and I smiled, surprising myself. Reed now called Gage a friend, and I could express joy in the face of dread.

"You sure about this?" I reiterated, still not convinced he'd find Vanore so easily, let alone persuade her to give me another spell.

"I owe you everything for risking your life for my pride. Few people would gamble their lives for someone they've just met." His chest heaved, and he stared into my eyes as if he was searching deep into my soul. "I meant what I said the other day about you and me."

"I know." No doubts existed anymore, but the problem didn't lie with his sincerity but my indecision about having more than one man. Damn, I wanted them, but it felt as if I dreamed the whole thing and I'd wake up alone again.

The flap of wings caught my attention, and I turned to see the gargoyle swooping past the window.

"You better go," I said. "I'm not sure how much longer Gage can outfly the creature."

"Stay safe, my Princess." He leaned in and kissed me like he had nothing left to lose. For the first time, it didn't bother me that he called me "Princess." I pressed myself closer, chest to chest, needing him, inhaling his scent. In his presence, my body and mind responded to him like an addiction.

In an instant, he drew away, blew me a kiss, and darted to the window. His eyes did a quick scan, then he scrambled outside. I rushed after him, my gaze shifting between him climbing down the wall and Gage, who steered the gargoyle across the ruins with the stone creature mere inches from capturing him.

My pulse drummed in my skull.

Help them!

I darted into the kitchen, tripping over my hair. Catching myself, I snatched a bag of dried bread from the pantry and scrambled back to the window.

"Hey! Over here." I tossed handfuls of food into the air, unable to see any birds in the vicinity. "Here birdie, birdie. I got food for you." I threw more morsels into the air when a long-necked crane flew out from the woodland to my right.

Another followed, and I threw the remains of food onto the ground.

Below, Reed careened around the back of the tower and vanished out of sight. Then Gage glided back toward me, bringing the gargoyle closer. The creature's face twisted as it eyed the birds.

"Go! Now!" I screamed.

He waved before swinging left and skimming over the tops of the trees, putting distance between him and the field. Damn, he was fast.

The birds fluttered out of reach as the gargoyle dove for them. They were well-practiced at ditching him.

I sagged against the wall as my heartbeat banged in my chest. For years, I'd wished for the universe to send someone to rescue me.

Now, I couldn't help but wonder if she'd listened and delivered Gage and Reed.

CHAPTER 15

The half-moon hung heavily in the heavens, and the wind whistled past, rustling the trees. I couldn't bring myself to leave the window or stop staring into the woods surrounding the tower. Reed had left for Tritonia and wouldn't be back for a while, but my stomach churned with unease. He'd mentioned asking Gage to help him make a quicker trip to Vanore. Did that mean the two were no longer trying to rip each other apart?

But how many bandage spells could one place over hexes before things went beyond haywire?

I exhaled loudly.

My scalp hurt, and I glanced back at Gingernuts pouncing on my hair. Then he darted through the place as if he were a bullet, bouncing off furniture and walls. Geez, someone was restless. After years stuck here, the only way I'd dealt with insanity was routine. Redecorating, running on the spot, stretching, meditation—anything to keep my mind occupied.

Back outside, several bats squeaked and flew toward the trees, probably searching for fruit. As my eyes followed them, my attention caught on a figure drenched in shadows. This part of the woodland stood about fifty feet from the tower, but was I imagining things? I squinted, studying the silhouette.

"Reed?" I whispered.

If he's back already, that means he failed.

"Thanks, Miss Obvious," I responded to myself.

Don't want you getting your hopes up again. Look how well that turned out last time.

"Okay, enough. I don't need a reminder of every single mistake I've made."

The figure shifted and stepped forward, wearing a cape and hood, just like the man in the mansion watching those being tortured.

Ice froze over my chest, and I scrambled to my feet because it was the same man. What the fuck was that sadistic bastard doing in the ruins? For the first time, part of me welcomed having the gargoyle for protection.

The stranger kept silent but stared up in my direction. No guards accompanied him that I could see, and if they snuck toward me, the gargoyle would chase them away. So, had the witch sent this man to check up on me? Or was she hiding somewhere, ready to toss another spell at me?

I scanned the empty field below. No one else emerged from the forest.

A strong gust of air blasted past, pulling at my hair. It threw the hood off the stranger's head. Pearl-white hair fell to his shoulders, fluttering in the breeze.

Wait! I stepped closer because I'd seen this man before. His wild hair, even the uneven posture where one shoulder stooped lower than the other. Years ago, we'd crossed paths.

He was the fucking henchman who'd killed my father when we'd gotten caught stealing Faye's golden wig. I gasped for air, hugging myself. Dread flowed through my veins like tar. Of course, the fuckwit would work with Faye. What the hell did he want?

I choked on my next inhale and couldn't stop shaking. What could I do? I had no one to call, so I'd fight alone to the end as I had my entire life.

Except... was he standing just far away for the gargoyle not to spot him? Or was he contemplating how to easily reach me without effort? Well, I wasn't going down without a fight. I'd stab him the moment he entered the tower.

That's right. Jab him in the neck. Payback is a bitch.

"Damn right!"

What was he doing? Was he going to gawk at me all night? I wished more than anything I'd taken knife-throwing classes. Looking down at the murderer had my blood boiling. All I could picture was my dad being dragged away by the back of his shirt as if he were a sack of potatoes, his pleas ignored. My patience hit a breaking point, and my words rushed out of me like an exploding dam.

"What do you want?"

"I heard you'd slipped past Faye's spell." His voice floated on the breeze, but it carried that sickly sweet tone I imagined perverted old men used to lure young kids into their carriages.

The man pulled the hood over his head.

"I wanted to see you and have questions for you." He rubbed his chin and remained in the shadows.

For the life of me, I didn't trust a thing that came from his mouth. What the fuck would a monster like him need to ask me?

No footfalls on the roof. Okay, he was being cautious about the gargoyle. Except wouldn't the witch protect him against the spell? Back in the mansion, he'd watched those shifters get beaten as if he were the king of the world. Was he working for the witch or vice versa?

"Like what? How I felt about you butchering my father? How much I love this prison that you and that bitch locked me in?" I trembled all over.

"Those matters don't interest me." He stood there, his arms dangling by his side, unnerved. He seemed like a dick who'd stalk someone for weeks on end before working out the most creative way to murder them.

For years I'd pictured myself facing the asses who'd destroyed my life, and within a few days, I'd found them both. And instead of fear, rage pumped through me that such fuckwits existed and continued to harass people. They didn't deserve a future.

"I have questions, too," I said. "Like, why kidnap innocent shifters and torture them? Are you a shifter hater? Did you get bullied as a child, and now you're the big man getting your revenge?"

"You have a wicked tongue, Elliana." He adjusted his groin. "Maybe I'll put it to good use." His voice climbed several octaves, and bile hit the back of my throat. Gross. So, was that his reason for his visit?

Footsteps boomed overhead, and the creep backed into the woods, but I wasn't ready to let him go. Maybe this was my chance to uncover the truth and understand why they'd locked me up. The more information I had, the better opportunity I'd have to discover how to overthrow them. And it piqued my interest... Why would this man even bother coming to visit me without the witch? Unless she was hiding, and he was toying with me?

Lure him out into the open. Get the gargoyle to take him down.

"You may be onto something," I whispered as I leaned out of the window.

"So you know my name," I replied. "What do I call you?"

No response.

"Asshole" sounds reasonable.

"Look. I'll answer anything you want," I said. "But you need to come into the tower. I can't keep shouting because my throat is getting sore." I chewed on my cheek, pacing back and forth in front of the window. Just picturing the dickhead butchered at the hands of the gargoyle had me smiling, and the eagerness to make this happen surged through me.

Hauling my hair into my arms, I pushed the long cords outside the window. The golden locks dropped and hung a few feet from the ground.

"Quickly. Climb up into the tower using my hair. Surely, the witch has protected a mere human by ensuring the gargoyle won't harm you? She wouldn't want you injured, right?"

He crossed his arms over his chest. "Who said I was a human?"

Was he a shifter? Or a warlock? When I'd seen him years ago, he'd behaved like the witch's bodyguard, following her instructions. He'd seemed to carry no magic.

Tell him you're hot and going to remove your clothes.

"Are you insane? I'm not stooping that low," I mumbled to myself.

It's clear what he's here for and it has zero to do with asking you questions.

A shiver trailed the length of my spine, and I shook. I'd die before I let him touch me, but he wouldn't make it to the tower if my plan worked.

Outside, he remained concealed in shadows.

"Or are you waiting for the witch to give you permission?" I taunted him. "Where is she?"

"It's just us two, child." His creepy tone returned, and when he stepped forward again, he had his cape open, revealing no shirt, just pants. He rubbed a hand over his lips as if he drooled. Disgusting.

Darkness plunged through me. My subconscious was right, and it took every inch of strength not to haul my hair back inside. Dealing with the devil came with dangers… but I wanted him to hurt, to scream with pain, to beg for his life just as my dad had done.

My mouth opened, but no words came. Two tries later and I found them.

"Well, what are you—"

A large shadow swooped overhead.

I jumped and pressed myself against the window's edge.

The gargoyle hurled through the air, darting after the man, who recoiled into the forest.

I held my breath. Please catch him.

Yes, beat the snot out of him.

Moments later, the white-haired man was tossed out of the woods and landed with a thump in the field. A roar gushed from his mouth, and he climbed to his feet, his cape falling around his feet. His torso shimmied, growing in size, white fur spurting across his body.

Shit, okay, so he was a shifter? Then why harm others like him?

The gargoyle burst out in pursuit, dragging broken branches caught on his wings behind him. He stormed toward the man, crouching forward, growling. Without hesitation, the gargoyle kicked him in the ribs, sending him across the field, rolling and spinning from the momentum.

I stayed glued on the action. "This is for killing my father."

The man slumped on the ground, swallowed by the oversized weeds.

A roar rattled through the night, and I flinched.

From within the folds of the grass, a white lion leaped out, his movement a blur. He slammed into the gargoyle's stomach, driving the creature backward. No one had ever stood up to the stone guard.

The gargoyle stumbled backward but was steadfast. As an undead, fear didn't play a role in its attacks.

The albino lion shook himself, his enormous mane swishing around his head. He stood taller than Reed in lion form and raised his head, unleashing a guttural growl. Except this was no ordinary lion. On top of his head were two bull-like horns, white as polished pearl. He had long, curved, saber-shaped canine fangs, but saber-tooth lions were extinct. His tail swung back and forth, tipped with an oversized scorpion's barb.

I gawked, my mouth falling open. It was as if the universe had crafted him by piecing together elements from other animals. I'd always assumed he was a human. Was this why he attacked others—to steal body parts with magic? I'd never heard of anyone born this way.

The animal pounced at the charging gargoyle, both caught in a tangle of limbs and wings and tails. They hit the ground hard, their hissing snarls leaving me covered in goosebumps.

Gingernuts hopped up on the windowsill, curious about the racket.

The lion flew into a tree trunk but scrambled to his feet and recoiled, scanning the woods behind him. He planned to run because maybe taking out the guard went against the witch's rules. But then again, he had to save himself. The stone creature closed the distance between them.

"Don't let him escape," I called out, gripping the wall as I half-leaned out to watch the battle.

His white tail struck the gargoyle's stone face, the scorpion barb hitting the guardian right in the eye. It shook its head, swiping at the affected pupil.

I bounced on my toes and cheered.

Stab him in the heart already.

"Yes."

But the gargoyle swung around, its wings beating, and swooped after him, wobbling at first, as if unable to keep its balance.

The white beast snarled, his ears flattened against his head, and he hurled himself upward at the stone guardian. The gargoyle pivoted his wings, bringing himself to a stop midair, and kicked the animal with its hind legs in the chest with such force, the shifter winced and smacked the ground with a thud. White vapors floated from his parted lips.

At once, the guardian tumbled to his knees, patting his eye over and over.

The lion staggered upward, stumbling about. While the animal limped away into the woods, the gargoyle climbed up and staggered after him.

I grasped my hair, clenching it, my eyes on the duo below, when a long strand floated away from me. I reached out and grabbed it, staring at it in astonishment, when the piece broke off in my hand. The rest floated away.

I rocked on the spot because my tresses were uncuttable, and I'd never shed before. I stared at the strand, twisting in the air like a worm slithering over salt. Staring back at the injured fighters, I wracked my brain for an explanation. The other gargoyle had been injured before by Dustin, and I hadn't lost any hair then, but now, I had when the white-haired man had gotten slammed.

"Oh, hell." My curse was connected to the lion's strength!

Scenario after scenario hammered in my mind. My hair had grown from the first day I'd been tossed into the tower, and I'd never understood why. They kept me guarded by the stone creature, protected. Did that mean the creep drew his power from my magical hair, whether it was on me or Gingernuts?

CHAPTER 16

REED

"I'm not your fucking prey. I'm not a fan of being carried this way." I called over my shoulder to Gage, who had his scaled arms wrapped around my chest. His wings made a clapping sound with each beat, and we jostled about as if riding bumpy waves.

He laughed in my ear. "Would you rather face me, Lion King? Groin to groin." Mirth wove through his words, and I gritted my teeth because he'd been rubbing himself against me on purpose for most of the trip. *Pervert.* We'd been flying for so long to reach Vanore because he'd insisted on a hundred stops to rest his wings. What sort of dragon was he?

"I swear, if I feel the slightest twitch against my ass, I'm jabbing you in the ribs, even if I fall to my death." Asking Gage to carry me to Tritonia was about saving time, but catching a carriage might have been more comfortable, even if it took longer.

His mouth lowered to my ear as he whispered, "Don't worry, pussycat. I don't swing your way."

I nudged him to back off, and his arms slackened. I slipped, and panic struck my chest as I grappled to clutch onto his arms. At once, he tightened his hold.

"Now, play nice." He burst out with laughter once again, and I swallowed my response, needing this to be over with already.

"We should have caught a carriage."

"Nah, would have taken too long. Anyway, do you hate dragons or something? What was with the attitude back in your territory when Elliana and I visited?"

"You trespassed and were throwing your weight around on my land. Of course, I was going to give you shit." Below us, the forest spread out in every direction. Farther in the distance, the bluest skies sparkled beneath the descending sun's orange glow. "Take us higher toward the cliff over there." I pointed to our right, where a mountain with a sheer rock face wall jutted upward.

"Geez, I need to rest."

"Again?"

"You're not fucking light. How much do you weigh? Five hundred pounds? You're a damn bull."

I shifted in his grip. "Four-fifty last time I checked. Lion shifters carry the weight of their animal form when in human form. Wait 'til you take on your dragon form—nothing will be able to pick up your fat dragon ass." I chuckled.

When Gage didn't respond, I figured I'd found a sore point, so I changed topics. He annoyed the hell out of me, but he'd agreed to carry me, and I'd seen how protective he was of Elliana. They were traits I expected in my pride—loyalty and willingness to fight to the death for your family.

"Anyway, what's the deal with you and Elliana?" I asked as he huffed behind me, his wings flapping double-time to ascend the cliff's edge.

"We used to date, and we're back together now."

I nodded and thought back to my kiss with Elliana, the tenderness in her touch and words, the admiration in her gaze. In her tower, she'd never pushed me away, so perhaps things weren't all rosy between her and Dragon Boy. But even if they were, I'd grown up with families made up of several parents. If several hearts joined, nothing else mattered but being with those people. Even if it came in the form of sharing. My mother had three husbands and would often tell me she loved them equally.

Such a system worked if everyone agreed, but my situation

with Elliana came with the complication of Gage. He adored her and might not accept a shared relationship. Well, come to think of it, Elliana might have issues with that, too.

What fucked-up thoughts when I ought to have been focusing on freeing Elliana before the witch returned, as well as finding my sister and missing pride members. Part of my reason for agreeing to come to Tritonia was that I hoped this Vanore could help with eradicating the purple-eyed witch. No guarantees, but I'd try anything.

Gage interrupted my thoughts.

"I know you've got a thing for Elliana. I've seen the way you stare at her, how you kissed in the tower."

Any second now, I expected him to drop me. Nothing would surprise me, but when he didn't, I said, "She's beautiful inside and out. I've never met anyone like her before, but if you insist she's only yours, I'll back off."

No response at first, then he sighed. "I think she'd have an issue with me making such a call on her behalf."

"I don't know a female who loves being told what to do or how to behave." I chuckled because all the women in my pride would snap someone's neck in a heartbeat if they showed a sign of threatening them. They were super protective of their families. After I'd taken over the pride from my father as his eldest son, I opened the rank to females to train as warriors.

A cluster of ravens zipped past us, and the breeze grew cooler the higher we climbed.

"Guess if Elliana felt the same way I did about her," Gage said with clipped words, as if the topic bugged him, "I'd be a full dragon by now."

"She's in a shitty situation and pushing you away until she's free."

Elliana had said something similar, and it made sense. Why drag someone you care for into danger? I adored her nurturing nature, even in times of hardship, and after years of being alone, she still thought of others. But she was a mystery, a woman trapped for so long that she spoke to herself, raised in cruelty, yet she stood tall. My pulse raged through me at knowing someone had done that to her.

"How long has she been talking to herself?" I asked.

"Since I met her. Figure it's her coping mechanism from being alone for so long. Doesn't make her any less amazing."

"Agree." When she was free and she spent more time with me and the others, she might heal and wouldn't need to talk to herself as much. But if she did, I'd still adore her.

We glided over the cliff's edge, where the trees were dense and thick, but in the distance, we found huts and a market buzzing with activity and voices. Already, the smell of barbecued meat found me.

"Shit, I could eat a horse right now. Put us down here, away from the markets."

Once we hit the ground and Gage released me, I stumbled forward on my numb legs. Pinpricks swarmed through me as the feeling returned. Leaning against a tree, I clenched my teeth from the tiny biting sensation. I patted down my shirt, sweaty under my pits and chest, where Gage's arms had hugged me like belts.

He stood across from me, his wings retracting and tucking into his shoulder blades, the iridescent scales across his body absorbing into his skin and vanishing. Shaking his arms, he stretched his spine from side to side, then kicked out his boots, drawing attention to his black pants held up by a golden-flame buckle on a belt.

"Is this where Vanore is?" Gage retrieved a crinkled blue top from his back pocket, unrolled it, and drew it over his head. Its golden buttons were an eyesore.

"Nope. We need to see someone else first so I can track down Vanore easily. I'm going to check with a friend who knows people."

"As long as you think it'll save us time," he said. "Don't want to leave Elliana alone for too long."

I pictured the witch returning for her and curled my hands into fists. If she laid a hand on her, I'd hunt the witch for the rest of her life.

"Kahlo's checking on her." My words growled. This affected so many people, like my sister and pride members still missing, and from what Elliana had told me, they'd been forced into slavery with magic. Was that the witch's intention all along? Create an army of brain-dead followers—to do what? Take over our land? Kill us? Except Elliana had also mentioned the man in the cape... the same one who'd dragged my sister away. And if he watched others getting hurt, he was someone supporting the witch. Or even controlling her?

"I gave my word to save Elliana." I didn't voice my other promise about making her mine. I always kept my word, and the only thing that would turn me away was if she chose Gage, insisting she only wanted him. For that, I'd admit defeat.

Gage stuck his chest out, staring my way as if I'd challenged him. "I plan to do the same."

"Good. Then she's one lucky woman... if we can get back to her in time." I pushed away from the tree, heading straight ahead, and Gage joined me.

"Why'd we have to stop so far away from the markets? I've been carrying your huge ass for the past day, so you know I'm tired."

"I appreciate your help, but I didn't want magic users seeing you. Dragons are sought after for ingredients, so I figure this allows us to blend in and avoid attention."

Without another word, we trekked through the forest with vines hanging from branches, greenery reaching our knees, and the muddy ground softening beneath each footstep. It must have rained recently because the strong scent of soil assaulted my nostrils.

"I read somewhere that lions were the fourth-largest cat... That must hurt not being number one, yet you all claim to be the king of the jungle and all that. Funny how a crossbreed between lions and tigers beat ya." Gage nudged me and smirked with his mocking expression.

I licked my teeth. If there was one thing Gage excelled at, it was getting under my skin. "We don't live in jungles. And ligers are part-lion, part-tiger, so that makes us top spot." I shoved my fists into the pockets of my pants. Gage wasn't the first to stereotype us. "Besides, you're just an evolved snake."

Gage huffed and cut me a glare. "Bull. We're the lords of the sky."

I laughed, rolling my head back, howling. "Haven't you read the histories where the first races in Haven Realm called dragons flying serpents in their scrolls and paintings? I think they're onto something."

"Yeah, not sure how much trust I place in those ancient texts. What did those people know? They believed a sudden change in weather was a demonic warning and would sacrifice virgins to the mountain gods for protection."

I eyed him as we marched onward. "You realize those so-called gods were dragons, right?"

"Hell, yeah." His smile stretched to his ears. "My ancestors had it right and were ecstatic. Those girls were not killed, I'm sure." He winked and climbed over an oversized log.

"Guess when you put it that way, I can see a benefit." I could excel at such a responsibility.

Voices reached us from up ahead, and we quickened our pace until we emerged from the woodland and entered a bustling market. Homes scattered across the ascending rock face. They'd been built inside the stone with windows carved out and wooden verandahs in front of each place. A few had clothes hanging off the railings. There had to be close to a hundred homes. To our right, Tritonia spilled out below, an abundance of forest and the dark sea farther still, the moon reflecting off the calm waters. In front of us, firefly lanterns swung in the breeze from dozens of poles, illuminating their fluttering wings.

Blankets covered the ground, displaying clothes, food, and other supplies for sale, and the sellers stood nearby. People were everywhere, carrying bags of merchandise and dragging kids along with them. Others circled a young boy performing a dance where he bounced up and down as if he had springs for shoes, yet he kept himself still and in control. Those who lived here were a combination of shifters, fae, and a few humans.

The surrounding chatter engulfed us, as did the aromas of

food. An older man wearing baggy pants and half a dozen beaded necklaces played a solo on a small drum strung from his neck as he walked through the marketplace. *Okay... Whatever floats his boat.* The smell of grilled sausages hit my nostrils, and my stomach growled.

"I'm starving." Gage drifted toward the food stalls, and I was right on his heels, eyeing the chargrilled corn and the grasshoppers on a skewer, but my attention fell on the meat rolled up in flatbread at a small stand nearby.

"Four of your meat wraps," Gage ordered. "And two home-brewed beers." He turned to me. "Is two enough?"

I nodded. "You bet."

Gage ripped one of the buttons from his shirt, and his top now lay open in a wide V across his chest. He placed it in the old man's palm. He glanced around and whispered, "It's real gold and more than enough to pay for the meal—plus lots of leftovers."

At first, the man frowned but inspected the button before biting down on it. With a massive grin and his eyes glinting, he stuffed the item in his pocket and rushed to prepare our meal.

I hadn't heard a single dragon story where the scaly creatures weren't obsessed with shiny objects and gold. Where he'd gotten it from was a different story. It wasn't as if he'd tell me if it was stolen. Or did the expensive stuff just get drawn to him like a magnet? I'd read about such things.

We stood at the edge of the market overlooking the land below, stuffing our mouths with the spicy meat drizzled with a minty yogurt sauce.

"How many people do you think have fallen off this cliff?" I asked, studying the steep dip a few feet in front of us. "They ought to fence it off for the kids."

"The real question is, who's been pushed off the edge?"

"True, true." I took another bite. He was right. No matter which realm I visited, every location had nasty pieces of work who wanted to cause harm or drama.

Finishing my wraps, I picked up the beer bottle from the

table and drank it in one go. I wiped my mouth, got up, and tossed the rubbish into a bin.

"That hit the spot. Now, let's do this."

"Okay." Gage faced the markets. "Who are we looking for?"

"My ex-girlfriend." I swallowed hard. "She's probably still pissed, so be warned."

CHAPTER 17

GAGE

"Where is your ex?" I asked, scratching my head. So many people crowded around us in the markets, stepping on my feet, talking non-stop.

Reed lifted his chin, staring past the mass. "Just farther down this aisle." Just as he finished, a blonde with the brightest yellow cat eyes stepped in his way, glaring, her lips twisted into a crooked line. In an instant, her palm struck out and slapped Reed across the face, loud and sharp. I cringed on the inside. The woman stormed off, vanishing into the crowds.

"Oh, damn, is that your ex? She hates you." I clapped Reed's shoulder. "What the hell did you do to upset her?"

"That's a different ex," he grumbled and rubbed his red cheek. "Fuck. She wanted me to marry her after we dated for two weeks."

I laughed, my stomach rolling with way too much enjoyment. "She's one of those loonies. You're better off. It's the clingy ones who sneak into your house at night to kill you. I had one who insisted on being with me every hour of the day, and it drove me crazy. This one time, I went to work, and I discovered her hiding behind a curtain, convinced I was cheating on her." I made a circular motion with my finger next to my temple. "A man needs alone time, you know? But damn, you didn't mess around."

Reed huffed and marched through the hordes of people, and I tracked after him. I shouldn't make fun of him because before I'd met Elliana, I'd had a different woman every few months, searching for the right person to love me, to help me become complete. With each girl, I'd expected this instant electricity, and *bang*—I'd be a dragon. But after years of misfortune, not only had I given up, but I'd been resigned to the fact I would never be more than a mutant with wings.

Elliana had changed my world. I craved her beyond just finding a mate. She'd had me hyped up on adrenaline to get under her skirt at first, but it was more than that. I'd grown delirious with curiosity to discover who she was and adored our in-depth conversations about the history of Haven Realm. Why were there seven territories? Where had all the different races come from? My theory was that Haven Realm was once part of a larger landmass that had broken up into multiple continents and drifted apart.

What I'd discovered was that I'd focused on the wrong element—finding my true mate had been about the practical need to transform and belong, not because I loved the women. Until Elliana. Now, whether I transformed or not was inconsequential. I'd accepted that fate long ago.

Reed halted near a baker, and I scanned the market stalls around us.

"Is she here?"

"At the end of this row," he said.

I glanced past several people to find a woman wearing an ankle-length black dress glued to her body, revealing every curve. Her chestnut hair was drawn into a messy ponytail, and dark makeup lay smudged under her eyes. She stood behind a table, shuffling a deck of cards.

"So, she's a fortuneteller," I whispered to Reed.

"A soothsayer."

"All right. She can tell us if we'll succeed. Excellent. Let's do this."

Reed didn't move. "When you're near her, keep your mind blank. Don't think about anything."

"How am I supposed to do that?" Not a moment passed where I wasn't pondering the miracles of life… or more like remembering Elliana's tight pussy gripping my cock. I adjusted myself. Fuck, shouldn't have thought that.

"Look." Reed lowered his voice. "She knows many witches and will gossip with anyone who listens, and we don't want the reason we need Vanore spreading to the purple-eyed demon, so focus on birds or how you collect gold."

I scoffed and rolled my eyes. "Don't tell me you believe that shit?" I didn't horde anything shiny in my tree house. And yes, I lived out of reach to avoid anyone finding my home—plus, I loved the height.

Reed's gaze dropped to the buttons on my shirt, then to my shiny buckle with an accusatory glare. "Yeah, right."

"Don't judge, man. You've been dating every crazy in Tritonia."

His mouth opened, but instead, a female voice called out, "Reed!"

We both twisted toward the dark-haired beauty, who beckoned him over with a curled finger. Just seeing her piercing eyes on Reed had me wanting to back away. Seemed every female dreamed of mating with a lion leader; that or it was something in the Tritonian water. I bet if I showed my dragon wings, I'd have them swarming all over me, too, but my heart belonged elsewhere.

Reed closed the distance to his ex, and I followed suit, passing a stall selling animal bones for spells. Yep, I'd need nothing from that shopkeeper unless they had a small enough bone to pick my teeth with.

"Ally." Reed turned on the charm as if he genuinely was pleased to see the woman.

She smiled and rounded the table, drawing him into a hug. Then without warning, her mouth pressed to his, and she gripped his shoulders, pressing herself against him. Reed pushed against her arms.

I approached to help a friend from the leech woman when they broke apart, Reed recoiling.

"Now that's what I call a reunion. Better than a slap in the face," I said.

Ally stood inches from me. Before I could respond, she snaked her iron arms around my neck and hauled me closer. Our mouths clashed, and a charge shot through my body, paralyzing me on the spot.

Sparks of panic detonated in my head, firing off scenarios of Reed's psycho ex prying into all of my thoughts. The time I'd stolen a treasure box from a group of pirates after I'd gotten drunk. Not my brightest moment, but I'd been sixteen. Or the time I'd dated two witches at the same time and sworn if they ever found out, they'd hex me into a frog. Then I remembered Reed's words about clearing my mind. *Fuck.* Okay, birds. Freaking big-ass vultures circling the skies, looking for carcasses to devour, like me. No, not me. *Shit.* Doves, yes, they were sweet until they pooped on your head. Eagles were more like it. Gliding through the heavens, diving for prey. Now, they were regal creatures.

At once, the frozen sensation melted off my body, and I stumbled backward, coughing to catch my breath. "What the fuck?"

"He's interesting." She licked her lips, flipping her hair over one shoulder. "But he has a strange obsession with birds." Her voice squeezed, as if she were a chipmunk. Now, that tone alone would have me running for the hills because while I was a patient man, pitched voices were my no-go zone. They drilled into my eardrums.

"Ally," Reed began, guiding her behind her desk to an area clear of crowds. They were chatting out of earshot, and I stood there, unsure if I ought to follow. Or would she read my mind up close? Unless only the kiss of doom gave her insight?

I pushed those thoughts aside and contemplated why chickens couldn't fly when they were in the avian family. With my mind distracted, I strolled toward Reed. At that exact moment, Ally slapped Reed, and I burst out laughing. Okay, call me a sadistic son of a bitch, but I couldn't help it. How many times could a man get hit by females in a night? Counting, we were at four for Reed. Never met someone who'd upset so many women in the same area.

Ally shoved past me, her bony elbow connecting with my ribs, and I winced, holding my side.

"What are your bones made of? Iron?" I called out.

Reed turned to me, his cheek bright red, and a growl rolled through his chest. His eyes shifted ever-so-slightly to his amber lion pupils, then back.

"Don't say a thing. Let's leave. We have a lead on Vanore. She hangs at the Moss Pit, a tavern on the water's edge in the cove."

While interest burned through me, I kept my trap shut, and we made haste to leave behind the market before any more of Reed's past showed their faces and beat him up. I smirked to myself.

By the time we'd taken flight, me gripping Reed tightly in my arms, curiosity was killing me.

"Okay, spill. What did you do to make her hit you?"

Reed sighed. "She promised to tell me where Vanore was seen last if I told her why I split up with her."

"And? What'd you say?" This drama was damn addictive.

"That I found her needy and didn't enjoy our kisses, knowing she pried into my thoughts."

"Ouch," I said, thrashing my wings as we glided downward. "You're lucky she didn't knee you in the balls."

"But it's the truth."

"For someone who's dated a lot, you're clueless. Have you heard of tact?"

"It's done, and I have zero intention of ever returning to see her again," he grumbled under his breath. "So, let's pretend that never happened."

Oh, I'd never forget that. I grinned widely as we glided onward. A light breeze buffeted under my wings, sending us into a turbulent ride.

"Keep going." Reed pointed ahead. "See the ocean bay? There should be a tavern close to the beach."

I rushed us forward, my breaths quickening and sweat dripping down my spine. The shore came out of nowhere fast, and I backpedaled, only to hit the sand in a crash landing. Reed tumbled from my arms and dropped to his knees. Barely catching myself, I gripped my hips and filled my lungs.

"That was a shit landing." Reed unleashed a snarl. The night must have been taking its toll on his preciousness.

"Hey." I gasped for air. "You're lucky you didn't end up in the water."

Nearby, foamy waves crashed against the coast, pulling at everything like greedy fingers, then dragging it back into its grasp. The briny smell wafted through on the breeze, and for those few moments, I had the urge to sit out here and dunk my feet in the sea. It wasn't often I visited the beach. When I was a child and went swimming, a damn jellyfish had stung me on the ass.

"You know mermaids live out here." I stared out, searching for a splash or tail, but the ocean lay tranquil tonight, the moon sitting high above the horizon and glistening across the surface of the water.

"As do mer-soldiers who'll stab you in the throat for laying eyes on their maidens." Reed strode up the beach and vanished into the forest, so I chased after him until we reached a wooden shack in the middle of nowhere.

The building stood wide with a sharp, pointy roof encased by enormous pines. The veranda out front circled the house, and the four windows glowed alight. A couple spilled out, arm in arm, stumbling down the steps, chuckling. They tripped, both crashing into a shrub. Reed hurried toward them until it was clear the pair had wasted no time and locked lips. My thoughts wandered to Elliana... What was she doing now? Was she still safe? Reed insisted Kahlo would check on her, which eased my worries, but only slightly.

We climbed the steps to the porch and entered. A young, beautiful female sang a harrowing ballad on a small stage at the rear of the room, and I drifted toward her, drawn by the tune. She wore a tight dress hugging her slender figure, her pearly white hair draped over her shoulders, and she poured her heart out into her song. Her fae ears poked out, one side pierced with several gold hoops. Their race was common in Tritonia and Darkwoods, but they kept to themselves. Their voices were angelic and hypnotized even the angriest beast. I swayed on the spot, my toe tapping the wooden floor. She met my eyes and winked.

So much mystery surrounded their race, but the juiciest rumor surrounded the death of one of the most powerful royal fae families. Apparently, the surviving princess was blamed for killing her parents and siblings. Before they could capture her and uncover the truth, she'd vanished, and many believed her to be hiding amid the normal folk. Whether she had committed the murder or not was up for speculation. Gossip insisted the other royal families in Haven Realm had put out a warrant on the princess. The person who brought her back alive for judgment would claim a portion of the riches that had once belonged to the fae royal family. Tempting, if I didn't feel pity for the princess—if she was alive.

Now, if she had been framed, which had always been my thoughts, I hoped the poor princess remained hidden. She'd had everyone chasing her down to capture her, then her relatives would murder her to claim the throne. Luckily for her, no one knew what she looked like. Fae princesses were forbidden to leave the kingdom and from showing their faces before wedlock.

I took a last glance at the woman on the stage with a thin waistline, decent boobs, and pale blue eyes. The sadness in her words mirrored in her gaze. I turned away.

Reed carried two metal mugs to a table in the far corner of the room. I sat across from him and drank half my homebrewed ale. Bitter, rich, and delicious.

"So what does Vanore look like?" I asked.

"Dreadlocks, dark skin, swirled tattoos across her cheeks, and golden canine teeth."

I doubted I'd miss anyone with those features. Several men slouched at the bar, chugging down drinks, a sword at the hip and wearing baggy pants and shirts. One wore a cap, his skin tanned, and he bore scars on his flesh from many battles. Most who lived by the water in Tritonia were pirates, voodoo witches, and mer-people. All kinds were welcome, unlike in Terra. The bigoted priestess deemed only humans pure and prohibited other races from entering their territory or her people from leaving. Didn't stop them, but they did so at the risk of life imprisonment.

"You think Elliana'll be okay until we return?" I asked. "I know Kahlo's there, but neither of them stands a chance against a witch." I shifted in my seat as Reed swung back his drink and waved at the barman for another round.

"We'll find a solution for Elliana and my pride if we have to visit every tavern in Tritonia."

I prayed it wouldn't come to that.

The barman arrived. He smiled with yellowed teeth and placed two drinks on the table. When he leaned over to collect the old mugs, his long beard brushed my arm. It was like barbed wire and so bushy, one could lose a bird in there. Behind him, a serving girl carried three plates piled high with fried shrimp, bread and butter, and a small roast. She set down the food and left us.

"A man of my taste." I ate a salty shrimp, the oily coating melting on my tongue. Gods, I was in heaven. I went in for two more.

"Are you going to pay the nice man?" Reed eyed one of my buttons. I gritted my teeth as the lion cut a large chunk of meat and placed it between two slices of bread.

"Here you go." I ripped off a button, but I might as well have worn nothing now as the shirt lay half open. "Should cover us for the food and many more drinks."

The man studied it as the other food merchant had and left us with a huge smile.

"My gold isn't a free-for-all." I reached out for the bread and made a shrimp sandwich with a lathering of butter. Despite my earlier meal, I salivated for more. "This is damn good."

Reed hummed as he took a big bite. The waitress returned with more plates piled high with dumplings, stew, and a fragrant, spicy rice dish scattered with diced sausages.

"You know, Kahlo once ate two whole leg roasts on his own. The man can put away food." Reed ladled himself a bowl of stew and ripped the bread into chunks for dipping.

"That's nothing," I added. "I got invited to a bear wedding, and those shifters scoffed down everything in sight. Anyway, their banquet was exquisite, and let's just say I went through twelve chickens marinated with a spicy coating. A guard checked on me as I sat there with a mountain of bones, curious who I'd butchered."

Reed's laughter came from deep inside his chest, his whole body shaking. "You're actually a decent shifter. Sorry for giving you shit before about your dragon side. Just never know who you can trust these days."

Filling my plate with rice and dumplings, I shrugged. "All water under the bridge. Plus, you're helping Elliana, and that means the world to me." Something about bonding with Reed over a meal warmed me. "Count me in to help save your sister and pride members once we help Elliana."

"Appreciate it."

We finished every morsel of food, and I slouched in my seat, my belly exploding. I contemplated loosening my belt, but I worried Reed would pawn my flame-shaped buckle for more food. Voices hummed through the tavern as more people swarmed the place.

"Ey, Ariella girl, hope I didn't miss your singing." A woman's voice reached me from two tables away, and I twisted my head to find the singer from the stage chatting with an older woman in a long dress, leaning on a cane for balance. Dreadlocks hung down to her waist. When Ariella hugged the lady, they turned enough for me to see the tattoos on her cheek.

Fire hit my chest, and I waved at Reed, but he was already on his feet, heading their way. So, I grabbed a nearby chair and piled the plates high on one end to make room to welcome her.

The middle-aged women eyed our plates. "How much in hell's name have you two been gorging?" When she spoke, her golden canine teeth shone in the candlelight. Yep, we had the right person.

"Vanore." I pulled out a seat for her to take.

"How do you know my name?"

I lifted my chin. "We're friends of Elliana, who I believe you know?"

She stared at me long and hard as if, any moment now, she'd deny knowing Elliana. With a small nod, she balanced on her cane, her other hand gripping the table, and sat in slow motion. Guess for a voodoo witch, she had little to fear if with a few whispered words, she'd curse us, so no wonder she came over to talk to us with such ease. Plus, we were in a packed tavern with Ariella singing once again from the stage.

"Ariella is beautiful, ey?" Vanore stated, reaching over and cupping my hand on the table with hers. "That child comes with death, and you have enough danger in your life, boy."

I squinted, trying to decipher her words. Had she sensed my thoughts about Ariella from our touch? My skin crawled, and I slid my arm back while she grinned, the corners of her eyes crinkling. The depth in her gaze told me this wasn't a woman to be swindled. She watched every minute detail and struck before you made a move.

"Told her why we're here."

Vanore's nose creased as she glanced around the room and out the window. "You give your word no stone monster follows you tonight?" Her voice quivered.

"I swear on my grave," Reed whispered. "You're safe."

"The devil broke me, and nothing will fix my ruined back. I want nothing more to do with that creature. So, does Elliana send you to fulfill her promise of payment?"

"We have the money, but considering the last spell didn't quite go to plan..." Reed explained. "We'll pay you the full amount owing for a new spell."

Vanore cleared her throat. "No deal. I provided a spell and got hurt for doing so. So, if you want a new potion, pay me for the first one, then we'll talk."

Reed shifted in his seat and dumped Elliana's bag of coins on the table in front of her. "There."

She was quick to collect the money before tucking it into a pocket in her dress.

Without waiting, I detailed our situation to Elliana, about how fucked up the initial incantation had gone. "Can you assist her again, please?"

Vanore huffed and laid her folded arms across her belly. "My whole life, I've been able to tell what people were. Take you two, a lion and dragon shifter. Your auras reveal your real forms, but Elliana was the only person I could never work out. She was human but is morphing into something else from all the magic twisted into her soul."

I could only imagine the enchantment had integrated into her so much, it had become part of her somehow.

"For a price, I will create a potion to deal with the gargoyle, but there is nothing I can do to eradicate the full hex. Just so you know, the witch who placed the curse will always remain connected to Elliana until whatever she cast is erased."

I swallowed the lump in my throat. "Anything you can do to free Elliana from the gargoyle gives us a fighting chance."

"Yes, part of a solution," Vanore said. "The witch who hexed Elliana owns the gargoyle, and she holds the true power over the creature. I cannot break that bond, but I can strengthen my magic to block the resurrection of the stone monster. I can't guarantee it won't eventually be broken because I don't know this witch's ability, but I'll use each of your blood to bind it with my power. It's the best I can offer. It might give you enough time to destroy the witch while keeping Elliana safe."

Dread circled in my gut like those goddamn earlier vultures on my mind. I exchanged looks with Reed.

"Is there anything you can do about the witch? A spell to kill her? Something to freeze her? Maybe we can lock her up somewhere? She's kidnapping shifters and using magic to turn them into her slaves." Reed's voice had dipped, and his agony came through his strangled tone. He was a shifter who lived by loyalty and keeping others protected.

"Ey, if I kill a witch, every magic caster will hunt me down.

We have rules we must abide by. The most I can do is offer a hex for the gargoyle."

"So there's nothing you can do?" Reed's face tightened, and I tensed. "For Elliana's safety. Do you want her to die?"

Vanore sighed, leaned forward, and scanned the room. "Few know this, but killing a witch is close to impossible. We wear a lot of protection armor, but I'm only telling you because I adore Elliana, and it kills me to see someone torture her this way for all these years. Chop off a witch's head and burn her to ashes. Only then will she die. Don't leave behind a single bone, or she will return."

No one spoke a word, but I stiffened in my seat, ready to do the deed.

"Now payment," Vanore said. "What will you offer me?"

"Gold," I said. "As much as you want."

She shook her head and stared at Reed. "I choose his mane."

I shuddered on the spot, and Reed leaned back, his face blanching. "What do you mean?" he asked. "As in, cut off my hair while I'm a lion?"

"No. You come to my home, and I put an incantation on you where you give me your mane."

He moved around in his seat, uncomfortable.

"What does that really mean?" I asked. "When he turns into a lion, he has no mane?"

"He won't have the ability to shift into his lion form." Her tone remained calm, despite just admitting payment to help Elliana came at the price of Reed losing his shifter side.

"No!" Reed declared.

Vanore raised herself to her feet, leaning on her cane. "Then you are wasting my time."

I took her wrist, stroking her hand, coaxing her to sit back down. If this gave Elliana the chance to gain freedom—even if it just gave us enough time to take her from the witch's grasp until we came up with a plan to kill the bitch—I refused to walk away. What if Kahlo couldn't find the dagger? What if the blade claimed the person who killed the stone creature, as it had Dustin?

"I'll offer you something else." The rest of my response refused to surface. It lingered on my mind, but this wasn't about me. "Take my dragon wings." Just hearing the words left me exhausted and shaking.

Vanore stared at both of us, and her wry smile didn't comfort me in the slightest. "You both care for the girl—that is clear. But I have no need for your wings."

"Your price is too steep," I said, my voice climbing. "Your spell isn't permanent and can be overruled, yet you would take Reed's lion self forever?"

Reed stared down at his lap, shadows marring his features.

"That is my fee. I seek what he has, and you ask what I want." She remained calm and not bothered in the slightest that she'd asked for a man's dignity.

Fire sped through my chest because this was ridiculous. "Dragon wings are rare." Silence. My skin pricked with anxiety.

"I'll throw in a magical knife that bursts into flames when it skewers someone," she said.

"A blade? We're talking about someone's shifter ability. Reed is a pride leader. How can he rule if he's turned into a human?" I inched to the edge of my seat, searing fire curling in my chest.

Reed spoke up, his voice dark and distant. "I'll do it."

Vanore lifted herself to her feet, as did Reed.

"You sure about this?" Unease settled in my stomach. Lions were proud bastards. "You're risking everything for a chance."

He looked my way, his face ashen and eyes barren. "Elliana risked her life by entering the mansion. Now it's my turn."

"Gingernuts," I called out, eyeing a lizard dashing under the pantry. "I found it!"

He meowed behind me as I ripped open the door and spotted the critter scurrying under a shelf. I dove after it, my foot slipping on my hair at my feet. I fell to my knees but grasped the critter. "Come here, you."

The little thing wriggled in my palm. "You don't want to be in here—trust me. You're better off outside." Plus, I didn't need Gingernuts leaping over me to chase the lizard as he had the previous night, startling me awake.

At first, the commotion made me think Gage or Reed had returned from their trip, only to discover a goddamn lizard dashing over my chest and Gingernuts using my ribcage as a springboard.

For the past day, I'd been sitting by the window, waiting, studying the woods for any sign. Still no men or the witch. Had her threat been empty?

I figured Gage had gone with Reed. Besides, it wasn't like him not to visit after everything I'd told him, our acrobatic sex act, and his promise to assist me. I didn't doubt his sincerity, yet with each passing moment, dread crept through me that something bad had happened to the three shifters.

Two more lizards ran from under the kitchen counter and

sprinted across the darkened living room. "Gingernuts! How many have you brought inside?" Or did they climb the walls? Though with the number I keep catching in the tower and now knowing Gingernuts goes outside, I would not be surprised if he was responsible. *Heavens, they better not be breeding.*

I sprinted after them, trampling on my hair strewn all over the room, when a shadow fell over the window. I shuddered on the spot and pivoted on my heels to face the stranger. My thoughts flew to the gargoyle coming to punish me. Except I hadn't left the prison in days. The lizard jumped out of my grasp, and my breaths ran ragged.

The figure climbed inside, except it wasn't Gage because there were no wings.

"Reed?"

His exhales were loud and quick, as if he'd been running. When he stepped closer, the kitchen light illuminating the stranger, I realized how wrong I'd been.

"Kahlo!"

He wore a loose shirt with black trousers and boots. I was drawn to his dark-brown hair and his liquid-green eyes that glimmered with golden flecks. With his gaze on me, his pupils grew vivid and wide. His distinct cheekbones and angular jaw had me tingling to reach out, cup the side of his face, and caress his shadowy stubble. I darted toward him and embraced him, beaming with joy to see someone.

"Thank the moon you're alive."

His muscular arms were cords around my body, lifting me off the ground, his fingers pressing into my back with an urgency that made me believe he'd missed me.

"Where can we talk without the gargoyle hearing?" he whispered,

When the gargoyle had ripped Reed out of the tower, it had happened after he'd raised his voice, so if we kept extra quiet, Kahlo should be safe. I dropped out of his hug and closed the window shutters. When I turned, he picked up a fistful of my blonde hair, staring at the length from my head to all around the room.

"Welcome to my curse." I took his large hand in mine and guided him to the farthest corner of my bedroom. I'd spent endless nights crying there after each of my beatings, and ironically, I'd transformed the spot into the most comfortable location in the tower.

A couch made up of oversized stacked cushions I'd tied together with ribbons sat in the corner. I'd covered the piece in a silk fabric the color of the sun to brighten the room.

"I keep having this stupid repetitive dream about the three of you as gargoyles." Heavens, I'd woken up the last two nights screaming and in a sweat.

Kahlo sat on one end of my cushion stack, the pillows compressing under him to half their size and his bent knees reaching his chest. His eyebrows pinched together as he checked behind me. I jumped on the opposite end to act as a counterweight. But my load did zilch. Instead, the fabric under me gave way, and I slid toward him. I yelped as my stomach lurched. I crashed into his side, and we both rolled off the couch, arms, legs, and hair tangled. We landed on our sides, his arms clasped around me, one across my rear. Bodies pressed together, side by side, facing each other. My hair had coiled around us, keeping us plastered.

"Oh shit, I'm so sorry." Heat crawled over my cheeks. "And that's my ass you're groping."

"I know." His eyes smirked devilishly. "And it's incredibly sexy. Anyway, sitting down is so overrated."

"This has never happened before." I couldn't help but laugh as I wriggled to unknot us, which failed miserably.

He chuckled again and lifted his side, releasing a bundle of my trapped hair, and his grip on me slackened. We fell apart onto our backs, staring up at the billows of fabric I'd hung from the ceiling. I lifted my hip, and he removed his trapped hand.

"Think there's a flaw in my couch creation." I didn't move as we remained on the floor. It was nice to lay alongside the sexy tiger shifter. "I need a frame to keep it sturdy. Anyway, how'd you get past the gargoyle?"

Darkness concealed his expression, but his eyes gleamed.

"I snuck in here super slowly, using the shadows. It helped that you made a racket in the tower, calling after someone named Gingernuts and something about lizards."

"You heard that?" Fire crawled up my neck. What else had I said? "My pet cat keeps bringing bugs and reptiles into the tower. And for some reason, when I sleep, all the critters insist on jumping into bed with me."

Kahlo arched a brow, and I expected a smartass comment, but he said nothing. Yep, someone had more restraint than me, so I changed topics.

"Have you heard from Reed?"

He shook his head. "But he and Gage are fine. If there's one thing you can count on when it comes to Reed, it's that he's a natural-born leader and knows how to tackle any situation. He has this way of always coming out of predicaments unscathed. Lucky bastard."

"Then I guess no news is good news."

Kahlo rolled onto his side and propped himself up on an elbow, the kitchen candlelight illuminating his face. His dark hair sat off his brow, revealing a healed scar running from his temple to his jawline.

I gingerly reached up and trailed the pad of my index finger along the smooth wound. "What happened?"

"Poacher caught me in a trap and thought it funny to cut me up."

"Fuck! Sure hope you ripped him a new one." Being a shifter came with dangers from every angle—other races, jealous animals, and poachers hunting down their next trophies.

"Don't worry." Kahlo clasped his fingers around mine and brought my palm to his lips, kissing it. "That human will never harm anyone again."

I preferred not to know how it had ended. My attention landed on Kahlo's lips, imagining myself falling under them, fantasizing about being with such a huge tiger shifter. What was it they said about men with big hands? Or was that feet? A spark rekindled down below, and it buzzed with such delight, I feared I'd moan out loud if he made a move to get closer.

Do you have any control?

Zilch. So, I diverted to a distraction.

"Have you been watching the mansion these past two days?"

"After checking on Reed's pride to ensure they arrived safely up north with the wolves, I traveled into the Darkwoods forest and tracked down the collector's hideout."

My stomach clenched, and I waited with bated breath. "And?"

His expression fell, as did my hopes. "The place had been ransacked. Someone had torched the bunker, everything in sight burned to a crisp. I searched for any sign of the knife, but I'm sorry, Elliana. I couldn't find it. It's either been destroyed or stolen."

Heaviness sunk through me. "That sucks."

"Been asking around for a dragon-tooth dagger, too. No luck."

"Thanks for checking." I forced a smile, even if it felt strained. "Guess it all comes down to whether Gage and Reed have luck tracking down Vanore."

His lips curled up. "They will, you'll see. I trust Reed with my life, and he'd risk his life for those he cares for."

Our breaths sounded through the silence, followed by tiny footfalls hitting the floorboards. Gingernuts chasing the lizards, no doubt.

Kahlo's chin jerked up, his eyes widened, and he froze.

"Relax." I laid a palm on his chest; his muscles might as well have been rocks, they were so hard. "That's just my cat, Gingernuts."

His narrowed eyes said so much, but I didn't want to get into it.

"Has the witch returned to the tower?" he asked instead. "My trip to the collector took longer than expected. I should have visited earlier."

"No, but the hooded man came last night."

Kahlo's nose wrinkled. "Did he harm you?" He scanned my body, as though searching for bruises.

Just remembering the incident had me squeezing Kahlo's arm.

"The bastard is not only an albino lion, but he has freaking bullhorns and a scorpion tail. I think he's using magic to siphon other shifters' abilities for his own."

Kahlo's demeanor darkened, eyes hooding and the bridge between his eyes wrinkling.

I stiffened. "And he's the fuckhead who killed my father thirteen years ago." My eyes itched with tears. So many years had passed since I'd lost my dad, yet finding the creep who'd destroyed my life had reopened the wounds. Rawness etched into my heart. I blinked my eyes fast to drive away the tears.

"Sorry about your father. Reed told me about your tragic past." He lowered his gaze momentarily, and I appreciated his respect. "I visited the mansion and found it empty. The ward had been removed, and I checked inside the house. Empty. All that remained was the heavy stench of a barnyard, blood, and the bitter stink of magic."

"Why would they run?" My head hurt trying to make sense of lunatics. "They discovered something else..." I pushed myself onto my side and faced Kahlo, our knees touching. "The hooded guy fought the gargoyle. He's one mean fucker and strong because he hurt the creature with his bare hands. But he also got hurt badly in return. And that's when a strand of my hair fell out of my head."

Kahlo's brow creased into a dozen lines; it was clear he didn't understand the significance.

"My hair is uncuttable, and I've never lost a strand—ever! Except at night. My magic is connected to that fucking monster who tortures others and can take on a gargoyle. He's taking strength from my magical hair. I'm beginning to believe I've been locked up this whole time to keep this damn hair alive for him."

"Shit!"

"I know! If we kill him and the witch, then not only do we stop the kidnappings, but it will break my hex."

Kahlo nodded, and his expression resembled that of a man

ready to head out to battle—focused and barren of emotions. Just get the job done.

"Those underground tunnels could lead to anywhere in the realm," I added, thinking back to my time in the mansion. "The question is, how the hell do we know which direction they traveled?"

"We visit other shifter colonies to determine who went missing from their packs and when." He brushed a loose strand of hair behind my ear, his rough fingers tender against my skin. "We might find a pattern to follow."

I nodded. The only thing that kept me together was having these three men in my life, offering to help me, studying me as if I might have put a spell on them. They'd shown me what it was to have someone close to care about, who looked out for me. While I was still getting to know Reed and Kahlo, they'd been kinder than people I'd known for years.

Kahlo could have been a jerk and not visited the collector's bunker, but he had—then came to check on me. Now, with the newfound revelation that my problem was linked to Reed's, it only made sense that we worked together.

You sure that's the only reason you want to work closely with them?

I rolled my eyes and refocused to find Kahlo studying me with curiosity.

"You comfortable here on the floor, or do you feel like a cup of tea? We can sit on the scattered cushions. You keep your voice low, okay?"

"Agreed." He climbed to his feet, untangling himself from my hair, and took my arm, drawing me upright in no time. "Nice place."

"Thanks." I padded barefoot across the tower to the kitchen and set the kettle with water on the stove. With a few more pieces of wood tossed into the flames, we'd have hot water soon enough.

"Milk?" Kahlo strode past me and opened the pantry door.

Gingernuts twirled around his legs, meowing.

"Think you have a fan. Funny, as he hissed at Reed." I grabbed the milk from the pantry.

"Animals have always been drawn toward me." He leaned down and picked up the cat, then stroked him against his chest. "Growing up, I'd have injured, abandoned, or scared animals often visit me. My mother would say I had a kind soul."

"So, you're like an animal whisperer. Do you help them?" Knowing he spent his time aiding critters in need made me all warm and fuzzy on the inside.

"Of course I do." He patted Gingernuts' head as the cat was purring and pressing himself against Kahlo's chest. He never snuggled with me, and I chased him around the house for a hug and kiss, yet with the tiger, he was all smooches. I eyed Gingernuts suspiciously, but he was too busy ogling up at Kahlo. *Traitor.*

Still holding my cat under an arm, Kahlo removed several jars from the pantry and placed them on the kitchen counter. He reached for a pot hanging off the metal rack on the wall and set it next to the milk, spices, and tea. He spoke softly and said, "I'll make my famous spiced chai tea?"

Curiosity burrowed through me, as I'd never had someone in the kitchen making tea for me. "Hell, yeah."

He busied himself, placing all the ingredients into the pan before retrieving the sugar. He brushed past me, and my skin hummed with a delicious tingle from his touch. Just thinking back to us tangled and bound in my bedroom had me buzzing. Kahlo had made no move, yet the intensity in his eyes had screamed the opposite. Not that I expected every man I drooled over to fall head over heels in love with me, but had Reed told him he intended to claim me?

"Gingernuts, are you going to sit there all night?" I scratched his head, and he pushed me away with a paw. "Oh, I see. That's how it is."

Kahlo chuckled under his breath. "My father used to make us this chai growing up." He placed the pot on the stove. "The smell reminds me of my parents."

"Where are they now?"

He shrugged but didn't elaborate.

"Do you live close to Reed?" I asked.

Kahlo leaned a hip against the counter and set Gingernuts on the floor before patting down his own chest of fur.

"I live all over the land and often visit Reed." He raised his voice for a fraction of time, and a footfall struck overhead.

I froze, my heart banging in my chest, and exchanged worried stares with Kahlo. Neither of us moved. After the longest excruciating moment with no further footsteps or the gargoyle charging in here, I exhaled.

"Okay, be extra, extra quiet."

I took the kettle off the stove and set it in the sink to stop it from boiling.

Kahlo stirred his pot with a wooden spoon in slow motion, and before long, he poured his brew into mugs and served me one.

The warm drink smelled heavenly, all cinnamon, nutmeg, and ginger sweet. I sipped the chai, hot and creamy on my tongue, and the spices filled my senses. "This is incredible. I may hire you as my personal tea maker."

He smirked and swallowed another gulp before heading across the room, right past the table and chairs to the open section where I set up my bedroom, sitting on the edge of my mattress. Okay, was he being presumptuous?

"In case you tangle us in your hair again, we'll end up somewhere more comfortable," he whispered.

There wasn't a trace of flirting in his words because he was serious. Okay, the desire was all in *my* mind.

Dirty hound dog.

"Whatever," I mumbled to myself as I joined Kahlo. Both of us sat on the bed, our slurping and gulping the only sounds. Gingernuts hopped up to join us.

With the last drop running down my throat, Kahlo took my cup and placed it along with his on the bedside table. He then turned to me and drew me onto the bed to lie down next to him, face to face, and a strange inkling hummed at the base of my gut. The kind that expected more from Kahlo, like his hands all over me. I almost laughed out loud. At my core, I found him adorable and sexy as hell, but the more time I got to spend with him, the more I caught glimpses of what made him more than that.

"Tell me who Elliana is," he said, his head resting on a bent arm.

I lay on my side, on my pillow, lost in his deep green eyes. Was this his way of flirting with women? Because I was into it. If Gage was here, he'd already have me stripped, while Reed... I hadn't worked him out, but considering our last couple of times together, I suspected we'd head in the same direction. But Kahlo was different. He was in no rush, as if auditioning me to fill a spot. Or was he keeping me company in case the witch turned up? And nothing more. But what would he do against her? Then again, who wanted to be alone if she returned? Not me.

Gingernuts crawled in between us and lay on his belly, gawking up at Kahlo, who stroked him. I rubbed Gingernuts' ears.

"Okay, where to start?" I said.

"From the beginning. Reed told me only snippets. I want to know what makes a beautiful woman like you tick. What you like, your favorite foods, what turns you on."

I arched a brow. "That last point might be controversial. My likes change." I smirked, remembering Gage's comment about him planning to watch me with Reed or Kahlo. How my pulse raced when one of the three men was close, and how for the life of me I couldn't work it out how I was attracted to Gage, Reed, and Kahlo at the same time. Had I misread the signs? Then why did they stare at me as if I was theirs?

His fingers grazed mine as I caressed Gingernuts, and the corners of his mouth lifted. There was something special about a powerful, laid-back man wearing a mischievous grin and having eyes only for me.

"Now you've got me super curious," he said.

"I have one question," I said, living dangerously here, my stomach in a swarm of jitters. Lying next to Kahlo, chatting, I felt drawn to him, and damn, he was sexy. I enjoyed flirting with him. "Would you ever share the woman you loved with another man?"

He studied me as shadows fell across his face. "Do you mean specifically what I would do or from a man's perspective in general?"

"You." I chewed on my cheek, butterflies swarming my gut.

"Funny you ask." Emotions lit up in his handsome eyes. His lower lip twitched, as if he fought to control himself from kissing me. "I had this exact conversation with Reed the other day."

"Oh, spill." Forget the humbleness that came with patience. I grinned wide and gnawed on my lower lip, eager to hear more, while my stomach did somersaults.

"You must know Reed intends to make you his own, but he also understands Gage is with you." His fingers intertwined with mine, warm and strong. "I told him that if I ever had a woman like you, I'd move a mountain to hold on to you for eternity. If you loved me with unyielding passion, I'd accept other men you brought into our bond. It would make us a stronger family, each of us looking out for each other."

My breaths floated into the air like smoke, and the world might as well have stopped, leaving just the two of us together. His stare pierced into me, as if declaring he had every intent of being with me, too.

CHAPTER 19

A faint voice sounded in the distance. It kept humming in my ears. I rolled onto my side to drown out the sound but bumped into someone in my bed. Then, last night crashed through me. Kahlo in my tower, us chatting late into the morning, and we must have fallen asleep. It was the first time a man had slept in my bed. He'd been fully clothed—no kisses had been exchanged. I wasn't sure how to feel about that, though I loved that Kahlo chatted and laughed with me instead of going straight for sex. Our conversations were incredibly in-depth about my past, his theory on why shifters had come into existence, and how he believed people could make themselves orgasm without a single touch, just by thought. Now, that left me ultra-curious to explore.

Again, voices came from outside.

I opened my eyes to find streaks of sunlight pouring in from the gaps around the shutters on the window.

Was it Reed and Gage? But if I heard them, so did the gargoyle. My heart slammed into my ribcage. I rushed out of bed, pushing aside the sheets and my hair while Kahlo remained asleep, Gingernuts snuggled against his back.

I rushed to the window and heaved open the shutters. A cool breeze swept over me, washing away the sleep from my eyes. At the bottom of the tower stood Reed and Gage out in the open.

The gargoyle's wings thrashed overhead, sending a gust of air toward me. It flew toward the shifters.

I shuddered and froze mid-descent, a scream pressing on my throat.

Before I could make sense of what was going on, I hauled my long hair behind me, which seemed to take forever, and shoved it outside. Then, I clambered out the window.

Ice filled my veins. I glanced over my shoulder halfway down as both men picked up a huge bucket of water. It glistened and glimmered beneath the sun as if jewels floated inside. Was it the spell from Vanore? They'd found her! Despite the joy, panic dug its claws into my heart. How long had they been calling me?

Moments from the stone creature slamming into them, the men tossed the water at the monster, drenching it from head to toe.

They both darted sideways as the gargoyle crashed into the wooden pail and fell to his knees.

In a hurry, I scrambled down the wall using the grooves in the stone, unable to stop staring down at the way the creature's granite body shimmered and sparkled. My breaths spiked.

He unleashed an ungodly hiss, and I shivered when I hit the ground. No one moved. The three of us watched from a distance, my pulse racing too fast. I clasped my stomach.

The gargoyle stumbled to his feet, its face twisted into a snarl, its eyes wide, its mouth parted, and its fangs exposed. But fear was etched on its expression. With wings wide, fingers reaching for its throat, it froze over. Gone were the glimmers, and now only a solid statue remained—as it had been during the nights I'd gone up on the roof to work out a way to destroy him.

Unable to move, I struggled to believe the spell might have worked, not after all my previous attempts, and how Dustin had become the gargoyle when he'd killed the first gargoyle. Fear strangled my insides. Had the two shifters risked their lives? I'd intended to deliver the final blow. Not them.

Gage and Reed strolled closer, and my attention whipped from the gargoyle to the men. How long had it taken before

Dustin had transformed into the stone guardian? A whisper of a moment.

I trembled all over.

Still nothing of a change on my men.

Emotions bubbled in my chest, ready to detonate. When Gage and Reed reached my side, I tried to speak, but it came out as a squeak.

"Do either of you feel strange?"

I patted Gage's smiling face and his chest, then turned to Reed, who refused to meet my stare. Why was he avoiding me? Regardless, I hugged him, never wanting to release him or Gage in case the spell took them. He hugged me, his embrace weak and not as strong as I remembered.

Still, the gargoyle hadn't disintegrated. Breaking free, I took Reed's and Gage's hands in mine. "Are you both sure you're all right?"

"Honey, I've never been better, so stop fretting. We've just freed you, sweetie," Gage said.

My breaths refused to calm down, and I studied Reed, his pasty cheeks, the forced smile he offered me.

"What's wrong, Reed?" I blurted out as I faced him.

Reed finally spoke in a soft voice, but the spark in his eyes no longer lingered. "I'm fine."

"See?" Gage said. "We're both okay, just exhausted and starving."

"You both sure?" Unease nagged me that all wasn't right. I sensed it under my skin like worms. They were hiding some-thing from me, and it killed me because I'd asked no one to risk their lives for me. So, what had they done?

"I'm famished," Reed said, and I nodded. "Let's go upstairs, and I'll make a king's breakfast." He kissed my knuckles and climbed up my tower while Gage embraced me from behind, his chin propped on my shoulder.

"Elliana, why aren't you excited?" he asked. "You're free."

Maybe it was everything happening so fast—I expected this to go wrong. I'd ruined the first spell from Vanore, so it hadn't gone as planned, but maybe this time, the incantation had worked as intended.

Still, Reed wasn't himself, so how could I celebrate?

I turned in Gage's embrace and wrapped my arms around his neck, letting myself drown in his warmth.

"You and Reed are fucking amazing. I love you both for everything you did," I said. "You found Vanore?"

"Yeah, we tracked her down at a tavern. Let's pack and leave the tower after breakfast and put as much distance between you and the witch as possible."

He kissed the top of my head, but I didn't want to leave his arms. It all felt too surreal. For years, I'd been trapped by the gargoyle, and all my attempts failed. And now we got rid of him so easily. What was I missing? My stomach hurt as if danger still lurked. Or had I been looking over my shoulder for so long, I forgot what freedom felt like? But I kept going back to how strange Reed behaved.

"Can you be honest with me?" I raised my head to face Gage. "What's wrong with Reed?"

He grasped my shoulders and faced me with a stern expression. "We're both exhausted from the long trip. Don't read too much into it, honey. Let's focus on getting you away from this place. That's the priority."

I stared back at the gargoyle, still a solid rock, and the first trickles of joy threaded through me. My whole body thrummed with excitement as tears bubbled in my eyes at the reality that the spell might have worked for once.

"Never cry again," Gage said, wiping my tears. "Today is the start of your new life, and I'm right here beside you."

I threw myself at him, hugging him harder this time, breaking into a laugh. "Oh, shit, you and Reed did it! Let's get up there and celebrate."

When we entered the tower, Kahlo was awake and sitting on the edge of the bed alongside Reed. Their whispers died the moment I climbed inside. Yep, I wasn't an idiot. Shit had gone down, and the men were keeping it from me, assuming I wouldn't approve or it'd piss me off or otherwise upset me. Most likely, all those things. The heaviness returned to my chest, constricting me. What had happened? And considering Gage had taken Reed's side by not telling me what had happened in Tritonia, the news had to be horrible. Pushing them for an answer wouldn't work, so I'd work on them to discover the truth.

With Gage's help, I reeled in the rest of my hair, letting it sprawl across the floor. Reed stared at my locks and released a long sigh. Was he okay?

"Okay, let's get food in your bellies." I headed to the kitchen, shaking because I wanted to scream at them. *Force* them to speak. But then, would they even tell me the truth or brush me away? I ought to be bellowing with excitement when, instead, tears prickled my eyes because something had happened to Reed.

"How can I help?" Gage collected the bread from the pantry and picked up a huge knife.

"When you finish that, can you dice cheese, please?"

He leaned toward me and whispered, "So, I noticed Kahlo might have stayed here for the night." His mouth pinched at the corners, and in all honesty, I didn't have time for this when my insides felt raw and as if someone had dragged barbed wire through me.

"So, what if he did?" I said. "He stayed in case the witch came around."

His expression didn't shift. "And did she?"

I returned to the basket of eggs on the counter and started breaking them into a bowl. "No."

"Good. Then after breakfast, you pack, and we leave for good." He sliced the bread. I could sense his jitters and the way he kept shifting on the spot. Then he neared me again and whispered, "Because if something happened between you and Kahlo, I'd be okay with sharing, but I'd be disappointed that I didn't get a chance to watch."

I froze, letting his words roll through my head. Kahlo had said the same about sharing, as had Reed. So, were the three of them talking about being with me together? Hell yeah, that made my day, along with seeing them get along so well. But when I looked over at Reed sitting across the tower, the way he slouched forward, his elbows on his thighs and his gaze miles away, an ache spiked through me.

* * *

"Are you fucking with us? That prick came here to hurt you?" Gage stopped buttering his bread, his jaw clenching. Reed's eyes burned with flames while Kahlo dug into his eggs since he'd already heard about the hooded guy paying me a visit.

I nodded and swallowed the food in my mouth before taking a sip of my tea. We sat around the small table, everyone diving into the food, while Gingernuts ate his portion in the kitchen. My knees bounced under the table. While this was a celebratory breakfast, partying was the last thing on my mind. Not when other shifters remained missing, including Reed's sister, and then there was the whole mystery of what had caused Reed's change in mood.

"You say the bastard stood up to the gargoyle?" Reed asked.

"In his lion form or whatever shifter he was. The hooded man was freaking strong, but I suspect the witch kept me alive this whole time because somehow my hair gives him strength."

"What the fuck for?" Gage stuffed a piece of cheese into his mouth and swallowed his food. "I haven't heard of an albino lion before, so where's he been hiding this whole time? Why did he now kidnap shifters?"

"Shifters have been going missing for years," Kahlo added. "But it was only one here and there, so most people put it down to random attacks or accidents. What if the same person was responsible for those as well?"

"And he's getting ready for a major assault?" Reed suggested.

"On who?" I cupped my warm mug and sipped the peppermint drink.

They all shrugged.

"As of right now," I said, "all we know is that he's strong, works with a powerful witch, and steals shifters to perhaps use them for his own personal army. And my curse is connected to him, so keeping me alive for my hair is crucial to his strength. But what does it all mean, and why is this happening?"

"Considering they're out of the mansion…" Reed gulped down his tea and wiped his mouth with a napkin. "I say we follow Kahlo's suggestion. We ask other shifter packs who's gone missing and when and if they've seen anything strange. Let's gather intelligence and regroup with a plan."

"Agreed," I said. Eventually, the witch would track me down. I wasn't stupid to think she'd leave me alone if my hair fed the hooded man with power. So the trick was striking first before they saw it coming. I wracked my brain, going over everything I'd seen at the mansion, trying to remember anything the asshole had said when he'd paid me a visit. I'd met him once before when I was eight. That event had taken place back in my home-town where I'd grown up. What if he and Faye were from there, too? What if someone else knew them?

"I grew up in Crosswind, a small village near the Tritonia border." I cleared my throat. "It's a hike up there, but that was where Faye and the albino shifter captured my father and me. What if they're from there? It might help us gain more insight into who we're dealing with. My father also had a friend there we'd visit sometimes, a woman who baked the most incredible cookies. She might know something."

Reed and Kahlo nodded their heads.

"Good idea," Gage said. "Especially since I plan to get Elliana away from here. I'll take her to Crosswind today, and I'll ask the shifters there."

Having Gage jump in and help meant the world because it wasn't as if every problem was only on my shoulders for a change.

"Perfect," Reed said. "Kahlo and I will split up and do the same near here. We'll meet you both in Crosswind tonight at a local tavern. Deal?"

"Yes," I said, and everyone dove back into the food.

The countdown was on, and a sense of adventure set in. I was ready to take on anything because, for once, I wasn't alone.

Adrenaline coursed through me at knowing I'd have someone to rely on, to catch me if I fell, to comfort me when shit got real.

Not to mention more of you to die.

I swallowed the boulder in my throat. She was right, but running away wasn't an option anymore. No more looking over my shoulder, waiting for Faye to find me. This was the moment we made a difference. My heart skipped a beat at the dangerous mission we were about to embark on.

Here were three gorgeous men who affected me in ways that left me floating on clouds, and I couldn't bear to have any of them harmed. This wasn't just about me anymore but ensuring they received their happy endings. Would I succeed? Being with them gave me the hope to believe in miracles.

By the time we finished eating and I'd packed everything away, the three men stood in the living room, Gage carrying my oversized backpack. Clothes, two of my favorite books, and food for the trip. Plus, gold coins. Gingernuts was already inside a bag with just his head popping out, meowing and not a fan of this arrangement. But he was coming with us wherever we went. He was family. I pushed the straps of my bag up my shoulders with my hair tucked away.

"Ready, Sugar Pops?" Gage asked.

I hurried toward the trio. Never in a million years would I have guessed where that first meeting in the lion territory would have led to. But my life had never been ordinary, and the unexpected was the norm.

"I can't tell you how incredible it's been to have all three of you in my life," I said as the men stared my way. Gage pulled me into a hug first, then Kahlo joined, and Reed closed the embrace. Me in the middle of these amazing men who caused my heart to race and who meant more to me than I could have ever imagined. The more time I spent with each, the more I cared about them and yearned to keep each for myself. But first, I had to work out what was wrong with Reed.

A niggling sensation wormed through my thoughts, well aware that good luck rarely accompanied me, but maybe the fortune from three shifters would balance me out.

"All right, let's do this," Kahlo said, his palm still on my lower back, stroking me in circles, reminding me how much I'd shared with him last night. Like my fears and how much I'd wanted to die after each dreadful beating by the gargoyle. Yet, he wasn't running away from my messed-up life.

"I'll be seeing you soon." He drew me into a hug, strong and powerful.

Reed's warm body pressed against me, and when I turned away from Kahlo, he threw his arms around me, as if any moment he might break down and tell me what had happened in Tritonia. Instead, he whispered, "Don't do anything crazy until I come for you." The joy in his words had me smiling to have his true self back, even if just for a few moments.

Kahlo collected Gingernuts to take him down the tower wall for me, and they both headed out the window, Gage after them.

"Time to leave, honey." Reed offered me his outstretched hand.

I followed him and took one last look at the tower—my prison and home for the past thirteen years. The paintings on the wall of a meadow and castle, the fabrics over the walls that looked more like a boudoir but better than stone walls, and even the corner where I'd cried so many times. I had known nothing else for so long, and now leaving felt bittersweet. While I had many memories attached to this place, I wouldn't miss it. I turned and followed Reed out the window.

Farewell.

CHAPTER 20

Gingernuts meowed from his bag. I drew him against my chest and scratched his head, which was sticking out. He shifted about, wriggling in there.

"We let you out, and you bolted. No more leaving until we get to Crosswind."

Gage gasped for air, his chest rising and falling while his cheeks glowed red. "Pretty sure you mean to say that you let him out, then I chased the damn cat like a madman through the woods."

"But you caught him, so that's what matters." I lifted Gingernuts to kiss his head, but the cat gave me a filthy look filled with retribution. "*Come on.* Did you want to stay alone in the tower?"

Gage huffed and picked up my other backpack off the ground before hightailing it up the narrow track amidst the forest.

"I still don't know why I can't fly us up into this town?"

"Because I don't want the locals spooked. This is one of a few human settlements in Darkwoods, and it's tucked in the corner of the realm. They don't welcome many shifters."

I marched after him while Gingernuts vanished into the bag and settled down. I supposed being chased by a dragon shifter had worn him out.

"So, do you have any relatives or family friends?" Gage asked.

"Just this woman my dad used to know. After Mom died, my dad and I traveled from place to place, and Crosswind was our last stop before our attack. Back then, only a handful of houses and shops made up the village. Dad said he might settle down there because it was so quaint."

Tire tracks from carriages had worn the path. Dad loved that it was quiet on this mountain and that the village overlooked the forest below. Plus, he used to say the area made him feel like a bird perched on top of the world. Just like the eagle-man with Faye. How long before she tracked me down? Would Vanore's spell be enough to halt Faye from resurrecting the gargoyle? Would we put an end to the kidnappings?

Lofty cypress trees swayed in the wind, and muddy clouds rolled across the heavens. I rushed to keep up with Gage and not get caught in the approaching storm.

"Reed is a decent man," Gage said.

My mouth fell open. "You gave him a compliment? Now I know something happened between you two in Tritonia."

He pushed the straps of the two bags he carried up over his shoulders. We'd made a quick visit to his treetop house so he could pack a few clothes for his travel. Gage suggested we leave Gingernuts there, but I couldn't. He wasn't familiar with the place, and he might run away. Plus, who would feed and snuggle him?

"I misjudged Reed. He's a ruler who'll make a difference in this world and to his pride. Who puts his members first when danger appears. Anyway,"—he looked my way with a genuine smile—"I like him and can see why you're attracted to him."

"Whoa, where is that coming from?" I gripped my hips, unsure I liked where this was going. "What exactly did you two discuss?"

He threw an arm around my shoulders and brought me closer. "What happens in Tritonia stays in Tritonia. But the man likes you a lot. And I'm okay with that."

Too many thoughts whirled through my head. "I don't even know what you're saying."

"That I care for you more than my life, and I think Reed does, too. So, if you date us both at the same time, I'm fine with it. But on the condition you let me watch him take you at least once." He winked, and I wasn't sure if I should have been aroused or shocked.

My cheeks heated and not because I was shy. Far from it, but I lost all ability to respond. I waited for my subconscious to crack a joke, but she remained silent and distant.

"While I love your openness, what if he doesn't want that? Or me?" What if I considered adding Kahlo into that mix? Would Gage be so accommodating?

Gage ruffled my hair, and I adjusted the bag holding all my tresses on my other shoulder.

"Honey, there's no doubt in my head you wouldn't want two incredible guys like Reed and me by your side always. Just not at the same time. That's where I draw the line, but observing I can do."

"Okay, so if you're that open, you'd be happy for me to bring more men into this mix?"

He cocked a brow, studying me, and he'd be dumb if he didn't sense my sarcasm. I hiked up the slope, my thighs stinging, saying nothing.

"Yeah, I'd welcome Kahlo, but I'd suggest capping it at three. I want you all to myself more than once a week."

My breath hitched, and I glanced up at his smirk, his chin high and his hooded eyes fixed on me.

"You surprise me," I said. "But I've made it clear to all three of you I have no intention of starting a relationship with anyone until I'm free. If we eradicate the hooded man and Faye's spell, heck, I'll be the first to take all three of you out on a date."

"Ha, knew it. You want all three of us!"

"You're confusing me. Was that all a game to get me to confess?" I didn't have it in me for tricks when relationships were second on my list of priorities over surviving.

"Nah, but I wanted to hear you say it, that's all."

We traveled in silence as the skies rumbled with the promise of heavy rain.

"So you're honestly telling me you would be okay with

sharing me?" I couldn't believe we were even having such a conversation. I'd always prayed to the universe to give me a chance to have a future with an amazing man. She'd given me three, so was I being greedy in thinking I could keep them, or was the idea to select one?

"Why choose?" Gage responded. "I've never had a real family, and I'm excited to have not only you but two close friends." He stared out into the distance as he spoke, not a flinch of disapproval or disgust.

Damn, he was serious, and I never would have imagined such words falling from his mouth. But when I thought about it, I understood. If he'd always craved a family, he'd see the notion of the four of us in a relationship as appealing.

"We should hold on to this thought until the other two arrive. They may not be so excited to share."

He made a scoffing sound. "Be prepared to be surprised."

At long last, we reached the top, and in front of us, the road wove across flat land. The smell of a wood fire wafted through the air. By the time we arrived in a village surrounded by a man-made river, familiarity struck me. We reached a stone bridge arching over swirling waters, shimmering in the sunlight.

Crosswind was no longer the place I remembered. It now resembled a bustling town with a maze of narrow winding streets, an endless array of houses, and merchants selling clothes and food on the street. Even a church poked out from the back. When Dad and I had arrived here all those years ago, I'd stolen a loaf of bread and cheese for us, and we'd sat by the river's edge that evening, sharing our meal. The silence of the locality meant tranquility. No streetlamps existed, either. Now, the reds, blues, and yellows of the painted homes reminded me of children's toys.

"You okay?" Gage brushed against me.

I nodded but couldn't speak. A farmer drew a single horse-drawn carriage filled with chopped wood toward us from the open field at our backs. We stepped aside as he passed us with a nod of his head and entered the town.

"Crosswind doesn't feel the same." I wasn't sure how to word it, but it had lost its charm and looked like any of the other places I'd visited. I'd always pictured the location as idealistic, picturesque, and quiet.

"Everything changes."

"Yeah, I know. Just expected something else, I guess." I pushed forward onto the crossing. "I'm being silly, holding on to the past from thirteen years ago."

He slid his hand into mine, and we strolled toward the busy town, where voices boomed and pungent smells from baking blended into a strange concoction.

"First thing, we find a tavern room and drop off our bags and Gingernuts. Then we mingle and ask locals about shifters and anything strange in the area. Even if that lion pride you mentioned earlier still lives near."

"Agree." However, I was still stunned at how fast a small place had blossomed. While advances were needed for the populace, there was something to be said about simplicity.

* * *

"How long do we wait for Reed and Kahlo to turn up?" Gage stuffed another piece of lamb roast into his mouth, lounging across from me at our table in the tavern.

"As long as it takes." I glanced out the window into the night, the light pattering of rain hitting the glass pane. A storm had rolled through town, then vanished just as quickly. I hoped Reed and Kahlo hadn't gotten caught in it.

Now, we waited for them in the tavern closest to the bridge, so we'd spot them. Crosswind now housed six bars. Torches lit up the street. It had to be close to midnight. No more couples or families wandered the streets. Just working women, two lingering nearby in tiny skirts, thigh-length stockings, and puffy shirts. Both had black hair tied in ponytails, so I assumed they were twins and potentially offering clients two-for-the-price-of-one deals. A seedy man wearing nothing but black in the shadows studied everyone who spoke with the ladies. The pimp.

Farther down the road lay the bridge, one light illuminating the passage, and still no sign of either shifter. I returned my attention to Gage, who'd eaten all night and now scoffed down the baked potatoes. How much did a shifter eat?

Despite the late hour, the tavern buzzed. Men were drinking and laughing with friends, while others fawned over the young women wearing just stockings with tiny dresses—leaving nothing to the imagination—selling pre-rolled cigarettes. They'd have no problem making killer sales tonight.

A fire blazed from the cobblestone fireplace across from the bar, throwing shadows over the darkened room. A band with flutes and drums played a tune in the opposite corner. Behind the bar, a row of six wooden barrels lined the walls, and the barman tended to orders.

"So, how do you feel about moving to White Peak? It's beautiful there, isolated, and so much to see." Gage wiped his mouth with a napkin, his legs reaching out beneath the table and clasping mine between his.

"For a vacation?" I didn't understand where he was going with this, yet his gaze held an intensity behind them.

"No, permanently. Start a new life with me, the other men if they want to."

"You'd be ready to leave behind your current home? What about your job and friends?" Besides, I had no intention of running away until I sorted out my shit.

He leaned back and threaded his fingers behind his head. In his black gambeson padded with studded sleeves with a matching undershirt, he screamed "chivalrous knight;" all he was missing was a sword and a pledge to a royal family. At heart, he was my knight in shining armor. His perfectly accentuated face had me admiring him, and his full lips parted in a provoking expression meant only for me.

"For you, yeah. I'll go anywhere. I have no attachments in Darkwoods." His eyes gleamed beneath the candlelight at our table. "Now that I understand why you've been pushing me away for years, I'm not leaving your side." His eyes seemed to scream his intensity and emotions, and I didn't doubt his words.

These weren't from a delusional man but someone devoted,

and it warmed me to have him stare at me with such hunger. For too long, I'd kept him at a distance, and even now, it terrified me to open my heart. What if we failed and Faye defeated me, locked me in a place where no one could find me? A shiver rattled through me. I couldn't bear to know Gage might spend his whole life searching for me. As much as it killed me, I hoped he could move on if that ever happened.

Though the way he stared at me now scared me that he wouldn't. Whether I gave in to him or not, he was still devoted to me, so maybe I ought to give in. My stomach tingled with the prospect. It would be a dream come true.

I scanned outside once again, and the rain had ceased.

Maybe part of the reason Gage had never turned into a true dragon was because of my hesitation. The guilt raked at my insides like claws, yet I couldn't change. Not when being with me still posed a danger to him. It sounded foolish in my head, but it was the only way to deal with the fear chiseling away at my sanity. If I died or vanished, I refused to take anyone down with me.

Just then, the front door to the tavern snapped open with a flurry of wind. Reed and Kahlo strolled inside, their hair and coats wet. Kahlo carried a bag over his shoulder. A beam of excitement lit my insides at their arrival, and I smiled as I waved them over.

They turned our way, both grinning, and came over. The two strong men had others eyeing them. Even the women stopped and glanced their way, whispering and giggling.

A strange fire spiked through my gut... Was that jealousy? Surely not.

"Fuck!" Kahlo blurted out as he took off his leather jacket and draped it on the bench he sat on. "Why the hell is this place on the tallest mountain in the world?" He puffed and pushed up the sleeves of his tunic-style shirt. The shirt was the color of midnight and open at his throat.

"You ran the whole way?" I asked.

"Sure did." Reed blew out a long breath. "Couldn't wait to see you." He winked, and my lips lifted. I adored how much he affected me, and it seemed he might be in a better mood than he had been back at my tower.

Gage got up. "Let me get you both drinks."

"And food." Kahlo sat next to me. "Sure hope Gage carried you up here."

"Have you ever tried making her do anything she doesn't want to?" Gage laughed and sauntered over to the bar. Already, several cigarette women gravitated to him as if he were free candy on offer.

Kahlo's thumb caressed my arm, drawing my attention to him while Reed drank down the rest of Gage's beer. Their presence distracted me in the best way, and it was incredible to have all three with me, knowing they were safe.

Reed's hip grazed mine as he took a seat on my other side. He leaned in, stealing a kiss, the kind that started as a peck but ended in something deeper and longer. I lost my breath and drifted off into the clouds. Our tongues tangled, and I moaned under him. If this was after not seeing him for a day, I'd love to see what happened after a week.

When he withdrew, my breaths sprinted. Then he grinned, his eyes devouring me, and the temperature in the room seemed to rise.

"I missed you."

"I missed you, too."

Kahlo huffed, and when I turned to him, I realized he'd shuffled closer on the bench and without hesitation, he combed his fingers through my hair, bringing me closer to his chest. Okay, this was new and oh-so-exciting. My heart skipped a beat, and when our mouths clashed, my hunger for him spiked. Both of us were lost in a jungle of sexual starvation. He held my head, and my palms plastered to his rock-hard chest, my insides tingling and diving south so fast, I was convinced that with a single stroke of his skin, I'd explode.

"Really?" Gage's words sliced through our connection, and I drew back, chewing on my lip, tasting both men, their muskiness lingering over me. He set down four mugs of beer, foam sloshing out over the rim and onto the table. "You want to draw any more attention to us?"

I followed his gaze to find the rest of the room staring at us. Heat hit my cheeks because I'd never flaunted my passion in front of others, but I'd just kissed two men in front of everyone.

"Now give me some of that sugar." Gage smirked and rounded the long wooden table before leaning over my shoulder, pressing his lips to mine. An inferno erupted between our bodies, and I was convinced that with these men all happy to share me, I might have just discovered a brand-new level of ecstasy. Who the hell didn't want three god-like men at their mercy?

"Bet they don't see that too often in this town," Gage said.

Jealous glares faced our way, and one man even groped his package. *Gross.* Okay, enough turning on other people.

With Gage back in his seat, we huddled close and drank as if an unquenchable thirst had set upon us.

"Any luck today?"

Reed shook his head. "Not a fucking hint. All the packs we visited had shifters missing over the past few weeks, but it's been quiet this week, as if suddenly the asses vanished. I don't know where my sister is or how to save her." He stared down at his beer, and I reached over, touching his thigh.

"We'll find her. There are four of us, and no matter what, we'll rescue her."

"My bet is they got a whiff of us snooping too close and changed tactics," Kahlo said. "Moved to a new location to steal other shifters." Kahlo gulped down half his beer in one go.

"Hopefully, that also means Faye won't return and find me gone soon, and if she does, she'll have trouble resurrecting the gargoyle." My knees bounced under the table. After being locked up for so many years, I didn't want to return to the prison ever again. I'd do anything to hold on to my freedom.

Kahlo cast an arm around my back, his attention reminding me he'd fight for me—they all would—and I'd do the same for them.

"We had little luck ourselves, but we've only asked store

owners," Gage piped up. "Tomorrow, we head out to find shifters living in the nearby woods."

The bartender arrived at our table carrying a silver tray piled high with dishes. A platter of cheeses and salami. Stuffed eggs. Roasted goose and vegetables. Blood sausages. Bread rolls served to each of us, the tops cut off, the insides scooped out and refilled with meat and potato stew. A side of corn cobs and a serving of fruit.

"Geez, that's a lot of food." I'd been eating non-stop most of the night but still planned to taste a few more of the dishes. "I'm going to grow into a hippopotamus if I keep eating this way."

"More of you to love," Gage smirked.

"Anything else ya lads will need?" the man with a goatee asked.

"Keep the beer flowing," Gage said, and everyone dug into their meals.

Several rounds of drinks later, I was laughing hysterically. My stomach roiled from too much chuckling, but what made it funnier was that I couldn't remember the joke. Something about a priest, a dragon shifter, and a giraffe walking into a tavern. Kahlo slammed his palm on the table, roaring in amusement, while Gage chortled, as if he might burst at any moment. But Reed simply smiled.

I was a big believer that alcohol brought out a person's real emotions. There'd be no more hiding. I couldn't stop glancing over at Reed, who was on his sixth pint and grew more withdrawn with each drink.

Someone shouted from within the tavern, and I flinched, turning around to find three burly men swinging punches at each other. The bartender was there poking them with a long stick, telling them to cut it out. "Take it outside, the lot of you."

Others sat around gawking, cheering on the battle. When the fighters toppled a table, taking down two more, like quick fire, the fight spread, and soon enough, half the place brawled.

Gage was on his feet, swaying, his eyes glazed over. He dusted his hands. "I've got this. Dealt with these kinds of scuffles at Brawl all the time."

"Don't." I reached out for him, but he'd already set off across the room. "Idiot."

"Leave it to me." Kahlo hiccupped and took two tries to stand before he finally got up.

My head swam, the room spinning around me, but you didn't see me get up to join a fight. I should have had only two drinks.

In the time I took to calm my whirling head, Gage and Kahlo were in the thick of the rampage, tossing people about as if they were toys. *Shit!* They were going to hurt someone.

A man picked up a chair and brought it down on Kahlo's back, but my mountain of a man jerked around and lifted the man off the ground by clenching his shirt.

"Don't!" I jumped up, and Reed had already darted across the room toward them. Someone punched him square in the face, and he stumbled back, shaking himself with shock.

His body trembled, and my worst fears squeezed my heart. They would transform into their animal forms. Panicked people would draw knives and other weapons to kill them if threatened. I hefted the bag with my hair and threaded my arms into the straps, then ran to Reed's side, but my feet wobbled. I crashed against a table before finding my balance again.

Kahlo had already ripped his shirt off and growled, his body transforming. I tottered toward him, tugging at his furry arm, but he fell to all fours, his trousers splitting as he morphed into a monstrous tiger, reaching my waist. Stripped and gorgeous, he was the epitome of beauty, except everyone backed away from him. He sniffed the air, his golden-green eyes scanning the room. Powerful muscles shifted beneath his shiny coat. Hot air floated from the corners of his mouth before his upper lip curled over long canines, and I flinched away at first. His broad nose creased, and he crouched low, his haunches high, ready to attack.

Oh, shit!

Knives were drawn by the surrounding men, and dread swallowed me.

"Don't hurt him." I stepped in front of Kahlo as Gage

exploded with a thundering growl, and his wings spread out, almost reaching either side of the wall.

Nothing made sense, and sweat dripped down my back as my attention darted between the panicked humans and the shifters.

All I needed now was for Reed to turn furry, and they'd be the perfect set of loose cannons. Except he remained there, his body shaking, his skin gleaming with sweat. Thank fuck he had control of himself.

The bartender turned to us with his stick, which might as well have been a pitchfork the way he poked it toward us. "Fuck off. Shifters aren't welcome in this tavern." Others screamed at us, brandishing weapons, and my stomach clenched. So this town hadn't changed, even if it had appeared so from the outside.

"Killers!" another man shouted.

"They won't hurt anyone," I called out. Sure, shifters were stronger, but this intolerance of different races was bullshit. "You're the ones holding the weapons."

The bartender glared my way, his shoulders curled forward and his earlier cheer replaced by repulsion. "Get out. You're all the same, coming into our town and killing humans."

Reed was at my side, his hooded expression dark and swimming in shadows. "Shifters came in here and attacked people?"

A man with a cut lip grunted. "Fucking abominations. Your kind attacked two men in the woods just yesterday."

Horror locked me on the spot, and I rubbed my eyes, trying to wade through my foggy head. "What did they look like?" Of course, my thoughts went straight to the hooded man.

"Freaks! Like that horned lion." He eyed Kahlo and Gage, who'd already retracted his wings.

I rocked on my heels. "Was he white, and did he also have a scorpion tail?"

The man's face warped, and his lips twisted. "Get the fuck out before we skewer you to the walls!" he yelled, not answering my question. But he didn't need to. It was too much of a coincidence not to recognize this as the same monster. Why were they hunting humans? Did they see them as a free feast, or had they stumbled into the wrong place?

Others raised their weapons and hooted for our destruction. I looped an arm over Kahlo's neck and pulled him away. Under my touch, he vibrated and transformed back into a man.

Everyone gawked with disgust while I watched in awe at the magnificence of this change. Within moments, Kahlo stood next to me, naked and delicious. The women lowered their gazes and smiled.

"Leave!" the drunk mob chanted, and we all turned for the door, retreating, my skin crawling. Reed collected our clothes and his bag from our table. No one had ever driven me out of a tavern before, but that rumble might have been exactly what we'd needed.

CHAPTER 21

We tottered out of the tavern.

"Asses," I mumbled. "Kicking us out."

Reed gave a naked Kahlo his long coat, but not before I glimpsed his... *Oh, my.* I tripped over my feet at how damn big he was, even without being erect. When I glanced up, he caught me looking and smirked with a knowing look that said, *It's all yours.*

My face burned, and I looked away.

Gage marched ahead, and we followed him along a windy road heading deeper into the town. A few torches lit the path, but no one else was around.

"Thank fuck we booked our rooms at another tavern," Gage explained.

"Well, that went south fast," I said, hugging myself against the cool breeze. "What the hell happened in there? Why did you transform?"

Kahlo shrugged, walking in a crooked line. "Control is hard when intoxicated, baby cakes." He slurred his words. "Plus, all that excitement of a fight got my tiger riled up." He roared and broke into a laugh. Okay, *someone* had had way too much to drink.

I nudged Reed in the arm. "Clearly, you're the only one with control." I offered him a smile, but in response, his expression soured.

"I gotta go." Without a response, he swung left and walked down a side alley, vanishing in the shadows.

I froze, my chest constricting. "Reed? What's going on?"

"I'll go after him." Gage bounced on his toes, full of energy. "We'll meet you both at the Old Reindeer Hunt tavern."

Confusion twisted inside me, and I glanced at Kahlo, who leaned a shoulder against the wall of a tailor's shop. He didn't seem bothered with Reed taking off.

"Okay," I said. "Let's move. I can't carry or roll you to our room." I looped my arm under his, but damn, he was so heavy. If we fell, he'd crush me. We traipsed down a dark road between two buildings, the place stinking of garbage. "Ever since those two returned from Tritonia, Reed's been acting strange. Have you noticed?"

Kahlo half-nodded, half-shrugged, but kept his lips tight.

"I know something happened, but I don't understand why he doesn't tell me. I can help him."

Kahlo sighed. "Babycakes, ain't nothing you can do to help him now."

"What do you mean?" I tightened my hold.

"He adores you but doesn't want you to see him struggling."

Damn men and their egos. I halted at the corner of a cobblestone street with several burning torches lighting up the residential houses spreading outward. Maybe I was wrong about his reaction being about his sister.

"Is he worried about his sister? I am, too, but we'll help her. Did you hear the bartender? A horned lion attacked them. That was the hooded man. He was here, so we're on the right track." That also meant Faye might be here, so I had to keep a low profile. Maybe I'd get a cape to conceal myself and my bag holding my hair.

"It's not that." He leaned to the side, and I pulled against his weight so he stayed upright.

"Then what? What the fuck is going on with Reed? Just tell

me." My fingers threaded with his. "Please, Kahlo." I batted my eyelashes.

For the longest moment, he said nothing, then all at once unleashed a guttural sigh. "You know why he didn't shift back in the bar?"

"Because he has more control than you and Reed?"

"Fuck that. He was dying to change—I saw it on him—but he can't. He told me he sold his mane and shifting ability for your gargoyle spell."

His words refused to process at first, but my body numbed, and my head screamed. "What the fuck? Why would he do that? I never…" I stumbled backward, my earlier meal threatening to hurl out. "Does he get it back?"

I studied Kahlo, pleading with him to say *yes*, but when he shook his head, my legs weakened beneath me, and I fell. My knees kissed the pavement, but I didn't sense the pain. Not when tears swarmed my eyes.

"He had no right," I cried out, furious that he'd give up something so precious for me. *Me!* The hypocrite who'd always played it safe. Who'd refused to get close to the three men who intrigued her in case it didn't work out. Yet they'd given their all, and Reed had sacrificed part of himself.

I sobbed into my hands.

Kahlo was at my side. "Don't cry. He's gifted you with what he had because you mean so much to him."

I raised my head, unable to stop the tears. "Why is he struggling then? He could barely look at me when he returned, and tonight, being unable to transform must have killed him." My heart splintered at what he'd given up.

Kahlo lifted me into his arms, cradling me against his chest, but I kept telling myself I didn't deserve his affection. Or anyone's. I was a nobody who'd burst into their world and brought chaos to torture them.

Luck has never been your friend.

The tears flowed because what did I offer anyone aside from danger and agony?

In Kahlo's arms, I melted against his chest, his warmth engulfing me, and I closed my eyes. I never should have accepted Reed's help to visit Tritonia. This was all on me... I destroyed everything I encountered. How was I supposed to face Reed when he couldn't stand being in my company?

"Is this the place?" he asked softly, his breath washing across my face.

Opening my eyes, I stared at a wooden studded door with a sign reading, "Old Reindeer Hunt," painted in yellow across a wooden plaque. "Yes." I untangled us and released myself from his hold. Maybe it was better for everyone if I put distance between us before I brought hell upon them. What if Faye and the psycho albino shifter turned up and took down all three men to retrieve me?

Smart idea. Staying means putting them in death's path.

Kahlo opened the door to the tavern, and I stepped into a room with only half a dozen patrons at the bar in a room glowing from the fireplace. I turned away and swung left toward the wooden staircase leading upstairs. Gage and I had booked the last two rooms available. Who would have thought this place sold out, but apparently many people traveled through the woods on their way into Tritonia and used Crosswind as their last stop before hiking into the next realm.

Upstairs, I dragged myself down the shadowy corridor dotted with paintings of horses and retrieved the bronze key from my pocket. Kahlo's footsteps echoed close behind. Our room spread out before us, with a large bed against the back wall taking up the majority of the space. To the left stood a writing desk and the bathroom, and at the opposite end was a couch. This was the extravagant room, so I'd hate to see the cheap version.

Where was Gingernuts hiding?

"I'm going back downstairs for a moment." Kahlo retreated to the door. "I'll be right back. Don't go anywhere."

Before I could respond, he left and shut the door behind him.

Silence permeated the air, yet my mind boomed with the

harrowing dread of what Reed had done. My chest might as well have been splitting in half because everything hurt. I hugged myself as I staggered to the window. Pulling back the curtain, I found Gingernuts fast asleep on the windowsill. Outside, torches illuminated the streets, and I searched them for movement... for Reed. Had Gage found him? What were they talking about? Or did everyone blame me?

I scratched Gingernuts' head and lowered the curtain to let him sleep. I took off my bag and released my hair, letting it tumble across the wooden floor.

Kahlo had insisted Reed's decision was a blessing from him, but I couldn't live with myself knowing he'd no longer rule his pride. He'd lost the side of him he cherished. I didn't remember pacing until Kahlo returned carrying a tray with a teapot, cups, and a plate of tiny cakes.

"I've got something for you." His cheery voice was a saw cutting through my heart. He went out of his way to brighten my mood when I'd caused his friend to give up his shifter side.

"Why are you being so nice?" I asked.

He set the platter on the coffee table in front of the couch and patted the seat next to him. With no hesitation, I joined him. I longed to hear that everything would be all right, that somehow the mess I'd created could be fixed.

Kahlo gave me a cup of milk tea, and I selected a shortbread cookie while he studied his creamy slice of tiered sponge cake.

"I have no idea how to make things right." I dunked my cookie into the drink and ate it in two bites, then washed the buttery sweetness down with tea. Setting the cup on the table, I toed my boots off and curled up on the sofa, facing Kahlo.

"Do you know what your name means?" He took several bites of his cake and swallowed without chewing.

"No idea."

"It means 'shining light.' You attract a lot of attention because people want to be near you. Reed knew exactly what he was doing, and for him to give up something so important says a lot. The man adores everything about you. I've known him for years, and I've never seen him smitten this way with anyone."

That earlier heaviness sunk deeper, and I hiccupped, my tears falling free. "That makes me feel worse."

Kahlo shuffled closer and collected me into his arms, our bodies pressed side to side, my knees bent and leaning over his thighs.

"Knowing someone cherishes you makes you cry? Guess I better not share how I feel about you." He clasped my waist, and I shivered, fully aware of how firmly he gripped me. I wasn't going anywhere because Kahlo's presence eased the dread drowning me.

"Now, you've got me curious," I said, well aware of what I was doing and didn't care. Like with Reed and Gage, Kahlo had me floating through the air, promising me ecstasy if I let down my guard. And right now, I yearned to escape.

Flirt.

He smirked, his eyes undressing me. "From your delicious mouth to your delicate shoulders to your curvy ass, I'm enthralled. At our first meet, I felt as if my head constantly spun in your presence. Ever since, I've had only you on my mind." Kahlo's free hand swept upward along my outer thigh, halting at my hip. An electric buzz jolted through me to have such a powerful man entranced with me, his fingers pressing into my skin. Was he going to rip off my clothes?

You sure do fantasize a lot.

Except with the hunger in his gaze, I doubted I alone shared this dream.

"Oh, yeah? What else?" My palms fell flat against his chest.

"You keep your distance from everyone, but you're the kind who'd risk your life to protect others." He closed in, his cheek grazing against mine, his nose against my neck, and he inhaled. A guttural rumble rolled through his chest, and my stomach fluttered with a thrill I'd only sensed in Gage's arms.

Something about each of the three shifters in my life had me drawn to them. But I always pushed them away, like when I'd broken up with Gage. I was scared of them getting hurt, but it had never occurred to me that letting down my guard might be worse. That they'd prove how much they adored me. Little did they know, I desired them as much as the world depended on sunlight… They were my salvation, my existence. But I'd let Reed down, and how long would it be before I hurt the others?

A quiver traveled through me.

I was sick of running away, exhausted of living with fear, tired of being alone. Why couldn't I have what I longed for? Right now, that was Kahlo, and not just for one night but for forever.

Kahlo's mouth nuzzled my earlobe, and I tingled all over. Shoving aside all doubts and worries, I climbed over him, straddling my thighs over his lap. With my arms sailing around his head, I pushed myself against him. Mouths clashed, teeth clinking. Chest to chest.

He groaned, his body curling around me, and his hardness pressed against the apex between my legs.

"You sure you're ready for this, Babycakes?" he breathed in my mouth, and hearing his guttural voice had me firing up.

"Fuck, yes. I've dreamed about you since I first saw you in the lion territory. Having your eyes on me made me so wet."

His fingers crept under my shirt, finding flesh and digging into my back. His hips lifted, and his cock caressed me.

"You're mine." He drew me closer. "Once I eat your sweet pussy, I'm not letting you go."

"I wouldn't expect anything less." I kissed him again, harder and faster.

His tongue swept with mine in a duel. He'd already worked open the cord on my vest along with the buttons on my shirt, then slipped them off my shoulders. Breaking away, he lowered his gaze to my chest, his eyes grinning. He grasped my breasts, his palms grazing my nipples.

"Lie back for me, gorgeous."

I lay at his mercy. He supported my back while running his lips ever so gently across my puckered nub. Arousal thrummed through me with rekindled urgency, titillating in the pit of my stomach. Taking his time, he took a nipple into his mouth, suckling on it. I groaned as fire sparked me from the inside-out.

I rocked against his hardness, and watching him moan and

enjoy me undid me. He licked my boobs, making them bounce, and he continued to do so, covering me in his saliva.

"Fuck, you smell so delicious." Up on his feet in a heartbeat, he set me on my wobbly legs. "I need to see all of you." He hooked his thumbs over the top of my trousers and underwear, tearing them down my legs, unbuttoning nothing. His strength stunned me, yet I still stepped out of my clothes, holding his shoulders for support.

Everything in me awakened with a desperation to be taken. Instead, Kahlo lowered to the floor, sitting with his back to the couch. He tilted his head back on the sofa cushion and took my wrist.

"Kiss me with your pink pussy. Sit on my face, Babycakes. Let me drown in your scent, in your juices."

Buzzing with excitement, I climbed up, one knee on either side of his head. I gripped the back of the couch and couldn't believe I was doing this.

"Fuck yes." He clasped my hips and pulled me lower.

The moment his tongue swept across my inner lips, I exploded with moans. I scrunched my toes as his fingers gripped my ass, and he sucked and licked every inch between my legs. Hearing a man like Kahlo get switched on by laying between my legs roused the inferno raging within. I was sure I'd explode.

Euphoria took hold of me, and when his tongue flicked my clit, I roared with a scream. His sounds were insatiable, his mouth intoxicating with no respite. I rocked myself over his face, my whole body stirring with shivers, my pebbled nipples aching in all the right ways.

When he drove my hips off his face, I moaned in protest, staring down at him.

"Not yet. I'm almost there."

He grinned, enjoying his teasing.

"I know you are." He moved out from under me, and I moved aside, but his palm was already on my back, sliding downward. He pushed aside my hair. "Stay there for me. I need to get you ready."

"For what? I'm so prepared."

"Bend over for me and show me your ass."

When his thumb traced down the crack of my rear, I gasped for air, suddenly super excited. "Oh, this is new."

"You're telling me your ass is still a virgin?" A finger swirled around my ass while others slipped lower.

I blushed, but right then, I was so turned on, I didn't care.

"Is that a problem?"

"Nope. Just more preparation if you're willing."

"You bet."

He covered my ass with his wetness, then inserted a finger into each of my entrances. I arched my back and groaned loudly from the vibrating pleasure swirling through me. He pumped into me faster, and I cried out.

"Oh, hell… feels amazing."

"You're so wet, Babycakes." He inserted two digits into my pussy, his thumb still in my rear, pumping into me so hard, I rocked back and forth. When a third pushed into me, I exploded on the inside. I convulsed, shaking so hard, I couldn't tell where I started and where I ended.

Kahlo withdrew, and I collapsed onto the couch, clutching my thighs tighter. He hugged me from behind, running his fingers down my stomach.

"You're killing me." I writhed against him, sweat pooling between us.

He walked us to the bed, laid me on my stomach, then rolled me over. He pried my knees apart.

"Touch yourself. Show me how you flick that pussy."

Gulping for air and buzzing as I still floated on my last orgasm, I watched him drag his shirt up and over his head. I slid my hand down my stomach, over the small amount of drenched hair, and to my inner folds.

Kahlo's gaze never left mine as he stepped out of his boots and dropped his pants. Standing there naked, he took his huge cock in his fist, stroking it once. Heavens, he was massive. And yes, no wonder I needed preparation to take him into me.

Clasping my ankles, he raised my legs up against his chest as he closed in. He grabbed my hips and lifted me to meet his dick with ease. His tip pressed forward, gliding into me, and I tensed.

"Don't keep me out. Relax. I won't hurt you."

With a deep inhale, I let myself fall under his spell and opened myself for him. He slithered in deeper, stretching me. I fisted the bedsheets, groaning, loving the sentinel of him opening me. When he patted my clit with a finger, I drowned under his lovemaking. He thrust forward, and I cried out with anticipation. Sliding in and out in slow motion, he rubbed me so deliciously on the inside that my libido twisted, strangling me with desire. The agony of needing more, the heightening surge of sexual thrill, escalated.

He held on to my hips and hammered into me faster, picking up his pace. My world trembled as I moaned with each thrust.

"Fuck me like you own me." The words came out because I wanted him to take me every which way.

Unrelenting, he pounded into me even faster. The slaps were songs to my ears, and I lost myself in a world of carnal desire. I jolted back and forth over him, my insides growing tighter, more tense. And at once, he pulled out, leaving me empty and barren.

"What are you doing?"

His sexy laughter had me following him as he climbed onto the bed and laid on his back. "Come," he demanded, and gods, who would have thought having him control me would turn me on to no end?

I rolled over and crawled toward him as he lay on the bed on his back, his dick erect and sticking up, waiting for me. I slid my breasts over his thighs, pressing his hardness between my cleavage, eliciting a deep rumble. I buzzed all over at his reaction. On hands and knees, I stared down at him and kissed him, tasting myself on him, needing to have him. The groan in his throat was the sexiest sound I'd ever heard.

When I came up for air, he smirked, tugging on my nipples, and I softened as the earlier arousal rose so fast, it stunned me.

"Get on top, but face away from me," he said. "I want to take you reverse tiger-style."

"Is that a real thing, or did you just make it up?" I turned away, driving my hair off the bed and climbing over his hips.

"It's real to me."

I positioned a leg over him before sitting on his shaft. "Shit, you're massive."

"And you love it."

"Yes, I do!" Leaning forward, I held on to his knees and raised myself up and down over his cock, my wetness coating the insides of my thighs. From his spot, he massaged my inner walls, skimming something inside me, provoking a new sensation.

Riding him quicker, I caressed myself on him. He kneaded my rear, stroking my other hole, and it wasn't long before he slid a finger inside, then two. The tightness only drove me faster toward the edge.

"That's it," he purred. "Fuck me hard, Babycakes."

Sweat dripped down my back, and I couldn't get enough as I rode him. He wriggled under me and slipped out. I readjusted to reclaim him, but his tip nudged my other entrance instead, and I groaned. Excited and ready.

He opened my cheeks and, in slow motion, pressed himself into my ass, the sensation covering me with excited goosebumps. I panted, loving how much the pain turned me on, the widening. He rocked my hips back and forth.

"Kahlo, I can't hold back anymore." The more he thrust me, the more I shuddered, and at once, an orgasm swooned within me, claiming me at the core.

He grunted behind me as he pulsed within me. Together, we soared with pleasure. I clasped him tight, thrashing as excitement burst through me.

At last, he pulled out of me, and I collapsed on the bed, heaving for air, shivers wracking my body.

Kahlo shifted about on the bed from behind me, the mattress bouncing until he joined me and drew me into his arms.

"You've just broken me," he whispered in my ear. "I can never be with any other after that."

And those words alone had me smiling so wide, my cheeks

hurt. Nothing else mattered in those moments of utter bliss except my determination to embrace the three men and never push them away again. I had to show them they meant the world to me.

CHAPTER 22

I woke with a smile on my face after a mesmerizing night of sex with Kahlo, but as sleep faded, reality pushed to the front of my mind. And the ache in my gut returned. I should have stopped Reed and Gage from going to Tritonia, should have made it clearer they weren't to give up anything. But hindsight was a fucking bitch, and no matter how much I cried, it didn't change the cold, hard facts. I needed to get myself into gear and get up. I turned toward Kahlo, but he wasn't in bed, only Gingernuts sleeping in a ball on his pillow. I patted him, but he grumbled and ducked his head deeper under his paw.

Was Kahlo out searching for Reed, or had they returned? I climbed out of bed, pushing my hair out of the way, and the sexy ache between my legs reminded me of Kahlo and how I craved to crawl into his arms. Perhaps I should have been out in the streets looking for Reed, but with the way he'd taken off, I wasn't so sure he wanted to see me. Our situation had been complicated enough; now, it was wrapped in barbed wire.

Except there was no more sitting back. I had to confront him, eventually. The guilt sat heavily in my chest. I stood and made my way to the bathroom, where I spotted a bowl of food and milk near the couch for Gingernuts. Kahlo was a keeper.

Once I got dressed, hair plaited and curled up into my bag, I threw it over my shoulder and marched out into the corridor. Nerves twirled in my stomach as I reached the next door. I knocked, but when no response came, I rushed downstairs. *Please let them have found Reed.*

I skipped down the steps and curved around the banister toward voices in the main tavern area. The place was mostly empty except for three men at a main table near the window drenched in sunlight. My men. I bounced on my toes at seeing Reed. He may not have wanted to talk to me, but fuck it, I was just happy he'd come back.

Pancakes with berries, bacon, and porridge bowls filled their table. Gage spotted me first and waved me over to sit on the long bench next to him. Across from him sat Kahlo and Reed. Both glanced my way, Kahlo smiling with a confidence that promised to pull me into his lap and keep me there forever. While Reed offered me a simple smile, enough to give me hope that he'd speak to me.

Gage stole a kiss as I plonked down next to him, and Kahlo's leg grazed mine under the table. "Morning, beautiful."

I grinned, adoring how they both watched me with so much admiration in their eyes, but my concern lay with Reed. So I addressed him right off, unable to sit there pretending otherwise.

"Reed, listen, I'm so sorry. I-I mean, you didn't have to give up your mane for me." I squirmed in my seat, the words not flowing as easily as I'd hoped.

"Don't—" he began, his brow furrowed.

"No, please hear me out. All three of you have come into my life, and I never imagined myself falling so hard for each of you. Hell, when I was younger, I used to beg the universe to send me a knight in shining armor. Someone to help me. But instead, she blessed me with the three of you." My throat dried, and I picked up the glass Gage had filled with orange juice. I gulped half down. "For too long, I believed the only way I kept others safe was to keep them at arm's length. Then, Reed, you showed me what a coward I've been. I stayed safe, thinking I protected those around me, but all I did was conceal my affection. If I'd been more open, then you would have understood how much each of you means to me. How if I lost any of you, I'd wish for the world to open and swallow me. Maybe then, you may have reconsidered sacrificing your lion and would have known I would never want you to do that." I finished the juice, unsure if I'd expressed myself well or whether I'd just rambled.

The men studied me, Kahlo chewing on bacon while Gage topped off my juice.

Reed, on the other side, also watched me, his posture stiff, clearly ready to argue his point. "That's where you're wrong," he finally said.

Gage piped up. "I'm with Reed on this one."

Kahlo nodded in agreement, his mouth full of food.

Of course, they'd stick together, as they'd done so ever since the trip to Tritonia, and I loved that they got along. But this ganging up against me would drive me insane.

"If you'd let your walls down earlier, I would have given up my mane quicker," Reed said, his eyes narrowing with that stubborn look. "I don't care if that pisses you off."

Biting my tongue, I gave him the chance to talk.

"I mean, I don't regret my sacrifice when I know it gives you a fighting chance to escape the gargoyle. Faye was returning for you, and if we'd sat back and done nothing, we might never have gotten the chance to protect you again." His voice was hard yet caring because the reasoning came from his heart.

"You had no right." I raised my voice. "I didn't want you sacrificing what's crucial to you. What about your pride? Will you lose them? What if you need to transform to protect your sister against other shifters?" Lava twisted within me.

He squared his shoulders. "I had every right. It was mine to do with as I pleased."

Fire lit up my veins, and I slid to the edge of my seat. "But not for me! I'm a nobody, and—"

"Never say that," Kahlo growled. "You're the first person I've met who brings me to life. For years, I've wandered alone, convinced I didn't deserve a family. I wasn't good enough because no one wanted a lone tiger. Even two tigresses I tracked down craved a leader who had a large pride, so they crossbred with other shifters rather than being with me. But when I'm with you, you carry no judgment in your eyes, and you see me for me. So, if someone asked me to give up my shifter side to help you, I'd do it in a heartbeat. It's about what's inside that counts."

Gage's hand was on my thigh. "I'd give up my dragon wings for you, honey. In fact, I offered them to Vanore, but she didn't want them."

Rawness spread through me. "You'd all sacrifice so much for me? Even after I drove each of you away? Shit, I'm like the worst person in the world."

"You entered the mansion at the risk of getting caught, and you were. It could have gone so much worse, yet you took that chance for me," Reed said. "So, what I did was my choice, and don't you dare hold yourself responsible."

I shifted in my seat, unable to get comfortable. "But last night you—"

Reed cut me off. "Last night, I was dealing with the outcome. I won't lie and say it's easy having lost what I lost, but I don't blame you."

Yet guilt cloaked around me, cutting into me. If it weren't for me, he wouldn't have done it. Studying the men with their strong expressions told me they weren't backing down in this argument. Still, it didn't sit right with me with one inch, but even if we argued until we were blue in the face, it wouldn't change the situation. Reed had given up his lion. His pride and sister remained kidnapped. The albino psycho and I were linked. Those were the issues to deal with.

My throat thickened, and the words struggled to come. I stretched across the table and grasped Reed's wrist.

"What you did for me was fucking stupid but also heroic, and I'm left in awe that you gave up so much. I love how much you care, and my admiration for you is endless. But once we find your pride and sister, I'll do everything in my power to get back your lion."

His eyes widened. "No—"

I waved a palm in his direction. "It's my decision, and I have every right to do so." My mouth curled upward, and it didn't take long for him to follow suit. "Until then"—I grabbed a piece of bacon and a slice of buttered bread—"no more secrets between us. Understand? We talk about everything."

They all nodded in reply.

The smoked meat was divine, and I was tired of talking about shit that still bugged me. But I meant every single word. I would visit Vanore and give her anything to return Reed's lion side, and I'd deal with any consequences of that then. For right now, I had to believe I'd be able to give Reed what he'd lost. Otherwise, I couldn't smile again.

"Speaking of being open..." Gage's voice brimmed with mirth. "I'd like to know what happened in your room last night. There were some interesting sounds coming out of there." He eyed me.

My mouth gaped open, and I sucked in a breath. Did they listen to me screaming like a siren from Kahlo ravaging me? My face was on fire while Kahlo puffed out his chest. He had his arms in front of his chest, as if he were steering a carriage.

"Well, I had her ass—"

"Shut up!" I tossed a piece of bread at him, which he caught and ate. "That's not the kind of sharing I'm talking about." Curling my fists in my lap, I was unsure what killed me more— the men discussing my sex marathon last night in front of me or the tingle in the apex of my thighs sparking alight, well aware Reed and Gage would get off on the update.

Bet you wouldn't complain, not after what you did last night.

Heavens, even my subconscious had me blushing.

Kahlo broke into a chuckle, deep down from his gut, then blew me a kiss. "Come on, Babycakes. They ought to know I took your virginity!"

My face must have reddened like a tomato because I felt hot.

"What are you talking about?" Gage blurted out. "I've been with..." He glanced at me and cocked an eyebrow. "Oh, I see. Honey, you're into the whole backdoor thing?" He waggled his eyebrows.

I gritted my teeth before stuffing food into my mouth. Yep, time to drown my embarrassment by gorging. I might even pass out from a food coma. Yay.

Reed smirked my way. "I'd definitely be interested in hearing more about last night. But first, we need to get moving. I need to find my sister and pride members."

"I know a friend of my dad living here in Crosswind. Yesterday, Gage and I visited her, but no one was home. I want to return there, as the woman used to love cats and maybe she can look after Gingernuts for a short time. She might have insight into the lion shifter who attacked the locals. Where he came from. Anything to help us."

"Sounds like as good a place as any to start." Gage pawed the fried meat dumplings and ate two without pause.

"While you do that, I'm heading out to visit a lion pride nearby," Reed said. "Kahlo, you with me?"

He nodded, and Gage nudged me. "Looks like you're stuck with me."

And just like that, I was ready to dive in and take down the assholes who'd played God with my life.

CHAPTER 23

"*Y*ou sure that woman lives here?" Gage fingered a wreath made of twigs on the front door.

I held back along the cobblestone footpath in the front yard, my bag on my back holding my hair, and scanned the sides of the house. I spotted a passage to our right and headed that way, Gage following and carrying Gingernuts in his bag.

The narrow corridor flanked by the stone house and a lofty fence led us to the rear of the property. The land opened outward into a garden wonderland. Rows of carrots, lettuce, turnips, and many more vegetables filled gardens in every direction, and farther yet stood a wooden shed with the door open. An oversized oak was behind the shed, a tire swing hanging from a branch. Someone had to live here by the look of those gardens.

"Hello! Remy, are you home?" I asked.

In response, a black cat slinked out from the shed, tail high and rubbing itself against the wall. An elderly woman with a green apron over a yellow dress emerged, her eyebrows raised. She met my gaze and studied Gage.

"Can I help you both?" Her voice was stern yet familiar and welcoming.

I sauntered toward her, my hands tucked into my pockets to

appear less threatening. "My name is Elliana, and you probably don't remember me, but you used to know my father, Thomas. You used to call him 'Tom Cat.'" I'd only met Remy a few times; she'd always roar with laughter at Dad's jokes. Heavens, what I wouldn't give to have those moments back. I swallowed the rock in my throat.

Her eyes wandered upward as she tapped her chin, her silvery hair waving in the breeze over her shoulders. "Yes, I remember him. He would try to sweet talk me, so I'd make him my tea cake. He'd say it was the best in all of Haven Realm." She laughed. "He was a charmer. And I remember you, but my, how you've grown."

Remy ambled forward, staring up at me, as she had to be at just under five feet. "How's your father? You both vanished, and I never saw you after."

At first, the words refused to come. I'd said them so many times, but looking into Remy's warming eyes reminded me of the wonderful man I missed so much.

"I'm sorry." My voice shook. "But my father has passed." I tried to smile, but holding it together grew harder when Remy clasped her chest and stared at me with glistening eyes.

"Dear, I'm sorry. He was a wonderful man."

"Thanks."

Gage approached us, offering me the distraction I yearned for, but it was Gingernuts who made his presence known with a long howl.

Remy gushed, reaching down for him, scratching his head. "Who is this?"

"Gingern…" I wasn't sure I could say his name to this elderly woman. "This is Ginger. He's a noisy boy often."

"And I'm Gage, the non-noisy one."

Remy laughed and patted Gage on the arm. "Come inside for a spot of tea."

By the time we'd settled down on a couch, we sipped chamomile tea. I released Gingernuts out of his bag, and he wasted no time running around the house, checking out every corner. He wasn't your typical scared feline.

"We're here to ask for information and perhaps your help," I began while Gage focused on doling a heap of cream on his scone, clearly making himself at home.

"Dear, your father was a gentle soul who'd always bring me a gift each time he visited. So I'll assist in any way I can." Her smile was contagious, and I suspected there had been more going on between her and Dad. But it was adorable. I wished more than ever that he was still alive and had time to make a future with Remy. Maybe I'd be able to experience a real family.

"I heard from folk in town that a lion shifter attacked a few locals," I said.

"Oh." Her hands clasped to her chest, and her white hair trembled as she nodded. "Tragic. The farmers had been hunting pheasants when a white lion with horns attacked them. Both farmers escaped with grave injuries. But we've had no attacks in town for so long."

"It's probably best if everyone stays in town for a while," Gage added.

Remy sipped from her cup. "The last time something like that happened, I was a child. A great battle had broken out between the lions in a local pride. It was horrendous." The cup quivered in her hands. "Their fight spilled into the town. People died, as did lion shifters. I remember the ground littered with bodies, the air ripe with death. But there was one beast, white as snow, who survived. Blood splattered his mane and face as he limped off."

"Do you think it's the same one who attacked the farmers?" Gage asked as he stuffed his mouth with half a scone.

She shrugged. "The recent attacks were by a creature with a scorpion tail, but the animal I'd seen all those years ago was just an albino lion. So angry and out of control." Her lips thinned as she shook her head in disapproval.

I exchanged glances with Gage, and I'd have bet we were thinking similar thoughts. It was the same fucking bastard.

"Did you ever find out why he killed his pride?"

"I've no idea, child, but after that day, I never saw him again. I hope whoever attacked those men doesn't return to the city. The council is talking about building a big wall-locked gate around this town now."

"It's sad it's come to that." I gulped my tea as Gingernuts brushed past my legs, then Remy's. She bent down and picked him up.

"For someone with only three legs, you sure run around a lot." She snuggled him, and there was no protest. I eyed him while he was busy getting hugged, but I knew the truth... He was pissed because I'd taken his long hair.

"I have a favor to ask. Could you look after Ginger for a week, maybe two, while I finish a few errands? I'll definitely be back for him, as I love him too much, and we've been through so much together."

He strolled across the table to me. Oh, had he finally forgiven me? I embraced him and kissed the top of his head.

"Of course, dear." Her voice softened, and her eyes glistened. "In honor of your dad, I'd do anything. Helps that I love cats." She smiled, leaving me feeling calm and at home.

"Did you hear that?" Warmth soaked right into my bones, knowing Gingernuts would be cared for. I ruffled his cheeks, fluffing them. "You'll stay here for a short while, and I'll be back. Be good, and bring no lizards into the house, okay?" He head-butted me in the arm.

"Thanks for your time." Gage was already on his feet and collecting our cups and saucers before taking them to the kitchen.

I followed suit and already missed Gingernuts. We hadn't been apart since I first lured him into the tower. We slept every day in my bed, snuggled up. We shared meals and played games. My chest constricted.

"Take care of him. He means everything to me. I'll be back as soon as I can." Remy nodded, and I hugged her, her small frame fragile but comforting. Thank you so much." When I broke away, she hobbled into the kitchen and pulled out a bag of cat treats, shaking the contents. Gingernuts was there in a flash.

Gage took my elbow and led me outside as I caught one last glimpse of my cat gorging on food. "He'll be fine," he said.

"I know. I'll just miss him." In no time, we left behind the residential part of town, making our way to the tavern, hoping Reed and Kahlo had returned.

People filled the streets in the shopping district with storefronts packed with merchandise, such as dried meats, ducks, and an array of miniature cakes. That one had me gawking. I reached out for Gage, but I found only empty air. He'd strolled into a store with herbs and crystals. I trailed after him.

Incense filled the store, and the array of skull-shaped goblets caught my attention. Why would anyone want to drink out of a skull? Maybe it was a joke gift for someone who had everything. Across the store, Gage chatted with the sales clerk. So, I took my time and looked around the store, investigating the crystals, the bath salts, and an array of other goodies. Eventually, Gage nudged me and nodded for us to leave.

Once we left the spiritual store behind, he smirked. "I got you a gift."

"Oh, really? What is it?"

He offered me the parcel, and I didn't waste time ripping it open to reveal a glass container the size of my palm filled with a pink liquid. I swished it around in the jar, and it bubbled. "What is it?"

"Shampoo."

I cut him a glare. "Are you fucking kidding me?"

He laughed, and he tossed an arm around me, drawing me closer. With a kiss on my nose, he said, "Maybe you should ask me what sort of shampoo it is."

"Okay, spill."

His eyes squinted. "The woman at the store does spells, and I asked her if she had something to help weaken hair so we can cut it. I told her there was a spell on your hair, and she made a quick concoction and gave me this."

I stared at Gage, giving him my best are you-fucking-insane look. "You realize my hair is a curse, and this perfumed-infused liquid soap won't undo that. But at the same time, I love the thought." Up on my tiptoes, I kissed his sweet lips.

"Let's go to the tavern and wash your hair. What have you got to lose?"

People waded past us, and it felt as if I missed something. He'd never asked to wash my hair before. "Are you trying to get me wet and naked?"

He winked my way and snaked an arm around my waist. "Let's get to our room quick. I swear my balls are blue." He stepped close behind me, my ass against his hardness, and I smirked.

"You've got a dilemma."

His mouth was on my ear. "Wrong. You do if we don't return soon. I'll be dragging you into a side lane and eating your pussy no matter who sees us."

My libido awakened with a start at his sexy promise. We rushed through the crowds to our tavern.

You didn't get enough, hey?

"Keep quiet. You're just jealous," I mumbled under my breath as Gage opened the door to the second bedroom, where he'd spend the night. This one was a similar size and layout to mine, except in here, the windows overlooked the ocean of residential homes instead of the storefronts.

"You know there's hot running water?" He peeled off his shirt, revealing a muscular chest and abs my palms tingled to touch.

"There's a lot of hair to wash, so I hope you're ready to work hard."

He was at my side, taking the bag off my back and freeing my locks.

"Honey, I'll be working you hard... don't you worry about that."

I wasn't sure how I felt about this, except the tightness rolling between my legs had me eager for whatever Gage had planned. He guided me into the bathroom and grabbed the metal lever near the tub, then pumped the lever up and down. Water gushed out from the faucet in spurts, splashing everything in sight. I laughed out loud before stripping down to my underwear, a white camisole, to avoid wetting my clothes. Lukewarm water half-filled the small tub, but I had no intention of getting in there and instead dragged my hair into the bathroom.

Gage's gaze sailed down my body and back, his eyes drowning in ecstasy as he licked his lips. "You're so beautiful, honey." He marched into the main room and collected the shampoo I'd left on the bed. In the meantime, I wet my hair starting from the end, working my way up.

"So, I'll lather," he stated and without waiting for my response, got on his knees behind me. He added the soap to the parts I'd wet, working them into a lathery mass. In all honestly, I'd only washed all my hair once, and it had taken two days, then another two to dry. So, I vowed to never try it again. Most days, I scrubbed the hair at my skull only, but I combed it weekly to remove the knots. I bent over the tub and scooped water over my tresses.

"If you're going to stick your ass in the air, you need to get naked," Gage teased.

I glanced over my shoulder at him, his arms covered in soap, but the bulge in his pants grabbed my attention. Call me horny, but having him study me with such sexiness had me clenching my thighs together. So, I did him a favor and pushed the underwear down my legs before kicking them aside. Then I turned my back to him, my legs apart as I bent over, my hand splashing about in the bath.

My skin tingled with my daringness and anticipation.

I didn't even sense him move, but I sensed his heat behind me, and the moment two fingers stroked my pussy, I melted. Gripping the edge of the tube, I spread my legs wider, and he didn't waste a moment to drive his fingers into me, fast and hard. I cried out.

"So fucking wet and all mine," he growled.

I wriggled, drowning in the euphoria shuddering through me. Within moments, his cock replaced his fingers. He pressed into me, spreading me with powerful thrusts that left me breathless. I screamed with pleasure, needing him as if my life depended on it.

He shoved my shirt up my back, and his palms found my

breasts, plucking at my pointed nipples. He never stopped pumping into me as he drew me upright and walked me toward the wall.

"Scream my name," he demanded as he jammed me up against the wall, my cheek pressed to the cold tiles, and his long cock thrust into me, rubbing me raw. So primal, I couldn't get enough of being dominated by these men. To have them control me, worship every inch of me.

His fingers dug into my hips as he pulled my ass toward him.

"Gage, oh fucking hell, you feel incredible." I drew in short, sharp breaths.

He drove into me so fast, I could no longer feel my legs, just him inside me, sliding in and out, opening me up with each plunge.

"Don't you dare stop!" Pinned beneath him, I rode the ecstasy tidal wave, moaning, never wanting the moment to end. I rocked my hips, meeting every slap. My nipples hardened, and a vibration thrummed within me, rising with a sudden spike. All at once, I tumbled over into an orgasmic bliss, shaking me at the core. The climax struck so damn fast, my entire world shuddered.

"That's it." Gage's groan had me quivering with elation. "Squeeze me with that sweet pussy."

Shattered, I trembled all over as juices flowed down my inner thighs while Gage pulsed inside me. Spent, I collapsed against the wall, but he collected me into his arms, wrapping me and bathing me in kisses down my neck.

"Fuck, Elliana. I love you."

My pulse banged so hard at hearing the most incredible three words. I turned around in his arms to face him, but the ends of my hair rose upward, curled into spears. Gage's mouth dropped open at the sight while terror jammed into my heart. What the hell had the shampoo done to my locks?

CHAPTER 24

KAHLO

"That was a waste of time." I nudged Reed as we passed crowds of people on the streets, standing around and blocking the path as they chatted with friends. "The local pride dispersed and moved away ages ago. I bet that decision wasn't of their own doing but due to someone forcing them." I side-stepped a man selling apples in the center of the road.

"Bet you're fucking right," Reed agreed. "But we got a name for the albino lion, which is a start."

"White Venom! Who the fuck calls themselves that?" I mimicked pulling my dick and gained a frown from a nearby older woman, so I dropped my arm and looked away. "A wanker, that's who."

"Yeah, but it tells us a lot. He's an arrogant son of a bitch who believes he's untouchable. He needs to show others he's better than them. That means he wants revenge for something."

I cut Reed a hard stare. "You got all the from a try-hard name?" My attention fell on a flower shop. Gorgeous white flowers mixed with pink ones filled the front window, and my thoughts soared to my Elliana. She'd been on my mind non-stop since our time together. "Give me a moment." I rushed into the store and bought the biggest bunch of flowers before heading back outside.

Reed arched an eyebrow. "You've got it bad for her, too?"

"Man, it's like she's tapped into my veins, and everything makes me think of her. The sun reminds me of her hair... even these flowers smell like her, and every time I hear laughter, I turn, hoping to see her. Hell, I've never felt this before, but I'm not embarrassed to admit I'm smitten. She deserves so much more than these, but I'll make it up to her once we deal with White Venom." I chuckled. "I can't even keep a straight face while saying that name."

Reed smirked, but I noticed his stiff demeanor.

"Listen," I said. "Hope you're not pissed that I spent the night with her last night."

"Nah, man," he said. "I told you that before. If we're sharing, I want it to be with you. Plus, I'll spend time with Elliana soon enough. I'm too worried about my sister right now, you know." His hands curled into fists at his sides. "It kills me to know she's out there under a spell, treated as a slave, or gods know what. I want to rip out the fucker's spine and shove it up his ass for harming my pride. For daring to harm Elliana."

"Shit, yeah." Without another word, we made our way through the town and finally reached Old Reindeer Hunt Tavern. Upstairs, I unlocked the room I'd shared with Elliana and found it empty. Nothing was out of place, and the bed remained unmade. Unease slithered through my gut. "Elliana?"

A thump hit the wall from next door, and my heart leaped into my mouth. I rushed into the corridor, Reed on my heels, and burst inside the room next door.

At first, I couldn't make sense of what I was staring at. I swung my head in every direction.

Blonde hair spread across the walls, ceiling, and floor. At the ends of the hair, they coiled into a dozen cords, moving, slithering around as if they were snakes.

And in the middle of the room stood Elliana on the bed, deliciously naked, and her tresses covering her breasts and across her hips. What had happened to her? Was it the witch trapping her?

"Hi there! It may not look it, but we're all right, really." She waved, her voice shaky and her face blushing as if caught red-handed doing the dirty, except this was something else. "Oh, are those flowers for me? They're gorgeous." A lock of hair snapped toward me. I recoiled, but the prehensile hair struck toward my wrist and wrapped around the bouquet, then ripped it from my grip.

"Hey, give them back!" I cried out.

It carried them over to Elliana, placing them in her grasp as if she were the queen of crazy. She smelled them and shrugged nervously.

"What the fuck's going on?" I hissed, my hands curled into fists. "Is the witch here? Did she hurt you?"

Reed stepped deeper into the room when the door behind us snapped shut, locking us inside.

"No witch. But funny story," Elliana said. "Gage bought me a supposed magical shampoo to help make my hair brittle and cuttable."

Gage laughed from our left, and I turned to find him plastered to the wall, golden hair pinning him there with only his face showing. "My mistake. Turns out it brought her hair to life, and now it does what she asks it to do, except there's a small glitch."

"And that is?" I scanned the room, wondering how in the world we were getting out of this.

"It seems to misinterpret what I ask it to do," Elliana smirked. "So I asked it to go back to normal and be limp, but that seemed to mean spreading itself across the room. Gage thinks it's trying to dry itself, which might mean it will stop moving after a while. But it's anyone's guess. So, we're just waiting, you know."

"This is some fucking weird shit," Reed said, his wide eyes glued on Elliana's nudity, his chest heaving with each breath.

Elliana sighed. "I say we stay relaxed and calm."

Which was close to impossible, given I was both turned on at seeing my beautiful love naked but disturbed by the hair with its own mind. I couldn't refocus my attention away from Elliana's gorgeous, dark blue eyes and the way the bridge of her petite nose scrunched up each time she worried. Her curvy form, tiny hips, and… Man, where was the wind to blow away the strands? I could stare at her naked for an eternity.

Two tentacles curled up my legs, rushing over my groin. I tensed and kicked it away.

"Oh, I wouldn't do that," Gage cried out. "It doesn't like being pushed around."

More of the slithering serpents surged toward me, and Reed backed away into a corner. Great help he was. I punched and bucked, but the restraints tightened around my wrists and ankles. "Fuck! Make it stop!" They dragged me across the room and curled around my chest, lifting me and shoving my back against the wall.

I thrashed and fought, but I might as well have been battling a giant. Slammed against the wall, hair swarmed over me like insects, covering every inch of me, and with only my head free. "Let me down!"

"Told you," Gage said.

"Sorry," Elliana said, wincing. "I'm trying to work out how to control it, but I figured I'd wait until the hair dries. Maybe then the spell will wear off."

"Reed? Do something!" I yelled, the restraints keeping me glued to the wall. Across from me, Gage was in the same predicament.

"Any suggestions?" Reed asked, scanning the room.

Elliana shrugged. "This is new territory for me, but let me try something." She shut her eyes and mumbled something under her breath. Was that her asking the hair to behave or talking to her alter ego?

At once, the blonde strips over her body fell away, revealing her perky breasts, flat stomach, and a small mound of light hair between her legs. I cheered, apparently out loud since everyone turned toward me.

"What? As if all of you didn't want that to happen?"

"I sure did." Gage wolf-whistled.

Reed grunted, and I twisted my head to find him caught up in the snake hair, throwing punches to no effect. None of us were going anywhere, but on the bright side, while we waited, we had the best eye candy in the world.

But instead of getting tied to the wall, the hair shoved Reed toward Elliana. He stumbled forward, and the locks scooped him up and placed him on the bed. Both stood there, threads of hair attached to each of them as if they were puppets, and we were about to watch an orchestrated show.

"What did you tell it to do?" Reed asked.

Her cheeks reddened, and she shyly looked down.

"Oh, you dirty girl," Gage called out. "You thought of getting it on with Reed, didn't you?"

"Is that how it works?" I asked. "Because I think all of us at once."

Gage piped in. "Hey, tiger man. Already told Reed I was into watching, but not joining in on male action."

I glared at Gage. "What are you yapping about?"

"Shut up," Elliana hissed.

"What did you ask the hair to do?" Reed repeated. The hair holding him tore at his shirt and pants, unbuttoning his clothes. He didn't fight, simply stared at Elliana, and all I could think was, *bring it on.*

"I told it to release all three of you, but then you popped into my head along with your promise." She cringed, but Reed reached out and lifted her chin with a finger.

"I meant every word." His shirt got torn off his back and his pants pulled down. Okay, we were about to get to the action.

Her lips pinched. "Yeah, but I couldn't stop my thoughts, and I pictured you naked." She lowered her voice. "With me and you doing stuff."

"Yes!" Gage yelled.

I flinched from his sudden outburst, my muscles tighter than my balls. "What the hell is your problem?" I hissed.

"They'll do the nasty and we get front-row seats. Tell me you don't want to see this?"

My blood soared, and my pants constricted at the thought. Reed was like my brother, but at the core, seeing my Babycakes taken by someone I trusted had me hard, and I needed this.

"I'm in."

"This isn't a show," Reed responded. "Maybe shut your eyes."

"Fuck that!" Gage laughed. "Now, if we're trapped here, at least get it on already."

Elliana collected Reed into her arms, both naked and pressed together, his arms gliding around her silky white skin. But in that same instant, the hair curled around their bodies.

She writhed. "Stop. I command you to end this."

All the hair slackened, cascading to the floor, along with Gage and me. I hit the floor. Elliana broke out in a laugh, and Reed right along with her. Both lay on the bed covered in blonde locks, staring only at each other. I didn't need a poke in the back to know where this was going. Reed's first time with Elliana should be alone without an audience—as much as I'd love to watch. But we weren't locked in place anymore. So we'd give him alone time. I snatched Gage by the elbow and hauled him to the door.

He frowned. With a sigh and his shoulders curled forward, he followed me outside into the corridor, and I shut the door.

"I need a fucking stiff drink after that," Gage blurted out.

"Not sure I'd use the word 'stiff' right now." I glanced down at my pants but laughed at how ridiculous the situation had become.

"I should have told Elliana the shampoo came with side effects." Gage clapped my back. "The shop assistant said it sometimes made the user horny. Didn't realize that meant her hair tapped into her thoughts and her lust."

Once we reached downstairs, I headed to the bar and took a seat, Gage by my side. I tried not to let my mind wander to the pleasures going on upstairs. Elliana was still mine, and I'd have her again.

"Makes sense her hair would pick Reed," said Gage. "He hasn't been with her yet. Plus, it wasn't as if it would select me since I'd just finished banging her."

"You did?" I twisted in my seat, adjusting myself. "Let me order drinks, then talk."

CHAPTER 25

"Oh heavens, Reed. Yes, right there." I threw my head back on the pillow as his magical fingers slid between my legs, gliding over my slickness. Ever since Gage had washed my hair and pinned me against the wall, I hadn't been able to stop the insatiable sexual hunger chewing on my libido. As much as I tried to control my thoughts, they kept slipping back to sex—me getting fucked, taken by all three men. So, my hair responded, holding on to them. And I couldn't say how horny I felt out loud because I was too damn embarrassed.

Now, with Reed lying next to me in bed, both of us stripped of clothes and my hair mostly dry, I needed the itch scratched before I detonated. He kneaded his fingers into my back as he dipped his mouth to my chest.

The flat of his tongue found my nipples, licking me before gently gnawing on my pebbled nubs. My skin pinpricked at the arousal coursing through me, but when he drew away, I groaned.

"Why are you stopping?"

He climbed off the bed, and my gaze settled on his erection.

"Hell, are all shifters built like bulls?"

His laughter tickled me, and he grabbed his cock, wide and long, the tip coated in pre-cum. His balls were tight, so why was he far away?

Fire consumed me, scorching me right in the apex of my legs, and I widened them. "Touch me."

"You're so swollen and sexy." But instead of reaching for me, he picked up a handful of my hair from the floor before leaning over me. His heat danced over me, and I moaned beneath him, kissing his chest. He took my wrists and tied each to the metal bedhead. "We're doing this my way."

I trembled at his dominance, squeezing my thighs together, but he *tsked*.

"No, that won't do at all." He bent my legs and prodded them open, pivoting my hips upward. Opening me to the nth degree, revealing every inch of my vulnerability, I panted for air. With my hair, he tied my bent legs in place, looping the hair to the bedhead.

"You okay with this?" he asked.

Having him stare down at me broke down all my hesitations —every single wall. Something about my pussy spread wide and being on display while Reed studied me had me buzzing with need. The muscles in my arms and legs ached slightly, but I didn't care when I floated with desire. He tugged on his cock several times before switching off the light and bathing us in complete darkness.

"Um, hello?" I couldn't see a thing, yet I lay exposed, and I thrummed with excitement, remembering Kahlo's words about coming to orgasm from thoughts alone. I believed every word.

"Where are you?" No response, but when a finger traced my wet pussy, I arched my back. "Please, Reed. I need you."

He pinched my clit, and I screamed with ecstasy, wriggling as much as my ties allowed. The bed beneath me indented from Reed climbing between my legs.

"You're such a tease, Lion-Man."

"And you're everything I've always wanted. I'm keeping my promise and claiming you as mine. Your love. Your tight pussy. Your perky breasts. Everything is mine."

I gasped for air as his breath washed over my inner thighs.

"Yes. Heavens, yes. Take me."

Without a response, the mattress shifted, and the next thing I knew, I felt his cock at my entrance, then with one thrust, he was deep inside me. I moaned loudly as he pressed forward, widening me. My ragged breaths quickened. He withdrew, then drove back in, quicker this time. I lifted my hips and welcomed his thrusting, his pace picking up. Excitement gripped hold of me, and all I could do was focus on our point of contact, the sound of him slapping against me, his muskiness flooding me. I teetered near the edge.

"Yes, Reed, please love me."

His hitched breath wasn't lost on me. I hadn't meant to use the 'l' word, goddess, but it was there at the front of my mind ever since Gage had revealed his feelings to me. Losing my three men would kill me, but did that mean my admiration, craving, and protectiveness over them was more than just me liking them?

Unrelenting, Reed fucked me, hammering into me, our exhales blending as one. I rode the wave that was Reed, drowning under him and adoring being claimed. A swell of arousal roused through me. When his mouth clasped over a breast, a surge of fire crashed through me. I unleashed a high-pitched moan, convulsing, my inner walls clenching around his cock. His hold never loosened.

He groaned, reaching his climax. Both of us shuddered with pleasure. The sensation caressed me on the inside, lingering long after the explosion that had moved me.

Reed collapsed on top of me. His mouth found mine, and I kissed him hard.

"Elliana," he whispered. "Nothing will ever come between us."

We lay there, spent, our breaths racing, hearts clanging, and all I could do was smile as joy flooded me. I'd always dreamed of finding my soul mate. I'd been blessed with three.

CHAPTER 26

A startled scream ripped me from my sleep. I jolted to a sitting position, gasping for air. Sunlight drenched the room, and I looked around to see my hair covered my three men. Gage and Reed lay on either side of me, with Kahlo spread out at my feet. Everyone wore clothes except me because they'd all insisted, and hell, I'd loved the way they'd all eyed me with starved expressions. Besides, I'd been too tired to argue. Gage and Kahlo had joined Reed and me in the room last night after our intense lovemaking session. Fortunately, once my hair had dried, it had stopped trying to control everyone. That was the last time I used a magical shampoo.

The shriek came again from outside, and I flinched. I climbed over Gage. He grumbled and tumbled out of bed as I darted to the window and pulled aside the curtain, partially blinded by the sunlight. I squinted and stared below at people darting through the streets, others yelling with panic, dragging children with them. They all ran toward the rear of the town.

"What the fuck's going on?" Gage's groggy voice washed across the back of my head.

I lifted my gaze to a figure flying in the distance. "What is that?" A bird? Except the wings were larger than any bird I'd seen.

"Son of a bitch." Gage cursed over my shoulder. "Is that an eagle shifter?"

Shuddering, I pressed closer against the window, gawking at the defined brown eagle wings. My stomach lurched at recognizing the eagle-man from the night Faye had captured me in the mansion. And that meant one thing.

The witch was here.

Panic rippling across my flesh, I spun around and cried out, "Reed, Kahlo, get up!"

I sprinted around, picking up my clothes and climbing into them. How had they found us? Or were they here to cause havoc for the local townspeople?

Reed snapped to his feet while Gage shoved Kahlo in the shoulder to get up. With everyone awake and out of bed, hair disheveled and all eyes on me, I spoke of my worst fears.

"Faye is in Crosswind. So, the albino shifter might be, too. Maybe they're attacking people. We need to help them." I slid into my pants, shirt, and vest, tightening the laces in the front of the vest with fumbling fingers, then searched the floor for my boots. One lay near the bed, the other across the room.

"*White Venom's* here?" Kahlo croaked and smirked as he picked up his top.

I stepped into my shoes, tucking my blade into my belt.

"Who's that?" Gage asked.

"The albino lion," Reed explained. "We found out from a nearby shifter he frequents this locality and attacks shifters often. The local pride has dispersed, as have most shifter groups in the vicinity."

Gage burst out laughing, holding his stomach. "White Venom?" His eyes teared up. "Who the fuck does he think he is? A hero?"

"Actually, more like the villain." I pulled my hair over my shoulder and said to myself, *move for me*. Nothing. All right, so maybe drying it had gotten rid of the craziness. I sure hoped so, as I didn't need that complication on top of everything else.

"Your hair behaving?" Kahlo asked.

"Seems the drying did the trick, but I'm worried water will trigger it again. I'm hoping it doesn't."

His brow marred. "We'll deal with that later."

I nodded and rushed into the bathroom for a quick visit. By the time I returned to the main room, everyone stood ready, with Gage still chuckling.

Reed faced me. "We've all agreed that we're going down to check this out. You stay here. If the witch wants you, then she can't see you."

I huffed, but Kahlo squared his shoulders. "We're not budging on this, Babycakes. You're the one in danger."

Before I could protest, the three marched out of the room and shut the door behind them. I paced back and forth, rage surging through me. I'd sat back my entire life, locked up, imprisoned, and here I was again. It might not be the tower, but I hated this wrapped-up-in-cotton-wool being thought of as fragile shit.

It's for your own safety.

"Fuck, I know that. But I hate it." I pulled the curtains aside and scanned the street, noting my three heroes sprinting against the flow of people. My chest tingled with how proud I was of them, but fear gripped my heart. What could they do against Faye? It could just be a few of their controlled slaves roughing up the locals. Except White Venom—he with the most ridiculous name ever—had been here the other day attacking farmers. I remember the way he watched those panthers get beaten up in the mansion, sitting there in his hooded cloak, enjoying the show. Bastard.

So if he was close, then we'd finish him off. If he died, then my curse should break. Except I'd seen him battle the stone creature, so what chance did I stand?

My three men vanished down a curved road, blocked from view by buildings. An ache settled just under my heart. I paced across the room. How long would I stay here, knowing they were out there in danger?

What could you do, anyway?

"I don't know." My voice wavered. "But I'm scared shitless of losing them." They were right; revealing myself was idiotic, and I had no plans of doing that. What I wouldn't give to have Gingernuts with me. He and I were practiced at being closed up together. He'd keep me company and entertain me. If everything went sour with me, hopefully, Gingernuts wouldn't be homeless.

Outside, more people scattered about, and the eagle-man had vanished. The men would have reached the bridge by now. What had they found? Would they be smart and suss out the scene first? Maybe retreat would be a decent option, though I remembered who I was dealing with. Three alpha shifters would attack first. I ran my hands through my knotted hair, but it felt greasy, as if the shampoo still hadn't come out and clung to my strands. I remembered the insane outcome yesterday where the tresses had taken control. Curiosity swirled within me, so I marched into the bathroom, put the plug into the tub, and pumped the metal handle. Water gushed out. What if water brought my hair to life again? It calmed down once it was dry? I had nothing to lose by trying since I seemed to still have shampoo residue in my hair, and I was curious. If I could better get control of my locks and force them to do my bidding, well, that would be interesting and give me an upper hand.

Can you imagine if water brought it back to life and you got caught in the rain? You'll turn into a sex-starved monster in front of everyone.

"Well, maybe it's better if you don't speak today. And it's not just sex-related, but about how I feel."

So you were super horny yesterday?

"Whatever. You know it's normal to have those feelings, especially around three hunks." I took a bundle of hair and dipped the tips into the water just as an explosion detonated behind me. The ground trembled, and I fell forward, my hands and half my hair falling in the tub. My heart slammed into my sternum, and I jumped up, turning around.

Rubble scattered all over the room, sunlight drenching the place, as if someone had peeled the roof off. *What the hell?* I reached for my knife on my belt and stepped closer in slow motion, my head poking out first.

The gargoyle stood in the gaping hole it had created in the wall. The enormous stone creature was glaring my way with its square shoulders, long arms, and trunk-like legs.

I pulled back fast and died a little as my insides turned to ice. My breaths refused to budge because my worst nightmare had returned. How? Vanore had said the spell would free me from the gargoyle. Reed had given up his fucking lion for this. Dread numbed my brain. I twitched, tears swimming in my eyes. This couldn't be happening.

Heavy footfalls hit the floor, and I backed into the farthest corner of the bathroom. Fear slammed into me. The creature filled the doorway, its shoulders rubbing the frame as it pushed inside.

I screamed. In a rush, it stormed closer and seized me by my shoulders. I struggled and kicked, shoving against the creature, but I might as well have been battling a boulder. It dragged me across the floor, and I struggled to keep up.

"Please don't do this. I'm—"

We flew out of the room through the hole in the wall, claws digging into my shoulders. The pain stung, but having him come for me fucking killed me. I writhed as the town below me was a swarm of activity. Several people swam across the river and darted into the woods. And just as we approached the bridge, my attention focused on the commotion. I gasped. My men faced a pack of half a dozen animals—panthers, lions, foxes, and wolves—encircling the gate to the city. The white-haired man stood proud, Faye by his side.

Anger surged through me because no way in hell would my men survive this.

"Run. Leave," I bellowed as we flew fifteen feet above them.

The men glanced up, and their eyes morphed into disks as they spotted my plight.

My hair fluttered around me, over my face and head. Higher still, the strands coiled into corded ropes, as they had yesterday. The sections I'd wet were alive, and they struck the gargoyle. There had been more shampoo still in my hair.

"Take it down!" I yelled as we passed the group below. The

dreadlock limbs constricted around the gargoyle's face, covering its eyes. We swayed in the air, my stomach swishing about. When my locks looped around the gargoyle's wings, heaving them together behind its back, we started dropping midair.

I screamed as the ground raced toward us. The creature hissed, its claws slackening. I shoved myself away from it and slammed into a perfectly positioned mass of bushes. My back spasmed, and I stung all over from the branches stabbing me. The ground shook from the gargoyle striking the ground close by.

When I stared at the creature, hatred riled through me, and the hair tightened over it.

Groaning, I staggered upright, ready to kiss Gage for his insane shampoo gift. Golden hair wound over the creature, binding its wings and legs. And no matter how much it fought, it wasn't moving. After all, my hair was unbreakable.

That also meant I remained stuck in this fucking conundrum, locked near the creature while I kept it contained.

I glared toward Faye and White Venom, who remained near the river. Across the bridge stood my three men, and they already crept toward us. For the life of me, I had no clue what to do next. I hadn't planned to show myself.

Faye and White Venom strolled toward me, the animals in their slavery parting for them to pass.

I lifted my chin when, in truth, I trembled in my boots. Around me, half my hair fluttered in the air, strewn across the ground because it hadn't gotten wet, but if it had been, I might have had an additional arsenal. Now, where was the rain when I needed it? Instead, the skies sparkled without a cloud in sight.

"I made a mistake," Faye called out. "I figured you'd stay put, but I can see you're a lot more devious than I gave you credit for."

"Yes, that's me. So, how about we call it a day, and we part ways?" I stood proud of myself for having escaped my tower at night for years without her detection.

White Venom chuckled, but nothing about the sound was hilarious. It covered me in shivers—and not the good kind.

"I want her tied up, shackled to the wall, so she never escapes again." He growled down at Faye, and she nodded, as if fearful of him. Why would a powerful witch cower before a shifter?

When he lifted Faye's chin with a thumb and stroked her cheek, I watched the way she stared into his eyes. That wasn't someone scared… nope. Someone smitten. Shit, she loved that monster? Had they been together all these years?

And studying their happy moment had me quivering with rage. They had no right, not with the chaos they brought upon people. They'd locked me up for thirteen fucking years so her lover boy could remain strong through my magical hair.

"You both disgust me." My words poured out just as I spotted Gage, wings wide, lifting into the air carrying a wooden barrel, water splashing out the side. Fuck, we were so perfect together because they knew what I needed. Kahlo was in animal form, huge, and together with Reed, they snuck up behind the shifters too busy watching me.

Except how the hell would we win this? I waved my hands in the air to ensure everyone watched me.

"Why the fuck are you harming shifters? Did someone upset poor Mr. White Venom? Which, by the way, is a shit nickname. Did you come up with it all by yourself, or did you open a dictionary and have Faye read you two random words?"

His face warped into a scowl, and his body shimmied with impending transformation.

Terror threaded through me. What was my plan again? I stepped backward as the gargoyle hissed from being tied up in a tangle of hair.

Faye laid a hand across White Venom's stomach, holding him back, but the man shoved her aside as if she were nothing more than a pawn in his game. She stumbled on her feet, and she didn't deserve my pity, but seeing her flushed face and the hurt in her eyes touched me. Except she'd decided to hook up with a psycho.

The moment a shadow flew overhead, the eagle-man shot into the air after Gage, but he'd already upturned the barrel.

Water came crashing down, splashing me and forcing me into a stagger.

"Take her and hold down her hair." White Venom waved for his army. The animals charged at me, their mouths gaping, their gazes wild with rage. And when I spotted a golden lioness taking the lead, I met familiar green eyes—just like Reed's. Hell, it was his sister.

Reed and Kahlo sprinted over the bridge, both slamming into the white-haired man, tackling him to the ground. Gage, partially transformed with his dragon wings fanned out, swooped down and snatched the witch, his claw tightly across her throat, covering her mouth and nose.

But the mob coming my way had me frozen on the spot because all I could imagine was me torn apart.

CHAPTER 27

Sweat and water coated me. I trembled, unable to stop. Half my hair swung outward, mirroring striking snakes, targeting the shifters coming my way. I brandished my knife, but I wasn't ready to kill them when they were innocents, trapped just like me.

The lioness leaped first, and I cried out. Two of my locks snapped around her head and torso, hurling her sideways. She winced, but I didn't have time. In every direction, my tresses flung toward the attackers. A panther slid under the assault and ran into my legs, knocking them out from under me. My arms flayed out, and I fell, but the bastard animal chomped down on my shin. Sharp, piercing torture shot through me, and I kicked the animal in the face with my free leg.

I screamed as a bear ran toward me on all fours, the ground thundering under him. My life flashed before my eyes. The last loose lock of hair struck him in the chest, driving me to a complete stop and choking him. He gasped for air, and yet the blue band around his neck glinted in the sunlight… If I removed those, they'd stop attacking me.

Another kick to the panther's face, and I dislodged my leg from its mouth. Someone might as well have poured acid over my wounds because they burned to an insane degree. I clenched my jawline through the pain, swallowing back the cries. Blood oozed out from the wound where the material and flesh had been torn. Agony lanced up my leg, my breaths sprinting.

The panther coiled back around to face me. Terror tangled with determination in my veins because, while scared, I'd fight to live.

Shifters surrounded me while the gargoyle bucked and battled to free himself from my hair.

Gripping the blade, I staggered upward, hobbling on one foot. If I was going down, it would be fighting. Snarls and roars drew my attention to Kahlo and Reed in battle with White Venom. Reed had the scorpion barb in both hands, battling to hold it back from stinging Kahlo, who had his mouth latched around the lion's neck. Blood smeared all over his white coat, tainting it. The monster groaned and whined. The panther coming for me turned to help his master.

Where had Gage taken Faye?

Movement to my side had a cheetah staggering to its feet, still wrapped in my hair. With my blade in hand, I hobbled toward the battle, each move sending stinging pain through my leg. At once, my hair pulled me back. I looked around to find it was still locked on the animals I'd shackled down behind me.

"Reed, Kahlo, stab him!" I shouted. A knife had to work. I lifted my blade to toss it to them just as the cheetah leaped at me. I recoiled, but it bit into my arm. I bellowed with excruciating pain and fell to my knees, the weapon dropping from my grasp. I shuddered and hit the animal in the face with my other hand, poking it in the eyes. The sharpness throttling down my arm catapulted me into a world of pain, my eyes tearing up. Shaking all over, I cried out as Gage fell out of the sky and smacked to the ground feet away, slumped and beaten.

"Gage!"

Faye was in the arms of the eagle-man and landed next to him with the grace of a bird. Her twisted lips curled upward, and she snatched a handful of Gage's hair and dragged him to his knees. He didn't make a sound, yet his defeated expression said it all. She grabbed a knife from her belt and pressed it to his throat.

"Stop!" Her voice echoed around us. "Or he dies."

The cheetah released me as if on command, and I cradled my hand, gnawing on my lip to ride the hurt. Except my heart split when I met Gage's eyes. A gash under his eye had blood smudging his cheek. More littered his body as he stood there in only his pants, his gaze hooded.

Reed and Kahlo stepped back from the lion, who stumbled, likely due to his bleeding neck. The beast raised his head and roared loudly. Two more shifters around me pulled free from my hair. If we had more time, we'd eventually weaken White Venom.

Then stab the fucker in the heart.

From within the town, crowds of people watched, clearly terrified and keeping their distance.

My world spun as I stared from Kahlo to Reed to Gage, battered and injured but ready to fight to the end.

"Little girl." Faye's stare pierced through me. "I've underestimated you for the last time. Release everyone from your hair. Now!"

Gage grunted as blood trickled from the blade pressed to his neck. Panic gripped me, and in my head, I called to my hair. *Release them. Free them. Please.*

My insides died at seeing the terror in Gage's expression.

"Don't hurt him," I pleaded. "Let all three of them go, and I'll come with you willingly. Please."

"Just fucking do as I say before my hand slips!" she shouted.

The white lion approached her side, already shifting into his human form, and in no time, he climbed to his feet, naked with blood dripping down his chest from the gashes around his neck. The sight of him sickened me.

"You protect these three shifters, but they're bloodthirsty animals." He belched, his nose creasing.

"And you're any different?" I hissed, my arms stiff by my side.

He cracked his neck. "I admit I'm a prick who loves to kill. But the animals you're protecting will do the same. A lion butchered my family in front of me with no mercy because my father dared to disagree with his pride hunting down humans.

For my parents' good deed, they were killed. So fuck them all." He growled, his shoulders hunching forward in a pose of attack. "Every shifter is a beast and deserves to be controlled. They will grovel at my feet."

I shuddered, unable to believe him. He had condemned so many for retribution against a few? "You're a fucking hypocrite." Anger boiled deep inside me, churning, hungry for destruction. "You butchered my father, doing to me what had been done to you, so how are you proving anything, you psychotic bastard?"

He shrugged and half-smiled, wiping away a line of blood rolling down his chest. "Sacrifices. Some had to be made in the process. And you were a nobody who had no family, so you wouldn't be missed. Now, you and your hair are an integral part of my success. You should be proud of that."

"Fuck you!" My throat thickened. Hate smothered me until I couldn't see straight.

The tightness across my scalp eased, and around me, my hair loosened. But now it coiled around my body as if hugging me, sensing the rawness swallowing me. I pushed against it, my pulse thumping in my veins. I didn't need it, not fucking now. But it kept hugging me, swathing me like a baby. *What the hell? Get off me!*

Fighting the tresses was impossible, and I faced my men. "Run! Get out of here."

Reed and Kahlo understood and already retreated toward the woods, sprinting away unseen, but Gage… My heart bled.

Just then, claws dug into my arms, the air of wings beating behind me. I cried out and glanced up at the gargoyle's stone underbelly.

It lifted me off into the air, and with my rushed breaths, I fought for release. *Hair, let go. Do it!* But it refused to budge.

We soared away from the chaos below, leaving my men at the mercy of madness.

* * *

"Don't!" I staggered to my feet, rushing toward the window inside my tower as a large plank of wood shifted over the covering. I slammed into it, banging my fists. "You can't do this. Please!" I cried out, aching everywhere, tears rolling down my cheeks.

Blackness encased me, and only tiny threads of sunlight pierced through. Hammering sounds echoed around me. They must have been nailing the covering in place.

"Don't worry, child," Faye called out from outside. "This is temporary, as you're moving locations. Should have done it long ago, but I felt pity for you. My mistake."

Bitch. You should have stabbed her when you had the chance.

I dropped to my knees, wracked with tears, unable to stop the sorrow burrowing through me. I'd failed myself, the men, everyone. The universe had dangled freedom in front of me, given me a taste, then ripped it away. It reminded me I wasn't worthy of anything but being locked up. I was forbidden from having a life.

Had Reed and Kahlo escaped? What about Gage? Would he become their slave?

Terror clawed at my heart, and darkness slithered through me. What would happen once I was completely closed in? I'd go insane because I couldn't do this. Not again. Not after I'd experienced joy, only to have it stolen away. The tears fell, and I felt barren. Useless. Shaking with rage.

I didn't remember how long I'd stayed there crying, but my eyes and throat had dried. There was nothing but silence outside. For years, I'd cried, been terrified of the gargoyle, and dreamed of freedom. But I couldn't sit back, knowing freedom was just there for the taking. I had nothing left to lose. There were no more options if I failed because Faye would ensure I was buried away for eternity, and she'd kill my three men. I had to stand up and fight to the bitter end because if I failed, I'd rather die than remain closed up. Fire coursed through me, and I curled my hands into balls, ready to battle. I'd finally found three men who adored me despite my faults.

Climbing to my feet, I straightened my posture and gawked

at the wooden plank covering the window. I pushed my palms against the panels, but the bite on my arm stung, and I winced.

Voices floated from outside, and I lifted myself on tiptoes, staring through a tiny gap. There were trees in the distance, but I couldn't see lower since I was too short. I grabbed a chair and got up in slow motion, as my injured leg still hurt like hell.

Down below in the field, Reed and Kahlo hid amid the trees' shadows. I burst with joy, bouncing on my toes at seeing them. They must have run the whole way to get here in time or maybe caught a carriage. But who cared… they had come to rescue me.

I climbed down and staggered into the kitchen, rummaging in the drawer, but I only found knives, so I grabbed one and slid a blade into the hole in the wooden barrier. Wriggling it didn't split the timber, but instead, the damn knife snapped free from the handle and vanished outside somewhere.

Backing up, I picked up a chair and tossed it at the entrance. A tiny chip fell away from the gap where I'd stuck the knife earlier. If I could make that bigger, maybe I could pry my fingers in there and break it off in pieces. But what could I use? I spun around the dark room, my hair coiling at my feet.

My strands still had shampoo stuck to the hair because I never had a chance to fully rinse it off! I hobbled into the bathroom and filled a bucket to start drenching my hair.

Yes, hurry up.

Without hesitation, I tossed the contents over my head. I yelped and trembled from the iciness digging into my flesh. "Hell, that was insane." I wet the rest of the hair, and already movement wriggled near my feet.

"Okay, my pretties. Time for you to show me what you can do." Back at the barricade, I said, "Break through this barrier." I repeated the words in my head, and my locks curled into separate limbs. They twisted in on each other into the shape of a fist and slammed into the plaque, over and over. Creaking sounded, and I bounced on my toes just as the next punch punctured through.

Shards of wood exploded outward, and sunlight poured into the tower. Best sight in the world. I darted to the window and glanced down at the two men still in the shadows, but they stared my way. I waved at them, but at this stage, I had zero ideas on the next move. Going down the tower shouldn't draw the gargoyle's attention as long as it didn't see Kahlo and Reed. Regardless of the risk, I needed to talk to them to find out about Gage.

I climbed out of the gaping hole and scaled down the granite wall, pushing past the sharpness digging into my bitten leg and arm, my heart in my throat. We had to find a way to stop Faye and White Venom. And if I could hold down the gargoyle with my wet hair once, dammit, I'd do it again and drag it around with me if that meant saving everyone.

Once I reached the bottom, stumbling in the bushes surrounding the tower, someone tsked behind me, and my veins turned to ice. That wasn't a sound either of my men would make.

I turned in slow motion and called out in my head to my hair, *Get ready to attack them and defend me.*

Faye stood there, hands on her hips, eagle-man tossing Gage to the ground, bloodied and bruised. White Venom stood near in human form, still naked and disgusting. Both glared my way, and instead of fear, rage fueled through me. I'd been afraid for so long that it now numbed me. Staring at the two who'd destroyed my life, I pictured them dead. My hair formed into multiple sharp blades facing the enemies, sitting as a halo around me.

"Gage!" My heart bled at seeing him slumped on the ground, gasping for air. He wasn't wearing a magical ring around his neck, but he was spent and too injured to fight back. One eye had puffed, his lip split open, multiple cuts on his face and chest bleeding everywhere. He grumbled but didn't look toward me.

A shadow fell over us... The gargoyle dove at us, and I cringed. "Stop!" Faye yelled as she flicked her hand toward the creature. It landed with a thump, frozen in place, glaring at me, as if any moment it would charge and rip me apart. Of course, she'd have control over it. The text I'd read said only the witch who brought it to life had power over it, so it would listen to her command.

"Oh, Elliana, you wasted no time escaping again, I see, but your tower is no longer yours. I have a wonderful basement with a prison cell that you can call home from now on." She shook her head, rubbing her chin. "And I was being kind by giving you a chance to enjoy life, but I was wrong. You threw it back in my face. Now you can live like a rat on scraps and in filth."

White Venom studied me as if I were something to devour, his gaze ravaging my body, and a shiver jolted through me.

"I've served my time twenty times over. I don't want to fight you, but I will." I stared at my tangled hair weapons, then back at my captors.

The white-haired fuck head snorted, his nose scrunching. "Don't kid yourself." He glanced down at Faye. "Get her out of here and locked up somewhere she can't escape. You promised me she'd never get out!" He growled and marched away, his shoulders curled forward. I chanced a glance toward the woods and found no sign of Reed or Kahlo.

Faye's jawline clenched. Behind her, Gage drew himself up on hands and knees. "You're welcome that I didn't leave him behind to die. I preferred for you to see his last moments." Faye kicked Gage in the ribs, and he crumbled into a ball, groaning in pain, spitting blood.

"Leave him alone," I cried out, my grief surging with every expelled breath. Tears bubbled at the edges of my eyes, but I couldn't fall apart. Not now. So I swallowed the boulder in my throat and released brave words. "Why do you let the lion belittle you?"

Her face warped. Okay, maybe not a great question.

"You know nothing about us, or how he treats me, the tender words he's said into my ears, what he's sacrificed for me."

I huffed. "Like making others suffer for his strength?"

Her eyes narrowed, and her mouth twisted into a crooked line.

"He sacrificed his life to save mine when I was poisoned. He gave me his life energy, so I restored him in a way by feeding him the life source from other shifters. A bull shifter lasted him a week, while the scorpion mere days before he got weak, but over time, his mane fell out. So when I found you with your father, you were the perfect solution with your long hair. The energy he takes from your hair keeps him alive and helped return his mane. As long as it kept growing and remained unharmed, you'd be a constant life source for him to draw from." She stared at him over her shoulder, and for the first time, a tenderness filled her voice. "I would do anything for him."

Anger surged through me as Gage shook, bleeding into the ground, and my insides ached to witness his struggle.

"And I'd do anything for the men I adore, but what you're doing is fucked up. Kidnapping shifters for him to get revenge. You took away years from me, so isn't that enough?"

"Everyone lives with injustice in this world. My Leon was assaulted as a child, mistreated…. so is it wrong to get payback?" She stepped toward Gage and clenched his hair in her fist once again, wrenching his head back.

My heart clenched. Blood trickled down Gage's cheek and chest. He trembled, but behind his eyes, an inferno bubbled.

"Tell me, child," Faye said, "if I was to slit your lover's throat now, would you not crave revenge?"

Hatred raced through me. I'd lived with it for years, yearned for retribution. But Faye's question struck a chord with me. Deep inside, I'd longed for them to suffer for taking my only family away, for stealing my life, and now they threatened my men. So, was I any different from Leon or Faye? The tug-o-war inside me ripped me into fragments because I'd always considered myself a victim. But all this shit had stemmed from someone else believing they'd been attacked without justification. My eyes pricked, thinking of what losing my dad had done to me. How my life would end if I now lost the three shifters who'd shown me how to open my heart again.

"I will spend the rest of my life hunting you down." I looked away and studied Gage, then Leon, who glared at us from a distance. "You and that monster let anger control you when all my father did was steal a golden wig. That wasn't worth his life or mine." I wiped my cheeks dry. "It wasn't enough to justify you destroying my future, but you're now ruining families for greed and power. That's no longer revenge for a past mistake." I lowered my voice. "He's become a psychotic madman who thinks he's above others. He's taking fucking slaves. No one has the right to do that." Curling my hands, hatred flowed through me, burning an inferno in my chest.

Movement came from my peripheral vision—Kahlo in tiger form, and Reed burst out of the woods and sprinted up behind Leon. My mouth opened to distract Faye when a dozen animals charged toward us from the woodland across the ruins. My stomach dropped, and a chill iced my veins.

The lioness—Reed's sister—panthers, and other creatures charged. Eagle-Man flew overhead and dropped two more men to the ground, already shifting. The bird squawked and dove mid-shift toward Kahlo and Gage. My pulse was in a frenzy as panic gripped me.

Leon roared at the attack, and Faye turned to face him, her body tense.

Without thought, my hair jutted outward, slamming into Faye's back and arms, twisting around her neck and covering her mouth. Her eyes morphed into round orbs in surprise.

Gage grasped her hand and dragged her to the ground alongside him, hands to her neck, choking her. But the eagle shifter swooped down, snatching him by the waist before hurling him across the field.

Terror bled through me, and I darted after him.

But the gargoyle hissed at my back. My heart skipped a beat, and I turned. It rushed me, its wings spreading outward like a great shadow taking over my world. And my knees weakened beneath me. Death was coming.

CHAPTER 28

My screams rang across the ruins, and I recoiled from the gargoyle, numbness threading through my mind.

The creature's arms struck out and seized my injured forearm as cords of my hair jerked toward it in attack. They wrapped around its wrists, binding them to its body, forcing me forward by its unrelenting grip. The creature thrashed against the restraints, crying out from the stabbing ache racing up my body. Fear shackled me while I pulled against its hold, both of us stumbling about. Its wings beat, and it lifted off the ground, dread smacking me in the chest.

"Stop its wings!" I called out, repeating the words in my head. But the stone monster dragged me upward by the arm, and when my toes left the ground, an agonizing ache jolted through my stretched shoulder. At once, my hair pulled my head backward, and I shrieked. Faye was on the ground getting dragged behind us, still locked in my tresses.

Pin down its wings, I bellowed in my head, swaying in the air, writhing for escape.

Hair fluttered in my face, swooping around me. In a breath's whisper, we dropped, and my stomach hit the back of my throat. I yelled out. We hit the ground, my legs crumbling beneath me, my wrist released. I scrambled backward on my ass, feeling no pain as dread knocked me about. The gargoyle fought my tresses. It had one wing clasped under the hair around its body. It yanked one of its arms free and tore at the golden cords binding it in place.

Faye moaned loudly, half-cocooned in my locks, lying on her side, flapping about like a fish out of water. With her mouth and hands disabled, her magic remained immobile, but how long before she escaped? Grunts escalated behind me, and I spun to find Reed and Kahlo brawling with the other shifters, all teeth and blood. Gage rushed to their aid, and I didn't see how in the world we could win this. We needed to escape.

Not while you're stuck with the gargoyle and Faye.

My gaze settled on Leon, glaring at Reed's back. The lion scratched the ground with a front paw, his head lowered with the bull horns pointed at Reed. Dread shook through me, and I darted toward him, wincing each time my foot hit the ground.

"Reed, watch out! Behind you!" I shouted, my insides icing over.

I willed strands of my hair to snake through the air. They caught Leon across his horn, winding tightly, and yanked him back. Normally, his immense strength should have enabled him to drag me along, but with me weighed down with the gargoyle and his love, his vigor failed him. They pulled me in three directions.

Leon roared with frustration, his nose creasing, saliva spitting from his mouth as he slashed at the air with a clawed paw. He thrashed and eyed me as a target. I trembled and needed him anchored away before he attacked me. I scanned the field and spotted half a granite wall from the old ruins. *Tie him to the stone.* The cord of hair locked onto him, shaking him and hauling him closer, strands hooked onto the parapet atop the decaying ruin. My hair wrenched him across the ground, his paws digging into the ground, his head forward, shaking to break loose.

The horn groaned under all the weight, and Leon screeched as if in pain. The tresses went taut, and a loud crack resonated. A fracture split along the base of his horn. *Oh, shit!* I'd underestimated the tension in the rope of my strands. The horn snapped clear off, flinging into the air. The lion fell to his knees, bleeding from the breakage.

His face contorted with malice, and he came for me, thundering like a bull.

Terror catapulted through me, shaking me, and I recoiled.

He reached me in seconds, and his deadly tail slammed the ground at my feet, missing me by inches. I jumped out of the way. Over and over, he struck, and I ducked each blow, but only within a whisper of my life. Desperate, I threw him backward while darts of my hair jabbed him in the face, the neck—anywhere to stop his assault. I wasn't ready to die.

I struck him in the eye, and he halted, shaking his large head, the shaggy mane billowing around his face, but his tail kept flinging around him, reaching for me. I backtracked, but my heel caught on a rock, and I fell backward, crying out, my hands flailing for balance. All I could think about was the lion attacking me, ripping me to shreds. I'd never see my men again, my future lost before it even began.

I hit the ground, and a piercing ache jolted up my spine. A loose lock caught the tip of Leon's tail, barely restraining him, tugging him away from me.

To my left, the witch wriggled against the grasp of my hair. Soon, she'd get free. To my right, the gargoyle fought his restraints, his second wing an inch from being freed. The gargoyle darted toward me so fast, I gasped. He snatched my wrist, trying to hoist me to my feet. All of it was too much. I couldn't hold all three at the same time.

"Help!" I wailed, scrambling backward as the lion's stinger hammered the ground near me. He growled with such intensity, it rippled my skin with goosebumps.

Gage was by my side within moments, punching the albino in the back like a wasp intent on stinging an animal to death. Leon turned with swiftness, his stinger aiming for my dragon. Gage punched Leon in the chin, but the lion didn't budge and stalked toward Gage, ready to finish him. He lunged and bit Gage in the thigh.

I fought against the gargoyle's grip, hauling against his

strength. "Gage! No!" I tossed out a thin lock at Leon, winding it around his neck, choking him.

The albino scratched at my hair, veins in his forehead bulging.

The gargoyle clawed at my shoulder. Piercing fire jolted down my back, and I lost my grip on the albino. He batted Gage with his paw, drawing blood, his tail poised, but Gage rolled away.

Leon's head jerked in my direction, and he loomed closer. Growling like a lion that had cornered a gazelle, he lifted his tail above his head. This was it. Fear stabbed my gut like a knife, twisting ever-so-slowly. Paralyzing dread spread through me as if it were ice. I twitched, fighting the impulse to just fall to my knees and cower. In the distance, shifters surrounded Reed and Kahlo while two panthers charged for Gage, who bellowed with rage.

My eyes swung to the scorpion barb, and I pictured myself being stabbed to death. Behind me, the gargoyle fought to loosen its wing, staggering on the spot but holding me in place with a solid grip. My throat thickened, and I heaved against the gargoyle's clutches.

But the barb rushed through the air, straight for my face, and I froze.

A lock of my hair snared around my free arm, jerking me sideways so fast, I lost my breath. My head spun as I cried out. A flurry of air rushed past my ear. The scorpion barb had missed me by inches but had struck the gargoyle in the chest. Fire scorched across my scalp as my hair had caught on White Venom's tail during the attack, and it was now trapped inside the gargoyle, held in place by the barb that had detached itself from the lion. Under the intense pain, I could no longer hold the witch or gargoyle at bay, and the cords restraining them slackened. They stumbled free.

Yet the gargoyle dropped to its knees, hissing, hands clasping its chest just above its heart. Reality punched me in the gut.

"Fuck! Yes!"

Leon had just stabbed the stone creature in the heart. I jerked around to find him staggering, his body shimmering and trans-forming back into human form. He was going to take the stone beast's place. I held my breath, waiting.

Faye rushed to her lover's side, crying, mumbling words I didn't understand. A spell, perhaps?

Leon yelled, fear coating his voice, his body shaking as he writhed on the ground.

I pulled my hair to free myself from the gargoyle, but it wasn't budging. Cold rushed ran through me.

Faye called out her enchantment, but nothing happened. She slammed the ground with her fists in frustration while Leon grabbed her hand, holding it to his chest. He had to know his end was coming.

Dust floated in the surrounding air, and I stared down at the gargoyle on his back, legs dissolving into particles. The hair connected to the gargoyle's heart darkened into a gray color like stone. And it spread toward me. Would I turn into a stone monster or disintegrate along with the creature?

"No. No. No!" I screamed as cracks formed in the gargoyle's features. It was vanishing, and Leon and I were about to take his place!

"Elliana!" Gage shouted, hobbling toward me, his shoulder ripped apart, blood coating his shoulders and shirt.

Was my fate sealed?

"Gage!" My voice rippled and shrieked.

His face paled when he reached me, his gaze swinging from me to the hair, to Faye praying over her lover, whose legs had already turned to stone. She screeched in agony and ran her hands over her lover's chest, her touch flaring with blue magic, but nothing made a difference. Part of the spell had originated with the first creation of a gargoyle, so Faye couldn't change the curse. Now, it backfired and had taken Leon.

"I'll get you out of this," Gage said, but his hand trembled against my shoulder.

"I've always loved you," I mumbled.

"Don't." He searched the ground. "Where the fuck's a knife when you need one?"

"Listen," I called out, tears blurring my vision, watching the gray crawling up my strands, closing in on me. "I was stupid to push you away and to never let myself be with you."

Gage grasped my hands, his face inches from me. "I'm going to save you. Don't you fucking leave me." His words hiccupped, and tears ran down his cheeks. Behind him, there was movement. Reed sprinted toward us while Kahlo fought an army of shifters. Suddenly, Gage shuddered uncontrollably and staggered backward, his limbs stretching, cracking.

"Gage!" I dove after him, but he'd stumbled too far, making gurgling sounds that terrified me.

Armed with a blade, Reed rushed to my side.

"Something's wrong with Gage!" I yelled.

"And you're in danger. Get on your knees." I did as he said, and he gently cradled the back of my head on his thighs. "Shit, Elliana." Determination pumped through his expression as he used the blade to hack at the lock connecting me to the gargoyle. The action pulled my hair, but he kept sawing.

My mind started to fail, refusing to kick into action when all I pictured was my death.

I watched with horror as the gray crept along my hair, ready to consume me. For killing a gargoyle, the price must be paid, and for that person to replace the stone creature. That person was me and Leon.

"I can't cut it," Reed hissed. "Lie flat on your back."

I followed his instructions because I had no other idea how we'd fight this. Reed knelt next to my head and slammed the long end of the blade down on my steely hair. An electric spark shuddered through my head, and I screamed.

My gaze landed on Leon embracing Faye, kissing her as the stone rushed up his arms and into her. It spread across her back and her head, locking them in an eternal kiss. *Shit!*

Reed kept hammering unrelenting while I bit down on my lip until I tasted blood, riding the agony, my eyes shut, crying out each time a jolt rocked through me.

A soft hand touched my cheek, and I flinched.

"It's okay," Reed said. "Open your eyes. I've cut it all off."

His smile coaxed me to stand up. He took my hand and lifted me to my feet with ease. I looked behind me to a mountain of my cut hair. My breaths raced, and I touched my head, finding every strand had been chopped off, and what remained hung to my neck. My long hair was gone. I sucked in a shaky breath.

"Oh, hell, you did it?" I leaped into Reed's arms, crying and laughing. "Faye's death must have broken my curse." I felt pity for her, but I was also glad she was gone. No matter what happened now, we'd saved Reed's sister, his pride, and the other kidnapped shifters.

Reed hugged me, kissing my face and neck. "You're free."

But in the distance, Kahlo was rushing toward us in his tiger form. An array of shifters writhed on the ground as eagle-man tumbled out of the sky near them, the blue rings around their necks fading until non-existent.

I broke from Reed's arms. "The pride is free!"

Where was Gage? I scanned the grounds and saw no sign of him. My stomach churned with an uneasy sensation until Reed groaned from behind me. My heart slammed into my ribcage, and I swung around to find my cut hair curling around his legs like snakes capturing their prey. It moved on its own. I rushed toward him, both of us ripping at the hair, but there was too much of it. It curled around his chest, and his panicked breaths had despair swallowing me.

"What's happening?" I couldn't stop pulling at the strands that had encircled Reed. It must have attacked him because he'd cut the hair.

A sudden hiss echoed in the air, and I shuddered, glancing behind me. Dread wove into my soul as I studied Faye and Leon, both stone gargoyles, their stony eyes on me.

"Fuck! No!" I shuddered. The spell had been broken. The shifters' controlling collars had broken. Yet these two moved toward me. My connection to the gargoyle remained? It had to be because of Faye's magic inside the creatures. I retreated alongside Reed, who was now completely cocooned in hair, his moans muffled. "Reed!" I yelled as I pulled at the hair, circling him, searching for any kind of give.

Faye and Leon approached, slower at first but soon speeding up.

Kahlo arrived, already in human form and naked, his breaths heaving, his face bloody.

"Help me! Reed is inside the hair," I cried and retreated toward the tower, letting Kahlo rescue his friend.

If the gargoyles were taking me, I couldn't let them injure anyone else. So I'd lead them away. Sweat drenched my skin, and my pulse throbbed through my veins.

When a roar thundered overhead, I flinched. Every fucking sound had me jumping, so what now?

Gold gleamed in the sunlight as a colossal shadow passed over us. A stream of fire burst free from the flying creature, but as I squinted, I realized what I was looking at.

"Gage?" Excitement riddled through me. Green and yellow scales glinted across his long, serpentine body, wings spanning out, claw tips dipped in gold. He was incredible, and I gasped in awe. Smoke poured from his nostrils. He curled toward us, his wings tucked in tight, and swooped in closer.

The gargoyles charged toward me. Terror shook me at the core.

Gage stormed lower and snatched up both creatures in his enormous mouth in one go. The swish of wind from his momentum crashed into me, sending me into the shrubs, where I stumbled and fell. My mouth fell open as Gage beat his wings like the furious pounding of my pulse.

He landed in the middle of the field, the ground shuddering under his weight. The stone creatures struggled, desperately trying to escape, but Gage sank his fangs into their bodies, crunching them as if they were pork rinds. Rocks fell from his teeth as he chewed on the monsters. A beam of light exploded from his mouth, then vanished just as quickly. The spell vanquished.

I exhaled long and loud, but it wasn't time to rest. Not yet. I spun and half-ran, half-stumbled toward Reed.

From within the cocoon of hair, a growl came. Kahlo pushed me behind him, standing in front of me, and I adored his protectiveness, but this was Reed in danger. He'd risk his life for me, so I would do the same for him.

The hair bundle shifted, expanding, growing. Then, a golden lion burst free. I stumbled into Kahlo, who held me close.

Reed landed several feet away, tilting his chin back and roaring so loud, the sound pierced my ears. In the distance, Gage unleashed a fireball into the air and rushed toward us. His body shrunk, pulling inward, and Reed's did the same. Before long, three naked men surrounded me.

"Oh, shit! I think we pulled this off," I said, hugging myself, still unable to believe we'd all survived.

"You're free," Kahlo said.

"And I'm a fucking dragon. Did you see that?" His hands flayed in the air, and I burst out laughing, joy flooding me because, for the first time in too long, I didn't fear what would happen next. I didn't understand where to go from here, but as long as we were together, I'd be fine.

I turned toward Reed, my insides beaming. "You got your lion back."

His smile touched his ears. "But I don't understand how."

Reaching for his hand, I intertwined my fingers with his while Kahlo cradled against my back and Reed clasped my other arm. "Faye had said the albino lion had given up his life to save her. And that my hair had not only fed him energy but helped him regrow the mane he lost. My cursed hair was connected to his mane, so when you cut it, you unleashed the magic. I'm guessing it must have chosen you to transfer the lion shifter ability because you'd touched it last."

"All I care about is that I'm back and I have you in my life." He kissed my knuckles gently, and I melted at his tenderness. My smile burst from within. I was no longer being worn by worries or obligations.

Gage bathed my arm in smooches. "You finally admitted your love, and my dragon evolved. I knew you were the one for me."

"I'm sorry it took so long."

Kahlo wrapped his arms around my stomach and rested his

chin on my shoulder, his lips on my cheek. "I finally have a family, thanks to you."

Just hearing the joy in their words had me choking for a response. Maybe I didn't need to say anything, but being held by my three men, there wasn't a single place I'd rather be. Who cared that we were bloody, injured—some of us naked. Kahlo was right. I'd found my family, too.

Reed broke free. "I need to check on my sister and pride." He took off, and we all followed, ready to do what was needed.

CHAPTER 29

FOUR DAYS LATER

"You sure they'll welcome us?" I asked, glancing around an open field surrounded by pines, the scent fresh, yet an eerie sensation crawled down my spine. We were in the Den. This was wolf territory, and no one walked in here without being taken down. Everyone knew the drill—wolves attacked when you entered their territory.

Kahlo threw an arm around my waist, drawing me against him. I adored his warmth, the way he stared at me as if only I existed.

"Babycakes, after all the fucked-up shit we went through, I'm ready to take on a wolf pack to protect you." He leaned down and kissed me, his fingers pressing into my back.

I softened against his rock-hard chest, my insides twisting into a knot at how much he affected me. And he was mine, never leaving my side.

Someone cleared their throat behind me, and I broke free to find Gage cocking an eyebrow.

"Really?" He leaned close and stole a kiss, but I laughed.

Movement drew my attention to four timber wolves standing twenty feet away. I shuddered in their presence because they were large beasts, and I bet more of them surrounded us. Reed strode ahead of us, his chest puffed out and proud, and damn, he had the sexiest ass, even in his trousers. Though I'd been getting used to seeing him naked.

From deeper in the woods, a man emerged dressed in simple black pants, no shoes or shirt. Built like a mountain, he swept the long, black hair off his brow with a hand, revealing the bluest eyes. My hand rose to my short, cropped hairstyle that was spiked across the top; I had every intention to keep it cropped.

"Oryn." Reed took the shifter into an embrace, patting his back. "How have you been keeping?"

"Better than you, my friend." Oryn broke the man-hug and studied Reed's bruised face, which was littered with healed cuts. That was no different to the rest of us, but we'd survived a brutal fight for our lives. Injuries healed, but coming back from death was impossible. Or at least I hoped because I wasn't ready to deal with Faye or Leon again or to see another gargoyle for the rest of my life.

Reed laughed. "We've dealt with a fuckhead, stopped a psycho witch, and saved my kidnapped pride members. Plus, I've found my beautiful and loving soulmate."

Just hearing him talk about me with such tenderness had me smirking. Oryn glanced over my way, and I waved, then felt stupid and dropped my hand.

"Hi, I'm Elliana. And this is Gage and Reed."

His expression beamed, and he turned back to Reed. "I see you took my lead and bonded with more than just a beauty."

Reed chuckled and looked our way. "It's the only way." He called us closer, and we joined them. Oryn towered over me, but it seemed all shifters did, and I had no problem with that. Not when I called three my own. I waited for a response from my mind, but my subconscious had fallen quiet ever since the battle four days ago. Not a sound. Had she pulled back, figuring I no longer needed her? Or was she tightly entwined with my curse? Though part of me missed her snarkiness.

"Come, the others are expecting you," Oryn said, and we

followed him deeper into the woods, the ground covered in dried pine needles. The wolves trailed behind us. Reed told me about a human female who'd once stumbled into this realm and had run into the three alphas who reign over the territory. They'd cared for her, and she'd aided them in fighting against a poison ailing their packs. She'd fallen for all three of them, and they'd loved her back. So, just like me and my men, she'd also taken three lovers.

Now, I couldn't wait to meet Scarlet, as she'd gone through shit before finding three shifters of her own. She might even offer me insight into how to handle all of mine, especially in the sleeping arrangement department. Did all of them share the bed every night or did she take turns sleeping with each? The four of us decided we'd live in Reed's territory, as he had a pride to lead and a family, and just knowing we were part of that made me smile. I'd been alone for so long, and now my life would change for the better.

Gage and Kahlo had taken charge of preparing to build us a new house on the land. They'd both insisted on creating privacy for us a little way from the rest of the pride, who lived in smaller huts. Joy blossomed inside me at the notion of the men close, stealing kisses at every moment, and never being alone again. I yearned for that more than anything else. And once we built the house, Gage was going to fly out and collect Gingernuts. I missed him so much.

When we emerged from the dense woods, a new world came into view, and my mouth dropped open. An open field lay before us with a giant oak tree in the middle. An enormous wooden house was cradled on the thick branches. A circular veranda surrounded the building, windows were covered in curtains, and a set of circular steps led up to the home.

Kahlo's fingers intertwined with mine.

"Wow! This is impressive," I said.

Gage took my other hand in his and kissed it. "We'll build you something bigger and grander. With a landing pad on the roof for me when I come in from my dragon escapades." He wiggled his eyebrows, and I leaned in against his chest.

"Would those involve plundering villages and stealing gold?" I giggled.

"Nope. Because you're coming with me, riding on my back."

Kahlo nudged Gage on the shoulder. "Not before we build her a seat and harness, or she'll fall off. I've seen your wild flying."

Gage's nose scrunched up. "I won't be a donkey wearing a saddle. Fuck that. She'll be safe on my back, but if you want to join us,"—he smirked—"I'll carry you in my mouth."

Kahlo burst out laughing. "You're hilarious."

Gage leaned closer to my ear. "He thinks I'm joking, but I'm not." Mirth danced through his words, and I loved the antics between the two, always trying to better one another, but they'd proven they cared for each other like brothers. While Reed might be the serious one of the bunch, when he let loose, he put these two to shame.

A loud squeal drew our attention to a crowd of at least two dozen men, women, and children rushing toward us. Reed hurried forward, and I cheered on the inside. This had to be his pride, safe and protected by the wolves. They circled him, each embracing him as he spoke to them, probably telling them about the good news. Oryn stood aside, as did many wolves in animal form. Were they his guards?

"Elliana!" Reed called out and waved us over. Uncertainty sat in my chest. Would the rest of his pride accept a human for his mate? Would they embrace him sharing me with two non-lion shifters?

The crowd parted for us, and Reed took me into his arms, kissing me quick, then turned to his people.

"This is my mate, Elliana. Each of you will have time to spend time with her, discover how incredible she is. She's going to move in with us, along with her two other mates, Gage and Kahlo."

I held my breath, scanning the faces, but no one frowned or booed. They studied me with awe, not bothered one inch about who I was. Just that their leader had found someone who made him smile with giddiness, who held him close and tight. They closed in, hugging me, sniffing me to take my scent, and offering words of gratitude.

A young girl approached me, and I crouched down to hug her. She whispered, "I like you. You make Reed smile more than I've ever seen him in the past." Warmth engulfed me. I'd brought out that kind of cheer in their leader. By the time I'd finished with the greetings, Kahlo hugged me from behind, his arms laced over my stomach.

"They love you," he cooed in my ear. "And who can blame them? You have me enchanted."

"They're so friendly and welcoming," I said. "I've never experienced so much kindness from anyone who didn't know me."

"Well, get used to it. Your life is about to change and for the better. And if you struggle, I'm there to catch you." His eyes smiled, and he wrapped me in his arms, making me adore his strength and warmth. Having three men who cared for me felt strange, but it was growing on me fast.

"Shall we head to the treehouse?" Gage asked. "Someone's calling us."

Kahlo and I turned around to see Oryn up on the balcony. "Come on up when you're ready."

"You go up. I'll join you soon," Reed said before returning to his pride. It made me proud to see his attention focused on his family and the care he put into showing them they mattered. That was the reason I was drawn to him. Sure, his attractiveness played a huge part, but discovering the real man underneath had me captivated.

Kahlo led me by the arm, Gage on our heels. Halfway up the circular steps, Gage had his hand on my ass, squeezing. When I glanced over my shoulder, he smirked.

"Just helping you up, Sugar Pops. Plus, it's rare we get to see you in a dress." He winked, and a tingle sparked in the pit of my stomach.

"Can't argue with that logic." Once we reached the landing, I gawked at the magnificent landscape spread out over the veranda railing. There was a carpet of greenery in every direction. Mountains jutted out in the distance, their snowcapped tips telling me that might be the White Peak realm, where the bear shifters lived. "Gorgeous."

"Yes, you are," Gage added.

"Wonderful to have you here." A female voice joined us, and we turned to a slender woman with chestnut hair reaching her waist. She was beautiful; even dressed in a simple V-neck dress that fell to her knees with long sleeves, she exuded a feminine goddess feel. "I'm Scarlet, and you must be Elliana." She closed the distance between us and took me into a hug without hesitation. She smelled of vanilla, freshness, and a touch of powder.

I held her against me, adoring her hospitality.

"I love having visitors over. Doesn't happen often enough." When she broke free, she turned to Kahlo. "Tiger shifter, right? I can see it in your eyes."

He laughed and embraced her before she faced Gage, who puffed out his chest.

"Bet you've never seen a real-life dragon?"

Her eyes widened, and she clasped her hands to her chest. "Oryn just told me, and I jumped up and down—literally." Her smile was contagious.

Gage didn't miss a beat, already pulling his shirt up and over his head.

Kahlo stepped closer and clasped a hand to his shoulder. "Best not to strip the moment you meet a woman, you know!" He chuckled, and Scarlet's reddening cheeks had me admiring her already.

"All right, I'll go back downstairs, but be ready to be stunned." Gage blew me a kiss, then vanished toward the steps.

A dark-haired man with soft features and a mischievous grin stepped outside, holding a baby wearing a yellow jumpsuit in his arms, maybe six months old.

"Did I hear someone say 'dragon?'" When he exchanged gazes, he nodded. I could see why Scarlet would have fallen for him. Aside from his strong cheekbones and gorgeous features, he carried a confidence about him. But with him holding a child, something in my chest shifted. I'd never given kids a second thought because my whole life had been about survival, but now things were different.

"Who is this gorgeousness?" I'd had no idea Scarlet had a child.

"I'm Nero," teased the grown man as he placed his baby in my arms. "And this is my angel, Autumn."

I cradled the little one, loving how tiny and soft she felt, and when she looked up at me with huge hazel eyes, I was mesmerized. Her face glowed as if she lit from inside-out.

"Hello there," I cooed. "Aren't you adorable?"

"That's what Scarlet says about me all the time." Nero took Scarlet into his arms, holding her against him, kissing her, making it clear the honeymoon was far from over between the pair.

Kahlo was at my back, staring down at Autumn, his finger running the length of her button nose. "Beautiful."

Just then, Oryn and another man joined us on the veranda, each carrying a baby and gravitating toward Scarlet. *Wow, three babies.* Their family was complete, and the way they stared at her showed how much they loved her.

"Hey, I'm Dagen." The new man shook Kahlo's hand and offered me a side hug, kissing me on the cheek. He was captivating with honey-colored hair that danced across his shoulders. Stubble covered his broad jawline, and a scar lined his temple and hairline. "And this here is Alexy, and he"—he pointed his chin to the baby in Oryn's arms—"is Jay."

"You're blessed with three tiny ones to love," I said.

"Don't get me wrong," Nero said. "I love them to bits, but even between the four of us, some nights, none of us get to sleep when these three wake up and decide it's feeding time."

Scarlet laughed. "I wouldn't change it for the world. But it'll get crazier." She rubbed her tiny belly, and her men drifted closer to her, watching her with awe and affection in their eyes. So much love that it made me gush.

"You're pregnant? Oh heavens, that's incredible. I'm so excited for you." I hurried over and half-hugged her, Autumn between us. "You've got the most beautiful family. Congratulations."

"Well, we had something to do with it," Oryn said, arching a brow, his laughter loud and boisterous.

"Congratulations to the whole family," I added.

Kahlo was there, hugging them, shaking hands, and I studied Scarlet's beaming expression. She loved being a mom. Maybe one day, I'd be one, too.

A roar sounded, and I flinched, but the noise set Autumn off, making her burst into tears, then the other two started as Gage glided overhead in his dragon form.

"Son of a bitch." Nero half-hung over the railing, gawking at Gage's splendorous golden form gleaming in the sunlight, his wings wide and stupendous.

With Autumn wailing in my arms, I followed the other two wolf shifters into the house filled with furniture. Paintings of the wilderness dotted the walls. Oryn and Dagen placed their babies in a triplet rocking bed, and I set down Autumn in hers. Oryn broke into a soft lullaby, and at once, the three of them silenced, their eyes transfixed on their father. Like them, I could sit there and listen to him until I fell asleep.

I retreated along with Dagen, and he grazed my arm. "Reed is the most honest man I've met, and he's lucky to have found someone who loves him."

"Thank you." I quivered with the reminder that Reed loved me. My heart ached at the thought of losing any of my men, and I couldn't deny that I had lost my heart to them all. "I'm the luckiest person in the world to have found Reed, Gage, and Kahlo."

"A shifter's love is unrelenting, so you're in fantastic company with your harem." He smirked and guided me outside. "I need to see that dragon. He's incredible."

Harem. I'd never given it proper thought to consider us more than a group that had bonded, but why wouldn't it be a harem as well? I had three men all to myself, though I wasn't sure how I felt about calling us that.

Out on the balcony, Reed turned up, and while everyone

ogled Gage doing somersaults in the air, he drew me into his embrace. Face to face, his lips grazed mine, and he kissed me with a passion I couldn't ignore. A fire sizzled through my veins.

There was nowhere else I'd rather be than with my men, looking forward to building a future together. Yep, this was just the beginning of a glorious new time in my life where I'd never be alone again, where I'd have someone to love me, and where, for the first time, I'd look forward to sleeping during the night. Kahlo joined us, and the three of us stared up at Gage's stunts. Damn, he was incredible, and all mine, all three of them, and I couldn't be happier.

* * *

"I saw the way you looked at those babies." Kahlo snuggled against my side as I lay in an oversized bed in a wolf hut. Scarlet had insisted we spend the night, so tomorrow, all of us could attend a wolf pack picnic. Our pride would join, so Reed's guard made haste to collect the rest from Darkwoods. Night had fallen, and we'd retreated, the four of us, to rest for the night. Though with the way all three men studied me, I wasn't sure how much sleep we'd get.

Gage lay on my other side, resting on a bent elbow, his fingers caressing my collarbone before dipping toward the bedsheet I'd covered myself in because they'd insisted we all sleep in the nude. Another reason I doubted we'd get any shut-eye.

"Have to agree," Gage said. "I watched you feeding Alexy and saw how it captivated you."

"I don't know what you're all talking about." Oh, I knew, yet I refused to admit that I loved the idea of having a baby. Telling the men that would mean opening up a different can of worms.

Reed crouched at the end of the bed, nude and studying like a predator. In a flash, he seized the blanket and ripped it off me, revealing my naked body.

"Hey." I gasped and reached for the sheet, but he'd tossed it aside.

"I'm with Kahlo and Gage. If you want a baby, then we need to get to work making one." Reed scooped up my foot and lifted it to his mouth. His tongue licked my toes, and I wriggled, giggling.

"Who said I wanted children right now? Just because I adored Scarlet's kids doesn't mean I'm ready." Lying between three hunks without a thread of fabric between us grew harder to ignore by the second. My skin prickled, and my nipples pebbled into balls. Especially with two men squished up against me, their hands roaming across my stomach, cupping my breasts.

Kahlo took one into his mouth, and I moaned, my head tilting back from the arousal stirring around my libido.

"That's fine," Gage added. "But I'm all up for practice runs, you know. Plus, you promised I'd get to watch Reed and Kahlo bringing you to orgasm."

I came up for air just as Reed parted my legs and slid a finger along my silkiness.

"Oh shit." With their touches, I'd lost my train of thought. "What were we talking about again?"

Kahlo released my breast. "Giving you a baby. Don't know about the rest of you, but I would love to be a father."

"Me, too," Reed and Gage responded in unison.

Three sets of eyes lingered on me.

Who was I kidding? Holding those little ones had had me cooing and dying to create a family of my own. I yearned to hold my children in my arms and help them grow into the most amazing people.

"I'm with you," I started, unable to believe what I'd said. But the smile on my lips hurt in all the right ways and I had no plan on retracting my words. "I must be drowning in lust because in your company, I float on clouds and would agree to anything."

Reed crouched between my thighs, inhaling me. "It's not lust, but love. And I've wanted nothing more than to make you mine for eternity." His mouth latched onto my pussy, and I arched my back, purring beneath his attentive tongue. To have both Gage and Kahlo watch him eating me turned me on beyond belief. I shuddered with arousal pulsing through me.

Kahlo blew warm air over my erect nipple, his hardness nestled against my thigh. "You mean the world to me, Babycakes, and I'm ready to do this." He suckled on a nipple, raising my temperature as I moaned so loud, I lost myself.

Gage's hand cupped my head and turned me to face him, the love in his eyes swallowing me. "I lost my heart to you long ago and knew one day, I'd finally make you mine. Now, you've made my dream a reality. Love you, honey." His mouth crashed with mine, hard and unrelenting, and I kissed him back with a vengeance. Needing him.

I rocked my hips back and forth, electricity burning within me at having three men devour me at once. If there was such a thing as fairy tales, I was living in one now. After all the years I'd been tortured, I still couldn't believe this turn of events, but I had plenty of time to work on letting it sink in. But right now I had other things to focus on.

Reed's tongue pressed into me, and I groaned, shaking as an orgasm rattled through me, owning me, claiming me, just like my men.

EPILOGUE

ONE WEEK LATER

"Gingernuts," I cooed and pried open my backpack. "Come out."

His tabby head popped up. I waited, hoping he wouldn't freak and run in a corner to hide. He'd adapted to the tower rather fast, and the gargoyle never scared him, so maybe he'd quickly feel comfortable in his new home.

His gorgeous, huge eyes scanned the living room, the circular couch, the fireplace, and even the open door to the veranda.

I scooped him up out of the bag to discover he wore an orange knitted sweatshirt and couldn't stop laughing. "You look adorable. Did Remy make that for you to keep you warm?"

I pressed him to my chest, kissing his head.

"Well, we're now living in the lion territory, and everyone knows you're joining us. So don't be scared." I stepped outside onto the wooden balcony, the afternoon sky streaked in oranges and blues. From the first floor, the open field spread out into the distance. Giant trees dotted the land, blossoming with flowers amid pale green leaves, while several older lions slept in the shade. The perfect view.

Gingernuts squirmed in my arms, so I set him down. On bent legs, he scurried across the veranda, sniffing the cushioned seats and the bird feeder in the corner, then stuck his head through the wooden railing and glanced down at Kahlo.

He carried a long plank of timber over his shoulder, his bare chest glistening. I leaned over the railing, gawking at the way his muscles shifted with each movement, his bulging bicep drawing my attention. I chewed on my lower lip and pictured me in his arms. I still couldn't believe my three men were building a freaking home for us. Two floors were complete. They weren't kidding when they mentioned making the place grand.

They worked on two additional levels, along with a landing pad for Gage after his scorching acrobatic stunts, a pool out the back for Kahlo, and a private cellar for Reed. He had shown me a sneak peek of his room… cushions everywhere, along with a few whips and ribbons on the walls for tying me up. Hell, I trembled with arousal just seeing his playroom… or as he called it, the Lion's lair.

I was getting a gazebo with flowers and cushioned lounges, giving me the perfect haven to enjoy the sun without fear. No more looking over my shoulder, and damn, I would finally get a tan. The tower was a thing of the past. With my blessing, Gage had torn apart the granite tower, bringing it down with the rest of the ruins. It put an end to one chapter of my life.

Khalo tossed the timber onto a pile with others, the noise drawing my attention.

"Hey, sexy," I said. "Shouldn't you be getting ready for our date?"

He glanced up, his smile widening. "Shouldn't you wear no underwear if you're in a skirt?"

I pushed down the fabric fluttering over my thighs in the balmy breeze. "I'll remember that for next time." I winked.

He stared at me with hunger. "Is that a promise?"

I burst out laughing as Gingernuts meowed and curled around my legs.

"How's the little one doing?" Kahlo asked.

He no longer cowered but watched a sparrow land on the bird feeder.

"He'll fit in easily."

"Meet you out back, then." Kahlo strolled around the house and out of sight when I sensed someone stepping outside to join me. I turned to find Mayse, Reed's sister, nineteen and beautiful, with golden curls framing her face. She shared her brother's brilliant green eyes.

"I finished your dress." She held onto a deep red gown with thin straps and a low-cut back. The tiny jewels beaded across the tight bust sparkled.

"Wow, it's stunning. You made this? Hell, you're talented and should open your own dress store. Women would flock to it."

Mayse's cheeks blushed, and she smirked, her eyes narrowing. "I don't know."

I reached over and touched the fabric, delicate under my fingers and lightly transparent. The men would go crazy when I wore this tonight. They were holding a special dinner date, just the four of us, to celebrate the start of our new life. Maysa had insisted on making me an outfit, but I'd never imagined something so impressive.

"I'll help you sell your creations," I said. "I happen to know a few people." Sarcasm lined my words. She handed me the gown, and I couldn't wait to get changed.

"When that witch controlled me," she began. "I knew what was going on but couldn't control my actions. I prayed that if I somehow escaped, I'd no longer waste my days hiding in the pride but do something with my life."

"Then it's set. We'll work on creating a line of women's fashion. Something sexy and sensual for the ladies." I wriggled my eyebrows.

Her eyes glistened, and she hugged me. I yanked my dress aside to avoid it getting crushed. "I'm so glad you're with my brother and living here. Now I have someone else to talk to about clothes."

"I'm the lucky one. You and the pride accepted me." I adored having someone I could consider a sister.

She broke away. "How could we not? You helped free me and the others. Now, get dressed. The backyard is ready, and the men should be there waiting."

"Thank you for everything." I stepped inside as she picked up Gingernuts and stroked his ears. Yep, this was what having a family felt like—secure, comforting, and my heart flooded with joy.

I changed clothes, combed my hair, and pinched my cheeks to add color to them. Spinning on the spot, the dress swirling around my ankles. On purpose, I wore nothing underneath, wanting to tantalize my shifters and have them squirming in their seats over dinner as they stared at me. My stomach tingled, and I hurried downstairs and out the back door into a field.

There I found a large round table decorated with flowers, candles, goblets, and jugs of wine. My attention fell on the three figures staring my way. Nerves claimed me, tightening in the pit of my stomach.

I lifted my chin with a smile and strutted toward them, placing an extra swing in my hips. All sets of eyes devoured every inch of me, their chests heaving for air as if I'd knocked the air out of their lungs.

"Hello!" I said nervously, the apex between my legs boiling and wet just from their stares.

Each of them approached me, Gage and Kahlo taking a hand while Reed stepped in front of me, his arms falling to my hips. They watched me, their gazes drowning.

"So, what do you think?" I broke the silence. "Don't keep a girl hanging. Do you like the dress?"

"I'm so fucking hard," Gage said, his touch sliding to my ass, squeezing. "I can't think straight. All the blood's gone to my dick."

I fake purred and winked at him while Kahlo had his mouth on my cheek and swept to my earlobe, licking me.

"I can see your sweet pussy through that dress. Fuck, do you know what you're doing to me?" He sucked in a rugged breath, and I quivered with desire.

"Don't you two have control?" Reed blurted as he bunched up my skirt at the front of my legs, lifting it and stroking his hand between my thighs. His fingers grazed my swollen lips, and my toes curled. When Reed dropped my dress, he stuck his fingers into his mouth and groaned as his eyes rolled back with ecstasy. "I suggest we start with dessert first."

The other two cheered, and I beamed to have their hands all over me. Their attentiveness, their excitement, their love. Yep, this was everything I'd ever dreamed of, and not only had I gained a family, but a fairy tale ending.

I brushed their hands away, then sidestepped around them before wandering toward the table, grinning. I glanced back, noting they all gawked at my ass.

"Who's ready for dessert?"

Their expressions sharpened, and they scrambled toward me while I giggled and burned from the inside out.

Bring it on.